The Misbegotten
Book 1 of An Assassin's Blade

Justin DePaoli

Cover Design by Eloise J. Knapp.
www.ekcoverdesign.com

Editing by Eliza Dee.
www.clioediting.com

Map Art by Jared Blando.
www.theredepic.com

MYRIOANT

ICERUN

the widowed path

EDENVALE

EAGLES CLAW

THE HOLE

ERIOR

the slavers

WATCHMEN'S BAY

THE TWIN MOUNTAINS

VEREUMENE

N

OLANDO

CHAPTER ONE

This wasn't how Death and I usually collaborated.

The man's eyes oscillated. His hands flew outward, knuckling into and spilling the mug of toxic wine. Had the gaunt bastard simply obeyed the very simple rules every man follows when gulping down my poison, his bony head would have fallen with a thump into the wooden table. And I could have stood, patted him on the back, told him it wasn't personal, and left the village where people shared suspicious relations with cows and pigs.

Instead, I blinked, which is about the only thing an assassin can do when the man he intends to silently kill thrashes about, jumps up from the table, wobbles around like he has wooden pegs for legs and then crashes shoulder-first into a cabinet.

Fuck, I thought.

Stained glass figurines and plates tumbled off the shelves, shattering into thousands of tiny bright green, blue, red and yellow fragments. It looked like a rainbow had been murdered.

One cabinet fell into the other, which fell into another, and by the time I thought my second *fuck*, they had all crashed to the floor into splintered wood. Harmon Fillick followed in short order, the side of his face striking the floorboards. The sound made my spine tingle — you never get used to that deadened crack. That cold slap of flesh. It's the kind of noise people don't wake up from, and if they do, they've got permanently scrambled eyes and a new habit of drooling.

"What was the point of that?" I said, hoping he was still alive so he could offer me closure.

He wasn't.

From behind the closed door, a girl shrieked. "He's channeling them! The gods!"

"It sounds like they're angry with him," a boy put in. "Maybe we should help."

"Don't be stupid!" the girl said. "What would you do to gods?"

"I'd... well, I'd... I dunno."

The little ones probably followed Harmon Fillick around enthusiastically — after they got over the frightening lack of meat on his bones — just as most kids shadow savants. Children find something intrinsically wondrous about people who heal others and are supposedly the closest connection to the gods.

Another boy chimed in. "Wot you doin'?"

"Ellie thinks Savant Fillick is talking to the gods," said the other boy cheerfully. "But they sound angry."

"Well o' course they angry. They gods. Why would they be happy?"

A thin line of blood snaked along a crack in the floorboards, trailing from Savant Fillick's newly fractured skull. The twerps outside continued chucking out ideas about what the gods wanted with the savant in the first place, and before long, more high-pitched, inquisitive voices joined the fray.

"Does the savant know you're all outside his door?" a husky voice called out.

"He's talking to the gods," the girl said. "I heard lots of noises. They're very angry, I bet. My mom makes lots of noises when she's angry."

"That's 'cause she's big and fat and when she moves, the ground shakes," a boy teased.

"Is not!" the girl said.

"Enough!" the man barked. "Or I'll snatch every one of you up and dump you off at your parents' feet."

A set of knuckles fell against the door. I edged a finger along the hilt of my sword.

"Savant, is everything all right in there?"

I dried my palms on the worn leather of my pants. Swinging a sword with sweaty hands rarely works out in your favor.

"Savant Fillick?"

The room was square. Solid walls enclosed me. Escaping unseen seemed unlikely, unless Skin and Bones had built a secret passage that led into the great wilderness.

The door moved. Its hinges creaked. Into the dank and dusty cottage swam slivers of pale light. A hand appeared in the crack, and the crack soon became a yawning gap as the man behind it spotted a thickening stream of blood creeping across the floor.

"Er, hello," I said, deepening my voice into what I hoped resembled a celestial boom. "Savant Fillick summoned me. I am the god of..." Which gods did these people believe in again? Wind, fire, water...? No, no, that's farther west. Maybe justice, death, vengeance, those fabulous caricatures?

So much for my godly impersonation. That's the problem with having two thousand bloody gods moseying around up beyond the clouds: too many to remember when you really need them.

The man's eyes bulged as they followed the outline of blood up to Savant Fillick. The tight ball in his throat plunged and bounced back up as he took a meaningful swallow. The lovely sound of steel scraping along a leather scabbard shaved away the silence. He took a step back and managed to scream one word.

"Ass!"

While it has long been thought by many that I am indeed an ass, this man hadn't intended to insult me. It just so happens you can't spell assassin without an ass or two, and you certainly can't intone the entire word when you have blood fountaining out of your opened throat.

The black blade that swiftly rived his flesh and in turn his voice winked out of sight behind the door frame.

"Never a moment too soon," I said.

My lovely Commander Vayle, second-in-command of the Black Rot, stepped over the man's collapsed body. I helped her drag him inside. The kids would probably be back soon and the last thing I needed was for a bunch of brats to shout at the top of their lungs that the gods were on a killing spree.

After getting the body inside, Vayle held up a burlap sack that looked about thirty months pregnant. "Fifteen skins," she said. "I would've gotten more, but I'd seen you attracted visitors. Tsk-tsk."

I sheathed my blade and tiptoed between the rivulets of Savant Fillick's blood. Cleaning dried blood off your boots is about as pleasant as wiping days-old dog shit off.

"Well," I said, "there's only about three hundred skins back at the Hole. How*ever* will you survive?"

"This wine," Vayle said, rapping her nail down the bag, "is much better than what we have at the

Hole. Very sweet and very wet. That's what Mrs. Whiskers claims."

"Mrs. Whiskers?"

Vayle pinched her sun-kissed cheek. "On account of the wispy whiskers that gather on her face."

I eyed her suspiciously. "Are you certain you didn't buy cat piss from a smooth-talking feline?"

Vayle had a look around at the chaos that had unfolded. "Are you certain you came here to assassinate a savant and not his house?"

"He didn't cooperate," I said, pushing her toward the door. "Let's get out of here."

She shoved a hand into my chest. "Wait here. I'll round up the horses."

Vayle sneaked out of the shack and returned a short while later, two horses in tow. They whipped their bushy tails about impatiently. I didn't blame them. They were probably eager to go back to the Hole and have a decent meal. This village had the kind of roughage that looked about as tasty as a plateful of pinecones.

I heaved myself up onto the saddle of my mare, Pormillia. I patted her mane and said, "Come on, pretty gir—"

"I told you!" a voice shrieked. "I told you they was angry!"

Vayle and I exchanged glances as a young girl with blond curls bounded up a dirt path, her little arms swinging furiously. When she reached the pond of blood outside Savant Fillick's house, she doubled over, mouth agape. Her big eyes looked as wet and fresh as the yolk of an egg.

Well, damn. Vayle and I had overlooked the fact that dragging a dead man inside doesn't help when he leaves behind bright red evidence.

"Why did they hurt him?" she asked us.

Now more children were running toward us. Along with a few larger figures, some of them wielding pitchforks, a couple holding crudely made swords.

"The gods hurt Savant Fillick," the girl cried.

"Don't you fuckin' ride off on me," a man hollered, pointing the blunt end of a club at us.

A pair of feet sliced through the crisp patches of grass behind me. I turned to see a dirty face with a wiry beard coming closer. He held a sword.

I clicked my heels. Pormillia lurched forward and broke into a trot that quickly transcended into a gallop. Vayle rode up beside me, leaning hard into her saddle, her chocolate hair whipping about her face.

Something landed with a thud behind us. Probably a rock or a club, one last desperate attempt by the villagers to see justice brought to their tiny hamlet. They would never know, but justice had already been delivered. Savant Fillick was a man whose hands had often wandered up the shirts of little girls and into the pants of little boys.

But I hadn't accepted the job based on the knightly virtue of honor. I wasn't an honorable assassin like my commander, who only took assignments where the end resulted in good old-fashioned justice. Pay me enough glittering gold and suddenly I forget most morals and beliefs I've ever had.

Once we were a half mile outside of the village, Vayle and I slowed our horses to a trot for the rest of the way.

She reached inside her burlap sack, took out a skin of wine and gulped. "It's not good for the little ones to see what they did."

"Blame it on the savant. Apparently his body's a fucking sponge for poison."

Vayle drained the rest of her wine and stuffed the skin back inside the sack. "Did you use the entire vial?"

"Did *I* use the entire vial?" I asked, incensed. "Of course I used the entire vial." I'd only been in the assassination business for fifteen bloody years.

When she looked away, I slipped a couple fingers inside my pocket, slid the vial out partway and took a peek, just to be sure.

A midnight blush smattered the sky as twilight came out to play. The mango sun angled itself behind a cylindrical hill. *My* cylindrical hill. Or, to be less selfish, *our* cylindrical hill. Home of the famous Black Rot kingdom known as the Hole. Really, less a kingdom, more a village, and rather infamous than famous.

I squinted at the crest of the hill. Two horses stood at the edge like guards at a post. White caparisons draped them.

"Hmm," I said, "messengers."

Having the Order of Messengers pass by the Hole wasn't unusual. Requests for assassinations often came through their hands, but they weren't the sort to pull up a seat, take a few skins of wine to the face and bullshit for hours. They dropped off their messages, collected payment if need be, and went on their way.

"Must be a message without ink," I said. Those were the type that were sent when the risk of a parchment falling into the wrong hands could be disastrous. "Probably a rich noble fuck who wants his liege to disappear."

"Or maybe someone wants a king to disappear," Vayle said, smirking.

I laughed. Years ago, under the veil of anonymity, someone had requested the Black Rot fetch the head of Dercy Daniser, Lord of the Daniser family and King of Watchmen's Bay. There are two kinds of people the Black Rot does not assassinate: children and kings. The former because even assassins have a smidgen of morality, and the latter because we are not suicidal.

See, the concept of life as an assassin is simple. You want the world to be on edge. You want families and lords and ladies and brothers and sisters and queens and kings to contend with one another and have the perfect amount of animosity for each other so that they hire mercenaries like yours truly to put blades in the throats of those they hate. What you absolutely don't want is for them to be so bold and desperate that they do the deed themselves, because then they don't need you. At that point, assassins become hindrances. And being a hindrance is not good for your life expectancy.

Pormillia aimed her nose toward the winding ramp of dirt and rock that twisted around the hill. Vayle's mare fell into position behind me. The path up was too narrow to ride two abreast, which is often inconvenient, but fantastic for defensive purposes.

I inhaled the sweet scent of burning pine deep into my lungs as we neared the plateau of the hill. Nothing quite like the smell of home.

The two messengers clad in snowy plate shifted in their saddles as Pormillia rocked forward onto the plateau.

"I'll be fucked if that isn't Grom," I said, shoving a playful elbow into the pauldron of the lankier of the two messengers.

"Astul," he replied, winking. Or maybe he was simply blinking. Hard to tell the difference when a man only has one eye.

"Been a couple years since you showed your ugly mug around here."

"Been running a new route recent—"

An explosive *whoosh* erupted across the way, followed by a plume of flames that licked high into the murky sky. Throaty laughter erupted soon after, and one of my Rots fell onto his back, cradling his stomach and probably trying not to piss himself. Apparently tossing a skin of wine into a fire is goddamn hilarious when you're drunk.

"They've been doing this all day," Grom said.

I shrugged. "You know what they say. When you're not killin', you're drinkin'. Well, that's what we say anyhow. Anyway, I'm guessing you're not here to watch in awe as a bunch of assassins make asses of themselves."

"King Chachant Verdan requested a verbal message be delivered to you."

My heart tap-danced in my chest. "*King* Chachant Verdan? Since when does Chachant go by that title?"

Grom cleared his throat. "Since his father was assassinated six days ago."

CHAPTER TWO

On the torn, piss-stained pages that smell of mothballs and tell you all about history, you find there are two kinds of king slayers. First, there are the sort who aren't particularly adept at clandestine operations and find themselves sitting in a torture chamber until they cough up a name or two. And then there are those sneaky assassins who wiggle their way in unseen and sneak back out just the same, leaving an empty throne in their wake.

The Verdan king slayer was apparently an example of the latter. After revealing Vileoux Verdan had been assassinated, the messenger went on to tell me his son, Chachant, had requested my assistance, which meant the new king had little information on the old king's death. He wouldn't send for *me* if he knew who was responsible — he'd simply march his army to war.

See, I'm not only an assassin, but a purveyor of information. Better to have two careers in case one goes to shit, I've always said. Plus, information will forever be a hot commodity.

I descended into the Hole, which was an actual hole, not some symbolic name

Dank and musty air clung to the rims of my nostrils and scurried inside like spiders hurrying into their funnels. Some would find the smell disturbingly similar to an abandoned cellar that was more cobwebs than stone. But for me, this was a place of tranquility.

A few pronged candelabra were stuck into patches of spongy mud along the walls, seething with orange-tipped flames that fought one another to show the way. Even with the help of fire, darkness was the Hole's closest friend. It embraced you down here, took you in like its guest and wrapped you up in an onyx hug.

I kept down a narrow hallway enclosed with wooden boards. A couple steps and one turn later, I was in a room that looked as if every bounty hunter had come to die here. I filled a few small purses with gold, hardly making a dent in the stockpile. After gathering some stale bread, skins of wine and bundles of wool, I emerged up top, with fresh sizzling timber burning the stink off my clothes.

"Shepherd," Big Gruff roared, invoking my name as the shepherd of assassins. Big Gruff always roared, never simply spoke. If you found yourself in a drunken brawl against him, you'd likely take your own fist to your jaw just to get it over with. Large and mean-looking was one possible description of Big Gruff. Monstrous with a dash of unhinging charm was a better one.

"You got a case of dead animal breath, big man," I said.

He flashed a massive grin and clenched my shoulder. "Somethin' 'bout the wine interactin' with my spittle. That's what Commander Vayle says, anyhow. Heard me a tale about you going up North to track down a king slayer."

"I see Vayle doesn't waste time informing on every one of my doings."

Big Gruff shrugged. "Eh, you were lookin' a bit blanched in the face when you came in from those messengers. Blame us, we started poking around and asking questions."

"Well, I don't expect to do any hunting for a king slayer," I said. "Probably just some information exchanging hands." I just hoped the information I'd provide — or rather, sell — would be helpful. If you've got a dead king on your hands, best to resolve the problem quick, before outlandish theories crop up and suspicions have five kingdoms marching to war.

He pulled me in close and leaned his thick beard in toward my face. "You want some company?"

By the tone of his voice, it almost sounded like a statement, rather than a question. "Think I'll get along fine on my own, thanks all the same."

Big Gruff pulled at his beard and smacked me on the back. "Only an offer! Always offerin' some muscle, you know Big Gruff." He laughed uneasily.

I blinked. "Oh, I know Big Gruff. I know that Big Gruff can't lie for shit. What's going on?"

"Goin' on? Oh, not a whole lot tonight, I reckon. Wine, tales, seeing whose stream of piss goes the farthest off the cliff, you know how it is."

I crossed my arms and waited.

"Oh," he said, feigning ignorance, "you mean what's goin' on with me askin' you—"

"Yes. That's what I mean."

He scratched his long mane of knotted hair. A stick fell out, which wasn't surprising. Bats were rumored to have nested in there.

"Ah, well, er… you know that job me and Kale had up near the Desert Hills a while back?"

"Was that the one where that one lord wanted the Rots to assassinate a god of lightning for killing village cows? And it turned out a farmhand was fixing steel swords to their heads during storms and conducting experiments?"

Big Gruff's eyes constricted as he thought. Finally, with an exasperated breath, he said, "No, no. I'm talkin' about the twin sisters who wanted each other dead. The one paid better than the other, you remember? Anyways, we was on our way back, got circled around in some woods near western Rime and came upon a big shack. Scared Kale and me somethin' bad. Ground looked like a big monster bucked it up with his shoulders. Singed circles all 'round, and these animals in cages — Astul, their legs were all twisted, eyes in threes and sixes, tongues split and sometimes missing altogether. Inside we found books about conjuration."

My upper and bottom teeth crashed against one another. "You came across some pretty damning evidence that conjurers lingered nearby and you didn't tell me? That's some fucking important information to leave out."

His huge face fell solemnly. "Me and Kale, we scooped up the books and got out of there. Camped for the night a long ways away. Had all the mind to bring 'em back here to the Hole, but... well, we got drunk. Woke up with the sun, but without the books."

"Lucky you didn't wake up with blood pouring out of your mouth," I said. "Do me a favor and don't keep anything about conjurers from me again."

He wagged his thick finger in the air. "You got it, Shepherd. Sure you don't want no protection?"

"I'm sure. Go get drunk and piss off the cliff."

He roared with laughter, slapped me on the shoulder and bumbled back to the group of Rots, who were playing spin the sword.

Conjurers, I thought. *Just what I fucking need.* Problem with conjurers is that you never find just one. There are always more. They're like vultures, except instead of being able to fly, they have the power to take your mind and conjure up thoughts you'd much rather not have floating around inside your head. There was a good reason why the Black Rot participated in their extinction several years ago. Too bad a few got away.

I paid Vayle a visit, told her I'd be back in a little while — which is a vague way of saying sometime in the next month — and mounted Pormillia, who was dressed in a black caparison embroidered with the red fist of the Black Rot.

The journey down the road from the Hole to Edenvaile, kingdom of the Verdans, is seven days if the Order of Messengers have the northern roads clear, and anywhere between twenty and never if they don't. And never doesn't mean that you turn back and go home. Never means your horse either breaks a leg or gets tired of shuffling through flank-high snow, bucks your sorry ass off and leaves for greener pastures.

On day three, Pormillia and I crossed the border of Rime. By this time, I was bundled up in wool and frozen snot dangled from my nose. Pormillia seemed content in the thick blanket I'd brought along for her.

Daytime in the North is a depressing sight. You don't expect much from a night sky. Maybe a few glittering stars and the occasional sliver of moonlight. But the day is the harbinger of timeless hope. The day will come, another sun will rise, the light will beat down the night! Well, not so much in Rime. The proverb here was, "Should the sun show itself, kiss your loved ones goodbye, for the apocalypse is sure to follow."

The sky was always a damp gray, and the wind sucked every feeling except pain from your body. A white canvas stretched endlessly across the fields, dotted with crystals that would probably look quite pretty if your mind could remember what that word meant.

But Lady Fortune had her eye out for Pormillia and me. The Order of Messengers had recently plowed the main road — you won't believe what an army of iron plows attached to the back of drawn carriages can do — and my four-legged girl trotted through the packed snow gracefully.

On day eight, the gray walls of Edenvaile sprung from a thick fog that had settled down from the white-capped mountains against which the kingdom nestled. Bowmen patrolled the parapet, lazily flinging one foot in front of the other. Boring job up there, since the city allowed passage during the day to anyone who wasn't hauling in siege equipment.

Pormillia tasted the air with her flaring nostrils, eagerly drinking in the cloying scent of spices that thickened in the air like broth in a soup. Hints of cinnamon and ginger and peppers and garlic and onions coalesced into a pleasant mixture that made me hunger for something other than the stale bread I'd been eating for the past eight days.

My mare stepped inside the gate and onto the cobblestone streets dusted with snow. The fancy flooring only continued if you kept straight and entered the market district, where merchants stood behind their stalls, their vigilant eyes combing through the sea of bodies, ready to feast on the first amateur who stupidly made eye contact. "Ma'am, gifts from the Pantheon here! Salted trout caught beneath the ice just this morning! Eyes big and juicy, might have eggs in her too!"

With a quick jerk of the reins, Pormillia turned onto a side street, kicking up a sea spray of snow and ice. She stopped before the stables, where I clambered off her.

A dirty-faced stable boy quickly led her to an open tie stall. I took a pouch of coins from a sack around the saddle, flicked him a gold piece and told him if he took good care of her there'd be more where that came from.

Then I went off to find someone who could grant me an audience with the king.

I'd been to Edenvaile my fair share. Vileoux Verdan knew how to accommodate an assassin. I'd drink my fill of wine, eat my fill of truffle cakes and carrot pies, and fuck my fill of whores — all without spending a coin. Of course, indulging in vices is never truly free. In return, I'd pass information to him.

This particular visit to Edenvaile felt... different. I couldn't walk one foot without having a new pair of eyes following me from beneath a steel-brimmed helmet. If my hand even brushed the hilt of my sword, bodies would shift. Mail coats would jingle. The city guard was more numerous than ever, and they apparently considered everyone a suspect.

Luckily for me, I was on good terms with the commander of the city guard, Wilhelm Arch, who mingled near the frozen steps that led to the keep.

"Wilhelm!" I said, putting a hand on the back of his breastplate. No less than twenty guards unsheathed their blades.

The clamor of the market district behind me went on, its patrons oblivious.

Wilhelm's nod placated the guards, and they went back to idly standing watch.

"If it isn't the Shepherd," he said. He gave a long, tired blink. The bags under his eyes were stretched and dark, falling away from his face. He seemed like he wanted to add something but couldn't quite find the words.

"Long days and longer nights?" I asked.

He wiped a scarred hand over his bald head. "Endless. Chachant hoped you would come. But he's not here presently."

"Will he be here presently in a few hours?"

"A couple weeks, if the storms aren't bad. Went south to Vereumene. Gathering of the five families is in a few days. Mydia is serving in his stead."

What a crock that gathering was. Established some forty years ago to ensure tempers wouldn't flare and escalate to another great war. Half the great families didn't bother showing, which is a hell of a feat when there's only five. Maybe a king being assassinated would persuade them to honor the gathering.

"I'm surprised Mydia wouldn't send a consul to discuss matters. I hear my face gives her the shivers."

Wilhelm wiped away a thin film of snot from his unkempt beard. "I've faith you two can act appropriately. She'll see you soon. At the present moment, she's... busy."

Busy. Yes, that was it, of course. After all, she was Chachant's sister and responsible now for presiding over the second largest kingdom of the world. Busy could mean many things: entertaining proposals from the court, meeting with ill-tempered vassals, or — more likely in Mydia's case — bathing in a golden tub while naked men pampered her with soft soaps.

I gazed across the way, beyond the market district and toward a squat oval building. It was a building whose occupants frowned at those who entered without pants, but as soon as you put some gold coins up on the counter, well... keeping them on was quite against the rules.

"I'll be busy myself," I said, winking at Wilhelm. "One of your men can fetch me when Mydia is ready, yeah?"

He blew air between his wind-burnt lips and muttered something, which I took for a yes, and so I skipped happily over to Edenvaile's best and only brothel. At least in my mind I skipped; I would never be caught physically swinging my legs as I jump to and fro. Assassins have reputations to keep.

After handing over more coins than I'd ever admit, a woman with smooth, radiant skin led me to a secluded room. Silk sheets and down pillows adorned the bed.

Her name was Nyla, and Nyla professed she had a knack for removing clothing. Her long fingers gently edged along the bulge in my pants. She smiled, unclasped a button, removed my shirt, stripped my pants — she got me naked, all right?

And that's all Nyla did. A fully clothed woman suddenly appeared in the doorway, gesturing for Nyla urgently. A few moments later, someone new ambled in. Shiny red hair cascaded down her back, and her full hips swung ever so slightly as she walked seductively toward the bed.

"I'm sorry," she said, her voice as delectable as melted chocolate. "I'm Marigold. There was a mix-up with Nyla. I hope you don't mind…" She subtly pushed her tits forward and sunk her pearly teeth into her lip.

Now, I was a paranoid man. Knowing the horror you yourself are capable of immediately makes you suspicious of everyone else and particularly of supposed brothel whore mix-ups. But I was a man all the same. A man who suffered from a weak will, a dry throat and a singular thought when a pair of pillowy breasts were shoved into his face.

There was a gasp and the feel of a soft, fleshy tip circling my tongue. Suspicions? What suspicions?

###

Climaxing and sleeping are as closely related as cuts and blood, and try as I might, the heaviness of my eyes got the better part of me. I awoke in the brothel atop stained sheets. Someone was calling my name.

After blinking away the bleariness, I realized that someone wore a mail shirt. And leather boots. Rather masculine face, too. To each his own, but that wasn't something I cared to see in a brothel.

"The presiding stewardess, Mydia Verdan, will see you now."

"The presiding stewardess?" I muttered. "Oh! Oh, right. Yes, yes. Mydia. Of course. I'll be right there."

The guard left, and I quickly hopped out of bed. Got myself dressed real quick and double-checked my pouch of coins. Looked good. If Marigold skimmed a few coins from the top, it wasn't noticeable. I would've liked to ensure I still had possession of all my belongings as well, but a woman impatiently peeking in implied this room was expecting a new visitor. So I simply tapped my belt to feel for two ebon swords — the most precious of my cargo — and went off.

The guard was waiting for me outside, along with hysteria — something I do not like the company of.

"He's still here!" a woman cawed. "Told ye he's still here! Still lurkin' around somewhere."

"Saw him breathin' just earlier," a man said. "A boy! That's all he was. How can ya kill a boy and live with yourself?"

The guard motioned toward the keep. "Follow me."

"What happened here?" I asked.

"Stable boy," guard said, peering back. "Took a dagger across the throat. Bled right out. No witnesses."

"That's strange," I said. "I couldn't move my fucking foot without drawing the attention of ten of you bastards, and yet a boy gets murdered in plain sight and no one sees a thing?"

He said nothing. Didn't even seem concerned.

I, along with my frosted breath, trailed the guard back to the tip of the market square and then up the steps into the courtyard of the keep. Two guardsmen opened the double-leaf doors, allowing us entry.

My armored courier led me to a twisting staircase laid with black carpet and trimmed with gold. Banners draped the walls, displaying the Verdan trio of golden swords resting against an inky sky. Inlaid torches spat at me, flinging the orange shadows of their curling flames along the banners. The swords glistened, as if real gold lay inside the cloth pennants.

Up another set of stairs and yet another we went, finally spilling out into a grand hallway with marble flooring and a painful display of grandiosity. There were chandeliers that sparkled and glittered, sculpted portraits of old Verdans who had kicked the bucket long ago, colorful paintings stretched across twenty-foot canvases. Funny thing is, these were the royal quarters. Only people who passed through were royal guardsmen, lords and ladies of the court, the Verdan family and visitors of the aforementioned. It was as if the only reason for this bombastic display of grandeur was to remind them just how privileged they were.

The guard stopped before a door with two guardsmen in full plate, swords sheathed. "Lady Mydia," he announced, "Astul, Shepherd of the Black Rot, has arrived."

"Bring him in," she said.

The door swung open, and I stepped forward, only to be yanked back. The two royal guardsmen entered first, and only then was I permitted entry. How fancy.

Mydia sat on a velvet-cushioned chair behind a small circular table. Silk brocade clung to her small frame of subtle curves. Silver and golden threads weaved in and out of the indigo fabric, and an emerald pendant nestled in her cleavage.

"Smells like lilacs in here," I said. "Just get out of a hot bath, by chance?"

She folded her hands and rested her arms on the table. "The scent was more intense and pleasant before you arrived and fouled it with the smell of sex. Just get done pleasuring your cock, by chance?"

I laughed, saw my way over to the table and had a seat across from Mydia. The guardsmen followed.

"Don't worry," I said, "you of all people know that I'm not a one-and-done man. There's more left, if you're eager."

Mydia flicked her head back, swinging her blond hair out of her eyes. "Once before, but never again."

Once before, indeed. Once before, her little heart throbbed for a bad man. Once before, her lips were mine, my tongue was hers. Once before was a long time ago, when I was younger and drunker. Lucky I still had my head after that little fling, and it was even more surprising that my relations with the Verdans remained intact.

"We can skip the pleasantries," I said, "and get on with what exactly your brother wants of me."

Mydia leaned forward, her heavy brows creased. "My father was poisoned. We discovered him lying belly up in his bed, lips the color of charcoal, throat scalded. The assassin left behind little evidence, but Chachant believes—"

A thunderous bang rippled across the floor as the backside of the door slammed into the wall.

"That's him," a voice bellowed.

One royal guardsman scooped Mydia out of her chair. The other locked his plated arms around my neck and threw me to the ground. I struggled for breath.

A contingent of city guardsmen and guardswomen paraded into the room, with Wilhelm at the head.

He stood over me. "Astul, you are being charged with the murder of thirteen-year-old Evan Tilman, a stable boy and son of Rory Tilman and Lana Tilman."

The guard relaxed his grip, allowing me to speak.

"Are you fucking mad?"

"We found your dagger beside his body," Wilhelm said.

"My bloody dagger is right—" I patted my hip and felt the sickening emptiness of a sheath.

Someone, it seemed, didn't want me to leave Edenvaile.

CHAPTER THREE

Wilhelm had stripped me of my belongings and stuffed me deep beneath the frozen earth. At least he was nice enough to give me a coat and wool pants, if only so I would survive long enough to watch a sword separate my head from my neck.

I had been underground for two days, shackled to a pillar in the kind of blunt darkness that even moles would consider overwhelming. Ice hung in the air like a humid vapor after a summer storm, too thick and heavy to drift away. And with it swirled the raw stench of piss, shit and disease. No place to relieve yourself here, except on the floor. Or in your own pants.

Guards came around occasionally and handed me wooden bowls filled with what looked to be white vomit. I asked them what it was, and they always said, "Food." If that was food, it was time to start looking into the benefits of starvation.

Few people joined me, aside from a man who wept occasionally and one who lamented about angels and demons. The latter was my opera singer and I his audience.

He would break the shroud of silence by preaching about good and evil, and I clapped and egged him on. It's not the crazies who talk to themselves nor the whimpers of those distraught and lost that sap you of your soul in a dungeon. It's the silence — the bitter emptiness, a void in which you start to lose your grip on what's real and what's an illusion. As long as people talked, even if they spouted nonsense, I was at ease.

Even laughs were had. Sometimes when the preacher of good and evil would speak of the heavens, I would tell him demons and devils were afoot and that I could see them. He gave some valuable advice about my situation, such as, "Don't let your feet fall into the hellish fires, or the demons will bite off your toes." Wise advice indeed.

My friend continued with his talk of evil well into the night, or morning, or afternoon… time had little meaning down here. The only thing that finally silenced him was the familiar pitter-patter of boots kicking along the stiff dirt floor. Odd timing, since a guard had given us some vomit — sorry, food — a short time before.

Something sounded different in those footsteps that drew nearer. They moved swiftly, marching headlong into the darkness with purpose.

"A demon approaches!" my preacher friend said.

Could've well been a demon, if such things existed. Shavings of menacing orange slowly reached into the blackness and extinguished it, thrusting it back.

"Repent!" the preacher cried. "Repent, and may the angels come! May they smite this foul spawn and lift us into the heavens!"

A slender figure bathed in the warmth of fire approached. She leaned her torch close to my face and hooked a strand of raven hair behind her ear.

"Aren't I too pretty to be a demon?" she asked.

"My, my. What a treat. They send Sybil Tath to check up on me. Or are they calling you a Verdan now, given you and Chachant have shacked up together for quite a while?"

Sybil Tath was the eldest daughter of Edmund Tath, king of Eaglesclaw and lord of one of the five great families.

She closed one of her big eyes and scrunched up her face, deep in thought like a playful child. "Hmm. No, I don't think it works like that. But if you're so interested in what they call me, I'll be sure to send word via the messengers when the wedding concludes."

"So the promise of a wedding lives," I said. "You know, people were starting to ask questions. After seven years of playing stuff-my-keep under the sheets together, word was getting around that you two would never marry. That maybe even… well, I'm not one for rumors, but people were getting the wrong idea about Chachant. That maybe he preferred a harsher touch, a few bristles on the face of his lover, something to stuff *his* keep."

I became suddenly aware that Sybil held something in her other hand. A bag of some sort. She clutched it tighter, similar to when some drunk clutched his mug tighter right before driving it into my face for spilling his ale.

"Who are these 'people?'" she asked.

"I'm not good with names, unless I killed you, fucked you, or drank with you before. Or, in your case, met you twenty bloody times."

"Twenty-one now, huh? I betcha it'll be the best meeting yet, too."

"It scares me when people say things like that."

She heaved a sack at my feet. The contents inside clangored like clashing steel. She knelt and fiddled with something in her pocket.

"I'm freeing you," she said.

A clasp around my ankles clicked and relaxed.

"In that case," I said, "I should inform you I only insult those I'm very good friends with."

"Mm hmm," she murmured.

She unlocked the clasp around my wrists, then unwound the steel chains from the pillar. As she worked hastily, the fog of her warm breath drifted into my hands and fingers and cheeks, thawing my flesh and bones. It smelled like a crop of flourishing mint.

"Get dressed," she ordered.

"Does Wilhelm know about this?"

"He does, although he does not agree with it. But I need your help, whether you killed a stable boy or not."

"For the record," I said, dressing myself with my leather armor and wools from inside the bag, "I didn't."

I straightened out my boys, which is another way of saying I sheathed my blade and the dagger Sybil had kindly returned to me.

"Your weapon is light," she said.

"Made of pure ebon. What's the saying? Light as air, cuts like... well, since there's nothing that cuts quite like ebon in this world, the simile hasn't been completed. Maybe I'll have you one crafted, as a thanks for freeing me. Of course, that depends on where you take me."

I wrapped a small pinch of fur around my neck.

"Last I heard," she said, "it would take half the Edenvaile vault to buy enough ebon for one sword."

"I know people."

"So I've heard."

"Speaking of the Edenvaile vault," I said, "Mydia and I never got to the point of discussing payment for information on your little king slayer problem. Now I'm not a stickler, Sybil. Since you freed me, I'm willing to part with whatever knowledge I have for a... mm, let's say, discounted price."

Sybil grabbed the empty bag from the floor and compressed it against her chest. "I would rather have your eyes and ears than what's between your head right now. Trust that you do not already have information that could help me."

"Is that what Chachant wants as well?"

"Does it matter? He's not here. And I promise you will be rewarded handsomely, so long as you are in agreement that forty thousand is a handsome payment."

I cleared my throat. "As in forty thousand coins that glitter gold? Well, then, what are you waiting on? Lead the way."

A whistling voice pierced the cold air. "I hear 'em! They skitter and scatter down the halls, mingle amongst us! The demons are here, friends. The demons have *come.*"

We passed by the preacher man, who shook his skinned head in disappointment.

I shrugged and said, "The gods rescued me."

Sybil's hissing torch carved out an orange-lit ramp of dirt that ascended quickly to the surface. We followed it and emerged into the slightly less cold air that coasted through the openness of Edenvaile.

The night sky resembled a placid lake whose pinpoints of winking light were the celestial equivalent to mosquitoes and sundry insects nipping at calm evening waters. It was a welcome sight, after being stuffed underground for days.

A temperamental wind brewed up around us, hawking and hunting for some sign of life to bury in a five-foot snowdrift.

"They're supplied and ready to go," Sybil said, motioning to two horses. She pulled her wool cowl down, tied it in place, and put a foot on the saddle strap.

I touched the mare with a chestnut face and golden eyes. My Pormillia. She nuzzled my palm affectionately.

"I saw her in the stables," Sybil said. "I remembered her eyes from your most recent visit." She heaved herself onto her horse. "Come, hurry."

We rode off for the gate, which was curiously opened. After we put it behind us, it closed with a thud.

We rode east for a while and then south at daybreak. During a quick breather to let the horses regather themselves, Sybil told me she knew a place we could rest comfortably. Comfort wasn't as much a concern of mine as getting answers to what had transpired in Edenvaile and why exactly the lover of Chachant Verdan had freed me in the dark of night. She had been obtusely vague, but she'd assured me I would receive the answers I desired. Answers and, even more importantly, a mountain of gold.

Around midday, we reached the toes of Mount Kor, near the southern tip of Rime. Here the snow lay as fine dust along the jagged rock and among bearberry and arctic moss.

Sybil circled around for a while, sniffing about like an elk hoping to pick up the scent of her mate. She eventually led us into a small cavern buried inside the descending mountain. The roof was painted the color of wheat, scarred with chalk lines as if someone had taken a dagger and scraped it all up. After walking into a cavern once and having a spider the size of both my hands fall on my head, I had a tendency to inspect ceilings with the thoroughness of a rock hound inspecting gems.

"It's warm in here," I said, feeling myself begin to sweat. "Oh, shit. Did I die and go to…"

Sybil laughed. She got off her horse. With a few hand signals, the beast sighed and lay down.

"It's a hot spring," she said. She dipped her finger into a wide natural basin, shored with smooth rock, and flicked it at me.

The hot sprinkles of water chased away the cold in my bones, which evacuated my body in the form of shivers.

I rubbed my hands in anticipation and climbed off Pormillia. Sidling up to the edge of the water, I knelt, opened my mouth and allowed the slow-rising steam to pour through me.

"I promise you," I said, unbuttoning my coat, "this has nothing to do with primal needs."

I kicked off my boots.

"Nor am I attempting to draw the ire of Chachant," I added, removing my socks.

With some manipulation of a buckle, my belt fell away from my waist and down around my ankles.

"And I certainly am not a ne'er-do-well who wishes to rape you," I explained, undoing my pants and kicking them across the way.

My leather jerkin clonked against the ground.

"And I have no interest in forcing Mother Nature to play the role of voyeur," I clarified, balling up my shirt and sending it to accompany my pants.

I slid a couple fingers beneath the band of my skivvies and nodded.

"So with all of that said, I hope you take no offense, but I'm getting naked."

And I did get naked. And I lowered myself into the hot spring, and I closed my eyes as the shivers descended all the way to my toes. The scalding water burned like fire, but, oh, it was a good pain.

I stretched my hands along the edge, submerged up to my chest. "Ohhh," I said with a pleasant sigh, "this — this is good."

A *plop* pried open my eyelid, and I watched as a bare Sybil Tath settled into the spring.

She caressed a wet hand up her arm and around her shoulders, washing away the grime. "How long do you think the walls of Edenvaile could withstand an assault from Braddock Glannondil's armies?"

"That... is a strange question to ask."

Sybil splashed a cupped hand of water onto her face. "Chachant is convinced Braddock is behind his father's death."

Suddenly the water didn't feel so warm anymore. "Your lover can't possibly be thinking of trotting off to war against a man with three times the army."

"What would you do if someone killed your father?"

"Write the good man a letter, thanking him." Of course, that was impossible, given I was the one who had ended his life. A bit of revenge for a childhood of black eyes, busted eardrums and a mother who walked about with a disfigured face till the day she took one punch too many. "But even if my father was a king who I loved dearly," I explained, "I damn well wouldn't mindlessly accuse the most powerful man in the world of assassinating him."

Sybil tilted her hair back into the spring, wringing out the oils. "I disagree. It's a hazardous accusation to make, granted, but not mindless, given Braddock's proposal."

"Did that proposal suggest poisoning a king with a flowing white beard and bushy brows? In that case, yes, it may just be probable that he did indeed poison Vileoux, along with half the northern lords."

Hair still soaking in the water, her eyes slanted toward mine. "He proposed to unite the five families under one crown. The Danisers agreed, but Vileoux rejected it. My father followed Vileoux, and the Rabthorns never officially made a decision."

Clearly, I needed better spies. Or more of them. This proposal should have reached my ears the moment it left the Glannondil kingdom of Erior.

"Why one crown?" I asked.

"It would prevent further destabilization of the realm if all five families allied together. There were various scenarios under which it would operate, from a more liberal arrangement where each kingdom would retain its local sovereignty, to a firmer hand that would..." She searched for the proper words — the proper *diplomatic* words.

"That would finger each kingdom," I said, "and if the kings and queens didn't scream in orgasmic glory when Braddock told them to, why, he'd march on their lands and annex them for treason. Am I close?"

Sybil lifted her head out of the water and leaned back against the rock edge. "More or less."

I thoughtfully scratched my itchy beard, flinging dandruff into the spring. There weren't many ways Braddock could benefit from cutting down Vileoux Verdan. Unless he wanted to...

"How's the North reacting to Chachant's claim to the throne?" I asked.

"Poorly," she said blankly. Not a muscle in her face twitched. That's how Sybil Tath was. She only allowed you to glean what she wanted, never her true feelings or thoughts. It was quite maddening.

"I imagine," I said. "Twenty-year-olds aren't given much respect." I thought about everything she'd said and ran through a scenario aloud. "So Braddock puts Vileoux in an early grave. Chachant ascends to the throne. He's got the face of a baby and the kingly experience of one, too. The infamous apostates that are the northern bannermen see this as their opportunity to make good on their own claim. Chaos erupts in the North. Braddock marches in to pacify it, puts a puppet on the throne. Now he's got the Danisers and this new king behind him. Rabthorns will get in line, weasels that they are. In the end, your father's resolve will weaken, and Braddock gets precisely what he desires. Makes sense. But there's a problem with the theory."

Sybil turned an eager ear toward me.

"Patrick Verdan," I said. "He's got the true claim and from what I hear the backing of many northern lords." Patrick had abdicated years ago, leaving behind his rightful heirship to the throne, but he still had the Verdan name. And he was the eldest.

"That's not the problem," Sybil said matter-of-factly. "The problem is Vileoux Verdan isn't dead."

"That," I explained, holding up a finger, "would be more than a problem."

Sybil gently propelled herself through the water, the sharp point of her nose pricking the steam as she floated over to the opposite edge. I caught a quick glimpse of her back before she turned.

"What is that?" I asked. "That mark on your back."

"A tree. I saw it in a dream once. Isn't it beautiful?" She turned and treated me to the entirety of the tattoo's elegance.

Beautiful... was not the word I would have used. No, it didn't look beautiful or artistic or grand. It looked... well, very, very real. As if I could reach out and touch its trunk that grew sideways and suddenly surged high into the air. As if I could hang from its boughs of thick, knotted branches and smell its bounty of yellow flowers. I blinked and shook my head, drawing myself back into the present.

"Anyway," I said. "Vileoux, er—"

"Isn't dead," Sybil said. "I saw his supposed dead body before Chachant did. Before anyone, except the guards. As I walked past his quarters, there was a loud bang, as if someone had fallen into a dresser or bedpost. I waited there as the guards called for him. There was no answer. They waited and called again. No answer. Eventually, they kicked in the door... and there he was, on the floor, stench of red wine in the air."

"Sounds like a lush fell and hit his head," I said.

She waved a finger in the general direction of her mouth. "His lips were black. Dried, burnt black...

awfully terrible looking. His throat, what I could see of it, was sooty, no pink at all."

I wiped a condensed layer of steam from my forehead. "Oils of camadan seed produce similar effects, but not as dramatic and certainly not as quick. And I don't know of any willing participant to take camadan-oil-spiked-wine to the face."

"Willing participant?"

"You told me Vileoux wasn't dead, so I'm assuming someone played his part."

"It was Vileoux who I saw dead in his room. It was Vileoux who I saw buried in the bitterly cold sarcophagus. I know the man. I know him!" she insisted. A rare glimpse into her emotions, or a calculated move to rouse me? "I've slept in his keep for seven years. It was him, and I am not mistaken."

"Fine," I said, hoping to temper her temper. "I'll take your word for it."

"When Chachant made way for Vereumene, I went into the ossuary to beg Vileoux — his spirit, if it remained — to help Chachant. To instill tranquility into his heart, lessen his hunger for revenge." She touched my shoulder, as if for support, or perhaps to steady me. "I bent over his sarcophagus, nudged the top ajar so I could see his face... there was nothing, Astul. It was empty. He had left."

"Or someone had taken him," I pointed out.

"Semantics," she said. She lifted herself out of the water and onto the ledge, airing out her naked body.

"Well, those are quite different things, you know. Leaving on your own accord, or being forced to—"

"Listen to me," Sybil said seriously, cutting me off, "I saw something the night Vileoux — or his body, whatever — went missing. You'll think I'm mental, but... I saw fire in the sky. It was a bird bathed in flames." Her eyes narrowed, and she forced a heavy swallow down her throat. "I swear upon my life."

"Which way did it go?"

"This way."

Silence captured us. Prior to about ten years ago, claiming you spotted a flaming bird in the sky was enough to have a savant start chiseling into your skull, hoping to pop whatever strange fungus or parasite had clamped onto your brain. But then the conjurers arrived, or rather appeared, and with them unnatural abominations that they both created and controlled. Mostly ridiculous things, really — two-tailed squirrels, lions with the teeth of a man, rotund ravens who couldn't soar for more than a few seconds without having to perch and catch their breath. Hadn't ever seen or heard of a flaming bird, but if it existed, it was undoubtedly born into this world from the minds of conjurers.

After a while — long after her body had dried and her hair began to frizz — she spoke. "Dead or alive, what would they want with him?"

"Dead? Not a whole lot. But alive?" I chuckled as a way to cope with the thought. "If you could take the mind of a king presumed to be dead, imagine the chaos you could unleash if he would happen to show up at, say… oh, I don't know, the gate of Edenvaile three weeks from now, eyes swollen, shirtless, rags for pants. Claims he was given a concoction to slow his heart to an undetectable pulse and then kidnapped. If war was your thing, that's the route I'd go."

Sybil frowned. "But *why*? What motivations would a couple of conjurers, or even a small colony, have for doing that?"

"None at all," I said. "Unless they're working with someone."

There was that face again. As cool and unmoving as stone itself.

"I got wind of a couple conjurers near here," I said. "It was a while ago, and my Rots disturbed them, so they likely moved. But it's not far from territory my brother patrols. He may have a lead on them that's helpful. Might not be the conjurers we're looking for, but it's something."

Sybil picked her feet up out of the spring, spun around on her butt and trudged over to her clothes. "Mm. So the tragic life of Astul — from the abusive father to the estranged brother — isn't quite so true, is it?"

"We haven't talked in several years. But I've kept eyes and ears on him. He may make poor choices, but he still shares my blood. That's got to count for something, right?"

Sybil began bouncing up and down, initiating the tried-and-true method of persuading your thighs to fit inside your pants. "I'm joining Chachant in Vereumene. I hope he's still there when I arrive. I'm worried he's not going there for a peaceful meeting."

"If he's expecting Serith Rabthorn to join him in a silly conquest against Braddock, he's going to be disappointed. Only way that bastard joins anyone is if there's a clear route to victory."

She combed a soothing hand through her snorting horse's mane. "My father detests Braddock, so Chachant already has an easy ally on his side." She paused and added, with emphasis, "Dercy will be in Vereumene, too."

"Won't ever happen," I said. "Dercy wouldn't ever go against Braddock."

"If Chachant plants the seed…"

"Fine," I relented. "Make sure it *doesn't* happen. Last thing I want while I'm in Erior is a bunch of knuckle-dragging armies to come pounding on the walls."

"Erior?" Sybil questioned. "You said your brother—"

"He's been in Erior for the last month, probably on leave. So I have the pleasant assignment of finagling my way into that bloody kingdom without alerting any of Braddock's court or the king himself."

Sybil raked her nails across her scalp, freshening up her hair. "What kind of naughty boy have you been to draw such ire from Braddock?"

"Offed his uncle," I answered. "He supposedly burned an entire field of some lord's crops as petty revenge. Some lord with very deep pockets who could afford a very expensive assassin. Botched it a bit and word got back to Braddock."

"Well, try not to get yourself caught, hmm? I like you, Astul." She smiled.

"You'll know if I do. He promised that if I was seen within two hundred miles of his walls, he would impale me, string the Glannondil banner up through my intestines and out of my mouth and then parade me across the whole of Mizridahl."

CHAPTER FOUR

The relationship between my brother and me was complicated, largely because I'd stabbed him five years ago. Despite my profession, I tried to reason without violence, but after he insisted on joining the Glannondil army — *good pay and free food, Astul!* — I socked him in the jaw. He tackled me, I kicked him, he spat in my face, yada, yada, yada, and I ended up taking a small chunk of flesh from his shoulder. It was hardly noteworthy in my opinion, but he made a big fuss about it, stormed off and told me never to talk to him again. Hopefully he wasn't serious.

Pormillia had valiantly trotted along for eight days, pushing on through the bogs and swampy marshes of the Paggle Badlands. There's a misleading name if I ever saw one.

The clomps of northern snow were in my distant past now. As I rode eastward, the quagmires dried up and the mud hardened into lush soil upon which meadows of rich green grass and rainbows of flowers grew. After another couple days, my girl and I arrived at what people around here affectionately called the capital of the world.

Its sixty-foot-high sheer walls, decorated with crimson banners featuring a grinning jackal, roosted upon the shoulders of Mount Poll, and behind it lay a skyline of sculpted peaks surging relentlessly into the clouds. When the sun was bright and would melt away the gray sky like ice, you could tilt your head till the back of your skull touched your shoulders and you still wouldn't have seen the conclusion of those bluffs. For all intents and purposes, life on this mountain ended right here. Go up much higher and you weren't coming down, at least not with the widely accepted definition of liveliness pulsing inside you.

I guided Pormillia inside the walls of Erior, and the capital of the world came alive.

It smelled like the sea was roasting in an iron pan of shallots and lard. A few more steps and the spunk of mutton and cloves nosed its way in, quickly elbowed aside by the sharpness of cinnamon pies and the sweetness of berry cakes.

The cobbles teemed with merchants and buyers, a haggle here, a thank-you-good-sir there. Crooks preyed upon the wide-eyed, explaining that this here stick, you see, you burn it at night and the fumes — quite strong, now, don't sniff them — they keep away vampires, werewolves and even ne'er-do-well fairies corrupted by ekle mog. What's ekle mog?

Oh, my, my, my dear sir, step over here and take a look at this contraption of string and wire, it's designed to blunt the essence of ekle mog which surrounds each and every one of us, and…

So on and so forth.

Rain began to fall, tinking off the garbage pails that Braddock implemented throughout the city to cut down on populations of opportunistic dogs. Then thunder came with all its bluster, and the wind whistled. Buying and selling and conning went on all the same. Storms weren't enough to shut business down here. Rain was a way of life and it often moved on as quickly as it came. Such is life near the sea.

I offered a stable boy a few coins to keep Pormillia in a stall without any neighbors. You never know what kind of horses will shack up next to yours in a city like this. Biters, kickers, spitters — my good girl didn't need any of that shit.

I took a secluded alley away from the hustle and bustle of the market. It's an experience going through the market, but one that's quite dulled when you realize the only reason this kingdom of riches exists is because of the embarrassment of resources it sits upon. And guess who has the luxury of mining and chopping and farming those resources? Slaves, the hidden pride and joy of Braddock Glannondil.

The dark alley spilled out into the heart of Erior. One artery led to the stepped plateaus which, if you climbed all three, would put you face-to-face with the keep. Another led to city's bathhouses and entertainment. And still another took you down a sloping path to the farmlands, where my brother most certainly was not located, but I'd find him later. I had a six-year-old promise to keep first.

Unless you fancy rows of corn, beanstalks, cows, sheep, and finally goats who do not know the meaning of personal space, the farmlands weren't particularly enticing for visitors of Erior. The smell of lemony heron and sweet custards was replaced by the repulsiveness of cow shit.

I studied the ground carefully as I walked, lest my foot plunge into an oily lumped mound that could take your breath away and never give it back.

"Gray roof, silver rooster," I whispered, scanning the rooftops. That's what the letter said many years ago. I squinted. "There you are."

I started that way, planting my foot in the ground of sunken mud… at least I hoped it was mud. All the men and boys stopped plowing and milking. Their narrow eyes moved as I did. One woman stood in the middle of her farm with her arms at her side. Her stomach rolled over her pants, although that very well could have been her breasts. There's a scary thought. I continued on toward the farmhouse, when she shrieked.

"Get off me damn crops, ya big legged lug!"

Fearful that she might charge me like a sex-deprived elk and grind my bones into her soil as fertilizer, I jumped to the side, gave her an uneasy smile, and nodded.

I walked up to the house with a silver rooster perched atop the gray roof. I knocked on the door twice and then opened it.

In hindsight, it's probably better to knock first, and then wait for the door to open. Especially if you aren't certain whether your good friend still lives there. It had, after all, been six years since he sent me that letter.

With the door swinging open and slamming against a wooden wall, another sort of slamming greeted me: the slamming of flesh on flesh.

Picture the cranky gal outside, except without clothes and doing her best to mimic a standing dog. Her pasty white blubber, covered with wrinkles and a few brown dots for good measure, jiggled and wriggled as her bony man, bald as a rat, pulled back and entered her again and again and again. His jutting ribs wimpled as he thrust, as if they were swinging back and forth, determined to break free of his decrepit body and find a healthier abdomen to live inside.

There were ancient grunts, throaty roars and sharp spankings. The sheets were bitten and balled up and kicked aside. Vigor apparently grows with age.

The woman's face slammed into the bed, twisting around as it did. She opened a twitchy eye, and that's when she saw me.

Her mouthful of rotting black gums produced the kind of shrill wail so piercing that if you would attempt to parrot it, you'd probably avulse the soft skin of your throat and raw your voice with a single screech. It was, in fact, the sort of wail that you'd expect to make if Death jumped out of the bushes late at night.

"Apologies," I coughed, "wrong house." I promptly turned, walked out and closed the door.

If I didn't have every bloody farmer looking at me before, I sure did now. Most had an angry look to them, the kind that foreigners often receive after accidentally eviscerating cultural morals when visiting another kingdom, and just before they get mauled to death by an angry mob.

A younger man nearby, however, was grinning.

"I'm looking for someone," I told him. "Goes by Rivon. Rather short, whitish-gray hair. Has a great fondness for roosters."

The man flashed me a crooked grin. "Yeah, yeah, the rooster keeper."

The rooster keeper?

"Up there on the Gleam," he explained. "Can't miss 'im, got a little home with some fencin' around it and 'bout twenty roosters. Plenty of fat hens too. Lots of eggs."

I thanked the man and hurried off to the second plateau, which was affectionately known as the Gleam.

The Gleam is where you went to get your fill of entertainment and cleanliness, but only if you were wealthy enough. Up here were enormous bathhouses with water that ranged from lukewarm to just a smidgen under a rolling boil. I used to anticipate relaxing in them before Braddock barred me from his kingdom. They shared the plateau with a theater, archery competitions, dirt rings for wrestling, horseshoe tracks, hammer-throwing events, and, apparently, a rooster coop.

Something strange caught my eye as I climbed up to the Gleam. The third plateau of Erior, where the keep was situated, bled out in a mishmash of crimson tents. Faint outlines of soldiers — hundreds and perhaps thousands — crowded amongst the tents, like a platoon that'd been mobilized for war. I'd have to ask my brother about this.

Near the far edge of the Gleam stood a triangular building with a roof that split into two sweeping panels anchored into the ground. As I approached, I was reprimanded by a symphony of angry crowing. In a wire pen that must've been thirty feet long, hens and roosters shuffled about, pushing their beaks up against the fence curiously. Or perhaps threateningly.

I knocked on the peeling cedar door of the house and waited. I wasn't going to make the same mistake twice.

An urgent pitter-pattering of feet droned from inside.

"One moment, please," a breathless voice called out. "Just one moment."

"An old friend is here to see you," I said.

"Yes, yes," he said automatically. "One moment, *please*."

The door creaked open, and an arm swung through, followed by a shoulder, and then a leg. Rivon Eyrie squeezed the rest of his tall, unwieldy self through the tight space like a kitten beneath a door frame. He quickly shut the door behind him, heaved a heavy breath and smiled uneasily, like a murderer hoping a pair of inquisitive guards standing before him hadn't seen the trail of blood leading into the kitchen.

He scratched the salty bristles on his face and poked a headful of silver hair forward in surprise. "Astul?"

His anxious smile twisted into one of joy, scrunching up all the wrinkles on his acorn face. He swung a birdlike arm behind my back and embraced me.

"Six years!" he said, taking me by the shoulders and probing me from head to toe with his eyes. "I'd say they'd been kind to you, but you look worn, old boy."

"Hunting down a king slayer will do that to you."

"A king slayer?"

"Let's go inside and I'll tell you all about it. And you can tell me how Rivon Eyrie went from a Rot to the rooster keeper of Erior."

His eyes swung side to side vigilantly, then he opened the door. "After you," he said.

He framed the doorway, forcing me to go around him. Soon as I stepped inside, he was at my heels.

He kicked the door shut and slid a crateful of heavy-looking ceramics in front of it.

"Interesting arrangement," I said, noting the peculiar emptiness of the room. Well, empty except for the cluster of drawn satchels and cloth bags bursting with pots and pans and cups and sheets and pillows and paintings and various knickknacks.

He chuckled nervously. "Bugs," he said.

"Bugs?"

"Oh, sure, sure. Got a nasty, er, infestation. Roaches, spiders, that sort of thing."

"I see. Does giving off the appearance that you're moving out scare them away?"

"It's the oils," he said, scratching his neck. "They, er... kill 'em off. The bugs, that is. Just got to apply them all around the house and in the morn you wake up with shells and corpses of, um..."

"Roaches and spiders," I reminded him.

He snapped his fingers. "Yes, yes, roaches and spiders. Don't want the oils touchin' all your belongings, though. Anyways, sit, sit. Have some peppermint tea with me."

He went over to the corner of the room and began rummaging through some bags.

"Hmm," he muttered. "Now I could have sworn I sat them on top here. Or maybe it was in this one."

"Rivon," I said.

"No, not here either," he said mindlessly. "Now where in the hells…"

"Rivon!"

He picked his head up and brushed his stringy hair from his eyes.

I pointed to the collection of bags littering a small table and both chairs. "It seems your chairs are in use."

"Oh, don't mind those things," he said, waving a dismissive hand. He plodded over to the table and tossed the bags to the floor. "Ah," he said, stuffing his hand inside a small pouch, "here they are."

He produced a thin leather casing that when opened up revealed bright green leaves.

"There, there," he said, pouring them onto the table. "Now, where is that pot…"

For the next twenty minutes, I twiddled my thumbs as Rivon raced around his house, riffling through his stowed-away possessions, cursing, muttering to himself that he ought to have really prepared this in a much more orderly fashion, and generally mumbling whatever four-letter word came to mind. He eventually found the teapot, but then he had to go fetch water from the well. And of course that meant meticulously sneaking out of and back into the house for no discernible reason.

Finally, the tea was steeped, warmed and poured into two clay cups that had handles carved into the shape of rooster tails.

"Enchanting," I said, nodding at the craftsmanship apparently inspired by a chicken fetish.

"Oh, yeah, yeah, got a potter 'round these parts to fix them up for me. For free too! Monetarily speaking. I did provide her with twenty-four extra-large eggs laid by Big Momma out back."

I sipped on the scalding tea, sighing as the coolness of peppermint soothed my throat and warmed my belly. "How long have you had bugs?"

He lowered his cup. "Bugs?"

"Roaches, spiders."

His eyes grew big. "Oh, oh. Yes, roaches and spiders, all around here. Infestation! Er, a couple days now. Started getting real bad for a couple days, yeah. Been hanging around here weeks, though, just a few here, a few there, you know how those little bastards are, *anyhow* what's this about a king slayer?"

"Someone put Vileoux in an early grave. I would have just waited for the old coot to die, but not all assassins are as patient."

Again, he lowered his cup and his eyes got big. "Killed him? Oh, my. No, no, never heard that. Word got around that he was dead, but I thought it must've been natural."

"More like magical," I said.

Rivon choked on his tea, spewing forth frothy peppermint and spittle into his hand.

"Are you all right?" I asked, watching him carefully.

He pounded his chest and licked his lips. "Fine, fine. Went down the wrong tubule there. Anyways, you said, er... magical?"

"Just a figure of speech," I explained, allaying the concern in his voice. "*Seems* almost magical to assassinate a king and get away with it nowadays."

"Right, right," he said. He pinched a nostril and snorted, sucking back up snot that his failed attempt at swallowing had shaken loose. "Does seem strange, grant you that. Wish you luck and all that, finding the killer. Nice of you stop by, Astul. I appreciate it."

He gave me a friendly nod, stood and began tidying up.

"Rivon," I said, remaining seated, "we've hardly talked."

"Haven't we? So sorry. Lose track of time nowadays. Days blend together with nights, nights with days, sun with the moon, moon with the sun." He rambled on, miming the clash of astral bodies with his hands. Tea spilled over the rim of his cup and splashed onto the floor. He didn't seem to realize.

Scooting out of the chair, I went up to him and steadied him with an arm around his shoulders. "Easy, old man. Come on, now, have a seat. When's the last time you slept?"

He counted his fingers. "Oh... oh, been three days, I think."

Must've been triple that since he had last showered. The must of slimy sweat caked on his skin and through the layers of his thin hair stung my eyes and made them water. I dropped him off in his chair and retreated to the other side of the table, where the stench wasn't so noticeable.

"Must be exhausting," I said, "tending to all these chickens. Do you supply all of Erior with eggs?"

"Oh, Gods, no. No, no. Only the royal family."

"Lotta hens for one family."

"Lotta mouths for that one family," he countered.

I leaned in sympathetically and touched his arm. "Rivon, this wasn't your dream, playing slave to a king. What happened? You were supposed to come here to the richest city of the world with all the coin you made as a Rot, and you told us — you said, I'm gonna live like a king, fuck like a rabbit, drink like I've got five mouths, ten stomachs and twenty livers, and I'll raise my roosters in peace. Instead, you're livin' like a glorified farmer and drink like an old man whose stomach can only handle weak tea. And you probably fuck like a eunuch, don't you?"

He thumbed the wiry bristles on his chin. "Priorities," he said vaguely, "they change, and…"

"Fuck off with all this bullshit. You're leavin', man. And you don't want anyone to know. Why?"

He touched his forehead to the table, sighed heavily, and picked his wary eyes up. His mouth moved, but nothing came out.

"Talk to me," I said. "I allowed you into the Rots when you couldn't fight for shit. Tried training you to swing a sword, and you never could grasp the concept. But damn if you weren't good at organizing the Hole, keeping morale high, procuring goods — you were like a fucking nanny and requisitions officer rolled into one. But that's not what the Rots have ever needed. I could've booted your ass out, but I let you stay. Because I liked you.

"And I let you leave our brotherhood to go live your golden years out in the capital of the world. Didn't ask for the gold back, the horse, the swords… nothing. Now I'm asking for something: what has you so scared that you're willing to abandon your roosters and your home?"

He covered his face with pruned hands and began weeping. "You'll… you'll never believe me." He struck the table with a closed fist. "You'll think I'm an old coot." Another fist, another strike. The table wobbled. "I'm not a fuckin' old coot, you got that?" His trembling lip curled out, and a row of bony teeth grimaced at me. "I know what I fuckin' saw!" He pointed a leathery finger at me accusatorily and shouted, "I know what I fuckin' saw!"

Tears sledded down his cheek and into his mouth. Born from fear? Or anger? Maybe both. Probably both.

"I believe anything these days, Rivon."

A louring scowl darkened his face. The room felt cold, bitter. Long gone was my friend's witless eloquence and the childlike playfulness. He looked like the kind of man beaten into submission by grief and tortured by horror.

"Always wondered why Braddock married that poor woman, Pristia," he said. "He had his pick of the lot. Could've gotten Mydia if he wanted. Or Dercy's girl. No, no, he takes the hand of a fisherman's daughter." He clenched his teeth and added, "And now, I *know* why."

This was not heading in a pleasant direction. I swung the cup of tea up to my mouth, throwing every drop of it back. Throat was still dry.

"About a week back," he explained, "I took my usual midnight stroll before lying down. Near the fountain, up there by the keep, she come running out. Mad running, like a woman gone batty. Arms were flinging up and down, her hair's going everywhere, her dress is flying up into her face, and she's got no britches on. Her eyes, Astul, they were white. I'd never seen white like this."

"Like snow?" I asked.

"No, no. Whiter than snow. Whiter than the hottest fire I've ever seen. So white, I couldn't see the pinpoints in there, just a solid... it looked like nothingness. Dead, maybe. Yeah, that's the word. Dead. Looked damned dead. But she was alive, Astul. She shrieked, hurt my ears, made my roosters crow. And then she saw me. She knew I'd witnessed it all. Guards shooed me away, ushered me back to my coop here."

I trailed a finger down my pimpled arm, hoping to push the bumps back into my skin. Didn't work so well. We're all children inside, scared of the unexplainable monsters of the night. Or in my case, the very explainable.

"Suppose that'll keep anyone up for a while," I said.

His head swung back and forth like the twine of a pendulum. "Not me, not then. You believe I fell right asleep after that, in my bed, in the arms of my lover?"

"Er," I stuttered, having a quick look around. "Your lover take the bed with her?"

"I burned the bitch."

I instinctively scooted back away from the table in surprise.

"Not her," he clarified. "The bed."

"Oh. Your lover already get a head start on you?"

"You could say that," he said morbidly. He wiped his nose and stared at the grains on the table. "Jumped right off the cliff four days ago. Out back here. Hit the cobbles below. Splattered into chunks and pieces and—"

"Rivon," I said, touching his shoulder.

"Shards of bone everywhere. Brain bits between the cobbles." He picked his head up and looked past me like I wasn't even there. "Do you know how much blood is in a body?"

There's no damn good answer for that question.

"A warning is what it was," he speculated. "Pristia seemed to follow me after that night. Any conversation, she was nearby, watching. Glaring at me. She took my lover's mind and ruined it… a warning that if I couldn't keep a secret, I was next."

The secret, of course, was that the queen of Erior was a conjurer. If conjurers aren't careful, their attempts at rooting around in another's mind can make them lose their own temporarily. Their eyes roll back, blood gets sucked right out of their face, and insanity grips them.

I drummed my finger on the table. "Fuck me."

"Yeeuup," Rivon said. "Been sayin' that myself."

"Braddock Glannondil is a scary enough man without a conjurer riffling around in his mind and pulling his strings."

Rivon clapped his hands and got up. "I'll be off soon. Faster I can get out of this terrible place, the better."

"I need your help."

He sighed and sat back down. "I was afraid you'd say that. I'm not killin' anyone, Astul. Positively refuse to do it. Absolutely under no circumstance will I—"

"I'm not asking you to kill someone," I said. "I'm asking you to help *me* kill someone. If you tell Pristia that you'll divulge what you saw, unless she gives you, I don't know, some sort of monetary gift — do you think she'll pay you a visit and take your mind?"

"That would be a likely scenario, very much so, yes."

"Good. Do it, tonight."

He held out a pair of placating hands. "Astul…"

"I need this, Rivon. Vileoux Verdan is dead and Braddock Glannondil is under the control of a conjurer. Something big is happening, old friend, and I'm not eager to see it come to fruition. Whatever the conjurers are planning, we need to stop them."

He cleared his throat. "Leaving here and going far, far away, I believe, is a fantastic solution, wouldn't you agree?"

"You can run as far as you want," I said, "but you'll still be living in a world where a bunch of misbegotten fucks can steal your mind at a moment's notice. If they can take a king, they can take a world. You don't want that. *I* don't want that."

He tilted his head back and then let it fall forward, sighing. "Will you kill her here, in my cottage?"

"That's the idea. Before she has the opportunity to take your mind, of course."

"Oh, of course," he said soberly.

You sever the connection between a conjurer and their victim when you sever the conjurer's head from their shoulders. Or cut open a big blue vein on their neck, whatever results in death first. Soon as I'd incapacitate Pristia, Braddock would regain the domain over his own mind. Whether he'd know what his wife had done to him, or even that his mind was ensnared, was another question entirely. That made this little plan slightly hazardous, given the punishment for murdering a queen would probably be… well, something very, very foul.

"I'll see you back here tonight. Keep safe." I got up from the table and walked to the door.

"Where are you going?" he asked.

"To have a meet-and-greet with my long-lost brother."

"Oh. Where?"

"… at the Stag Tavern."

"Ah. When?"

I cocked my head. "Uh, now?"

"I see. What for?"

"Why are you so damn inquisitive?" I asked. "To catch up on the past five years."

"Oh. Right. Well, I'll be waiting for you. Twiddling my thumbs." His voice trailed off into a faint whisper. "Counting my blessings. Praying to the gods. Writing down my last words…"

"Rivon," I said. "You'll be fine. I'll be fine. I'm good at assassinations. It's what I do, remember?"

His mouth fidgeted. "Have you ever assassinated a conjurer acting as a queen?"

"A first for everything." I smiled reassuringly, opened the door and left.

The thing about killing a conjurer is you never quite know what you're getting into. Most of them can only conjure thoughts in a person's mind, and even then only when their victim is overcome with some sort of emotional malaise. Fear, guilt, sadness, that sort of thing. But there have been some incidents, including the involvement of myself and the Rots, where a conjurer has delved into unsettling conjurations, including but not limited to rivening the ground, collapsing a roof, and turning a playful fox into an orange-faced murdering fiend responsible for the partial loss of my little toe.

Point is, it's generally beneficial to bring along some help when fighting a conjurer, just in case. Which is where my brother would come in. I didn't need him so much for information anymore, but rather as an extra sword.

I just had to convince him the queen he swore allegiance to was a conjurer.

CHAPTER FIVE

Vayle had once told me that if you look hard enough at the bottom of a mug, you'll find the answers to all your problems. And if you don't, well, you'll fall into a drunken stupor and won't have to deal with them until the next day, in which case you can try again. I believe philosophers call that a logic loop, or perhaps a vicious circle.

After downing a third mug of oyster ale, the answer to my problems walked through the creaky door of the Stag Tavern. Or rather *an* answer.

He was bigger in the shoulders than I remembered, carried himself well. He had the long, sullen face of my mother and the crooked nose of a soldier who'd gotten busted up a few times.

I waved at him from a secluded corner of the tavern.

He looked around, probably contemplating whether he should skip out, but then resigned himself to the fact that I'd chase him out the door like a gull after bread.

He trudged across the wooden floor of the tavern, squeezing between rowdy drunks and whizzing barmaids. Candles and torches throughout the tavern illuminated his pale face, ghostly as always. It was as if he was born allergic to the sun.

"Another storm?" I said as he approached. Water puddled under his soggy rags.

He crossed his arms, tongued his cheek and held my eyes for a long time.

Finally, he said, "Thought I'd made it clear that I didn't want to see you again."

I snapped my fingers at a passing bar hand. "Two more oysters."

My brother turned to protest, but the bubbly boy was already bounding into the crowd again.

"Come on, enjoy yourself," I said. "Have a seat and talk to your long-lost brother."

"You haven't been lost long enough," he said.

Look at him now, I thought. Standing there with all sorts of confidence, throwing out snappy quips — why, it could make an older brother's heart swell with love. Not mine, of course. I wasn't the loving type. But he could always earn my respect, even if he did have that stupid grinning jackal fastened to his cloak.

"I don't have much time," Anton said. "So if you were passing through to say hello, well… hello, goodbye and it would probably be better if you skipped this kingdom on your way back."

The bar hand pranced by and traded two mugs for payment. I slid him an extra gold piece upon noticing the ale sloshing against the rim; you always appreciate a filler.

"Mmm mmm!" I mummed, inhaling the charred nautical fumes. "Makes you feel like a pirate. Sit and drink with me, and don't lie to me again. Soldiers on leave might worry about their next assignment, if it's going to be in the sunless jungles of the Sedan Woods or the relentless sandstorms of the Desert Hills, but they don't worry about time, because they've got lots of it."

Anton swung his long mane behind his ears, sighed and kicked the chair out from the table. "Lord Braddock knows we're brothers. If I'm seen with you after what you did to his uncle…"

I snorted. "*Lord* Braddock?" He licked his lips incredulously. "All right, all right. Fine. You call him whatever you wish. He *is* your lord now."

"Being part of this army has given me purpose. It's given me direction. These men are my brothers. My *real* brothers. Not whatever you masquerade around as."

I drank. "Still stuck on that knife I put through your shoulder?"

He cast a glance off to the side and shook his head. "Just like you, Astul. Pretend all the shit you put me through after mum and dad died didn't happen. You sit here and drink your fill, insult the way I've lived my life. Don't you dare pretend I was given a different opportunity in this world."

I leaned back, letting pent-up years of ire and resentment roll off my shoulders. "Well, you could have—"

"I couldn't have done a thing! You ran off into the wilds and left me behind with Aunt Jo and Uncle Timmon. What could they possibly give me except stale bread and some tea? Poorer than mum and dad and just as drunk, that's the kind you left me with."

I drank. "You were a pipsqueak, and I was fifteen. Fuck me for trying to protect you. I expected to die out there, running around in the trees and mountains of fuck knows where. Never intended to establish the Black Rot. Just so long as I sniffed some freedom and keeled over somewhere other than home, that was fine by me. I wanted better for you, Anton."

He threw his arms onto the table. "Then why not let me join the Rot?"

I drank. No, chugged. The faster this ale went to my head, the better. "Killing's a dangerous game."

"Tell me the truth."

"You really want the truth?" I asked, dumping the rest of the ale into my bloated belly. "Truth is if you bungle up one time, you're a dead man. You think we've got it all. Our pick of whores, vaults full of gold, bellies full of tender meats, and pure, unadulterated freedom. You wouldn't be far off. But one slip of your hand, a simple miscalculation of one's intentions… and your head's cut clean off. Or you're sitting in a dungeon, taking kicks to your balls till your cock spurts blood. Who would want that for their own kin?"

He folded his hands. "Especially a kin who isn't good enough. That's the reason you never wanted me." He shrugged indifferently and added, "I know. I was the kid who couldn't run through the woods without hitting his head off a branch, couldn't scale a tree without crying about the heights. Awkward as they come, clumsy as they make 'em. But look at me now." He spread his arms proudly and began shouting. "Just look!"

The tavern quieted and its patrons regarded us hopefully, mugs and skins in hand, waiting for the outburst to flare into a brawl they could pick sides and join in on.

"Emotional outbursts," I whispered to my brother, "are unbecoming of a Red Sentinel officer. Congratulations for the rank, and please, don't mistake my praise for satire."

He lowered his head and scooted closer to the table. Realizing that fists wouldn't be hurling into jaws anytime soon, the drunks went back to drinking, laughing and adding aitches to esses.

"How'd you know?" Anton asked.

I stretched across the table and flicked the pin fastened to his cloak. "Grunts don't wear these. Also, I know everywhere you've been and everything you've accomplished since you joined this army. And, if you don't mind keeping this between you and me, it's made me proud."

He scratched his cleanly shaven face. "I appreciate the... the gesture. Even if it doesn't sound much like you. But I know you didn't risk coming here to tell me this."

"Who the hell here knows my face? Braddock and maybe a couple lords and ladies of the court? I'm not much for meandering up to the third plateau and kissing rings or whatever it is they force you to do up there to show respect, so I feel pretty fucking safe. Invincible, you might say."

Anton finally took a sip from his mug. "I'd say the drink has a lot to do with that."

Speaking of which. I flagged a barmaid down and had her bring me another ale. I'd sleep well tonight. "But you aren't entirely inaccurate. Stopped by to see an old friend."

"And who might that be?"

"I'll spell it out for you," I said. "Eye tee apostrophe ess. Eh ess ee see are ee tee."

Anton scribbled the letters onto the table. Then he chuckled. "You're a bastard."

Smiling, I winked. "Haven't been here for a few years, but it's changed. A lot more... force is present. Looks like you've got an army up there on the third plateau."

"Sentinels were all ordered back. Same with the Red Guard. You oughta see some of the cities around here. They say red tents are gushing out of the walls like blood."

The barmaid brought me my ale, and I quickly wetted my lips. "My brother's one of the lucky ones, is he? Gets to sleep in the capital of the world, instead of one of its boroughs."

He snorted. "Not terribly lucky. You should see the keep up above. Surrounded by tents and fire pits. Not enough room here, either."

"Must be a reason for all this mobilization," I suggested.

"Sure," he said. "I'll spell it out for you. Eye tee apostrophe ess."

I reached across and gave him a brotherly punch in the shoulder. "You don't know shit anyway."

He furrowed his brows. "Don't be so sure."

It wasn't worth pressing him farther. There's only one reason a king mobilizes his entire army, and it's sure as shit not to play parade the troops through the streets and hand sweets to little boys and girls. Braddock had a history of clashes with minor families in nearby provinces, but he'd always send a few outfits of cavalry to deal with the problem, never the full weight of his impressive army.

He was readying himself for war. Or more accurately, Pristia was readying him for war.

"Pristia," I said, "you know her well?"

"The queen? No, not at all. I'm an officer of the Red Sentinels, not a member of the court."

"So you don't have, oh… feelings of love or devotion or any of those sappy emotions for her?"

With squinted eyes and a cocked head, he asked, "What are you getting at?"

"She needs to die."

He pushed his mug away, groaned and went to stand. "I can't hear this. I can't listen to this sort of—" He wanted to say treason. It lay at the tip of his tongue, but instead he swallowed it and replaced it with "this sort of talk."

I grasped his wrist and yanked him back into the chair. "Your queen is a conjurer."

He blinked, allowed the word to register in his mind, and then closed his eyes. "I knew you had an ulterior motive for being here."

"She's got your king by the balls, or by the mind, really. And I think she's responsible for Vileoux Verdan's disappearance."

"You're whacked," he said. "Straight out of your mind, brother. Completely whacked."

I ignored him and continued on. "I don't know why, and I don't know what the endgame is. Won't have a bloody chance to figure that out, either, if we don't free the most powerful king in the world from her grasp."

He threw up his hands and stood. "I'm done."

"Anton! I need your help."

"Done. Goodbye, Astul."

"I'll prove it you," I said.

He licked his chops and chuckled. "I've gotta hear this. How do you prove that the queen of Erior is a"—he chuckled again and rubbed his temples—"a conjurer?"

Just before I could explain the details of this glorious plan, a bizarre hush fell over the tavern. Silence among drunks is about as common as singing among mutes: it takes no small miracle for it to occur. Well, a miracle, or, as I discovered, the appearance of a king.

Braddock Glannondil waddled into the tavern, flanked by a contingent of the Red Sentinels. Been a while since I'd seen that puffy face, those blubbery arms and fingers full of heavy rings.

The floor planks cried under his weighty frame. His crimson cloak dragged behind him as he hobbled through the red-faced drunks who fanned out in respect, or fear.

I hid my eyes behind my mug and swore silently. The jackal himself staggered toward me, a hunter sniffing out the scent of his prey effortlessly.

Anton stuffed his hands deep into his pockets. His jaw shivered as the lumbering footsteps behind him thudded closer.

"A brotherly chat?" Braddock asked, his weathered voice stabbing inside my skull like a harrowing headache. He slapped his hand on my brother's shoulder.

"Lord Braddock," my brother said. "I was…"

"Going to bind his hands and bring him to me?"

Anton swallowed. His brows twitched. "Yes, my Lord. Of course."

I rose from the table. "Leave him alone, you fat fuck. You wanted my head, and now here I am. My brother doesn't have a part in this."

A wicked grin split Braddock's lips. "The truth is much more interesting, Shepherd. Every morning the roosters crow, and on this morning, one of them told me I might find you two here. Brother and brother, planning a coup. I'm afraid your old friend, Rivon, swears allegiance to me now."

Betrayal needled itself into my flesh, numbing the tips of my fingers, sucking the feeling from my toes, wringing the air from my lungs.

"Are you afraid?" Braddock asked. "Afraid to die? Don't be. I'm not going to make good on my promise to string my banner up through your guts. Rivon suggested a much better idea for punishment."

"Are you going to torture me?"

Braddock pointed to himself innocently. "Me? No. But those I send you to… I cannot speak for them."

CHAPTER SIX

There's nothing quite like riding in the back of a wooden cart with your hands roped together behind your back. Every bump sent my ass into the air, only to come crashing back down on the splintery seat. Turns were great fun. Without a hand to brace myself, my head would careen into the side posts. Hopefully I wouldn't be dribbling and answering questions with grunts by the end of this journey.

The despair my brother and I displayed didn't go unnoticed by nature. The sun had gone into hiding and took the warmth with it. The clouds shifted from a milky white to a gloomy gray, spewing out fat drops of rain. This was the kind of rain you feel exploding on the back of your neck, ice oozing out and shivering across your shoulders.

We'd left Erior first thing in the morning, loaded into a cart like fish plucked from the ocean and on the way to cutting boards. Braddock wasn't even kind enough to make an appearance and wish us well. Neither was the enigma, Rivon Eyrie. So many questions for that man. The easy way out was to call him treasonous, hold a grudge till I died — which very well could happen sooner than later — and be done with it. But the danger at looking at the world through a black-and-white lens is that you miss the grays, and it's there, in that bleak prism, you find the twists and turns that give reason to the unreasonable, imagination to the unimaginable, and logic to the illogical.

Anton sat across from me, head slumped like a knight unseated during a joust. Dull-eyed and droopy-faced. It was eerily similar to the way he looked when our father and mother were at our feet, bloodied and lifeless. The only thing missing was tears.

I was always stronger than my brother. It seemed like nothing could undo me. An assassin doesn't live for thirty years without finding himself in a few... unfortunate situations. Retaining control is vital.

Even when it seems like everything has been stolen from you and your well of luck has gone dry, there's always a way out. I usually knew of those ways, although sometimes they snuck up on me, like Sybil freeing me from Edenvaile's prison.

But Writmire Fields — my destination — made my situation grim. Slavers controlled the fields, populating them with rapists, murderers, thieves and other societal misfits that get shipped to them for free. In exchange for the humanitarian aid, the donors get reduced rates on goods bought from the slavers. It's the game at its finest.

"My face itches," Anton said.

"Why are you telling me? I can try to kick you to relieve the itch, if that's what you want."

"You've done quite enough."

"Thought I could trust an old Rot."

Bump went the wagon, and smack went our heads. Anton grumbled. "An old Rot?"

"Rivon," I explained.

"He's a bloody rooster keeper."

"Look out!" I hollered, sliding across the seat and into my brother. A long patch of dimpled mud lay up ahead. The wagon plodded over it, rickety wheels tumbling into the deep dimples and rocking the cedar frame like an angry gale spurning a baby bird's first flight. Sitting close to my brother allowed us to hook our legs together, centering us on the seat so we wouldn't end up with cracked skulls and be dead behind the eyes before we arrived at the slavers' camp.

The barren field leveled out again. "Anyway," I said, "he was a Rot before he was Erior's lead fowl attendant. He'd never do this to me willingly… Pristia likely had her grubby hand in it."

My brother sighed disgustingly. "Oh, would you stop with the nonsense? Pristia's not a conjurer, you dolt."

I offered up my best admonishing grin. "Just like you, Anton. Pretend the world's a perfect little haven. Nothing's wrong. Everything's well and good."

"Better than living my life in raging suspicion, you unstable, paranoid fuck."

Oh, if I had my hands free. "Paranoid? *Paranoid?* If you heard the mess I was told about Vileoux's death—"

"Hear, hear, hear," my brother said. "Did you actually *see* anything?"

I spun around so hard and fast, my knee slammed into the side of the cart. "Did I see anything? *Did I see anything?*"

"Shut your bloody mouths," one of the transport guards said. "Fuckin' road's hell as it is, I don't need a splitting skull to go along with it."

Anton laughed quietly at me. "You didn't. Tell me otherwise. Go ahead. Tell me you saw evidence that Edenvaile's king was murdered. Don't even go into all the things you heard. Just tell me you at least saw him lying in a sarcophagus, dead."

"Something big is coming, Anton. I'm sorry you don't have the wherewithal to perceive that."

"I'm sure," he said in a patronizing tone. "War *is* pretty big, after all. If you want my theory, it's that the Verdans are playing a game of keep-away with Vileoux, pretending he's dead. They don't like that the Glannondils are so powerful, so they're going to play the assassination card, blaming it on Lord Braddock.

A few agreements later, alliances are made, war breaks out, and the world is restructured. No conjurers, no silly magic. Just old-fashioned bloodlust."

The horses at the head of the cart snorted, and an inquisitive rabbit hopped out of the way. "Just one problem," I said. "Rivon Eyrie."

"Would you let it go? He played you, brother. He's not a Rot anymore. He's trying to climb the ranks, swindle himself into the court. He did himself a big favor by turning you in. I respect it, actually."

Poor Anton, one eye black and the other white, forever and for always, it seemed. "I saw the hopelessness in his eyes, heard the loss of life in his voice. I felt the dread, the primal terror in his words. This wasn't an act. Something — *someone* — disturbed him, deeply."

"Acting is a skill," Anton said. "Like a blade, one can sharpen it till it sings."

"Even if that were true, he would never forget the Black Rot."

My brother shifted in the seat. "Climbing the ranks is more important to him than old friendships."

"That's not what I mean. Have you wondered why, if your dear Lord Braddock seethed with so much hatred for me, he never sent a small excursion to the Hole? Why, if anyone else had the mind to off his uncle, he'd bring the wrath of the Glannondils down upon them. But he gift-wrapped me nothing more than a thinly veiled threat."

"You always told me the Hole is impregnable."

"It is," I agreed. "But what's stopping a small platoon of cavalry from waiting nearby, till I clamber on down from my hill." I leaned close. "*Fear*, that's what. Do you know why spiders instill such fear in so many?"

Anton looked annoyed.

"They're the true embodiment of darkness," I said. "They lurk in the emptiness, the dank, the shadows, the places your eyes can't see and your mind doesn't like to go. They're silent as a wisp, despite skittering across your floors, spinning their webs, spawning their alien young. And they're everywhere, in every nook of the world. Worst of all, they're unpredictable. You never know in which direction they'll scurry, where they'll move to next. But they're always there, aren't they? And so it is with the Black Rot, with one tiny difference."

"Your assassins don't have eight legs?" Anton said.

I smiled. "If you hunt us, the entire colony will swarm you. Kill me in action? Fair enough, but don't you dare make an example out of me. Don't you dare hunt me down. Kingdoms have rotted away from the inside out because some pompous lord wanted to make an example of the darkness. But you cannot control what your eyes cannot see. Rivon knows this. He was a part of it. He wouldn't risk his life to climb another step up the royal ladder. Something bigger than you, bigger than me, bigger than the five families is brewing right now. I just hope we live long enough to see what it is."

"Living isn't in our future," Anton said. "I would have taken the beheading if I could. I've heard of these slavers before. You won't get out of here alive, Astul. No one does. Not even the Shepherd of the Black Rot."

I nodded, and not sarcastically. I had my faith, but sometimes that's just a nice thing to have. It doesn't really do anything.

During the night, we continued on into the Dead Marshes, where the seaside mountains vanished, replaced by thick curtains of trees, some stretching so far into the air it looked as though they wanted to give a reach-around to the moon.

By morning, the road we traveled turned from overgrown grass and weeds to a still swamp. The cart would stop every fifty feet it seemed, and our Glannondil escorts would get out, clean the caked-on mud from the wheels and swear at the gods when they stopped again minutes later.

Small stretches of vomit-colored clay eventually lead us through the marshes, surrounded by submerged blades of grass, circular gatherings of lilies and more water than mud. The horizon suffered a mangled death as we drew closer, with a massacre of splintered and limbless charred trees eschewing the blue from the sky. Vines and thorned creepers hung from them, some so big and knotted you'd swear they were eldritch serpents lying in wait. The whole land had a subtle green tint to it, whether from the bile of bogs or something more perverse.

The marshes soon ended, and our royal caravan came to a stop, in front of a gate. Even if you were born in a piss-poor village and hadn't ever ventured outside until now, you would have a word to describe this gate, and that word, undoubtedly, would be lame. It was nothing but a bunch of wooden stakes crookedly pounded into the ground, topped off with spikes for good measure.

"Smell that?" I asked my brother.

"I'd rather not," he said, shielding his nostrils with a shoulder.

"I'll give you a guess as to what kind of shit it is you're smelling. Here's a hint: it ain't coming from no cow."

Boy, was it rotten. Like a heap of city garbage warmed by the sun, drizzled with a few cupfuls of infected pus and garnished with chopped-up, liquefied necrotic flesh.

A man clad in leather armor and with goat horns for shoulder spikes opened the gate. "Two? That's it? Lost six this week and I get two to replace 'em?"

His voice sounded as though he was digging into the pit of his stomach for the deepest tone he could muster.

"All Lord Braddock could send," answered the driver. "He needs his own slaves."

"I'll fuckin' not doubt he does," the man said. "But you tell 'im if he keeps sendin' me this horseshit, there ain't gonna be a discount no more. I want five next time. Got it?"

"Yeah, yeah. We'll tell him. These two are brothers."

The slaver welcomed us with a toothless grin. "Brotherly love, eh?"

He walked up to the cart and put a fist into my shirt, pulling me off and so graciously tossing my face into the stiff ground. Another hand slapped my shirt, and just like that, back on my feet.

Anton and I found ourselves inside the walls, sitting against a building streaked with white stains that looked awfully similar to bird shit.

"Sit," the slaver said.

Next to us were a few other unfortunate souls, staring with wide eyes at an outrageously large slaver who approached. Those slavers, I didn't know where they came from, but I assumed they were crafted out of mountains. Goddamn giants. He asked each man and woman their names and their story. They all answered with a whimper, licking their lips and giving a nice, hard swallow at the end. Some were thieves, others rapists, and one had murdered a lord's son.

Finally, the big man's eyes fell on me. "And you?"

"Some call me the fat skinner on account of how I have a penchant for stabbing fat bellies like yours. Say, do you have a brother? I remember poking a blade in a man who quite resembled you—sweaty, oily face, two chins, scraggly patch of hair on his neck that looked like it belonged on the bottom of his ass. I bet he was your twin."

"Look at this," the slaver said, cackling. "A funny man we got with us. I need to laugh, it's good for you, yeah?" He cracked his whip across my face and bellowed a laugh that shook his shoulders. "Oh, it does feel good to laugh!"

The whip snagged a thin film of flesh from my cheek. I touched it with my finger, only to receive another lashing, this time on my hand. I grunted, but managed a smile. "Tell me, when's the last time you saw your cock?"

The slaver closed that stupid, oversized mouth of his and nodded. He went off behind the building and emerged with an orange-tipped iron poker.

"Usually we do this after, but you're a special case, I see."

He walked up, leaned in and pressed the poker into my chest. I heard a sizzling sound, like skewered bacon with grease dripping into a fire. And then I felt it. And smelled it. The putridness of scorched skin made me retch, but bending over pushed the poker deeper into my chest.

The pain... unimaginable. Felt it in my fingertips, burning in my eyes. It spread, coursing through and broiling every nerve in my body. I was being cooked alive, and wriggling, screaming, shrieking... none of it helped.

Finally, the hissing fled and the poker was yanked away. And I lay on my side, gritting my teeth and crying.

"You won't last the week," the slaver said. "Rise up, you're all getting it now."

I lay there as those around me stood. My brother was first. He squealed like a stuck pig and jumped back, driving his foot into my shoulder and falling on top of me.

"Why the fuck did you do that?" he asked me.

Anton and I were thrown into the fields within the walls. Our first job was to group logs according to size. The logs had already been cut and hauled in by other slaves. Fairly easy job, except when the logs are thicker than you. From what I gleaned, the slavers didn't much care if we talked, so I kept close to my brother.

"Look for a way out," I said.

"I'm *sure* I'll find one," he snapped back.

"There's a reason I did what I did. Look around you."

His head swiveled around, jauntily looking every which way. The boy had the brain of a dog whose parents were siblings.

"Subtly," I snapped.

"They're looking this way," he said.

"At me. They're watching me, not you, not anyone else. I didn't take an extra ten seconds of a hot poker in the chest for the hell of it. You have a bit of freedom in here because of me. Scan the wall, check for weaknesses… look for a way out."

Anton nodded. Finally, he understood. Damn near had to hit him over the head with one of those logs, but he got it.

We didn't talk for the rest of the day, minding our own business, picking up logs, stacking them in place and wheelbarrowing them over to one of three enormous pits. One was for small logs, one for medium and the last for the large variety.

Simple enough. For a lumberjack. I, unfortunately, was an assassin. My arms were nearly numb halfway into the day, and logs were dropping from my grasp like leaves from a tree in autumn. One almost landed on my foot. The slavers would laugh loud enough for everyone to hear and tell me to pick the damn thing up and get back to work.

At night, we slept on the ground, where we worked. We must have looked like black birds sitting in rows along tree branches. In the morning, it was back to business. Slaves carried in logs from outside the walls, and we separated them again. We ate once a day, carrying shallow wooden bowls we were given during initiation and filling them up once — and only once — with broth. Sometimes the broth had bits of bread, sometimes bits of dirt.

Filling our bowls with water from the wells was more common than filling them with food, but not enough to keep your throat from feeling like sand for most of the day.

When the sun fell, we slept on grass cool and moist from piss and dew. Jagged wood chips littered the ground, always getting caught in the bends of your knees and elbows.

It'd been five days of this shit. My brother claimed this place had no weakness, no way to escape. I was starting to believe him.

On the sixth day, a cart edged along the wall and stopped at the gate. More friends to play with.

There were four of them, and the slavers led them inside the walls. They all looked hopeless, except one woman. Furious would be the best word to describe her. I dropped off a log into the pit and squinted.

Why, I knew that face. Not so much the furious part, but the features. The thin lips, small forehead, plump dimples. And the hair... oh, I'd definitely seen that hair before. Black as a raven's plumage.

What, exactly, was Sybil Tath doing here?

CHAPTER SEVEN

The nice thing about slavery was that I had time. Time to cry, time to reflect miserably, time to… well, time to watch the sky and wonder, are there always so many birds up there? Was this simply one of those instances when you stand atop a seaside cliff, look out thoughtfully and invariably comment on just how massive the ocean is?

Or was this really just a fuckload of birds? Blue birds, red birds, yellow-tailed birds, big birds, small birds — didn't matter. They flocked together in droves, smothering the blue sky with their assortment of colors and sizes, and they all came from the east. Sometimes their furious squawks would quiet for a while as they settled into the boughs of the forests beyond the camp, but then more would pass through, thrashing the quiet air above, flapping and crying, shitting on all of us down below.

I watched the birds as I lugged logs into pits.
Or more accurately, I watched the sky, waiting for it
to darken into evening blush and then the crisp blue
of twilight. Soon it would be dark, time to sleep. Not
for me, though. For this slave, the day was just
beginning.

Exhaustion had most of the camp in its grip.
Snores murmured around me, and bodies writhed as
the nightmares came. One of the new arrivals wept.
As I crawled through the bird-shit-encrusted grass
and jagged wood chips, I came upon him. He could
have served as a distraction, someone who would
inevitably attract the slavers so they wouldn't have the
wherewithal to see me sneaking about. But as it so
happens, humanity rises up within me once in a while
— wholly unwelcome, mind you.

I put a hand on his ribs. "Stuff your shirt into
your mouth," I whispered. "Or they'll hear you, and
they'll beat you until you cry all your tears out. You
ever try to cry when you don't have tears?"

He sniffled and shook his shaggy head.

"There's pain for you. Go on, do it."

The youngster balled up the elongated neck of
his shirt and bit down on it. Then he wailed some
more, but he'd only disturb his neighbors now, and
they were fast asleep, enjoying their nightmares.

I continued on like a snake through the camp,
slithering and coiling around limbs and toes, heads
and shoulders. Onward toward the east gate, where
during the day the salt miners filled up buckets and

lucky lads and lasses would bring them in and fill the beds of trading wagons. Lucky lasses like Sybil Tath.

My breath abandoned me with each risked glance toward the drunk slavers on watch, near the front of the camp. One of the tall ones, all legs and arms, would lurch out of his seat occasionally and rush the front row like an elephant issuing a onetime warning. A slave jumped once. Got himself accused of plotting escape. Never heard from him again, aside from his cries that went on until morning.

All this crawling on my elbows and belly reminded me of a drunken bet with Vayle one night at the Hole, to prove who was more limber and coordinated while tunneling beneath hot-iron spits. That's also the reason I have a very large burn on the back of my calf.

No spits above me here, though. Nothing but the sky and… birds. They were still at it, flying in from the east, chirping away, as if to apologize for the disruption.

A bit more slithering around and I came to a woman who whispered to herself.

"Sybil Tath," I said.

She turned on her side and shoved her head forward in surprised delight. "Astul!"

"We tend to meet under unfortunate circumstances."

"What are you doing here?" she asked.

"Long story. And you?"

"A longer story. Come closer, I'll tell you about it."

We curled up together and removed our shirts, tossing them over our heads like blankets so they would dull our voices.

Her arms were warm and comforting, if gritty and crusted over with grime and sweat. Her green eyes were like verdant candles, a soothing flame inside our little cave.

She was eager to know about my time in Erior, or if I'd made it at all. I provided all the details, minus the bits about Rivon, Pristia being a conjurer and Braddock Glannondil mobilizing his army for war. Otherwise known as the important bits. If she needed that information — something I would judge — I'd tell her. I trusted her, mostly, but the golden rule of being a purveyor of information is that you always keep some things close to your chest.

"How did he know you were there, under his nose?" she asked.

"Doesn't matter now. I imagine your voyage here is a much more interesting story."

"I was ambushed as I left Vereumene," she said. "Captured and sold to the slavers. I expected to depart with Chachant, but"—the verdant flames of her eyes flickered angrily—"he lied to me. The meeting of the five kingdoms had been called off when Dercy and Braddock informed the families they could not attend this year. He went to Vereumene solely to ask for Serith Rabthorn's hand in war."

Her pimpled arms prickled mine, and a subtle shiver transferred between our pressed shoulders.

"He's a bloody fool," I said.

Sybil blinked, extinguishing the flame. Her eyes were a dull leafy green now, empty of excitement, void of anger. Back to being diplomatic, apparently. "He was rushed into kingship at the age of twenty. You cannot blame him entirely. And Braddock is not helping matters. I heard he's mobilized both the Sentinels and the Red Guard. Is that true?"

"Who told you that?"

"Serith's advisers. I could not talk to the king himself, because he is…" Her lips moved, as if in search of an explanation, but there was only silence.

My nostrils flared. "What? Serith is what? Please don't tell me he's dead. Anything but dead. Catatonic, mute, deaf, addicted to sleepy herbs, *anything* but dead. The last thing I need — that *we* need — is another dead king."

Her head seesawed from one shoulder to the other as she thought. "Wacky. Yes, that's it."

"Wacky?"

"He cries incessantly, becomes angry with the color white and has tried repeatedly to stab himself in the heart with his fingernail. I believe wacky is the proper word. It's as if his mind has been—"

"Ruined?" I interrupted.

"Yes."

Old age can ruin a mind, and Serith was an old man. But like aging itself, the process is often slow. A forgotten word here, a misplaced face there, and then you're forgetting how to get to your chambers from your throne. I did a job for the man several months ago, and his mind seemed all snuggly and pieced together. He must've deteriorated quickly, or even instantly. Short of taking a hammer to the skull, there aren't many ways that happens. In fact, I only knew of one.

"Chachant is on his way to Watchmen's Bay," Sybil said, "according to Serith's advisers."

"We've got to get out of this place, Sybil."

"How?"

"In the morning. If the three of us can overrun a slaver, grab his weapon, we could make a run for it."

More birds flew overhead.

"Who's the third?" Sybil asked.

More squawking and flapping. "Have you noticed how many birds there are?"

"Probably migrating. Who is the third person helping us?"

"From east to west? I know the western shores have nicer beaches, but I don't think birds concern themselves with the value of land or the softness of sand beneath their feet."

"Astul," she said, touching my cheek softly. "Who is the third—"

"My brother."

She went on about something or another, but all I could hear was the crowing, the whistling and the piercing screeches that sounded off menacingly like drums of war.

Migrating? No, most certainly not. I'd seen migrating birds before. Lazy bunch of fucks they are. They circle in the air, stop to rest for a while in the trees, venture leisurely like they're taking in the sights. These birds were flying hard, as if away from something that traveled a lot faster than snow. A lot meaner too.

"Feet on the ground!"

That voice was the third sound I'd heard, coming immediately after a solid thud of a boot punching right between my ribs and the subsequent groggy "Ergh" that slipped out of my mouth. I rolled onto my side.

"Feet on the ground!"

Another boot, placed expertly between the ribs once again. I rolled onto my other side, clutching my stomach.

"Put your feet on the ground!"

Another boot, this one catching me right across the jaw. With a now-stabbing headache, stiff mouth and bruised ribs, I got the idea and put my bloody feet on the bloody ground.

It was at that point it came to my attention I hadn't, as planned, made it back to my brother last night. Apparently Sybil's warmth had made a sleepy boy out of me.

A big bastard slaver had his chubby arm around her, holding her tight to his blubber. Same fucker who'd branded me. Went by the name of Shroden.

"The fat skinner!" he brayed. "Should've known it'd be the fat skinner. Always the one causing me trouble. Fancy yourself a pair of perky tits, do you now?"

He slid the back of his fingers along Sybil's chest. She tried to turn, but he held her firmly.

"I'm known to venture great distances in my sleep," I said, squinting through the sun that just *had* to position itself right in front of my eyes. Bright lights do splitting headaches no good. Learned that many years ago, after my first hangover.

"You," Shroden said, pointing at me with a grotesque nail sheathed in some sort of rotting yellow, "you like to play games. Big game player where you come from, hmm?"

"I'm sorry," I said, bowing my head. "I'll get back to work immediately and go at it twice as hard today."

He looked around, undoubtedly trying to untie the knot of confusing thoughts in his head.

"Tryin' to play another game," he asserted.

"I'm not," I said, and that was the truth. I wasn't the sole focus of his ire anymore; I couldn't afford to play games.

"You won't fool me." He peered out into the crowd of slaves. "Brother of the fat skinner, where are you? Come out, now. There you are. Come here, come here."

Anton wound his way through the bodies, stepping up beside me. White and black dumplings streaked his hair, courtesy of the birds. His eye twitched. Had it always done that? No.

Shroden fisted Sybil's hair and wrenched her head back. He burrowed a nail into her chest, a smidgen above her breasts and slowly edged it up her neck. "We're going to play a game, fat skinner. It's called pick 'em. You pick to save your brother, and I'll take your little crush here every which way, and after I'm done with her, the rest of the camp can have her." He tugged on the lobe of her ear with the seductiveness of a corpse. "She'll be so full of seeds, she'll be sproutin' from the mouth."

He hee-hawed like a cleft-lipped donkey, tits bouncing and flabs jiggling.

Sybil's neck pulsed, but her face was as cool as a sword swallower at a festival.

"Or you could save her the pleasure," Shroden said, his brows twitching suggestively. "But the price... it's expensive, fat skinner." He palmed the pommel of a sheathed blade and produced a rusted dagger. "Payment is your brother's life."

Anton and I glanced at one another. His eyes glistened, and for the first time since we'd arrived at the camp, there was life in them. Hope. The paradoxical kind.

"Do it," Anton urged. "Save the woman, kill me."

Crows. Cackling and yapping as they knifed through the sky, blurring the golden morning with the blackness of night. As they fled into the forests of the west, a low rumble drummed from the east.

"Choose, fat skinner," Shroden spat. "Or I'll choose for you."

"Kill me!" Anton pleaded.

It sounded like mountains were moving, shifting rivers and displacing the earth. The ground grumbled into the soles of my bare feet, and the wood chips quivered.

Shroden felt it too. He looked toward the gate and beyond, into the dense forest.

My brother lurched forward and grabbed the dagger from the slaver's hand.

He pointed the oxidized tip at his stomach. "I start it. You finish it. You won't have a choice, unless you want to see me suffer."

"Anton! Wait."

Big brother instincts kicked in, and my hand swung for his wrist. Little brother was too agile. He leaped back, steadied his feet and plunged the dagger into his belly.

Thunder boomed behind me, and blood spilled in front.

Haziness filtered across my eyes, as if I was looking at the world through frosted glass. A mist of limbs raced through the field like apparitions, seemingly drifting along without heads or torsos. I'd been a long time since I cried. Forgot just how disfigured the world looks through tears.

I blinked them away as Anton fell to his knees, dagger still buried in his belly. A sanguine smile touched his lips, and he pointed a bloody finger at me.

"You were right," he rasped. "They came for you."

An army of horses barreled out from the forest, draped with caparisons bearing a red fist. Heading the charge was my commander of the Black Rot, and beside her Rivon Eyrie.

I'd like to say I raised my hand for a sheath and sword to be thrown at my feet. I'd like to say I chased down Shroden, cut him off at the knees and then hacked his massive head clean off, right over the wall. I'd like to say the reputation that preceded me — that brutal, savage reputation that an assassin earns over the years — was reinforced as I ran my fingers over the warmth of slaver blood and tasted my revenge.

But life, she enjoys her irony. Killing going on all around me, swords clangoring, my Rots decapitating limbs and appendages, and there I was, most feared assassin in the world, Shepherd of the Black Rot, a man so dreadful that even Braddock Glannondil waited for me to come to him to make good on his promise — on my knees, eyes welling and nose running into my gaped mouth.

"We can save you," I told my brother, reaching a shivering hand out and gingerly touching his shoulder.

Slavers shrieked as swords carved them into puzzles of missing flesh. Shrill laments of innocent slaves caught between pounding hooves and serrated blades echoed in my skull.

"It went deep, Astul," Anton said. "I made sure of it." He laid a bloody hand over my arm reassuringly. "I wanted this. It was freedom, brother… freedom from this terrible place."

"Couldn't you hear it?" I asked him. "Couldn't you bloody hear it? The thunder coming from the forest, the birds, didn't you see them? Something was coming." I shoved an arm across my nose, wiping up the snot and tears. "Why couldn't you fucking wait?"

He regarded my screams with a smile. "Hope, I'd… I'd lost it. Couldn't see anything but the walls. Couldn't hear anything but the voices telling me to find a way out, and out meant…" He looked at the dagger in his belly and winced. "Pain's gettin' bad."

Through the unabating wetness of my eyes, I watched as my fingers swam to the unwrapped hilt of the dagger.

Something fell to the ground next to me, rolled over and rattled like steel. A belt.

"And this," a voice said.

A long leather scabbard crashed onto the belt.

I turned to see Vayle. She nodded and walked toward a group of Rots and mumbled something. The hysteria had ended. The battle was over, the slavers dead, and the slaves — those who survived — shivered on the ground in terror.

An ebon dagger lay inside the sheath affixed to the belt.

"You deserve better than a rusted blade," I told my brother.

He was on his elbows now, panting. "Just make it quick, Astul. It's, *ah!* The pain is overwhelming."

I straightened him, grabbed hold of the rusted dagger and counted.

"One." And I pulled. Pain isn't as bad when you don't expect it.

Anton nonetheless cried in agony as his gut spat its fluids through the vertical gouge. No, that's not quite right. He roared. Roared like a great beast stuck with a barrage of arrows.

With a fist in his sweaty, crusted hair, I tilted his head back. The twin blue veins snaking up his throat pulsed faster than a man can blink.

"I love you, Anton," I said, pressing the ebon dagger into position. "I always have, you bloody bastard."

We shared a laugh that shook the tears from our eyes.

"Goodbye, big brother," he said.

A quick draw of breath into your lungs, and... hold it. Thumb on the crossguard for leverage. Relax the hand. Steady now. Close your eyes, set your jaw. And cut.

There it was, that familiar feeling of slicing into butter. Usually I was behind my target, but I couldn't do that to my brother. I opened my eyes as his warmth sprayed into my face.

He glugged for a moment, and then fell into my arms. A clean cut across the throat gives you about ten seconds. I'd learned to end it in three, thankfully.

I laid him on the ground, angling his face toward the blue sky. And then, with a lick of my lips and the taste of copper on my tongue, I went off to find a shovel... and then, Rivon Eyrie.

The Rots aren't known as a quiet bunch, but they are smart, which means they know when to put their heads down and shut their mouths. This was a particularly good time to do just that, as I walked past a loitering few, cleaning the blood from my face with the help of an unsullied shirt belonging to a trampled slaver.

They kept their eyes low and their questions to themselves, for now. It was a matter of respect. You don't know how a man will react after killing his brother, so it's best to let silence linger, because silence is to the soul what food is to the belly.

Wise men — or those who think they're wise — say you've gotta move on after a tragedy. So that's what I did. I moved. Onward. Toward a silver-haired man who received me with a hard swallow and a hand on his hilt.

"Allow me," Rivon said, "to, er, well… explain." He pushed himself away from a shed and rubbed his hands nervously.

Vayle emerged from the building, with Sybil in tow. They held bundles of tattered linens in their hands.

"These," Vayle said, head buried in the clothes, "should keep the young and old warm at nights, until they reach Specure Village."

"That's a good six-day walk," I said. I looked back at the slaves, who were sitting on the ground, knees pulled up to their chins. "Some will survive, I suppose."

Sybil seemed to shrink in size when she saw me. "I'm sorry about your brother."

"It's done and buried. Quite literally, actually. I'll forget all about it once I can wash his stench from my face and clothes."

"Listen, listen," Rivon said. "You gave me only two options, see. Well, no. No, that's not entirely true, I suppose. Three options. One, let you kill Pristia."

"Which would have been the preferred route," I said.

Rivon steepled his hands in front of his chest in a pleading manner. "And we'd be no closer to finding out what kind of mess we're in. Vileoux Verdan was not brought to Erior, I promise you that. He's out there somewhere, mucking about as a corpse or the gods know what, mingling with conjurers, undoubtedly. Something very big is happening, Astul, bigger than the events unfolding in Erior. We can't go killing queens willy-nilly without knowing what the big picture is, see?"

"Why didn't you tell me this while we drank tea out of ceramic roosters?"

Rivon blushed. "I… those cups were gifts," he explained to Vayle and Sybil. "And, for your information, you would have ignored me or argued. I know this because you are a very stubborn man."

Vayle shrugged in agreement. "He's got you there."

"So," Rivon said, "when you went to the tavern to meet your brother, I had an audience with Braddock, and I informed him you were here, *which*, by the way, he would have discovered inevitably, after you killed his wife, and I highly doubt"—he threw his finger into the air as if he was testing the wind direction—"he would have done anything except string his banner up through your intestines as promised. I begged and pleaded, on account of our prior friendship, that he save your life and instead, er… well, send you to be tortured by the slavers. He agreed. It was not my intention for your brother to meet his end. I am sorry."

"Yes," I said, "you rather fucked up there, didn't you?"

His shoulders sagged. "I'm a rooster keeper. I've spent the past six years working out why my hens won't eat, why the eggs are soft and flaky, why my roosters aren't crowing. I didn't give it a second thought that your brother might perish here. I don't think that way anymore, Astul. I am a very simple man now."

"So why, if you're such a simple man," I asked, "are you here right now?"

Vayle stepped forward. "He was responsible for orchestrating your retrieval," she said, in a tone that suggested I ought to apologize for being an ass.

I looked off into the camp, where a mound of dirt concealed my brother's body. "I suppose he would have died marching to Braddock's war, if not here. I'm not going to offer my thanks, Rivon, but I understand."

He laid a hand on my shoulder. "I would like to stay with you, until this all ends."

I chuckled. "I don't even know where we go next."

"To Vereumene," Vayle said confidently.

Vayle may have been second-in-command of the Black Rot, but I couldn't recall a time when I ever refused one of her schemes, mostly because they were often inconceivably perfect.

My commander was ever the strategist. I had the creative touch, the one whose ideas would often be grand in scale, but Vayle was the one who brought the crushing reality to most of them. We worked well together.

Still, questions abounded. "What's in Vereumene except a blabbering idiot of a king?"

"According to Miss Tath here," Vayle said, "someone very interesting."

"You didn't tell me everything last night?"

"I did," Sybil said. "But after you went on about the birds, you stopped listening to me."

"Well, who is it?" Rivon asked.

Sybil tucked a stray hair behind her ear. "Serith Rabthorn's daughter."

I blinked. "Serith Rabthorn doesn't have a daughter. No fertile seed, no son, no daughter, no lineage — the man laments about his family's nonexistent future every time you talk to him."

"Go figure," Vayle said. "A Rabthorn lied."

"What's this hidden daughter going to tell us?" Rivon asked.

"I think something very important," Sybil said. "Considering she's a conjurer."

CHAPTER EIGHT

Sybil Tath and I parted ways again. She went off to Watchmen's Bay, chasing her lover boy in attempt to stop him from asking for Dercy Daniser's help in a war against Braddock, and the Black Rot descended into the colorless South.

There was rock as smooth as glass and as black and brittle as the crispy corpse of a rabbit strung up and forgotten about over a campfire. Nature had packed it into the form of mountains that were said to be so tall you could stand on top of them and finger the clouds. But time had worn them into disfigured hills, chopped off at the head and thinning around the waist. They had shed their glazed black skin across the flat expanse, creating a harrowing land that glinted like a demonic eye when burnished by the sun.

This place used to be the site of an old volcano. Now, it looked like it belonged to a population of pyromaniacs who'd run a few too many experiments.

My horse, who I'd borrowed from the slavers, crunched across the rocks. Her hooves crushed the slag into dust that smelled like ancient smoke.

Rivon coughed as we trudged through Crillick, home of Vereumene. His lungs weren't as good as they used to be, when he smoked every leafy herb rumored to induce psychosis. Probably because he used to smoke every leafy herb rumored to induce psychosis.

A few more nights of hoofing it over volcanic rock — a total of ten since we'd left Writmire Fields — and the circular outer wall of Vereumene greeted us through the fog of morning. An accessory parapet intersected the middle of the wall and rose far over the city, eventually forming a cross armed with trebuchets and catapults. Enormous nets were anchored into the rotund crags that surrounded the kingdom, snagging falling rock.

Vayle tilted her head back and poured the last of her wine — her fifth skin in as many hours — down her throat, then tossed the skin behind her.

"Knackered yet?" I asked.

"Perfectly subdued," she said, winking.

With a hand in the air, I idled the advancing swarm of Rots behind me, stopping well short of the wall, in case a jittery city guardsmen let his finger slip from the twine of his bow.

"City's closed," hollered a voice.

"Open it," I replied. "We're here to have a chat with your king."

"Said the city's closed. No visitors."

"Look—"

"Wait," Vayle whispered, shushing me. She guided her mare in front of mine. "We, the Black Rot, seek an audience with the honorable Lord Serith Rabthorn, King of Vereumene, Lord of the Rabthorn family, and Gate of the South. If it pleases his lordship, only the Shepherd will enter."

I side-eyed her. "You and your fancy language."

"The word you are looking for is diplomatic."

Behind the crossed parapet, a tiny figure appeared on an equally tiny balcony bolted into the high-rising rectangular keep itself.

"Did I hear that right? Black Rot? Open the gate for our friends. We are a welcoming kingdom, mm… not a… mm… come in, come in." He turned and vanished inside the keep.

Vayle and I looked at one another. "Thought he couldn't speak?" I said.

"Sounds like he's not cured just yet."

The weighty doors of the gate creaked open, and the Black Rot set on a path toward the walls. I swung around on my saddle and said to the guys and gals of the Rot, "Don't drink the water here. Seriously."

"Well, Shepherd," Kale said, "we're going to have to get proper fucked then on wine and ale."

Some of the Rots belted out ragged laughs.

"There's always tea," I said.

"Tea has water," Kale countered.

"Yes. Boiled water."

"Not a big drinker of hot drinks in the South. Unless it's mead, of course. Honey preferred."

This may well have been the South in the cusp of an early spring, but the dregs of winter hadn't dissipated quite yet. We trotted headlong into an autumn wind, the kind just cool enough to make you wish you had something covering your arms.

"Not sure I like this," Rivon said cautiously. "No, no. Not sure whatsoever."

"What's your problem?" I asked.

"Gives me the pimplies, this place does. Look at it, just look! A very, very depressing place, mm hmm."

He gave his lips a good tonguing and swiveled his eyes back and forth, perhaps hoping to spot something that reminded him of Erior. Unfortunately for Rivon, Vereumene was no capital of the world. But dredge of the world? It was in the running, if not the only one sprinting.

The guards received us with as much indifference as the walls. They barely recognized our presence, as if they had more important matters to attend, such as how they'd feed their family on the pittance Serith paid them.

As we passed under the looming shadow of the parapet above, the sphere of the city opened up into a mess of haphazardly laid volcanic paths, buildings rotting at their foundation, roofs collapsing, doors barely attached to the hinges. This place was never a jewel, but it didn't look like this seven months ago.

"Strangely empty," Vayle said.

Dust bunnies sewn to life with sticks and chunks of fermented fruit bounded along the streets, sticking themselves beneath signs and propped-open doors.

"Looks to me like everyone went out for a jolly walk," Rivon said.

Serith Rabthorn greeted us at the steps of the keep. "The entirety of the Black Rot?" he asked, clapping his hands together in welcoming fashion.

"We're having a family get-together," I said.

He smiled the smile of Death, which wasn't a large effort to imagine, given he had about as much flesh left on his decrepit face as a deer has fur after meeting a skinner. He wore a cream robe, or more accurately, the cream robe wore him. Thin white hair, frayed at the ends, greased at the roots, lay in a clomped mess at his shoulders.

Serith painfully unwound his bony fingers from each other. "Tell me. What is the occasion?"

"I was hoping we could indulge in a little chitchat. It's been a while, after all."

He smiled. "Of course, Shepherd. Your men"—as he examined the Rots, his eye caught the red hair of Malivvie—"and women will find plenty of…" He looked longingly into his abandoned kingdom. "Oh. Well, as we were."

He forced his cadaverous body to shift from right to left and then back again. It was like moving a diseased tree you fully expected to crumble into a mess of rotting bark and limbs. He shuffled his feet along the black pressed stones, toward his keep.

I clambered down from my mare and adjusted my belt. "Rest your horses," I told the Rots. "And set up camp here. Do not enter any of the buildings."

"Wot if they're offerin' free ale?" Auren asked.

"Even then." I turned to Vayle. "Find his daughter while I play entertain the king."

She smirked. "Have fun."

"I'm sure," I muttered, following Serith.

The old king took us into the empty throne room, the creased eye of the Rabthorn fox resting on the many tapestries that hung from the columns.

Up a few steps, around a couple corners, down a hallway, quick right turn, sharp left and we stopped inside a room. A finely sanded table lay inside, beneath a golden chandelier. Dozens of pronged candles burned on shelves at both sides of the room. Six barrels spread out in rows of two and stacked upon each other sat under the left shelf, which was filled to the back with clay amphorae.

"Pick your color of poison," Serith said. He tapped a quavering finger on the amphorae. "Red, purple, white."

"Red," I said. He filled an iron stein with the sweet smell of glazed strawberries. I didn't dare taste it until Serith wet his mouth first — a small habit you pick up when people are out to poison you.

Serith took a seat, groaning as he lowered himself onto the chair. "I've learned a few things in my life. You cannot be certain that a man stabbed through the chest will die. You cannot be certain that those you trust will not be swayed by gold. You cannot even be certain that your cock won't betray you when you get to be my age." He snorted. "But you can be certain that when the Black Rot comes, they'll foul your air."

I leaned back and sipped the wine. "I hardly think that's fair. The last time I came around, I brought with me the head of the bastard who killed your friend, as you requested."

Serith's mouth twisted. "You brought me the head of a wolf."

I nodded. "Exactly. Of course, we couldn't be sure. He did die while hunting, so who knows. It could have been a boar, a wolf, a bear — do you have bears here? At any rate, it could have been anything, but you'd like to think it was a wolf, wouldn't you? Who wants to be killed by a pig? And a bear? Gods, you'd think you could spot one of those from a half mile away. But wolves… they slink through the woods, eying their prey for half a day, and then they strike without notice, without sound, without sight."

Serith tilted back his head and pressed the stein to his mouth. He wiped his lips. "Drink."

I smiled and tapped a finger on the stein. "I like to savor my wine."

His heavy-lidded eyes closed, and his teeth began chattering. His lips formed words, but only air squeaked out.

"My apologies" he said, smiling devilishly. "So why are you here, Shepherd? To kill me?"

"You would have never let me in if you thought that's why I was here."

"Not unless," he said, lifting an emaciated finger sagely, "it is my wish to die."

He stared hard into my eyes, trying to pry loose a few words through intimidation. But I remained silent, and I was rewarded with a throaty laugh that quickly turned into a choking cough.

Serith pounded his chest until his hacking stopped. "It's not an outlandish wish, death. Is it? The process has already begun."

"A man like you," I said, "I wouldn't be surprised if this is all a ruse. Just to show you can pull the wool over even the Reaper's eyes when he comes for you and discovers you have quite a bit of life left in your bones."

Serith smiled and sipped from his stein. "I could use someone like you on my council. My advisers all walk around with a twig stuck up their butts."

I swirled my wine around into a funnel. "Advisers and guards, that's about all you have left, it seems. And I'm not even sure about the former, given the emptiness of your keep. Your people all run away from you?"

"I dispersed them into the north, far away from Vereumene. Forcing them out, all the men who weren't guards, all the lasses, the kiddies, that was the best decision I've made in the past twenty years. And the first one too. With my own mind."

I leaned back comfortably. "Lookie there, Serith Rabthorn knew why I came to visit him all along."

He rolled his eyes. "Of course I knew. Can you fault me for trying to get other information out from between those ears of yours? No, I knew from the moment I heard your voice. The Black Rot arriving not two weeks after Sybil Tath discovers me shattered and stuttering like a mad fool? That's no coincidence."

I finally took a drink of the wine. The aftertaste lingered bitterly on my tongue, but otherwise it'd do a fine job of letting my mind soar into the clouds.

"I've a lot of questions," I said. "Lots and lots of questions."

"You would do well to remember, Shepherd, that a conversation with me is never a one-sided affair. Just as the Rots must be paid to kill, I must be paid to talk."

I shrugged. "There's plenty of gold in my coffers."

"I don't want monetary payments. I want my daughter's safety guaranteed when you leave here.

You will take her with you. You will protect her. You will not let harm come to her, in any way, from any hand — natural or occult."

"Your daughter?" I said, feigning ignorance. "Oh, that daughter. The one you claimed you never had? The one who, if I'm not mistaken, is rumored to be a... what do you call them?" I snapped my fingers and said, "Oh, right. A conjurer."

Serith heaved his arms onto the table and set his jaw in a way that said he was done talking until I agreed to the stipulation.

Hauling around a conjurer is dangerous business, but sometimes you've have to make compromises when procuring information. "Fine. Consider it done. I'll protect your little girl. Now tell me why the world never knew about her until now."

Serith lowered his head and thumbed his flaky brows. "Her name is Lysa. Born early, barely breathing out of the womb. Nilly and I concealed her birth; it's a painful thing, Shepherd, to tell the world that after fifteen years of assumed infertility, you finally bore a child, only to have her die in the crib."

"And yet she lives."

He grunted. "I wish she hadn't. I'd heard that conjurers can heal the mind, and the mind can heal the body."

"You enlisted the help of a bloody conjurer?"

"What could go wrong? If he harmed her, I'd kill him. She was going to die anyhow, Shepherd. I thought—"

"You thought someone who forages around in the mind, twisting thoughts, perverting desires, erasing memories — you thought no harm could come of conscripting someone like that?"

He leaned forward, baring his shriveled teeth. "I was desperate! A father would do anything to save his daughter. I never thought he would take advantage of my weak fortitude and corrupt me. I remember losing my grip on my thoughts, feeling the shadows pass over me... and then... there's just bits and pieces of the last twenty years. Fragments of time."

"How'd you snap out of it?"

"You'll have to ask my daughter that. I'm told she's responsible; killed the one who took my mind. She won't talk to me. She blames me for what she says is a pain that will never go away."

"Are you afraid she'll kill herself? Is that why I'm tasked with being her guardian angel?"

"No," Serith said. "There's a war coming, and she is the heir to my throne. If she is found here, she will be raped, tortured and hung in the city square. I ruined my life to save hers; I will not give up now."

I had the rim of the stein pressed to my lips, and there it stayed as that dreadful word hung in the air like a bad stench. "War?"

"I'm told my bannermen have abandoned me for my cousin, Kane Calbid. He's blamed me for many... unfortunate happenings, most recently for secretly supplanting various lords under the Rabthorn banner."

I nodded my head. "That sounds like something a Rabthorn would do."

"I don't know if I did it or not. I can't remember. But my bannermen shouldn't have believed that. Thirty years ago, they'd have called for Kane's head and catapulted it over my walls." Serith tossed up his hands. "Now, after twenty years of kingship that I cannot recall, they proclaim him a visionary, an heir to the South. Ten thousand men are marching on my walls."

The emptiness of Vereumene now made sense. "You mean to surrender to Kane Calbid, don't you?"

He smiled. "I mean to give the city to the true heir of my throne. Let Kane Calbid gallop inside my walls and chop off my head. My daughter will remain. She will survive. She will lay claim to her queenship when Kane least expects it; she is a Rabthorn, after all. Deceit runs in her blood."

"And the way of a conjurer nests in her heart."

"Don't forget your promise, Shepherd — to keep that heart beating no matter what. They say, after all, that your word is gold."

Indeed, my word is gold. But just as gold is only good in the hands of a living man, my word does not apply to those who are not around to see it undone. And Serith Rabthorn would be dead soon enough. As would his daughter, unless she got to explaining just what a conjurer had been doing here twenty years ago, taking over the mind of a king. Because the more I learned, the more it seemed this whole ordeal was part of a plan that had long ago been put into motion.

The trouble with conjurers isn't that they think differently. Most people don't give a sack of cow hooves how you think, so long as you don't flaunt it. The trouble with conjurers isn't that they behave differently, either. Most people are indifferent to those who collect rats as test subjects, in an attempt to pervert their minds, so long as they do so in the privacy of their own home. The trouble with conjurers is that they don't have the decency to be different far away from the public eye.

They trot into villages, claiming they can heal the broken and disturbed. Problem is, humanity hasn't survived this long without being inherently distrustful. If some jolly old conjurer with gray hair and a red smile can root around in your mind, capturing the hurtful memories, erasing the heartaches, obliterating the troubled past, then surely some ne'er-do-well could root around in there and accomplish the opposite. And that line of thinking cultivates fear. Fear spreads like fire. Fear opens the door to chaos. And soon you've got yourself an entire world more than willing to rid itself of a potential problem, and the conjurer massacre begins.

Too bad we never tried to learn about them before our attempt at hunting them to extinction. It would, for example, have been prudent to know that apparently a daughter of a king could be turned into a conjurer. Prevailing thought said the mind-fuckers were born that way, like freaks with six thumbs and dwarfs with stubby legs.

What else didn't we know about them? What special little surprises would I find by sitting down for a nice chat with Lysa Rabthorn? Well, first I had to find her.

Outside the keep, Vayle was talking to a few Rots, pointing vaguely beyond the walls. She dismissed them, wheeled around with a skin of wine and saw me.

"The guards were kind enough to allow us to hunt their land," she said, walking over. "A river runs two hours east of here, is that right?"

"East..." I said with hesitation, "or west. One of those two directions."

"Oh, well. I told them to hurry back if they don't find anything. Hopefully they do; everyone is tired of stale bread. Something hot will do them good. Did you boys have fun gossiping with one another?"

Always the jester, my commander. "I've had more fun talking to squirrels. Can't say they provide more interesting information than Serith, though."

After giving her the rundown of Serith's divulgence, she flattened her finger on her lips and said, "Now I understand why Lysa appeared a broken girl. She committed murder only weeks ago. Your first one, it stays with you, as I am sure you will recall."

"Mm," I grunted. "Where is she?"

"Come, this way."

A slow patter of rain fell onto the black cobbles, kicking up volcanic dust like linens beaten into submission by handmaidens.

Vayle pointed to the city center with her chin. "Unless Nilly Rabthorn has two daughters, or is playing mother to an orphan, I believe that is her and Lysa."

The two were sitting on a bench beneath the rising shadows of wall-to-wall buildings.

"That's Nilly all right," I said. "Let's have us a friendly meet-and-greet with the queen and her conjurer daughter, hmm?"

"Astul," Vayle said, restricting my stride with a tug of my arm. "Wait. I will talk to her."

"Er…"

"*You* listen."

"Well, if you're that eager to get inside her mind, I suppose we can both interject from time to—"

"No," she said firmly. "Trust me, yes?"

"Never have I ever not," I said. "But remember to ask about her earliest memory, who this conjurer was she killed, if she heard about this plan that's seemingly been put into action, why she doesn't appear to be following it, why—"

"Astul. I know. Trust me. Please."

I rubbed my hands together and offered up a weak, apologetic smile. "Right. Sorry." While it was the absolute truth that distrust was something I never felt for Vayle, I was not accommodated to playing second-in-command. What if she didn't dig deep enough? What if she couldn't pry the information from Lysa? You often only get one shot at these things, before your target clams up and swallows the pearl. Hmm… maybe I needed to revisit my definition of trust.

Letting my commander take the lead, I fell in behind. The assumed Lysa Rabthorn kept her head down, but her eyes banked hard toward our approaching footsteps, wary as an abandoned animal who'd been spurned by humans one too many times.

Nilly was massaging her daughter's knee. She stopped when our shadows scurried over the bench like an unwelcome cloud. The queen's blond hair had been chopped off at her ears. Her round face, which used to be so colorful and tight, now sagged into a droopiness of pale depression.

Vayle bowed her head. "Lady Nilly Rabthorn, it is always a pleasure."

With a voice steeped in the kind of sorrow that bards sing about in morbid ballads, she said, "I thought that perhaps Kane Calbid sent the Black Rot here to kill us."

"We are not in the business of killing queens or kings," Vayle said.

I simply smiled and nodded. Was that the proper thing to do? Was I trying too hard? Dammit, this onlooker stuff was more difficult than it seemed. See, had it been me, I would have said the same as Vayle, and then looked slyly at Lysa and remarked, "Or conjurers." On second thought, seeing how vulnerable the girl was, maybe Vayle had the right idea of shutting me up.

"Am I to presume," Vayle said, crouching, "that this is the Lady Lysa Rabthorn?"

The nineteen-year-old woman with the color of strawberries rippling through her blond hair and a beauty mark on her cheek looked up. "Lysa," she said slowly, "will be fine. I am not a lady."

Nilly sighed heavily and continued massaging her daughter's knee.

"You are a Rabthorn, though, are you not?" Vayle asked.

Lysa seemingly thought about this, searching the thin lines of rain for answers.

"I do not believe my daughter wishes to speak," Nilly said.

"It's vital that she does," Vayle explained.

"Why?" Lysa asked. "Because I am a conjurer? And you wish to know what sort of monster I resemble?"

"I want to protect this world. I want to keep it from imploding on itself, and given recent events, that's proving difficult. I'm hoping you can shed some light as to why the conjurers took you as a baby, and what they're doing now."

Lysa clammed up, as I expected.

Vayle took the young woman's hand in hers. "I understand how you feel, Lysa."

Oh, that crafty commander of mine. If you ever want to draw the ire of someone, wait until the person is wallowing in sadness and then go up to them and tell them you understand how they feel.

"You," Lysa said, her tone accusatory and vicious, "cannot possibly... *possibly* understand how I feel."

Vayle sat her butt on the dirty ground and folded her hands. "You feel you've been cheated of life. You wish your parents would have ended it in the womb, and you hate them for not doing so. You hate them for allowing you to become a tool, a plaything, a slave. You've not seen happiness but for glimpses, and those glimpses anger you. And even now that you're free of your chains, you've yet to know peace. You feel empty, alone and afraid without them, don't you? You feel that perhaps... perhaps you cannot live like this."

The fury on Lysa's face softened, and she appeared inquisitive, like curiosity had up and struck her right across the forehead.

Vayle soothed her fingers. "I know how you feel because I lived your life."

"You're a conjurer?"

"A slave," Vayle answered. "In my past life. Forced to use my hands to clean and cook, my mouth to service, my back to bathe men. They wanted us unable to read and unable to think. They wanted us to depend on them. I defied them. I learned to read, and I snuck books inside the nomadic camp sites. I was lashed for it, raped, beaten until my eyes swelled shut. And when I finally broke free… I wasn't happy, because all I understood was the life of a slave. Being a free girl was suddenly very scary, much more so than fearing the whip or the hard fists of a drunken man."

Silence lingered. And then, Lysa spoke. "Do you believe that I'm not like them? I'm not like the conjurers that did this."

"Why did they want you?" Vayle asked.

"To help them, but I don't want to help them. I want to help people who are broken. They gave me a gift, Miss—"

"Vayle," Vayle said.

"Miss Vayle. I cannot give the gift back, and I don't want to. I want to use it for good, the way I was told conjurers had always done. But I do feel very alone in this world. It scares me."

"Your father said you killed the man responsible for all this. Is that true?"

"Yes," Lysa said shakily. She side-eyed Nilly and continued. "Well, he wasn't responsible for me. Lots of conjurers are responsible for making me one of them. I was an experiment. They'd never done it before, they claimed. But he was responsible for ruining my dad. For ruining my mom."

She blinked a tear from her eye and stared unrelentingly at the volcanic cobbles. "Did you know most conjurers can't control the domain of two minds at once? It breaks them, sooner or later. And it broke him, that awful, awful man. Siggy was his name. He began sleeping most of the day, mumbling when awake, on the edge of mindlessness." She glanced up, eyes swollen and swirling with blood. "I went into his room. With a knife." She licked her lips. "I held my breath. And I moved it across his throat. Like this."

She mimed the ripping of her knife across her throat. And again. And again, each laceration more violent than the last.

"You wanted to free your father and mother, didn't you?" Vayle said.

Lysa sniffled. "It wasn't the only way. I'm a conjurer too. I could have reversed the effects. I could have searched their minds, yanked out the thoughts and emotions and feelings and all the bad things Siggy planted inside them. Or maybe I couldn't have. They're still husks, even now. It's been too long. Nineteen years under a conjurer's control... I don't know that there's any good left in them anymore."

Nilly covered her eyes, and began choking on tears.

Interesting. Not the crying, but Lysa's revelation. That was a good piece of information to know, in case we were able to wrangle a few conjurers and get them on our side. Which, admittedly, seemed unlikely.

"Why," Vayle asked, "did the conjurers need your help, Lysa?"

"I was to be the queen of the South. There was to be war between the South and North. They abandoned those plans for me many years ago."

Vayle stood. "What could they gain from war?"

"This world," Lysa said blankly.

CHAPTER NINE

What a fan-fuck-tastic day. First I discover Kane Calbid will be assaulting the walls of Vereumene in short order, and then Lysa Rabthorn informs me the conjurers intend to incite a great war that sucks in every family, major and minor. And then after the war ends, those goat-fucking conjurers sweep in and pick up the pieces, taking my world for their own.

But something wasn't adding up. If the conjurers did manage to accomplish their goal of a great war — which was looking likely — they'd still need a sizeable force to come in and obliterate the remaining armies and families, even if most of them were weakened. You can't exactly procure a conjurer army when the vast majority of your people have been wiped out. Unless… well, maybe they didn't come from Mizridahl. Perhaps they came *to* Mizridahl.

The long-standing theory was that conjurers originated from a cult somewhere in the South; that's where they showed up first, near the shores. If they sailed here, that would mean they had their own world. Own cities, own people. Hmm. That's a slightly more terrifying thought than having Braddock Glannondil string his banner up through my intestines.

But first things first. Pristia, Braddock's wife, needed to die. If the old hag would keel over before the Glannondil army marched off to war, maybe Braddock would come to and realize he was about to commit the kind of blunder that would have his name next to those of the sort of kings who'd single-handedly dismantled their own empires.

I had the perfect plan for how to make that happen. The idea was simple. Lure the Glannondil armies out of Erior with, oh... let's say five thousand men. Then, a smaller number, perhaps one hundred assassins from, oh, I don't know... the Black Rot, for example, could sneak inside the empty walls, find Pristia and cut her down. Voi-fucking-la.

Now, the obvious problem may seem to lie in obtaining five thousand men. While I had not yet discovered the secret to breeding five thousand boys and subsequently jettisoning them all into adulthood instantaneously, I did know that a ten-thousand-strong army was conveniently marching my way. Inconveniently, it would likely shatter the walls I took shelter behind and slaughter everyone that joined me.

But here's the rub: the leader of this army, Kane Calbid, wanted Serith Rabthorn's throne.

Unbeknownst to my hopeful new-pal-to-be, Kane, Serith had all but transferred his kingship over. For all Kane knew, Serith's army was waiting on him here, ready to fortify the walls and bunker down for the long haul. His spies would discover the truth soon enough, but if I could reach him before then and offer my assistance in letting him into the kingdom with nary a sword swung on his behalf, he might well agree to my terms.

And the terms would be simple: I'd need half his men for a short excursion to the northeast, to avenge my brother's death by obliterating all slaver camps along the coast — a harmless endeavor for his skilled soldiers. The truth is that I would use those men to knock on Braddock's door, feign an attack, then make him chase us all over. But the truth is optional in these sort of negotiations.

This plan was greeted with a healthy dose of skepticism from Big Gruff, a silent *wow* from Kale, and an "Are you fucking drunk?" from Vayle, who very rarely uses the fuck word.

But as they sipped and gulped and threw back wine before licking flames under a black sky, they all came to see it as I did. We had no other choice. If we couldn't stop this war from happening and prevent the conjurers from taking our home... we would likely be their slaves. They'd imprison us, take our minds and use our blades to hunt down rebellious families who hadn't sworn their servitude to the conjurers. Even if we could run free forever, darting from beyond the reach of their shadows, what kind of life is that? One I'd sooner end willingly than live until the Reaper calls my name.

After convincing Serith to let us stay in Vereumene for two weeks — under the guise that my guys and gals needed rest and it'd be awfully difficult to protect his daughter while fatigued — I penned a letter to Kane, gave it to Big Gruff and sent him to a messenger camp about a day's ride west. The mountain of a man returned several days later, with a reply in tow.

It said this.

I accept your proposal. Seven days. Nightfall.

Kane Calbid.

Huh. Well, I suppose I could never fault a man for being simple and succinct.

"When'd you get this?" I asked Big Gruff.

"'Ey," he hollered toward a Rot repositioning a spit above a fire, "is that trout? Big lake trout? I smell it!"

I smacked Big Gruff upside his big head. "Listen, man! This is important. When'd you get this letter?"

He counted silently on his big, hairy fingers. "Let's figger this out. I get there in one day. Send 'er out with a messenger. And then... er, let's see. Yeah, yeah. Ten days later, I get it back. Then I sleep a night there — ale is woo-hoo strong, let me tell you that, Shepherd — then I come here today, rode hard all through the mornin'. But... I gotta know. Is that trout? You know how much I love trout."

Afraid foam would begin to percolate out from his jowls and he'd go rabid in the eyes, I told him yes, he was smelling trout, and then released the Rot-turned-beast.

Hmm. Ten days for Big Gruff to receive a reply meant it probably took five days for it to get to Kane and five more to get back. Big Gruff spent a day at the camp and another day to get the letter to me. Well, surprise, surprise. Today was day seven. Time to pretty up this plan of mine and get it ready for its first and only date.

A shiver tore through me, and I slapped myself like I was putting out flames. In reality, I was brushing off the grime that soiled my body, the filth that wrapped me up in a big, dung-filled hug, and the muck I slowly sunk into like quicksand. I felt dirty, all right? Real fuckin' dirty. Putting this plan into action meant I was playing the game. There are plenty of games in this world, but most people only play two. The first is a game that everyone participates in. You don't have a choice. Soon as you pop your head out of your mother's womb, you're in it, baby — you're playing the game of survival.

The second game, it doesn't have an official title, but it revolves around power: trying to obtain it, attempting to increase it, or, if you enjoy playing the first game, trying to lose it.

I enjoyed the game of survival. Living's pretty nice, as it turns out. But generally, if you're a fucker-up of the whole realm stability thing, your stay in this world will be quite short. Aiding a usurper and then using half his ten-thousand-strong army for my cause, that… that's not good for realm stability. But it was the only choice I had if I wanted to keep surviving.

I sipped hot tea as I walked into the bleakness of underground. Years ago Serith's court had ordered the construction of a new sewer system, but plans had changed and now all that remained of that sanitary promise was a big hole in the ground. At the far end, where a wall of dirt lay piled high, a shadow sat by its lonesome.

"I heard a whisper you might be here," I said. "I'm surprised to find you alone. Your mother seems to follow you wherever you go."

"She is sleeping," Lysa answered. "She sleeps much of the time. It's better that way."

"Do you love your mother? Your father?"

"I've tried, but"—she looked at me, hazel slits in the darkness—"why are you asking me this?"

"Your father has asked me to protect you. I don't know if he's told you, but this city—"

"I don't need someone to protect me," she spat. "And it doesn't take a great deal of independent thought to understand my father intends to surrender to Kane Calbid. You have still not answered my question. Why did you ask me if I loved my parents?"

Boy, this girl didn't take kindly to being given the runaround. I appreciated the no-nonsense type, but only if they were on my side. And I wasn't sure which side Lysa was on yet.

"Things," I said, "may happen to your father. And—"

She lifted a hand, silencing me. "You might have too much cowardice in you to plainly tell me you intend to kill my father on behalf of Kane Calbid, or as part of a larger scheme. But I am not a coward. I will tell you the truth: No, Mr. Assassin, I do not intend to avenge his death in any form and certainly not by obliterating your mind. I also do not intend to allow you to protect me under the guise of perverting my gift into a weapon of war.

"I will leave this place soon, so do what you must. I have a gift, Mr. Assassin, and it can be used for good. It can be used to help those in the throes of despair. My mother and my father are too far gone, but the little boy who lost his puppy, the little girl whose father never returned from war, the farmers whose crops have been ravaged — their sanity can be restored. I *am* a conjurer, Mr. Assassin. One unlike you have ever seen. Goodbye."

I sat there dumbfounded as the nineteen-year-old girl verbally slapped me across my face and promptly got up and walked away. I had clearly underestimated Lysa Rabthorn, and it saddened me she was not on my side. But thankfully she didn't play sides, and fear of her retribution was one less worry on my mind.

A small band of rainclouds arrived near noon, and then… I wasn't sure what happened. I became less intrigued by my surroundings and more lost in my thoughts, until the encroaching darkness of night had me on my feet, walking my camp and prepping my assassins.

Satisfied my men and ladies knew their roles, I went off toward the gate, where winding ramps led up to the parapet.

I took no more than two steps when my commander caught up to me.

"You're sober now," she said.

"And you're not," I replied.

"Sober as I'll ever be. You haven't changed your mind about a thing?"

"No."

"This isn't justice," she said sharply.

I looked around, just in case a city guardsman was lurking about. Convinced we were alone, I stabbed a meaningful finger in her chest, right between her breasts. "Honor and justice might keep you afloat in this life, Vayle, but they do nothing for me. And they've never been the foundation of the Black Rot. You can pick and choose jobs as you will, only accept ones that make you all hot and bothered with the idea of justice, but what happens here tonight is necessary for the survival of the Black Rot as a whole. One will never be greater than the whole."

Shaking her head, she threw a hand toward the general direction of the city gate. "Set them free. There's less than two hundred of them. Kane Calbid won't care if there are two hundred guards sworn to Serith running free. He won't pursue them; they can… they can rejoin their wives, their mothers, fathers, brothers… their babies! Everyone who Serith allowed to leave this city."

"That's not the agreement I made with Kane."

"Fuck your agreement. He's going to see a dead king. That's not good enough for him? Hell, Astul, why can't these men lay down their arms soon as you do the deed? Allow them to surrender to Kane's armies."

She'd been needling me about this for days, although not with quite so much vigor. It was getting tiresome. I slammed my hand against the wooden siding of a building in frustration, punching it straight through.

"You know why?" I said, much too loudly. Spit flung on the tail of my words. "Because all it takes is one proud guardsman, the man who thinks his destiny is to protect the bloody king. And suddenly the city guard sees us as unrightful usurpers, and the Rots are fighting two hundred well-armed men. We won't escape without injury. I won't let that happen. The guards will die with their backs turned, unable to mount a resistance, unable to harm our Rots."

Through gnashed teeth, she said, "We could have gone about this systematically."

"We didn't and we won't."

"We could have convinced Serith to dissolve the city guard."

"He's batshit insane. Wouldn't have worked. He's convinced they took an oath and that perishing under Kane Calbid's assault is the only proper way for their contract to expire."

"Using Lysa as a negotiation point would have made him think otherwise."

A sense of profound anger rose up in my stomach like a bad burn after a hot meal. "I'm done with this conversation. It's over. It's getting late. It's time to end this."

She blew air out her nose like a disgruntled dog. "You don't think this is the right decision, either. You don't know what the right decision is, do you? Look at you! You're smitten with anger. When you're confident, I've seen you deflect criticism like plate deflects steel. You laugh at it, and give it a wink and move on. You're... you're scared, aren't you, Astul? Scared that I'm right. Scared that—"

"Maybe I fucking am," I spat. "Let's drop the shit, can we, Vayle? Letting these men go free, or making them surrender to Kane Calbid, whatever it is you want to do with them, has just as many pitfalls. It'll end with their butchering all the same. At least this decision will save their families and our Rots. The guardsmen themselves will die quickly, and Kane Calbid will honor our agreement."

"I hope you understand," she said, "you will be the one who will live with the misery of butchering two hundred lives, of widowing two hundred wives, of orphaning hundreds of children when the wives lose their minds. And all to better your position in the game. Our position. It's not an easy thing to endure, a scarred past. Trust me, hmm?"

"I can handle it," I said.

She smiled gloomily. "I'm sure you can." She took a drink of her wine. "I've handled it for years. It's easy at first. Starts out as nightmares that you wake up from and forget about as you eat your breakfast. But soon, they linger a little longer. A little longer. A little longer, till you go to sleep with the same horrors you awoke with." She bit her lip as she regarded her skin of wine. "Soon you drink to chase away the nightmares. Then you drink to chase away the headaches. Then the sickness. Then the shakes."

"I won't let that happen," I said.

"You won't have a choice. But I'll be here for you when it happens, forever and for always, because I love you, Astul, as much as a friend can. I've been with you for fifteen years, and it's been the greatest time of my life. But it makes me very sad to know that in those fifteen years"—her mouth twisted into a frown—"you haven't grown one bit."

She twirled around, drank her wine, and walked back toward the encampment.

I hadn't grown? I hadn't grown? A wooden pail lay nearby. I turned it upside down, stood on top of it and yelled, "Look at me now! I've grown!"

Suddenly realizing that was something I would've done when I was ten, in response to my mother telling me I needed to grow up, I became frustrated, jumped down and walked hastily toward the parapet.

I stayed there for a while, pacing the stones, kicking the crenellations, bullshitting with the few guards that meandered around. One man, with a scar on his cheek and a shaky hand, told me he never even said goodbye to his son and wife as they fled to the safety of Austrick. Didn't want the last memory his son had of his face to be slathered with rust from the helmet he wore.

He contemplated running, but said one of his fellow guardsmen would probably stick him before he'd make it out the gate.

It was then I knew I'd made the right decision. But I wondered if I couldn't have snuck it in my proposal to Kane that the guardsmen would be allowed to go free. Maybe I should have. Of course, that would have required me to think of others. Regret coagulated in my stomach like syrup, heavy and sickening. *Goddammit, Vayle*, I thought. *This is your fault I feel like this.*

I peered out into the field of rock that looked like an idle ocean of ink. Sometimes when the moon was swapping between clouds, its pale bulb would gleam off the placid water, as if you could swim over to it, touch its dimpled surface and then burrow into its clutches. What would it be like, to be all alone up there? Peaceful, probably. All alone, one tiny speck looking out into whatever lies beyond.

All alone… much like the forward-moving silhouette that crested a ridge in the distance. There he was, Kane Calbid's scout, coming to see that the deed would be done.

I descended down from the parapet and took the long walk to the keep. The guards allowed me entry, and a short while later, Serith Rabthorn walked beside me, persuaded to take a stroll along the battlements.

As we emerged from the doors of the keep, I coyly glanced to the right. The campfires were hissing as spit grease dripped onto the embers, but the Rots had all vanished.

We passed a building with a thatched roof on the way to the parapet ramp. The corners of the wall and the severe angle of the roof were such that they concealed an alleyway nestled between that building and its neighbor. Even I, who knew what lay waiting in that passage, couldn't see them. As invisible as the wind and silent as poison.

"We're leaving in the morning," I told Serith, placing my hand under his arm so he could climb the ramp without falling and breaking his brittle face.

"Oh," he said anciently. "Tomorrow? Oh, that's... that's good. With—" He blinked and looked at me for help.

"With your daughter," I confirmed.

He was either regressing again, or he had good days and bad days.

Once on the parapet, he steadied himself on the crenellations, running his bony fingers across the scaly-textured stone.

"Where will you go?" he asked.

I ignored that question, instead brushing a hand along his back, straightening him toward the field.

"It's a beautiful night, isn't it?" I said.

He leaned forward, both hands on the crenellations. "Eyes are no good anymore, but good enough to see a messenger on this beautiful night."

"It's not a messenger," I whispered.

I glimpsed to my right. Then my left. Closest guard was twenty feet away and moving farther.

The familiarity of ice coursing through veins numbed all physical sensations, except the hands. They were wet as always, one dripping sweat down my pants, the other dampening the hilt of my ebon blade.

They say you get used to this job. They lie.

"I promised you I would protect your daughter," I said lowly. "But I promised nothing more. At least you can take comfort in knowing you're my first."

Mind ruined and dying, he couldn't understand. "Your first? What am I your first for?"

Ebon hissed against its leather scabbard. A helmet turned twenty feet away, eyes widening deep under the brim.

"Never killed a king before," I said. "Till now."

I wrapped my arm around his shoulders, turning his sickly body inward toward mine. And then... I slit his throat. His eyes were scrambled, mouth agape. His arms flung outward like snapped strings. Broken at the knees, his body almost crumbled onto the parapet in a heap. *Almost.* Before it could, I punched my boot into his back, then gave him another kick. And off the battlements he tumbled, a whizz of blood trailing in his wake.

The guards atop the parapet tried to rush me. But arrows climb faster than feet can run, and the contingent of Rots hiding in the alleyway had ambushed them.

Some guards cried far below, but it was mostly singing steel and the deadened thumps of bodies that disturbed the silent night. Thing is, once your throat is severed, then so is your voice. You can wail all you want, but it comes out a soft, wet gurgle that no one can hear. It was better that way.

I didn't hear Serith crash into the rocks his kingdom was built upon. But looking out over the edge, I spotted him lying in a mangled fashion, personal belongings, such as his skull, rather broken.

Strangely, this didn't seem to convince Kane Calbid's scout that the king of Vereumene was dead. He continued riding for the walls. Maybe he wanted to see Serith's face up close. Not much left of it now.

Hmm. He was going the wrong way now, toward the gate, rather than toward Serith's body.

I squinted at the approaching horse. Was that a… oh, fuck me. A white caparison featuring a golden galloping horse lay across the saddle.

Serith was right. A messenger rode up to the gates, which meant Kane Calbid's scout hadn't seen shit, because Kane Calbid's scout wasn't even bloody here yet. And when he did arrive, there'd be nothing to show him. He'd never risk his life coming so close to the wall to see Serith's body.

"This better be a fucking good message," I hollered.

The messenger sat up tall in his saddle. "The Order of Messengers comes on the behalf of Braddock Glannondil, King of Erior, Lord of the Glannondil Family, Gate of the East. He requests entry into the kingdom of Vereumene, governed by Lord Serith Rabthorn—" He paused. "Or the presiding steward."

Huh. Well, as far as messages go, you can't get much worse than that. Far as news goes, you can't hear much worse than that. Far as life goes, you can't experience much worse than that.

"And Braddock is where?" I asked.

"A day's ride away," the messenger said.

Huh. What do you know? You can hear worse.

"Well," I muttered to myself, "suppose tomorrow's as good a day as any to die."

CHAPTER TEN

A king rides alone for only two reasons. One, his kingdom has been sacked and there's a good price for his head and an even better price if you can haul the treasonous bastard in alive. Or two, his cohort of royal guardsmen were murdered, but the king managed to slink away like a fox. Braddock Glannondil has the shape of a two-legged engorged tick and the agility of one who'd just drunk the blood of a wino, so option two was rather… unlikely.

Which was why I was quite distressed when the rotund lord of the Glannondil family came galloping through the fields of sleek volcanic rock, his morning shadow his only companion. If Erior had been sacked, the conjurers were probably responsible, which meant I was now fighting for… well, nothing, really. It'd all be over.

His horse trotted inside the gate, where I stood waiting.

Braddock clambered down, his loose-fitting plated gorget jangling against his hauberk, which bore the grinning jackal lying in wait in a field of crimson.

My Rots regarded him warily, their eyes carefully following his feet and his hands.

Just as the impetuosity of the ocean swallows up the shore with complete disregard for the shells, Braddock marched through the bloodied bodies of slain guardsmen, making no attempt to avoid dragging his feet across their carcasses or kicking their limp skulls.

He held up a helmet he carried in his hand. "Is one of your Rots a skilled blacksmith? Bloody thing's been slamming into my head since I left Erior. Finally had to take it off."

Silence. It was of the sharp, uncomfortable variety — the sort that's preceded and followed by thinned eyes and hands that grip hilts a little tighter.

"Oh, piss off," Braddock barked. "If you got it in you, go on and kill me. But know that I've got an army behind me that will enjoy ripping the gristle right from your bone."

"I believe," Vayle said, standing beside me, "we're all just wondering why the king of Erior is here. Alone."

In true Braddock fashion, he plunged his hand deep inside his trousers and whipped it out. "You see this cock right here?" he said, shaking the head at Vayle like it'd spit corrosive poison at her. "I can hold piss in this cock for twenty hours." He stuffed his manhood back inside his pants. "None of my men can go twelve without bemoaning pains in their groins, then they soak the ground for five fuckin' minutes. I don't have time for that bullshit. I ride alone, because I ride fast."

"May I ask why the urgency?" Vayle said. Her diplomatic language spun confusion on Braddock's face. He had come in here expecting a confrontation, not acceptance.

After considering her question for a short while, he said, "There is a girl here who goes by the name of Lysa."

"Yeah, yeah," I said. "Lysa Rabthorn, the nonexistent daughter of Serith Rabthorn. We know a little about her."

Braddock pretended that little revelation didn't churn his stomach as butterflies fluttered in surprise. And I pretended that his search for Lysa didn't churn my stomach as butterflies fluttered in dread. Pristia had obviously sent him after hearing word of Lysa's rebellion. But why send the king himself? And why, if Braddock was telling the truth, send an army to trail him?

"You got a quiet place to talk in this shithole"—he shifted his swollen bags for eyes toward me—"king of Vereumene?" He grinned.

"I think we can find somewhere," I said. "But let's make it clear. I'm not a king."

I nodded my head toward the keep and walked that way.

"Alone," Braddock requested, as it became evident Vayle was joining us.

I turned and silently dismissed my commander. Dissent drew her mouth into a tight band of wrinkles, but she accepted my order without causing a fuss. She didn't care about being included, it wasn't that. She feared for my safety. The conjurers obviously had secrets we had never been privy to, and if they could turn Lysa Rabthorn into one of them, what could they do with the most powerful king in the world? But I needed information from Braddock, and perhaps he'd let something slip if it was just me and him, bullshitting back and forth.

I led him to the keep and up the wooden steps inside, to the room where Serith and I had last sat and talked.

Only one candle remained lit. I used its wick to set fire to the others. The wax lay low around the candlesticks, and the flames coughed sickly, spewing a sputtering marmalade glow that expanded and contracted throughout the room.

I grabbed an amphora of wine and waved it in front of Braddock's face. "A taste of venom to start off this unlikely meeting? It's good, I promise. I've had some."

He grunted. I topped off two chalices and sat them on the table. I wasn't much into playing servant or entertainer, but wine's a great lubricator for getting fat secrets to fit through thin lips.

"This wine," Braddock said, sniffing it into his wide nostrils, "did you drink it before or after you murdered the king of Vereumene?"

I sat and folded my hands innocently on the table. "I'm afraid I don't know anything about that."

"Then this meeting will be quick," Braddock said, swiping the chalice to his mouth. "I thought we could strike a partnership, Astul. If you can't even admit that your killers down there, or assassins, whatever the fuck you call them, butchered themselves some city guardsmen while you kicked Serith right off his bloody wall, then I've not got much hope of you telling me where Lysa is, do I?"

"Wait, wait, wait," I said, holding up my hand. "Let's ignore that preposterous shit about a partnership for a moment and focus on how you came to know about the events that unfolded last night. I'll go ahead and admit Serith's as dead as your old wife, though I think I was doing him a favor. Thing is, you were a day's ride away when that happened. Who told you?"

Braddock scratched the edge of his long thumbnail along the corner of his nose, scraping off something that looked as though it smelled unpleasant. "The messenger."

"The messenger? The messenger who said he was with the Order of Messengers? The Order of Messengers that requires each of its messengers to take an oath that their tongues reveal only the information their senders permit? Is this the messenger you speak of? Because I sure as shit didn't grant him the permission to reveal anything."

Braddock laughed and slammed his palm onto the table. "Power of coin, Shepherd. Oaths don't mean a damn thing when you can buy 'em. If the Order was serious about their oaths, they'd cut the tongues right from the mouths of their messengers. Not a good recruitment strategy there, though."

"Also not a good strategy to approach a man for a partnership after you sent him to a slaver camp. Look at what they gifted me with."

I pulled up my shirt to reveal the branded S on my chest. Scar tissue had shined it up real nice.

"But you survived," Braddock pointed out. "Something not many men could claim after they plotted to kill a king's wife." He hefted his elbows onto the table, rattling the thin supports, then shoved his wine aside. "Get this rat piss out of here. I didn't want to have you die in my kingdom, you know. The last thing I needed was for the Black Rot to come avenge their fallen shepherd. I had more than enough on my plate."

"Like secretly assassinating a northern king, perhaps? Or was it preparing your armies for the long march to Edenvaile?"

"I played no part in Vileoux's death," Braddock said, wagging his finger. "None whatsoever."

"Well," I said softly, "of course *you* didn't. I know that it wasn't *you*." I'd seen this kind of thing work once before, on a man who claimed it wasn't him who killed his mother, but instead a young boy named Phillip. Phillip was one of the many who lived inside the man's head.

"You think you're clever," Braddock said, his voice a low rumble of thunder. He leaned forward. "You think you're full of wit. Here you are, an adventurer, an assassin, a man who's broken free from society's domain. You're of greater intellect and greater wisdom than us sheep being led to the slaughter, blind to the strings being pulled. Allow me to pierce your veil, Shepherd: I know Pristia was a conjurer. I'd always known."

"Er, was?"

"She's dead." He thrust his fat hand across the table and snatched back his rat piss. He drank it all in one sizeable gulp, then threw himself against the backing of the chair in a defeated fashion. "Three years ago we married. One year and two days after my Gale had left this world. I knew before then what Pristia was. Over and over she spoon-fed me the dreadful memories of my wife's last few years, dredging them up from the deep. "Oh, Braddock," she would say, "it must be awful to look me in the eyes as you spill your seed inside me, knowing that it should be Gale whose loins ache from your thrusts." Each night, each morning… every day, she would force me to recount those years. She was trying to break me."

Hmm. Maybe Braddock Glannondil was cleverer than I gave him credit for.

In their bid to arrange peace when this world attempted to make them extinct, conjurers asserted that they could not influence healthy minds. Only the broken, the weakened and the deranged could succumb to their thoughts — the very people who they wished to help mend, or so they claimed. That's all well and good, but the problem is not a soul makes it through life thoroughly intact. Experience cracks you. The years chisel away at your psyche. All it sometimes takes is a reminder of the past to shatter you. Anyone can become broken, weakened and deranged with enough pushing — that's a scary thought when you've conjurers lurking about. Even scarier when they're the ones capable of doing the pushing.

"But I'm like a fuckin' wall, Shepherd," Braddock said. "I don't break easily. I'd buried Gale a hundred times 'fore I dug the hole. Wasn't a bloody thing Pristia could say that I hadn't already thought and then beat those thoughts into submission. But I knew what she was trying to do, dammit, and I'll be fuck all if I let a conjurer sneak about freely in my kingdom."

"Er. Well. That's precisely what you did. You should have killed her on the spot."

"If you knew a spy was pissin' about in your shithole of a base, would you kill him?" Before I could answer, Braddock continued. "Or, would you follow him back to his camp to discover where he came from and what his plans were? I wanted to know these conjurers were up to. I wanted to know their grand plan. And so I played along, allowing Pristia to command my every move, as if the thoughts she tried planting in my mind had uprooted my own."

I tilted my head. "And? What'd you find out?"

He chuckled sardonically. "Get Lysa in here. She'll tell you better than I can."

"Did she pay a visit to Erior and tell you the story of how the conjurers want this world for their own? Yeah, I already heard about it."

"She did visit. Pristia brought her there, to teach her a few tricks of the trade. When she realized I wasn't taken, she spilled her guts. And she told me more than that." His jaw shifted subtly. "She told me *how* they would take this world for their own."

"Right, right," I said in the impatient tones of someone who was being read the same story twice, "we're going to fight each other, kill one another and poof! The conjurers pop in, or fly in, or make whatever sort of fantastical appearance they please, and they clean up the mess. Got it. Heard it. Understand it."

Braddock folded his hands. "So you also know that they're bringing an army with them?"

"Figured something of the sort. Must have one hell of a place to hide an army big enough to sweep across Mizridahl, though."

"They do, in Lith."

I drew back. "Lith? Where the fuck is Lith?" I'd been across most of Mizridahl, and the lands I hadn't graced with my presence I nevertheless knew the names of. Lith wasn't registering at all.

"About five hundred miles across the ocean," Braddock said matter-of-factly.

I blinked.

"Ah," he said derisively, "I guess you haven't heard about everything."

"Five hundred miles across—" I stopped midsentence. I cocked my head toward the door. "Do you hear that?"

Braddock let his eyes fall into his lap as he concentrated intensely. "Sounds like"—the edge of his mouth curled up like the jowl of a pudgy dog unsure of the foreign food in his bowl—"like wind."

Sounded like wind all right, if wind was being pushed and pulled, twisted and pounded. Through the walls of the keep came a *whoosh*. A heavy, constant *whoosh* that percussed louder as the seconds passed. An ominous *whoosh* that prickled the hairs on my neck and sucked the spit right from my mouth.

I stared at my chalice. The tiny red ring that formed around its stem, thanks to sloppily poured wine, jittered like pond water wavering under a subtle gust. I peered in over the rim of the cup and watched as the liquid inside sloshed about more violently now.

I jumped up and hurried to the door. The king of Erior followed me through the hallway, down the rickety staircases and eventually to the hollow chamber before the keep doors. Down there was where I felt it the fiercest. In my toes and in my chest, a deep, shallow *whoosh* that climbed up my legs and swept over my rib cage.

Unsheathed ebon blade in hand, I opened the doors.

I stepped outside. A smarter man than I would have backed into the keep, shut the doors, shuffled under a table and prayed that just a few of the gods people worship were real and, more importantly, merciful.

But I stood there. How could something like this exist?

The sky crawled with fiery wings, plumes of thin flames crushed under the pressure of the air as the birds swooped downward.

My Rots ran. They ran from the birds. They ran from the talons aiming for their heads.

They ran from their world that was on fire.

CHAPTER ELEVEN

I blinked. Well, I tried to. It's a terribly difficult thing to do when crusty blood seals your eyelids. I leaned forward, but a steel chain looped around my waist tethered me to a pillar, immobilizing me. Rusty iron clasps bound my ankles and wrists.

A faint orange glow bled into the blackness. I saw my hands, but the shadows concealed all else. Bits of jagged rock needled my back. A puddle gathered on the dusty dirt floor under my crotch. I tried ignoring the fact I'd probably—

"Looks like ya wetted yerself there," croaked a man.

"What do you have, the eyes of a feline? Can't see shit in here. Where am I?"

There was a metallic jingling followed by a dry cough. "Well, you musta got hit pretty hard over the head. Yer in a dungeon. Some of the fellas call it the House o' Death. 'Course, that was when they was still

156

living that they called it that. Only you and me down here now. Dark at first, I'll give you that, but them eyes of yours'll come around."

I squinted but still couldn't see the man. "What city? Vereumene? Erior? Did that fat bastard Braddock Glannondil con me?"

"Er, sorry? Don't know none of those names. Where you from? Way out in the wilds? Yer in Lith. Well, under Lith, actually. They say the conjurers have quite a city up there, but you wouldn't know it from down here, would ya? Name's Tylik, by the way."

"Conjurers," I said aloud. "Oh, fuck me."

I traced a swollen bump the size of a pear jutting out from the side of my head. Last thing I remembered was a broiling heat sizzling the hairs of my neck, immediately before a pair of heavy feet — talons, perhaps — punched into my back and drove my face into the unforgiving floor of volcanic rock. Actually, I remembered what happened just before that as well. I remembered my eyes looking helplessly toward the keep doors that were shutting as Braddock Glannondil heaved them closed in terror.

"Heard you was a shepherd," Tylik said. "All the guards been talkin' about is you. And the crummy food they have to eat, but they always talk about that. Ever since I been here, mm, what, fifteen years now?"

I opened my mouth to speak. How foolish of me to think I actually had a place in the conversation.

"Maybe seventeen years," the man said. "Somewhere between fifteen and seventeen. What do you shepherd? Goats? Lots of goats 'round here. Or maybe you're from the West, lots of cows out there. Well, not anymore, but way back when there were. You know, I even heard of duck shepherds. Someone might have been lyin' to me about that, though."

"Assassins," I said bluntly.

"Oh."

My eyes slowly acclimated to the darkness, lifting the foggy veil enough that a thin outline of the man who called himself Tylik appeared. Like morning mist evaporating under the sun's burning eye, the shadows surrounding him melted, revealing less a man and more a thing. He slumped against a pillar and fiddled with hands so bony I wasn't convinced his corpse hadn't been reanimated. If flaming birds can exist, then nothing's out of the question.

"Call me Astul," I said after a while. "I come from a place called Mizridahl. Ever heard of it?"

"Misery-what? No, I don't think I have."

I kicked my foot out. The bracelet bit into the bone of my ankle. No getting out of this. "What's this land called, Tylik? The whole land, the world. What's it called?"

The man smacked his lips and wagged his finger, as if he was trying to usher out the words. "Oh, my. My, my, my. So it's true? Guards said you was from across the water, but I didn't believe 'em. They been tryin' to make us believe there's another world on the other side since I was a little one, and they still tryin' to get the young'uns to believe it. Say gold coins grow from trees, say there are more apples and pies and fish and cakes and cows than you could ever eat, more water and wine than you could ever drink."

Gold from trees? I needed to find these trees when I got back to Mizridahl. If I got back. "Sounds like a nice place," I said.

Tylik coughed a raspy laugh. "Always knew it wasn't true. Probably suffer just like us, don't ya? Eatin' roots and hoping there's some water in the dirty, stringy things. Truthfully, I didn't doubt there was another world somewhere. It ain't that hard to believe, y'know? But a place where water runs free and you can stuff your belly till you get big and fat? Naw. You'd have to be a fool to believe that. Scary thing is, lots of young'uns think it's true nowadays. Anyways, no real name for the whole world here. Just north, south, east, west, that sorta thing, and the names of the cities and provinces, o' course."

It had been years since I talked to a stranger without having an ulterior motive. It was rather… comforting.

"What about you, Tylik? Any young'uns of your own?"

The man snorted and paused. When someone hesitates to answer your question, you've already got your answer. "A boy and a girl," he said. "They wanted to make my little boy"—he drew in a deep breath—"wanted to make him a conjurer. Know what that does to yer mind? Ruins it, I hear. Naw. I know it does. Seen folk before they were conjurers and after, and they ain't the same, lemme tell you that." Tylik grumbled throatily and added, "So I planned to leave, see. Over to the West, on the beaches, where the conjurers don't control. Yet. But one of the townsfolk, they spilled my plans. Probably got a big reward, too."

"They arrested you?" I asked.

The silhouette of the man's head nodded. "Sure did. Conspiracy against the Council of Conjurers, they claimed. Thought I'd die real quick, but here I am." Tylik hacked and cleared his throat. "Say, Astul — or do you prefer to be called the Shepherd?"

The Shepherd, I thought. What did I shepherd? A bunch of assassins to their death? Fantastic shepherd I was, killing off my herd. Do that as a town's goat keeper and they'd stone you. Come to think of it, a stoning seemed like a better outcome than whatever the conjurers had in mind.

"Astul is fine," I said.

"Well, Astul, you seem all right, far as assassins go. When them guards feed us, they put it between us and expect us to fight like starving pups. Is why they put us so close together. Well, one reason. I'd much like to not fight for the food, if ya don't mind sharing half."

Before I could accept Tylik's proposal, something squeaked. Something thundered from above, like a door shuddering against its frame.

Hot, orange swirls illuminated a series of steep steps and streaked along the dungeon floor. Mashed chunks of waste were piled halfway up Tylik's pillar. And a foul green gunk puddled before him. It seemed to ooze from his toes. Well, where his toes should've been. Something had eaten off the tips, leaving behind some fleshy nubs glazed over with a swampy ichor.

Two men stumbled down the steps. One carried a torch and waved it disconcertingly.

"Take a whiff, boy," said one of them. "This is your life now. Just wait till Captain Gorge makes you clean this shit up."

There was a groan, followed by, "Clean it up?"

The other man laughed and stopped few paces away from my pillar. He pointed the torch at me and elbowed his partner. "Go tell 'er he's up. And move your ass. I don't wanna stay down here in this shithole any longer than I needs to."

For a moment that could only be measured in the quickness of a spark splitting from a piece of charred wood, the underling boy looked at Tylik. Poor kid's mouth tightened, and his nostrils flared. Whatever innocence he had left was now gone.

"You know," I said to the tall guard in front of me, "it'd smell a whole lot cheerier in here if you'd sprinkle some rose petals. Maybe plant some lavender in the dirt."

The man smiled. Discombobulated teeth filled his mouth, curling and pointing in directions teeth ought to not curl and point. "I only gots to smell it when I feed you dogs."

I didn't know what the guard's name was, but Crooked Tooth sounded like a good one.

Crooked Tooth shoved his torch close to Tylik, and the poor man jumped back in horror, whimpering.

"You're a tough one, aren't you?" I said. "You remind me of a big, fat slaver. He'd poke his slaves and torment them, and they couldn't do a thing about it. Till one day my assassins rode into camp and butchered him."

Crooked Tooth crouched down in front of me, the flames from his torch shimmering off his greasy, angular cheeks. "You wait till you see where your assassins are now."

A door opened and shut, and a pair of feet raced down the steps.

"She says bring him up. No burns, she says."

"Yer lucky," Crooked Tooth told me, grasping the clasp around my ankle and producing a key. "If it were up to me, I woulda burned off your little toes." He nodded toward Tylik. "Just like I did to him."

After freeing me from the chains and clasps, Crooked Tooth hooked a hand under my arm and yanked me to my feet. He and the young guard escorted me up the stone steps and into the great outdoors of Lith.

The dungeon door swung open and a gaudy light stabbed into my eyes. I kept my head down, shielding it from the midday sun hot as any I'd ever felt, until a passing cloud offered me reprieve.

I expected to emerge into the city of Lith itself, with a congregation of buildings above me and cobblestone paths beneath my feet. Or perhaps inside a heavily fortified keep. But an unbridled wilderness of yellow grass lay before me, with a dense gathering of flowering trees off in the distance. And then Crooked Tooth wrenched my arm, turning me around, and the city of Lith swallowed me up.

Two enormous hills mirrored one another, each rolling to a jagged peak. In their bosom sprawled a mass of structures strung together in orderly fashion like the wax cells of a honeycomb. Thatched-roof houses ran along the outer edge and clung to the slopes of the hills as if they were trees that stupidly took root on the face of mountains.

Strangely, the streets were empty.

"Is Lith home to ghosts, by chance?" I asked.

The toe of a leather boot scuffed the back of my calf. My feet crisscrossed one another, dropping me to my knees in the dry, crunchy grass.

"Ain't nothin' said about kickin' your ass," said Crooked Tooth. "Shaddup."

Both men yanked me to my feet, and we continued walking. In the thick of the silence, voices droned from within the deep recesses of the city. Hundreds, thousands of voices. The hiss of jeers and the thunder of applause.

A chill crawled up my spine like a jittery spider. Funny thing to feel cold inside when sweat pours down your face and your skin feels ablaze. The worst kind of shivers are those rooted in a hidden terror. At least when snow's falling and ice is underfoot, you know why your teeth are chattering and your skin is bumpy.

We walked toward a cove embedded inside one of the hills, where something glittered and sparkled as the sun came out to play again.

It was a tower.

Now, I'd seen my fair share of towers. They're usually made of dull gray stone and are about as artistic as what flows down a latrine during a storm. But what lay in that cove was a tower unlike any I'd ever witnessed and one I wouldn't even have thought to imagine.

It spiraled high into the air, crowned with what looked like a massive halo. Its walls were constructed from stained glass, etched with intricate designs. Light seemed to bend around the tower, reflecting multicolored prisms of blues and purples and yellows and reds and pinks and oranges.

Before the tower emerged a tree that looked as though it'd been crafted from celestial hands. Its trunk curiously threaded horizontally across the ground, for at least twenty feet, before rising vertically into a canopy of golden flowers that seemed to wink at me. I had the faintest notion I'd seen that tree before, but nothing like this grew in Mizridahl.

The guards pushed me onward toward the tower centered by two massive black banners. A white outline of a *C* with a shrewd eye carved in the middle was inscribed upon them. We eventually came to the tower and stepped inside. We went up a winding staircase made of stained glass with a golden-brown hue. Every fifteen feet or so, the steps spilled out into a circular platform or, if you continued walking them like we did, they went around and around and up and up.

When we could go no farther, a door greeted us. Two guards posted there opened it, and Crooked Tooth flung me into the halo.

The door closed.

The halo, as it turned out, was an enclosed balcony of stained glass. Not a fun place to find yourself in, suspended over the earth in something that can crack and shatter. Glass in Mizridahl was used only in the keeps of queens and kings as bombastic shards of art. It typically didn't separate you from Death's embrace.

A woman with a weighty, resonant voice said, "Do you know how it was made?"

She walked across the prismatic surface in silk slippers. A translucent white dress dragged behind her.

"Fifty years ago, the Council of Conjurers took the bones of those who resisted our rise to power, and we ground them into sand and made them into glass." She tucked a strand of auburn hair behind her ear and touched my arm with smooth, luxurious fingers. "Does that seem mad to you?"

I forced a swallow past the lump in my throat. "Ruining innocent minds seems mad to me."

She furrowed her brows. Her long face reminded me of a girl I chased after before I made a living killing people. Except that girl didn't have quite the same glow to her cheeks, the fullness to her lips or the shimmering hazel of her eyes.

"We all have our reasons, Astul, Shepherd of the Black Rot. Consider yourself. You murder, but you don't do it haphazardly, do you? It's logical. It's reasonable. It's certainly not madness, is it?"

I peeled my eyes away from the illustrious lady and prowled the far glass wall.

"Fascinating structure, don't you think?" said the woman. She sneaked behind me in silence and grazed my shoulder with a craggy nail.

Tucked far away in a gully along the opposing hill, a lion raced across a rectangular plot of dirt. It ducked between stone pillars, trailing a horse and the man riding it. As it lurched for its prize, two spears soared from behind it. One missed, but the other impaled the beast's skull, driving its head into the ground. The lion tumbled over and skidded lifelessly into a pillar. Every seat in the arena emptied as the people jumped and enthusiastically applauded.

"That was just to set the mood," the woman said.

"Who are you?" I asked.

The woman curled her hand around my shoulders, as if I was her child and she was showing me the grandeur of an exotic kingdom. The thought of some royal twit demeaning me made my mind twitch, but that was it. I'd always dreamed, in a sick sort of way, of being held captive by a pompous king or queen, just so I'd see the horror on their face as they discovered I was not like the proper, obedient underlings they were so accustomed to commanding. I'd refuse their orders, kick them, spit on them, show that Astul, Shepherd of the Black Rot, did not lose his pride, ever.

But somewhere between Mizridahl and Lith, my pride decided to jump ship. I stood there passively. My skin tingled.

"Look," the woman said.

The lion had been carried off, and now in the center of the arena stood a group of what looked like barbarians dressed in rags.

"Do you recognize them?" she asked. She clicked her tongue. "Those are your Rots."

I shrugged her hand off my back and lifted my chin defiantly. "Lay a finger on them and—"

"Shh," she said. She lifted a finger to my face, but I swatted it away.

I smiled as the revelation dawned on me. "I know what this is. This is a ploy, isn't it? A ploy to weaken my mind so you can take it. I don't know why you'd want me, though. I'm just an assassin, a drifter who's not all that important to the conjurers' endgame."

"Assassins," she said, "are very important. They can kill kings. They can start wars."

I licked my lips and punched a finger into the stained glass. "Those are not my Rots. What are there, fifty of them out there? Black Rot's a hundred strong. You could've at least made your lie more believable with some research."

She frowned. "Regretfully, the phoenixes that swept across Vereumene were unable to retrieve everyone they'd come for. But I won't allow that to spoil the fun." She pulled at my hand. "Walk with me, Astul."

She led me out of the room and down the steps, eventually exiting the tower. A carriage drawn by two black stallions waited for us. As I climbed inside, a bizarre event transpired in my mind, one that I seemed unable to control.

She's not evil, a voice told me.

You could strangle her before the guards could separate you, said another voice.

Maybe she has her reasons. Just like you.

She means to ruin your mind. She deserves to die.

Back and forth the voices went, until they bled into one.

She's much more respectable than Braddock Glannondil or Dercy Daniser or any of the others. She fights for what she wants.

A good point.

Do what she asks.
That's the best choice possible.

As if I had awoken from a dreadful nightmare, I found myself standing on a platform, thankfully not one made of glass. They were staring at me. Forty of them. Maybe fifty. I didn't know the exact number, but anything greater than zero was too many. Dust stuck to their bloodied faces. I could have listed them off by name, but why torture myself?

Rivon Eyrie's cheek was missing. His eyes were swollen, but through the puffiness he saw me. And he looked away, out of embarrassment… or anger.

The air inside the arena was stuffy. Voices trembled in my skull. Hundreds and thousands of them, talking about nonsense, or about what surprises the murderers and rapists inside the arena would face.

"You have two choices," said the woman, who seemed to materialize from the ether and appear right next to me. "Willingly help me take Mizridahl and I will spare your Rots. Or I will kill them and force you to help me."

I closed my eyes. As the words formed in my mind, I felt weak and pathetic. A feeble, woeful man. But I said them anyway. "What do you want me to do?"

"Assassinate Braddock Glannondil. That's it. Then you and your Rots can do whatever is that you do. Nothing changes. Even the conjurers could use assassins, you know."

The Black Rot was my life. The Rots were my only friends and my only family. Aiding a foreign enemy in the takeover of your homeland would seem preposterous to most, but so long as I kept what I held so dearly — the only thing I held so dearly — the reputation that would follow didn't matter.

"Consider it done," I said.

The woman turned her head, and there were screams.

Metal spikes surged from the center of the arena. They plunged through feet and calves and rears and stomachs, driving through throats and scattering bits of white skull and spongy brains along the dirt.

My stomach churned and twisted, and I fell to my knees. I gasped for air.

"I am Amielle, queen of the conjurers," said the woman. "And you, Shepherd of the Black Rot, will be the key to saving my people. Your mind will be mine."

Through gritted teeth and sobbing breaths, I cried, "I fucking said I'd help you!"

Amielle smiled. "The first step to subservience is hopelessness." She paused. "Isn't that right?"

"You'll learn, boy," said a man with a grizzled voice.

That voice… I'd heard it before. I turned around. Disbelief stifled my tears. It didn't seem real. Life didn't seem real. Smiling like he hadn't died with poison in his belly, Vileoux Verdan looked at me.

CHAPTER TWELVE

They screamed. Piercing screams, like a hawk's cry. The wails of terror turned to gurgling shrieks as blood fountained out of their mouths.

Or maybe they didn't really scream. They could have just toppled over as their heads rolled away from their bodies.

Sometimes that's what the visions showed me. Sometimes not.

The rot of flesh was heavy in the air. A steel chain jangled and clattered against itself. Tylik fidgeted beside me. He had said nothing since Amielle's guards returned me to this dungeon. He could probably smell the acrid stench of hopelessness as it permeated my pores like sweat.

Tylik cleared his throat raspily. He coughed and pounded his chest. The retching echoed endlessly in this prison, cutting through the veil of blackness and banking off the cold floor and stone walls.

Too bad the darkness doesn't engulf your mind with a black cloud like it does your eyes. It'd be a lot easier to escape the terrors you've seen if you could simply pinch a candle and stare into nothingness.

Desperate to escape my thoughts, I decided to indulge in something I excelled at: bullshit. "You know, Tylik, we may live longer than anyone has ever lived. Hell, I'd wager we might live forever."

"Mm. Don't know 'bout that. Go on and take a peek at my toes; they ain't the toes of a man who'll be living forever."

"We'll live forever," I insisted.

"How d'ya figure?"

I looked in his general direction. "Because Death would sooner abandon his duties than step foot into this shithole."

Tylik coughed a hearty, throaty laugh. "Might be right. Ya might be damn right about that." He hacked up what sounded like a bellyful of phlegm, pounded his chest again and sighed heavily. "Say, Astul. What would you do if you got back to that misery-place, yer homeland?"

"Oh, I suspect I'll return," I said. "I just don't think I'll return with the same mind I left with."

"Pity."

"They're going to take my world, Tylik. And there's nothing I can do about it."

"Hmm. I ought to think someone'll step up to the occasion. Lots of stories 'bout heroes and such, you know. And seems to me that heroes always appear at the very last moment."

I chuckled. "And it's in stories where heroes stay. They never come out to play in the real world. Got a king on my side back in Mizridahl, most powerful one there is, too. But he'll have the North bearing down on him. He'll be forced into war, and the conjurers will sweep in and pick up the pieces. Only person who can stop that is Patrick Verdan."

Tylik clapped. "See there? A hero, just like I said."

Maybe if he didn't sit atop a bloody mountain, secluded from civilization, I thought. Patrick Verdan, now there's a man with a good story to tell. He and Vileoux saw eye to eye about as often as two blind men. Their hatred for one another had led to Patrick's abdication, and with him he took a sizeable chunk of Edenvaile's populace. Ran 'em right up the western ridge, climbed a mountain and claimed an abandoned fortress he would name Icerun. The interesting part isn't that he and most of his people survived, but that his abdication damn near caused a civil war in the North. The lords of the North were eagerly awaiting Patrick's future crowning and the more liberal policies he'd bring. Patrick eventually placated them, but many promised that if he ever wanted to make a claim on the throne, he'd have their full backing.

What I wouldn't give to see Patrick round those lords up now and overthrow Chachant. An alliance between Braddock and the North was the only way to stymie the conjurers.

I told Tylik all of this, and he listened earnestly. Then, he drew in a deep breath, like an old man about to embark on a story of his prime years when he wrestled with lions and made wolves submit to him.

"I'm sixty-two years young," he said. "Now, 'bout… oh, fifty years ago, that's when the conjurers came. Just appeared, like they'd been born from rock or even air. They say they can heal broken minds, don't you know? And people 'round here, well… same as on that misery-place, I'd think — lots o' broken minds. Was all a scheme, in the end. Just a way to recruit our innocent children. Then they start doin' it openly, just comin' into villages and taking kids and if you resist, why, you get put in shackles, like me.

"Now, way before, the shackles were rope and the dungeons were above the soil. They put you in these big open chambers surrounded by wooden spikes. But see, these prisoners, they'd manage to send word back to their families. Rich families would hire mercenaries to free their loved ones, and poorer ones would round up the whole brigade — even the fat aunts and lazy not-good-for-nothin' uncles — and they'd storm the place. Sometimes you'd be freed, sometimes killed. Them's the odds, though."

Tylik sniffed the air. "Anyhow, just a long story to get on with my point that it'd sure be nice if there was a way we could do that nowadays."

Hopeless dreams did not impress me, nor were they a rallying cry to improve my current situation. It would be nice to send for help, but it'd also be nice to sprout wings and take to the sky, and while I'm at it, I would take a pinch of fiery breath and a smattering of scaly armor so arrows and swords would deflect harmlessly off of me.

Nonetheless, Tylik was a genuine man — one of the only I'd known — and it seemed the very least I should do was entertain him. "I'm afraid whoever would receive my letters would either smile, overcome with glee, or just as likely use the paper as kindling."

"Mm. No family? No little lady who has your heart?"

"Lots of little ladies have something of mine, but it's not my heart. Much of my family is dead, thanks to the conjurers."

"Gots to be someone who cares about you," Tylik pressed.

I considered what I had accomplished in my life. The memories were mostly foggy now, like looking at the moving pieces of the world through a marred scope. I saw bits and morsels, and I remembered them well enough, and I was fond of most of them. But something nagged me. It was big and sharp and quite painful. I believe they call it regret.

"I made a name for myself," I explained. "Built a reputation. Kings, queens, lords, ladies, village leaders, savants, goatherds, farmers — they knew me. And many of them wanted me and my Rots for... unscrupulous reasons. Because we delivered. We were feared and with fear comes respect. But I am, in the end, an assassin. I am not celebrated. I am replaceable if need be. I've never left anything in anyone's heart except perhaps anger, resentment and respect. Those things won't bring people searching for you when you go missing, though."

Tylik clicked his tongue. "Seems to me a man like you don't much care about that sort of thing."

I shrugged my clasped wrists. "No, I don't. Well, I didn't. I suppose knowing your mind will be taken away from you is a sobering thought that brings about strange feelings."

The outline of Tylik's head was not visible, but I distinctly felt him nodding in agreement.

"Mm hmm," he said. "Strange feelings indeed. You'll start feelin' calm about it soon enough. I got a theory about that. See, I think it's your mind's way of giving up. Can't get out, right? So no use in making your last few years miserable. Guards'll do that to you just fine, believe me."

My fingers skittered across the dirty floor in boredom. A sharp spine scraped against my knuckle. The momentum of my hand dislodged it, spinning it into my ankle. I leaned forward and picked it up. Holding it close to my eyes, I examined it carefully.

I laughed. Only while sitting in the abyss of a dungeon could a man possibly find curiosity with a thin rock chip — a wafer, really. The pointy end had a nice bite to it, but not enough to stick through a guard's throat. Great tool for drawing a little blood, though. Could trace a few tattoos into your flesh, maybe dig up those annoying moles.

Maybe even write a poem across your arm, give yourself something to read…

I passed the rock between my hands. Tylik spoke, but I ignored him, opting to give this sharp stone my full attention. I followed its craggy edges that formed the shape of a teardrop with a severe point.

I held it like the disfigured quill that it was and pressed it into the soft flesh of my hand. I pressed until a trickle of warmth slid down to my thumb and dripped onto the floor. It stung as I angled it and gently etched a letter into my skin.

The blackness of this place allowed me only a vague glimpse into my art, but it appeared eligible, if a little crude thanks to the raw, red tissue surrounding it.

"I miss the birds," Tylik said. "Their singing and—"

"Tylik," I interrupted, "you were a farmer, right?"

"Farmer is generous," he said. He coughed and added, "Like to think of myself as a fielder. I had a field. One cow, one row of corn and one row of tomatoes. Not much of a farm, if ya ask me."

"Fine, but you used tools to carve up the land and sow your seeds, yeah?"

"Of course."

I gave a satisfying nod, even though he couldn't see me. "Could you still do it now, with those old hands? Pretend for a moment your toes were not rotting off. Pretend you were home, in your field. Could you till the dirt? Pull a harrow across the soil? Could you carve up the land to sow your crops?"

"I suppose so," Tylik said. "Hands are a slight bit shaky now — I reckon from all this sittin' around. But they work."

"Good. Because I need you to carve my flesh."

"Er. What?"

A looped chain tethered me to the pillar. I scooted across the floor, toward Tylik's voice, moving around the pillar like a fish caught in a maelstrom. "Can you slide toward me?"

Tylik made a series of grunts — some bordering on the edge of painful whimpers. When he spoke again, his voice sounded nearer. Better yet, the faint outline of his shadowy silhouette materialized.

"Stretch your hand out," I said. "Far as you can."

A swollen stub with tendrils at the end lurched toward me. I placed the rock in his palm. "I'm going around the other side of the pillar so my back is facing you."

"Astul, what is the meaning of this? I don't understand."

I scooted my ass along the stony floor. "Conjurers want me alive, to do their bidding. They aren't going to kill me." My chains clangored and scraped against the pillar. All this moving was not helping my urgent need to piss. "They're going to take my mind. But I know someone who may be able to take it right back, if she's still alive. I need a way to deliver her a message. And what better way to conceal that message than having it on me at all times?"

I took my soiled shirt off.

"I… I don't like hurtin' people," Tylik said, his voice trembling.

"It's a mild pain. It's relieving, in a way. Start in the middle so my shirt will cover the words entirely. And press firmly: make me scar."

Tylik swallowed loudly. "Aren't you scared they'll find out?"

I turned back, my chin on my shoulder. "Of course I am. But that's no reason not to try. Now, can you reach?"

There was a grunt and a groan and a grumble. The cool prick of the rock stabbed lightly beneath my shoulders.

"Good," I said. "A little lower. Yes, right there. Write these words… actually, better yet. Can you draw? A riddle or puzzle, to throw off the conjurers if they see this."

He hesitated. "That depends. Drew a heart once, for my love. She thought it looked rather like a bum."

"Right. Let's just go back to the words. Are you ready?"

"Suppose so."

After some time of sitting in solemn silence and trying not to think about how badly my back burned from being cut open, the door to the world above croaked and creaked. A rivulet of fire flooded into the dusty dungeon, glinting off the unfashionable iron bracelets attached to my ankles and wrists.

"Food," Tylik said, with a hint of demented happiness in his voice, like a man whose only joy came from a few morsels of ground-up mice tails.

A pair of feet tread carefully down the steps. Not slowly, but carefully. The nuances between the two are subtle, but obvious to anyone who's spent a lifetime of sneaking around. Whoever was the owner of those feet cared greatly about arriving at his destination silently.

He or she or it moved like a placid river that you know in your heart of hearts is being swept toward the sea, but you can't for the life of you figure out which way the sea is.

"I don't think it's food," I said.

"Mm," Tylik grunted.

The fingertips of orange flames flickered closer, scrawling designs on the chalky floor, reaching and stretching and swooping over bits of loose rock. Finally, the toe of a leather boot appeared and then another.

"Uncle," the voice whispered. It sounded familiar. "Are you awake?"

"Don't sleep much," Tylik answered.

Burbling flames came into view, licking the damp air and expunging every shadow they came across. They cast a glow that illuminated the torch they raged from and the face of the man who carried it. Or perhaps the face of the boy who carried it.

"Was wond'rin' what you were doin' as a conjurer guard," Tylik said. "Figured they'd turned ya into a slave."

The conjurer guard was the young lad who'd helped Crooked Tooth haul me up to have a quaint meeting with Amielle.

"You two are familiar with one another?" I asked. "How nice."

"He's my nephew," Tylik said. "His name's Karem."

"I'm here to break you out," Karem said.

What a courageous act. It was too bad the voice did not match the intentions. The boy was scared shitless. He couldn't even hold the torch steady. It wavered like a battered ship on the ocean. Confidence begets success, and if you don't have much of the former, you probably won't see much of the latter.

"How do you plan to free him?" I asked.

Karem looked at me, eyes wide and face smeared with dirt. He dangled a key. "Gots this. Figure it's dark up there. Not much going on, so we can sneak out." He turned back to Tylik. "Dalleria is doing well, and Evander is too. I promised I would return their father to them, and I will make good on that."

The darkness between Tylik and me sped away as the reach of the flames pushed onward. The older man raised his head and looked at me with tired, heavy eyes. "I will only go if you free my friend here as well."

A better man than I may have jumped up — as much as one can jump when tethered to a pillar — and put on a show about how this was madness and to leave him here and don't risk it. But I was not that kind of man. I sat silently, enjoying the confusion that twisted and wrinkled on Karem's oval face.

"We create more risk by bringing others, but—"

"He is my friend," Tylik said. "I will not leave him behind."

Karem nodded. He knelt and stabbed his key into the thick iron locks along the chains woven around Tylik's body.

"I'm curious, Tylik," I said. "Can you walk?"

The old man's eyes thinned at the sight of his toes, which were swamped with a congealed green liquid. "Mm. Can't say I've tried in quite some time."

"Karem," I asked, "are you scared of death?"

The boy made his way over to me, holding his iron key out proudly. "I'm sorry?"

"Death. Are you scared of it? Or him, if you prefer. It's just that you don't look the type who can carry a grown man for more than a half mile."

"I will carry him the whole night without stopping, if need be."

"We'll see soon enough."

Karem glared at me. I hoped I had offended him. He looked like the kind of kid who'd been doubted his entire life. He was scrawny and pale. The hair on his face looked in a perpetual state of confusion as to whether it should grow properly or not at all. His voice was a bit squeaky. He was the kind of kid who, if you expressed doubt in his abilities, would do every bloody thing in his power to prove you wrong, if just to spite you.

A few twists of Karem's hand later, followed by a few clicks, and I could once again raise my hands over my head. More importantly, I could stand. Unfortunately, as I did, the code engraved into my back widened like the innocence of a virgin. It hurt. Quite badly.

I cursed under my breath.

"I am going to lift you, Uncle," Karem said, his voice steeped in uncertainty.

I snapped my fingers to grab his attention. "Here, give me it. I'll be your torchbearer."

Karem's eyes trailed from my feet to my head.

"This is a strange time to express distrust," I said. "I am already free. If I wanted to, I could have snatched the torch right from your grasp, put it to the back of your hair and watched as you went up in flames. But I've been a good boy, haven't I?"

"Give him the torch, Karem," Tylik said.

With uncertainty distorting his mouth, Karem passed me the fiery rod. He knelt and wrapped his thin arms around his uncle's sickly body. He rose up onto shaky knees, his uncle's nearly lifeless corpse slung over his shoulder like a sack of wheat. Poor Tylik... he resembled decrepit livestock being hauled to the butcher's knife. His head hung, chin animatedly bouncing off his nephew's back as he was carried toward the steps.

"You go ahead," Karem said. "You are the torchbearer, after all."

"That's all well and good," I said, "but I'm afraid I have as much sense of direction here as a eunuch has in a brothel."

"Keep left when we emerge, along a hillside. The moon is full tonight, so you should see a small outcropping of low-hanging trees in the distance. Go towards them, away from the city of Lith. Once we reach the forest, we should be free."

"Good berries grow on them trees," Tylik explained. "Real good ones. Blue ones, red ones, yella ones. Yellas are a bit sour, but some savants crush them and make 'em into a paste. Claims it can make holes in yer skin heal faster, but I don't know about all that."

I grinned and pushed past Karem, up the crooked wooden planks that ascended in an uneven fashion to the surface. The door at the top was already open.

"Cover your trail next time," I told Karem.

"I thought I closed it."

I stopped and turned. A gust of fire swirled around me. "Did you?"

Karem licked his lips. His pebbly eyes scoured the wooden plank at his feet. "Maybe I didn't. I... tonight has been a blur."

I poked my head out, hopeful not to see a band of guards ready to impale us with pikes. A gentle breeze tickled the fuzzy beard on my face. It seemed clear.

"Come on," I said. "Kick the door closed behind you this time."

With Karem and his skeleton of an uncle behind me, I crept around the craggy face of a hill that sped upwards into a mountain of jagged summits. The moon looked like an albino cherry, its stem a thin crescent cloud pausing overhead.

My hand trailed along jutting rocks and dense wet mud as I slowly led the way. The percussions of a terrified heart pounded in my ears. I spent my life portraying a man whose courage and intimidation could not be possessed by fear, and I did a pretty damn good job of it. But inside, far away from prying eyes, I was as scared as any when the time came to stick a blade in a man's belly or put my plan of escape into action. I just didn't show it. But here, in an unfamiliar land, with a city of mind-leeching conjurers on the other side of the hill… well, my fingers trembled a little.

There was a whisper behind me. "That's the outcropping, over there. Do you see it?"

"What do you suppose that is, then?"

There was an eye-blinking silence, which is the type of silence one experiences when your mouth is agape, but all you can do is blink your eyes and wish away the horrible thing you're staring at.

Finally, I said, "I'd venture a guess that it's a torch." Another blink. "Coming quite quickly." Another blink. "You could perhaps even suggest it's galloping."

"Oh my fuck," Karem cursed, which was an interesting way of showing surprise. If I lived through whatever barreled toward us, I'd have to remember it. "Someone must have seen us." Panic clung to his words.

Against the inky horizon, silhouettes tumbled toward us, a ball of fire heading the charge. The silence that draped over the land fled, chased away by disturbing stampeding hooves. A hunt had commenced.

I spun around, desperate to find something from the landscape with which I could work. Back toward the entrance of the dungeon, a small patch of earth ramped up into a discombobulated formation of dirt and rock, surrounded by flat land. It looked like the straggler of a hill that'd been struck by explosive lightning.

The hooves of assailing horses thundered closer.

"Stay here," I told Karem. "I'm going to draw them wide and away from you. When they pass, run your ass to those trees and get the fuck away from here." I grabbed Karem by the collar of his shirt. "You run like you're going to lose your legs tomorrow. You run like you want to see your uncle live. You run to be the hero of your little village. Understand?"

A steely resolve iced over the boy's eyes. His jaw tightened. "Yes."

I patted Tylik's shoulder. "Take care, my friend. If I live through this madness, I'll come back and take the toes from that bloody ogre who took yours."

The torch fire flared across Tylik's sloped forehead. His eyes welled up. With a shattered voice, he said, "Thank you. Truly, thank you."

The rumbling intensified, reverberating into the soles of my feet. The shadows drew closer, their outlines blacker, larger. It was time to set fire to the night.

I ran away from the hillside, in a large swooping pattern. I centered my eyes on the queer rock formation, putting everything I had into each stride.

The flames from the torch crackled and burbled, streaking through the night.

The deafening blows of hooves striking the mud were catching me. Their thuds and booms nipped at my ankles. The percussions enveloped me. My entire body quaked.

It's a terrifying thing to be in such a silent place that you hear only the rasping of your breath and the monsters that chase you. It's even more harrowing when you know there's no escape, only a prolonging of your inevitable end.

I jumped onto the twisted structure of rock and dirt, climbing up as high as I could. I felt like a preacher about to deliver a sermon to his faithful followers. Except my followers were the kind a captain of a ship has on the day of his mutiny.

Like the impetus of a toxic wave, the shadows of the beasts and their riders crescendoed over the land, coming to an abrupt halt before me.

"Oh, you got to be fuckin' me here," a man said, his face partially covered with steel. He held a small torch that glowed menacingly against the black sky. His voice was gratingly familiar.

Crooked Tooth.

The other two men remained silent, their mail-covered hands tightly woven around their steeds' reins.

"Get your bloody ass down from there, or I'm comin' up there and yankin' you down. And I'll make yer pretty li'l face turn inside out."

I wagged the torch insultingly in front of him. "I would highly recommend another approach. You see this here? This fire. Fire burns. Fire bad. Hurts. Ahh! Ouch! Ooo! Hurts! Do you understand any of this?"

With a big, bad huff and an angry frown, Crooked Tooth clambered down from his horse. He withdrew a sword and shoved his torch forward. "Eh? I got one too."

"That's impressive. But I have the higher ground. By all means, haul your gaunt self up here, but I think it would be prudent to negotiate. Hammer out a deal. Strike an agreement. What do you say?"

The vast number of sentences clearly spun Crooked Tooth into a whirlwind of confusion. His eyes seemed to dilate and narrow, and his cheeks twitched.

He looked at his pals. "One of you go tell the queen. See wot she wants to do with 'im."

Both men pulled their left hands back, rearing their steeds around.

"*One* of you!" Crooked Tooth roared. He pointed to the closest one. "Go."

The horse galloped away with its rider. I watched as its shadows sunk into the black horizon, hopeful it didn't stop suddenly and pick up two stragglers. When it continued onward, beyond the bend of the hill, a celebratory sigh of relief washed over me.

I sat on a smooth rock and cracked my
knuckles. Equally bored, Crooked Tooth chewed his
nails, or what were left of his nails. His fingers
resembled stubs, the tips of which had been gnawed
down to soft flesh.

I hummed a little tune, counted the dimples on
the moon and attempted to snatch stray sparks as
they darted like fireflies from the torch when finally
the air rumbled with crashing hooves. Two horses
blinked in from the black horizon, galloping my way.

Crooked Tooth straightened himself like a good
boy. His pal dismounted and followed suit.
Apparently no matter the world, the bullshit of
royalty stinks the same.

Looking more like a ranger than a queen,
Amielle and her trailing guard stopped up short of the
overgrowth of earth and rock I was perched upon.
She climbed down from her chestnut steed and sidled
over in front of Crooked Tooth, a lopsided grin on
her pale face. A dull green tunic wrapped around her,
the familiar *C* centered with a devious eye embossed
upon her breasts. Her auburn hair looked frizzy, as if
she'd just woken up.

With a voice of honey, she said, "The Shepherd
does not disappoint. Who freed you?"

"The god of imprisonment," I said. "He was
craving irony."

Amielle side-eyed Crooked Tooth. "Have you
checked the dungeon for Tylik?"

The ogre's massive nostrils flared. "Uh. No. I, er… no. But he got no feet, so don't think he's goin' nowhere." He became visibly distraught as the silence tugged at him. "But I can go put an eye down there and see."

"That would be good," Amielle said dismissively. She looked at his two friends. "You can join him."

Crooked Tooth and company took to their horses and obediently ambled over to the dungeon entrance.

"If I gave you a weapon," Amielle said, "would you attempt to use it on me?"

I traced a circle around my jugular. "I'd stick you right here."

A haunting grin cut across her scarlet lips. She held her palm toward the sky. Her chest heaved and her jaw shifted. A spark the color of a bloody orange flickered in her hand. It rose above her flesh, swirling into a growing ball of searing heat. The light from my torch melted into the ball's intensely blinding illumination.

"How much do you truly know about us? About the conjurers?"

I shrugged, pretending that the sudden appearance of an ensorcelled sphere of flames did not shake me. "I've slaughtered your kind before. Hundreds of them. You're nothing special; just a bunch of mutated freaks who can steal the thoughts of the innocent and mold them into monsters.

Conjurers made me a very rich man, though. Everyone in Mizridahl wanted them dead, and I gladly made everyone's dreams come true."

Amielle shook her head like a disappointed mother. "They were supposed to spread our name in peace. And they did, until you barbarians murdered them. And what for? Hmm? Why did they die? For showing you we can mend the broken and piece back together the shattered?"

"Is that why your conjurers ruined Serith Rabthorn's mind? And his wife's? And what of Lysa Rabthorn? You experimented with her, tried making her become one of your obedient freaks. Didn't turn out like you'd hoped, did it?"

"I once met a boy," she said, ignoring me, "who lost his mother in a tragic fire. His thoughts were dark. Hopeless. He lived in a world where nightmares slowly drowned him. I took his nightmares and showed them the power of a conjurer. I hid his horrors and rediscovered his hope. I made him better."

Her words did nothing to me. I knew the truth, even if she wanted to conceal it. "The most horrific tyrants I've ever seen have been those who have mixed morals and power. We're helping, they say — helping spread the good word of our god by cutting off the heads of those who don't believe in him. We're helping, they say — helping the king enforce his virtuous ideals by slaughtering anyone who won't bend the knee before him. It's the easiest way to obtain control: by wielding your power under the guise of help. I've never been fooled by it, and I won't be fooled by it this time."

"Sometimes," she said, "you must adopt the mind of a tyrant to achieve your goals. Even if those goals are pure. History does not bother itself with how progress was made, only *that* progress was made. Five hundred years from now, when my people have enjoyed generations of prosperity on your lands, they will not recall that I bludgeoned an entire world's worth of cultures and societies. They will eat their abundance of food, drink their abundance of drink and live happily until the end of their days, hailing Amielle Scorticia as their goddess."

A sense of pride struck me like an unlikely bolt of lightning on a cold winter night. Chauvinism was not an emotion that often moved me. Ever since I was a boy, I'd held civil zealotry in little regard. If a lord from the North wanted to take over our little village, I thought, then I would simply run away into the woods. I didn't care for "my people." I cared for myself. But this... this was different. The conjurers, they didn't belong in my world. They didn't belong in any world. For them to march in and eradicate all I'd known... no. No, that wasn't going to happen.

I stood tall and wagged my torch at her. "People will remember you in much the same way they remember a bee buzzing around their flowers. Here one day, gone the next, leaving nothing of significance behind. I'll make certain of it."

A shrill laugh bolted from Amielle's throat. "I can churn the wind that will extinguish your light."

Intense concentration wrinkled across her forehead. A foreboding howl bounded from the cliffs and from the forest, from the north and from the south. It surrounded me like the eye of a tornado. The air whipped about tumultuously, pulling at the rags on my body, yanking the hair from my eyes.

The flames in my hand sizzled.

They hissed.

They died.

Blackness entrapped me.

"And you think," Amielle said, her face invisible, "that you can stop me? I can conjure the earth to rumble and eviscerate the rock on which you stand."

As the raging wind quieted, an uncomfortable sensation trembled in my feet. No matter a man's profession — assassin, jester, stable boy, ring polisher — feeling the ground shift beneath your toes is a sign you will not be having a very good day.

Beneath the earth, something roared without pause. The hard shell of the jagged rock I stood on began to give way to the powerful storm beneath the surface. Cracks crawled across the top, deepening into massive gorges.

I dropped my unlit torch and held my arms out, balancing myself as my body began to sway uneasily. Stuck in the impermeable blackness like a rat in a blanketed cage, I felt the world around me begin to buckle. The ground thundered now, and the outcropping of earth and rock that served as my gracious host was ground up into morsels by whatever hell was rising from below.

Air rushed past my face, which is another way of saying I was bucked into the air and approaching the unforgiving ground quickly.

Holding my hands out, I braced myself for impact. Luckily my face was the third body part to thud into the densely packed mud and not the first. Still, the bridge of my nose twisted into an unhealthy curve, and my jaw felt like I'd gotten kicked by a horse.

"And you think," Amielle said, gasping, "that you can stop me?" She sounded like she was standing over me. "I can rive the sky and show you—"

I threw a hand in the air, my face still buried in the mud. "I get it. You can do a lot of wacky shit."

The haunting warmth of her body surrounded me. She knelt beside my head and conjured a tiny speck of flame that idled above her fingertips, illuminating her eyes, which were whiter than snow. "I will break you, Astul. You will not leave my world with your mind intact."

I hauled my face off the ground and offered her my best crooked grin. "People have been trying to break me my entire life. Good luck. You'd best pray that you're successful. Otherwise, I've got a blade with your name on it. I will kill you."

She vomited — a symptom of the exhaustion that comes with the use of a conjurer's perverted powers — then licked her lips. "A conjurer never dies."

"I know a few who impaled themselves on my sword that would disagree with you."

A wretched smile formed on her lips stained with yellow bile. "A conjurer never dies," she said again. She stood up and walked away, one hand cupping her stomach, the other pressing firmly against her temple.

A heaviness sunk into my mind. And I fell asleep.

CHAPTER THIRTEEN

My mother used to tell me that having a routine would save me from becoming a vagrant one day. Waking up once again in a cold, dark room with unforgiving stone slabs beneath me, I wanted to shout, "Well, lookie here, Mother. I finally found a routine: being knocked unconscious and then coming to in a place rats keep their distance from." Really fantastic thing these routines were.

To be fair, the dungeon did lack the acrid smell of piss this time around. And the stone wasn't quite as cold. In fact, it felt quite strange: gritty and uneven, as if tiny specks of sand dotted its surface. And was that a breeze? Something resembling wind certainly rippled through my hair. Speaking of hair, hard bubbles of blood were dried to mine. Upon a bit of inspection with my fingers, perhaps it was mud.

Hmm. My hands were free. Strange. Amielle's preference since I'd gotten here was to toss a chain around every movable body part and clasp it into place with ridiculously large iron locks.

Wiggling my ankles uncovered another interesting twist: they weren't bound either.

A fat drop of water — gods, I hoped it was water — splashed onto the bridge of my nose.

It did not fall from the ceiling, because there was no ceiling. If I was a gambling man — and I certainly was — I would have bet Rivon's roosters it was the sky that towered above me. Pinpricks of glittering light stretched across the black canvas, the moon full and fat and bright. That's not to say it provided me with a whole lot of light, though, thanks to a gargantuan wall blotting out most of its pearly sheen.

That wall seemed familiar. Hauntingly familiar. It looked like an imposing curtain of stone rising high into the air, cylindrical spikes overlooking tiers of seating. If you were a suicidal bird who fancied putting a pike through your body, this would be the place.

Hauling myself off the ground, I stretched my stiff arms and walked carefully into the shadows. That's when it hit me.

The smell. Damn near knocked me right back to the floor. I reeled around and covered my nose, but it was no use. I knew this feeling. It greeted me when I awoke from drinking a smidgen more than the perfect amount of wine — the perfect amount of wine being whatever amount doesn't make you dry-heave and want to kill yourself when you open your eyes in the morning.

I hurled nothing but a few globs of spit into the air and, unfortunately, onto my toes. Better than chunks of food, which was impossible given I hadn't eaten in two fucking days.

Wiping the slobber from my lips, I turned back around, this time prepared to face whatever rank scent of death wafted through this place.

And make no mistake. It was the scent of death. Worse than that. It smelled like a beast had been gutted, strung out in the hot sun and left to rot while a murder of crows had shat upon its corpse. It choked the breath from my lungs. But I pressed on with a demented curiosity.

My feet sunk into a cool bed of sand. As if I'd ventured out from a concealed room, more of my surroundings revealed themselves in the form of two more walls that curled around to form a half circle, meeting with the first wall.

As I stepped forward and spun around, the circle suddenly completed itself. That was the moment my heart tried to plunge through my stomach.

Rows upon rows of empty stone blocks serving as seats were staggered upon one another. I'd seen this place before, from afar. I had no interest in ever seeing it again. I wished I was back in the dungeon, chained to a pillar.

A gentle voice droned from behind me. "Rested up, I hope?"

I turned slowly and instinctively reached for my sword. Instead, I found my hip without a sheathed blade attached to it — one of an assassin's worst feelings.

A fiery gold hue streaked across the sand. A thin man walked along the outer edge, a torch in his hand. He stopped before ornate wooden posts that were spaced every ten feet or so. He touched the fire to them, and *whoosh*. They became alive with flame.

With each one he lit, a ghastly glow of orange brightened the arena, revealing more of its features. Revealing the source of the acrid stench that sunk into my lungs like an unwelcome parasite.

Scattered around the blood-stained pillars that reached into the heavens were the empty husks of men and women I'd recruited, trained and fought with. Assassins with whom I shared grandiose stories over skins of wine and barrels of ale. *Friends* who had, against all odds, managed to thread themselves into my heart. Friends who didn't deserve this fate. Friends whose death I was responsible for.

Most of them lay facedown, and that was good. But some... they gazed into my soul with their lifeless eyes. I shook my head, desperate to erase their smiling faces that turned to horror and terror as the spikes from the arena surged into the soles of their feet and through their calves, tearing through their ribs and arms and necks and heads and...

"Is this how your queen thinks she can break me?" I asked of the man who finished lighting the torches. "You may as well save yourself the trouble and drag yourself back to her quarters fit for a princess and deliver her this message: I cannot be broken. I *will not* be broken."

The dull flames from the man's torch illuminated his oval face. His sunken eyes sagged into unsightly bags. The skin on his chubby face looked as if it was slowly succumbing to the invisible force that yanked everything downward.

"Queen Amielle tasks you with cleaning the aftermath of the arena spectacle." He nodded at a wheelbarrow. "You may wheel the bodies to the front of the arena, where you will stack them in preparation for burning."

"Tell her she's got a better chance at convincing a fish to drown itself."

The man folded his hands together. "The queen has made it clear that you cannot leave here until you complete this task. You do not want to stay here. The stench is not something you grow accustomed to. I have tried."

The man placed his torch in a bronze lion-carved brazier affixed to the wall. He slipped into the shadows and returned with a cloth and small bucket. He knelt before a pillar, dipped the cloth into the bucket and began washing off the dried blood.

"You're not a conjurer, are you?" I asked.

He rubbed the cloth in a slow circle, over and over again. "I am the arena custodian."

I laughed at the absurdity. "What's the catch here?"

Without interrupting his studious cleaning, he said, "Pardon?"

"Your queen can't possibly expect me to stay put like a good little boy because a custodian tells me to."

"Ah," he said, dipping the cloth back into the bucket. "You want to leave. You may try, but the queen has posted guards outside the parameter. Standard response when I am given prisoners to help clean up after a rather... dramatic day here at the arena. Although she does not usually assign specific tasks as she has with you."

"These are my friends," I said. "My friends! Dead because of her."

The man sniffed and waddled on his knees to another dollop of blood. "I am sorry to hear that. But it would seem to me that you would find it considerably easier to burn their bodies rather than stare at them and smell their remains."

Taking stock of my situation put me in regretful agreement. I might have been the most stubborn man alive, but I wasn't getting out of here anytime soon. And I was probably playing right into Amielle's plan. If I remained here long enough, the madness would overtake me. And she'd win.

I took the wheelbarrow and placed it in the middle of the fallen Rots, and then I pulled my shirt up over my nose. One by one, I turned over the men and women who weren't yet lying facedown. When I finished, water clouded my eyes and an overwhelming sadness squeezed my heart.

I was never on friendly terms with sadness. That terrible tightness in my chest and the sandiness of my throat reminded me of being a wee little boy and watching my father pound his fist into my mother's face. I *hated* sadness.

Anger — yeah, that was what I indulged in. Anger drove me like air drives a fire. Anger put my feet on the ground in the morning and slashed my blade across the throats of my targets. Anger threw back the wine into my belly and coursed the adrenaline through my veins. Anger is what created the Black Rot. Anger for my father. Anger for the rigid world that expected me to put on a happy face and do as some bloody lord demanded.

Anger impelled me through the most difficult times in my life. With my fists clenched and knuckles white, I decided there in the arena anger would impel me once more.

With the fury known only to those who suffer through gross injustice, I heaved the bodies of the Black Rot into the wheelbarrow. Only two fit inside at a time. I dumped the first load off and came back for another. Dumped them off on top of the first two and came back for another, refusing to pause.

Refusing to feel sad. Refusing to feel anything except hatred and anger toward the conjurers.

I thought of nothing but how to reap my justice. And somewhere in those obsessive thoughts — perhaps after dumping eight or ten Rots in the pile — I heard a voice unlike any I'd ever heard before.

It hissed and clawed at the fabric of my mind. *Kill yourself*, it said. A whisper, then a shout. *KILL YOURSELF, ASTUL. It's the only way. If you kill yourself, she can't use you.*

I ignored the thought and pressed on.

It returned with a vengeance. I cupped the sides of my head and rocked back and forth as the voice felt like a hot knife threading into my skull.

This was a waste, it said. *Why did you even do this? WHY DID YOU EVEN DO THIS?*

It felt like an eternity before the agony in my head retreated. When I opened my eyes, a blazing sun blinded me. I brushed a hand through my hair, raining sweat down upon my arms. I picked myself up from where I had apparently collapsed into the sand and had a look around.

The deceased Rots were all piled up now, although I had no recollection of doing the deed.

A jolly whistle carried throughout the arena, followed by a gruff voice unfit for singing.

It's a good life.
Yes, it's a good life.
A good life for me.

It's not a bad life.
No, not a bad life.
Not a bad life for me.

Two mules dragged a cart into the arena. A goblin of a man directed them to the stacked bodies. He clambered down from his driver's seat and tugged on the reins, guiding the mules closer. An enormous wooden wagon was attached to the back of the cart.

The man poked a long fingernail into the mass of limbs. Seemingly satisfied, he nodded and went around the other side. He hauled off and threw his shoulder into the bodies, toppling them over. Some fell into the cart, their elbows and arms and ankles and knees cracking off the edge as they toppled inside. Others slid right off and collapsed into the sand, kicking a thin film of dust into the air.

"Get the fuck off them," I cried.

The man jumped in surprise. "Whoa! Hey. Who are you?"

"What are you doing with them? They're supposed to be burned."

The goblin scraped a long yellow fingernail across his doughy jaw. "Er. Don't think so. I wouldn't be here if they were ta be burned. What's wrong with 'em that the poor bastards need set on fire, anyhow? Bugs? Bit o' disease?"

Pinching my eyes shut, I drew in a deep breath. Clearly this was all an illusion. It was make-believe, all part of Amielle's grand plan to break me.

"You're not even real, are you?" I suggested. "You're just a vision in my head."

One of the man's unruly eyebrows inclined. He bent down slowly, keeping his focus on me as if I was an unhinged and unpredictable specimen.

"All right," he said. "*All* right. Just calm down, huh? Nice and easy here. My name is Yurkie, and I collect the bodies from the arena once a week. Now, if there's lots of maimin' going on and they pile up quicker than that, I sometimes make an appearance twice a week, but no more." He grabbed the wrist of one of my Rots and then his ankle. With a grunt, he picked the dead assassin up and threw him into the cart like he was a maimed deer.

"Ain't doing nothing to you," he said. "You have my promise."

"Those are my Rots!" I shouted.

I ran toward him, unsure of what I was going to do, but it was going to be something, dammit. Something mean. Something violent. Something born in anger.

But like a boomerang thrown through the air, the voice that had crawled through and pricked my mind once again returned.

ASTUL, SHE DIDN'T TAKE ALL OF THE ROTS. You can save them. You can save the ones that are left. YOU CAN SAVE THEM!

The ground beneath me had vanished. It must've. A chasm swallowed the arena, digesting the sand into a black mist that clung to my eyes as I tumbled down, down, down into the dark, ominous abyss.

Think of it, the voice said. Its tone had changed from aggressively hopeless to sweet and charming not unlike the melody of a songbird. *Conjurers need assassins too. When they take Mizridahl, pockets of rebels will fight them. The Black Rot would be the hand of the conjurers.*

I said a word. I swore I said it. I opened my mouth and I pushed my lips out and I screamed it. I cried it. But it didn't come out.

No! That was the word, the rejection for the heresy the voice in my mind proposed. But all I could do was think it.

A cold, bitter wind rushed past me as I plummeted into the darkness, my body somersaulting into what seemed like a bottomless crater where it became colder and colder the farther down I went.

It would be no different than now, the voice said. *Simply a different head wearing the crown. You don't truly care about Mizridahl's fate. Do you? You're not a hero, are you? You're a hired sword. Nothing more.*

The thoughts the voice induced bred in my mind like mosquitoes in a dank river. Slowly and methodically they spread, blanketing and suffocating everything that I believed. That I valued.

Or perhaps this was part of the game. A trick to make me think these thoughts weren't my own when they truly were.

Reality slipped from my grasp.

There was turmoil within my soul. I could feel it. What did it mean?

I was standing now. No, leaning against a wall made of glass. A warm resplendent glow chased away the darkness and thawed the glacier air.

The voice pricked my mind. It'd changed again. It seemed nearer, a physical manifestation. It sounded familiar.

"I'm happy you came to your senses."

I wiped a hand over my face and blinked away the sweat from my eyes. I was suddenly in a glass chamber, and at the forefront of the chamber stood the queen of the conjurers.

"It *pleases* me that you came to your senses," Amielle said.

She was wearing a long, flowing dress cut from the finest silk and embellished with rubies and glittering gems. Her beauty weakened my knees, and I knelt before her as she placed herself in front of me.

She offered her hand, and I took it willingly. Eagerly.

Holding her fingers gingerly, I kissed the top of her hand and bowed to my queen.

"I've always had a thing for sensible action," I said.

Amielle smiled a charming smile and stuck her nail beneath my chin, lifting me to my feet. She placed a parchment in my hand and fitted me with two daggers. She threaded whispers into my mind. She armed me with a brilliant scheme.

She kissed my forehead. "The Black Rot will forever have a place in my world. I promise you. Now, off. You've a king to kill and a world to change."

CHAPTER FOURTEEN

I rode upon a fire that raged over a churning sea and under roiling gray clouds. Not even a downpour of rain could extinguish the flames that wrapped around the bird's body and colored its wings in a magnificent orange glow.

The phoenix sped across the wide expanse of ocean at speeds unimaginable to my mind.

The jagged coast of Mizridahl appeared before nightfall. The mystical bird carried me over the Twin Mountains that spanned the southern stretch for hundreds of miles and beyond the Hush Forest, where the trees gather so densely, your voice is muffled into a whisper no matter how loudly you speak.

Soon after twilight streaked across the sky, the phoenix made its controlled descent. What did it look like from the ground? A meteor? Death and destruction sent from the gods?

The bird of fire swooped downward at a speed so fast, the uneven earth seemed to vault itself upwards at us. Small campfires burned between what must've been hundreds of pitched tents. Bodies moved between them; they looked like tiny dots at first, and then ants, and then a mass of waving limbs pointing weapons to the sky.

Arrows whistled past me. The phoenix twirled effortlessly between the barbed tips, spiraling downward, quickly approaching the enormous camp bristling with banners featuring a grinning jackal placed against a crimson sky.

Men poured from their tents like bees from a hive, bunching into uncoordinated groups.

The phoenix slowed and made itself perpendicular to the ground. It landed softly on the outskirts of the camp.

The arrows stopped flying.

I patted the bird's head and clambered down.

Steel armor clangored as Glannondil soldiers rushed toward me, their swords drawn.

An uncomfortable sensation jabbed at my mind. I felt like something was very wrong. Fortunately, the discomfort was quieted when a fat man pushed through the oncoming drove of soldiers with the confidence of a king.

He came to an abrupt stop. "Astul? You're fucking me."

"I've returned," I said. *I've returned?* I thought. *That doesn't sound like me. Where's the moxie? Where's the zest?*

"Gods," Braddock said, waddling my way. He slapped his thick hands on my shoulders. He inspected me closely. "You're alive, are you? Brain still in your skull, legs attached, hands aren't cut off — I'll be bloody damned." Grinning, he added, "Don't ever tell anyone I was happy to see you."

"I escaped with one of their birds," I said. Reaching into my pocket, I produced a tightly folded parchment. "And their plans for war."

Braddock's eyes widened. He urged me to follow him with a waving hand. "Come."

We walked past orderly rows of Glannondil soldiers. Some stared at me in amazement as if I'd returned from the dead, while others clenched their swords and kept a close eye on the phoenix, who pruned wild flames from her feathers. They extinguished into chalky smoke as they fell to the ground.

Braddock led us into a large tent. Inside, candles burned and massive maps were flattened across tables. He took the parchment from me and unfolded it across one of the tables.

"What is this?" he asked, pointing to the various diagrams written in red ink on the map.

"If I were a guessing man," I said, "probably their route to war. Or perhaps they simply enjoy drawing red lines with arrows pointing to the kingdoms of the major families. What do you think?"

There it is, I thought, *now you sound like yourself.* Problem was, I still didn't *feel* like myself. Anytime I'd ever seen the pale, chubby face of Braddock Glannondil, a dash of annoyance and a hulking scoop of hatred had embedded themselves within me. I faintly remembered how it felt, but it seemed now, as I sat across from the king of Erior, apathy overtook me.

Why?

"They can't possibly have the numbers for this kind of attack," Braddock said, leaning over the map studiously.

"Numbers are something *we* don't have. Let's see what we *do* have: a boy king skipping across Mizridahl to dole out justice for perceived wrongdoings. An idiot in Edmund Tath, who'll follow him. And Dercy Daniser, a king who refused to march on a lord for acting out on a claim to the throne. Oh, and the Gate of the South is wide fuckin' open now that Serith is… well, wherever I put his body. The conjurers don't need numbers when we are as fit for a grand war as you are for a skimpy dress."

Braddock's eyes narrowed on the map. "Dercy will help us," he said confidently. "He prefers to avoid trouble, but there's no avoiding this. Chachant and Edmund, on the other hand—"

"Are likely going to war with you if Sybil doesn't reach her lover in time."

Braddock nodded. "I've been told all about Sybil Tath."

The gears were turning in his thick skull. Soon, smoke would begin billowing out of his ears and his eyes would turn red and he'd cackle maniacally as his overly complex scheme would come to life.

A throaty sigh rumbled through the tent. Braddock peeled himself away from the map. "I need time." He turned and added, "Go find one of my servants. They will give you a bed and a bath."

A bed and a bath? How lovely. I trusted Braddock would make his decision soon, so I didn't press him further. Soon he would decide to march — whether to Watchmen's Bay in an attempt to enlist the Danisers, or back to Erior in hopes he could turtle and withstand the assault. Didn't much matter where he marched, simply that he did. The march would tire his men and strain his supplies. And just before he reached his destination — that point where morale is at its lowest and food comes in the form of grass and seeds — I'd kill him. The mighty army of Erior would fall into disrepair, and my queen would be happy.

As I sought out a servant for my bath and bed, I couldn't help but admire the vastness of the Glannondil war camp.

Red tents were sprawled out for a mile in each direction. Mules and horses chugged along beaten paths between the tents, pulling wagons full of food, weapons, armor and clothing. Most of the soldiers were idle, sitting with their knees up to their chins or lying on their backs and bullshitting with one another in front of the campfires that raged beneath a starlit sky. Some sat in wide circles, with women behind them sifting through their hair, searching for fleas and ticks and lice.

Suddenly, a voice blared from behind me. "Back from the dead!"

The hairs on my neck sprung to their feet. I spun around and shook my head in disbelief. "Never felt better," I said.

Wagging a skin of wine and swaying happily, Vayle approached me with the smile only a drunk woman can offer. She slapped my cheeks. "Look at you. Alive! Did you convince those flaming birds to bring you back?"

A harrowing pang needled my head. Pressing on my temples and grimacing, I said, "Something like that."

Vayle put her hand on my shoulder. "Astul? Are you all right?"

Something's wrong with me, I thought. But that wasn't what I said. What I said, with the conviction of a priest declaring his god is just and true, was, "I feel fine."

And the pain vanished.

But the faint perception I was suffering from emotional malaise did not.

The Black Rot's second-in-command stood before me — my best friend stood before me — and

I was forced to feign a smile. Relief and joy should have washed over me, but there was nothing. Just a cold, unmistakable emptiness.

Vayle eyed me suspiciously. She seemed to sober up instantly. "What did they do to you?"

"They imprisoned me. But I escaped. The Rots"—I paused, feeling compelled to do so for effect—"they weren't so lucky."

"They understood the risks," Vayle said. "And we're still fifty strong. Those… things, they didn't take everyone." She took a swig of wine. "Would you like to see them? I have them patrolling the wilderness, searching for conjurer spies."

The world around me spun sickeningly, tossing me into crushing consternation. Sundry worries proliferated in my mind — worries I couldn't quite grasp or understand. It was as if a parasite was in there, rooting around, and suddenly came across something he found to be quite alarming.

"That's good that they're alive," I said.

Vayle regarded me coolly. "Are you sure you're feeling all right?"

I slapped her leather jerkin. "I just need a bath and to lie down for a while."

She tongued her cheek. "Right."

A woman in a stained dress walked past. Vayle grabbed her by the elbow.

"Miss, please get this man a hot bath. He's in desperate need." Reaching into her pocket, Vayle produced a coin and offered it to the woman.

She put her hands up and shook her head. "No, ma'am. That's not necessary, promise."

"Take it," Vayle said. "I don't care how the Glannondils treat their servants; the Black Rot is a respectful bunch."

Unfamiliar generosity scooped the corner of the servant's mouth up into an uneasy smile. "Thank you, ma'am."

Vayle scrutinized me with narrow eyes, and then she turned and went off. I watched her until I couldn't see her wobbly footwork any longer, which was the exact moment she slipped inside Braddock Glannondil's tent.

Inside a vaulted tent, the servant helped me out of my clothes. She brought in cauldrons from outside and poured scalding water into a round copper tub sitting on casters.

After filling it halfway, she guided me over like I was a wounded soldier incapable of finding my way. Steam undulated from the frothy water. I lifted my foot and cautiously dipped a toe inside. A scorching warmth shot up my leg and enveloped me in what was possibly the most relaxing sensation I'd ever felt.

I settled into the copper tub, stretching out as much as the limited space allowed. The servant took a hard bar of soap mottled with bits of flowers and herbs and dabbed it into the water. Then she gently rubbed it up and down the front of my body. Dirt and grime and other unsightly filth washed away into the tub, muddying the water.

She held my wrist in her soft fingers and rubbed the soap up my arm.

"Smells divine," I said, closing my eyes and inhaling the swirling steam into my lungs.

She said nothing, although I imagined she was smiling and nodding along.

When she finally did speak, her voice was soft and apologetic. "Sir, can you please lean forward? I must bathe your back."

I was going to explain that I was not at all a sir, but I figured what the hell? I'd roll with it and enjoy the pampering.

So I leaned forward, and waited for her to smooth the tension from my shoulders.

And I waited.

And I waited.

And I waited.

Finally, she spoke. "Um. I am sorry. I... must get more soap."

She scampered out of the tent, arms flapping. Almost as if in a panic.

That was mildly concerning, but hot baths have a way of making you forget about your worries and allowing you to enjoy the moment. And it was a fabulous moment.

Until the servant returned with Braddock Glannondil and Vayle in tow.

"Have your mothers taught you anything about privacy?" I asked.

Braddock's sword clangored against his armor. He knelt down beside the tub and threw a heavy hand into my shoulders, lurching me forward.

"What the piss are you—"

He stabbed a fat finger into my back, and I yowled as a searing pain burned my flesh.

"Taken," Braddock said, as if he was reading a page from a book. "Find L. Rabthorn."

Once again the world around me churned. Candles flipped upside down and waves rippled across the surface of the tub. Voices became muddled, as if their hosts were underwater.

"Smarter than he looks," Braddock said. "Get him up. Bind his hands and ankles, and bring him to my quarters. I'll fetch Lysa."

Any control I might have had over my body was mysteriously wrested away. My body thrashed about as someone grabbed my arms and hoisted me out of the tub. My body snarled and kicked and cursed as they pinned me to the floor. My body spat and swore and swung my legs at them as they tied a rope around my wrists.

My body did all of this, without conscious input from my mind. Something impelled me. Something controlled me.

It is a terrifying feeling trying to scream, only to discover that whatever has invaded your mind has managed to mute your conscious voice. You do what

it tells you to do. You show the emotions it tells you
to show. You say what it tells you to say.

A blurriness sealed over my eyes. When it
dissipated, I found myself lying on a table, arms and
ankles bound. A leather strap stretched tightly across
my stomach, preventing me from rolling off.

"You don't have to do this!" a woman cried.

"She damn well does," Braddock said.

"He's right," another woman said stoutly. "I
would save everyone if I could. I know the terrors of
it all."

She appeared before me, a familiar face.

"Close your eyes," she said.

I spat in her face, which elicited a solid fist
punching itself squarely into my stomach.

"Don't do that!" she said. "It's not his fault."
She leaned down and soothed a hand across my
forehead.

My body suddenly entered a calm and tranquil
state.

My eyes were closed, but still I saw her face. It
came and went, returning for brief moments.

A sense of weightlessness claimed me. Slowly,
my mind drifted away. Far, far away, where neither
dreams nor nightmares, neither worries nor pleasures
could seize it.

I fell into a deep, calm stupor, but I was
strangely aware time was passing by. An awful lot of
time seemed to pass me by when finally I could feel
the warmth of my body once again.

I awoke a different man. That is to say I awoke with the absolute impression I was Astul, Shepherd of the Black Rot, and not some imposter.

But there was a problem. A woman was crying hysterically, bent over on the floor. She cradled a girl in her arms.

Not just any girl, but Lysa Rabthorn.

She looked dead.

CHAPTER FIFTEEN

Resting my weary bones in a Glannondil tent within a Glannondil war camp — now that was a scenario I'd quicker believe to be an inhumane method of inflicting the greatest pain possible than a reality that I gladly accepted.

Globules of morning dew clung to the tips of brown grass I trudged through. The rays of the mango-colored sun sledded down from the barbed peaks of the Twin Mountains, flattening across the expanse of a pitted landscape that stretched for fifty miles or so, where the crushed rocks, dirty clay and choppy hills eventually mellowed into something less virulent in appearance. Although the brown grass that resulted wasn't particularly eye-pleasing.

I ducked into a small tent and nodded to Nilly Rabthorn. She did not look at me. She was sitting at her daughter's bedside, wrinkled hand tightly grasping the young girl's. Her eyes were withdrawn into dark, swollen sockets.

What can you possibly say to a woman whose daughter saved your life and in the process almost killed herself? What can you say to a woman who wasn't quite all there anymore? Probably the best course of action was to say nothing and wait to be spoken to.

Nilly never looked up, but she eventually spoke. "The savant says she'll make it. But… I wonder if she'll have her mind. Or if she'll be a husk. Like me." She brushed a mollifying hand over her daughter's head. "I can't help to think that your mind was not worth saving. Not for this."

"If I were in your position," I said, "I would probably agree with you. Tell Lysa when she wakes up that I am thankful."

Nilly fell silent again, and figuring our talk had been exhausted, I left her to mourn.

Outside, Glannondil soldiers prepped for the long trek to… where exactly were they going? I headed to Braddock's tent. Before popping my head inside, I announced my arrival, eager to avoid a scandalous situation in which the fat king was changing out of his trousers. I was not eager to wreck my mind so soon after regaining control over it.

"Yeah?" Braddock hollered in response. "Well, get your ass in here, then."

Inside the tent, the king of Erior had his elbows on a table and his face sitting on his fists. He was looking at a map covered in rocks. A man who looked like he had a sword shoved up his ass flanked him.

Vayle sat comfortably in a chair off to the side.

"What are you planning to do?" I asked. "Attack them with rocks?"

"He lost his war-planning pieces," Vayle said. "So now we plan with rocks. Fascinating."

The man behind Braddock lifted his chin smugly. An outrageous mustache curled thinly beneath his nose, curved around his tiny mouth and shot straight out to his jaw. Sometimes you know precisely how a man will talk and act based on what's growing from his face.

"This is a war council," he said. "Respect the proceedings."

"We're not in Erior, Rommel," Braddock reminded him. "Drop the act."

I went over to the table. "If you keep this charm up," I told Braddock, "I might start to like you. Please don't make me do that. By the way, thanks for, er — you know. That whole getting-my-mind-back business."

Braddock side-eyed me, gave a curt nod and then went back to his map. He tapped a rock with a nail that desperately needed trimming. "The gray ones are the Glannondils. The black ones — well, the darker ones — are the conjurers. These rocks with the white chalk are the Verdans. The vertical rocks are the Taths, and the pebbles here are the Danisers."

"This looks ridiculous," I said. "And I'm not talking about your collection of rocks. Why are your people hugging the west coast?"

Vayle rose from her chair. I hadn't noticed how hungover she looked until she held her stomach and dry-heaved. Regathering herself, she said, "It's the seventh alternate strategy. There are more to come."

Braddock backed away from the table in disgust, flinging his hands behind his head and sighing deeply. "We're goddamned blind. Blind fucking soldiers marching to war in a headlong fog." He picked something off the small table beside his bed and tossed it at my feet. "I assume this map you gave me is false."

I picked it up and gave it a look over. "I'd guess so. I remember very little about my mind being wrested from my control, other than it was an unpleasant experience. It's unlikely the queen of the conjurers gives me her actual plans for war. What if they were to fall into the wrong hands?"

"The queen of the conjurers?" Braddock asked, sounding concerned. "You met the bitch behind this movement?"

I shrugged. "Met her? We're practically best friends."

Suspecting everyone in the tent was now eating out of my hand, I channeled the power of an old storytelling grandfather and divulged everything I knew about the conjurers and the blighted land on which they lived. About their oh-feel-so-sorry-for-me story of how their lands were empty of game and how the rivers were drying.

"Fuck up your world and go take someone else's," Braddock said. "Is that how it is? Why did they send you back? To lead me on a wild chase so they could conquer the other four families without my involvement?"

"To kill you," I said bluntly. "That much I remember."

Braddock crossed his arms.

"Don't be so offended," I said. "It wasn't my idea. Now, back to this war. We still have Lysa's word that the conjurers intended to come through Vereumene and Edenvaile. Or would at least ignite the war from those two kingdoms. That's what we should plan for."

"That plan's as old as my grandad's piss," Braddock said. "I've talked to Lysa. That was the conjurers' intention when they were set on her being the catalyst for this bloody war. They moved on from that a long time ago, when they tried fucking with me."

I grabbed a rock from the map, tossed it mindlessly into the air and caught it. "Then let's force them back to that plan of action. Look, their entire scheme is predicated on a massive war between the great families. If we can pacify Chachant's bloodthirst for you, we pacify the entire North and the East. That won't stop the conjurers from attacking Mizridahl — they depend on our world for their survival — but it forces their hand. They'll try to take both the North and South. The North because it's always a hair's width away from shattering into chaos, and the South because it's already in ruin. Take your men south, and—"

Rommel spoke up. "Vereumene is deserted. There are scores of factions appearing across the South with every report our scouts send, and Kane Calbid's claim for the throne isn't helping matters. It would be an impossible land to defend."

"Kane Calbid," Vayle said. "Recruit him."

"The only way he helps," I said, "is if Braddock promises not to interfere with his claim."

Braddock made the pouty face of a child who was just refused his third cake of the day. "I'm not enthused with the idea. Kane Calbid is a reactive man. It would be better to back the claim of someone who is calm. Level-headed."

"Someone whose strings you can pull?" I asserted.

He glared me.

"We don't have the luxury to choose," Vayle said, diffusing the situation. "If Kane provides his men, he and Braddock can hold the South."

"And the North?" Rommel inquired.

Vayle walked around to the front of the map. "The North," she said, picking up several rocks and placing them on Edenvaile, "is held by Dercy, Edmund and Chachant."

"Big assumption," Braddock said, "that the three can rally their bannermen to fight a war against things most believe don't exist anymore. We have little evidence to prove they do."

"Then let us do the job for them," Vayle said. "Perhaps their bannermen won't risk a war for something they cannot see. But they will for greater power. They will for a promise of a new title. They will for a promise of greater wealth. If that means removing the head on which a crown sits and shifting the seats of power around, then so be it. That's what we do."

Braddock paced. "Assassinating Dercy, Edmund and Chachant would be—"

"Brilliant," I put in. "If you can put aside your petty morals."

"It would be madness!" Rommel said, beside himself. "You could have five, ten... twenty claims for the throne all at once! It would be utter madness."

"Easier to clean up that mess," I said, "than it would be to clean up our corpses after the conjurers sweep through. And in case you're not aware, it's quite impossible to clean up your own corpse."

"What of the West and East?" Braddock said. "I'll be damned if they take Erior from me."

"They won't want to," I said. "They need bodies. The East doesn't have many families who don't swear allegiance to you and who haven't already provided you with their battlements. The West is a little sketchier, but if they move in from Watchmen's

Bay or Eaglesclaw, they'd run headlong into either you and Kane or Chachant, Dercy and Edmund. Or whoever we replace them with."

Braddock poured a pail of water into a hollowed-out gourd. "It's better than any damn plan I've come up with so far."

Rommel's lips moved, but there were no words. A good boy knows when his advice is no longer wanted.

"I'll deal with Kane Calbid," Braddock said, sipping his water. "I only have a contingent of the Red Sentinels here. The rest of them, along with my bannermen, are awaiting orders. I'll send for them right away."

"Send Lysa Rabthorn back to Erior too," I said, "where she'll be safe. She shouldn't be out here."

"Already had it in mind," Braddock said.

I turned to Vayle. "How many Rots do we have?"

"Fifty-some."

"Let's split them. Half go to Golden Coast, half to Hoarvous. They get to the highlords and promise them whatever they have to. You and me, we're taking the North."

Braddock pinched a sputtering candle. "By yourselves? This isn't a job where you assassinate some goatherd. You need to pull the entirety of the North together."

"I know just the man for that job," I said. Letting Braddock hunger for the answer for moment, I then added, "Patrick Verdan."

The armor wasn't my own, but it was satisfactory. One can't hope for more than that when dealing with Glannondils.

I put on a mail shirt, a leather jerkin, leather chaps and, as one might guess, leather boots. I was a man of variety if nothing else.

I stuffed some heavy wools into a burlap sack in preparation for the abuse the northern weather would dole out, double-checked my hips for swords and my ankles for daggers. Thankfully the weapons were of ebon. On a less blissful note, they had belonged to my Rots, who had been taken from Vereumene and murdered in Amielle's arena.

I strolled out into the camp, where tents were now coming down and horses and mules were being fitted for the short journey to Kane Calbid.

One steed in particular looked at me with hopelessness in its chestnut eyes. I patted its head and leaned in for a whisper. "Don't worry, old boy. I hear they're more fans of sheep than horses. But by the gods, if one sneaks up behind you and drops his trousers, you kick him hard and true."

The horse snorted, which I took for a hearty laugh.

Near the edge of the camp was a wide circle of tents that appeared removed from the rest, as if they had been ostracized for perceived faults.

"Look there!" said Wevel Pilfast, a Rot who I personally trained eleven years ago. "A man so foul not even Death wanted him!"

The small mob of darkly dressed and oily-haired Rots bellowed with laughter.

I smiled. "I hear you delicate little flowers were so scared when those flaming birds came through, you pissed yourselves while running away."

"Too fucking busy running to worry about pissing," Elima said.

I kicked some ash that had escaped a fire pit. "I hear that," I said, looking at my feet. "Commander Vayle catch all of you up on the plan?"

"Aye," Wevel said, "I'm leadin' the crawl through the Golden Coast, and Evandra's taking the others through Hoarvous."

I nodded at my feet. "Good. That's... that's good." I rubbed my hands together and tried get the courage to look at their faces while I spoke. But I guess I was too much of a coward. "Look, what happened in Vereumene... the Rots there who were taken. They, uh—" I began talking wildly with my hands, as if the words spiraled around me and I had to snag them from the air.

"We figured they were dead," Elima said. "Figured you were too. It's what we signed up for, Shepherd. We know the risks."

My tongue stabbed my cheek in frustration. I lifted my head and shook it silently. Then, I said, "You're wrong. You signed up for freedom. You all joined the Black Rot to experience life in its purest form: free and unrestricted. Maybe some of you have personal reasons as well, like Commander Vayle and her pursuit of justice. But above all, you wanted freedom. Freedom that you cannot find inside walls. Freedom that kings and lords withhold from you."

I licked my lips and continued on. "The most I've asked of any of you was that you do not kill kings and you do not kill children, and on occasion I'd request your company to cut down some lord who thought it wise to threaten our family. And perhaps a small amount of your coin went into the vault as tax. But otherwise you were free. Free to take whatever job came your way. Free to spend your gold as you liked, drink to your fill, fuck till you couldn't stand anymore. I'm sorry I have stolen that freedom from you here today. I'm sorry I stole that freedom from your fellow Rots who died in another land, far away from here."

"Oi, fuuuuck that," bellowed a Rot. "You didn't steal nothin' from us, Shepherd. We followed you willingly. Still do. We'll follow you till that bastard Death tells us we can't follow you no more."

"We trust you, Astul," another put in. "We were all gettin' too used to petty assassinations anyways. Now we're on the world stage."

"That's right! We fucked villages and even little kingdoms before, but never did fuck the world."

"Hear, hear. We get to fuck the world, boys."

"Right up the arse!"

Evandra cocked her head. "Why's it always the ass with you, Baurel?"

"Bet you it's protectionism," Wevel said.

"Protectionism?"

"Right, right. Protectionism. In case he gets with a guy dressed up as a lady, see. Since he's all about the ass, he can still have his fun. Protectionism."

"That ain't it!" Baurel shouted.

With an unexpected smile on my lips, I slunk back off into the camp. I hoped that wouldn't be the last time I saw my friends. But the fact was this plan Vayle and I had concocted… it was the sort of plan you make when you've got nothing else. The kind in which you shrug your shoulders and throw it out there, knowing it's better than nothing, but not by much.

Waiting for the Glannondils to ready me and Vayle each a horse, the two of us sat in Braddock's tent.

The king of Erior chomped a stale piece of bread in half and chewed it vigorously, probably imagining it to be a fat chunk of the greasy sausage he dined on regularly.

"What was it like there?" Braddock asked. "Being with the conjurers?"

The memories put a scowl on my face. "An unforgettable time that I hope to soon forget."

"What was the land like? Similar to here? The people, did they speak like us?"

"I was shackled to a pillar in a dark, cold dungeon for most of the time, at least most of the time I recall. The only man who I regularly gossiped with had no toes, but yes, he spoke just like you and me. And the land? Entirely unremarkable, except for a tree. It was the biggest tree I'd ever seen. It lurched out sideways for a while and then surged straight up into a mess of branches and golden flowers. It was serene, and it reminded me of something I still cannot remember."

A smile touched Braddock's lips, which never ceased to unhinge me. "Reminds me of a girl. Finest lover I've ever had. Friskier and wilder than Gale. She had small tattoo of a—"

"Tree," I said, barely able to move the word past my shrinking throat.

"No, not quite," Braddock said. "It was of a blooming field on her—"

"Back," I said dreadfully.

"Er, no. On her thigh. Anyway, her hair was the most brilliant shade of—"

"Black," I said, as the memories instilled trepidation into my heart. "Raven black."

"Red," Braddock said, sounding annoyed. "Quite not black."

"And she was tall and slender," I said, ignoring him. I ignored everything based in my immediate reality. My eyes were fixated in one position, like those of a man who'd crept over that line you don't come back from, where insanity seeps into your veins forevermore.

"Short and rather squat," Braddock said. "I feel confident in saying you have never had the pleasure of meeting her."

"Her eyes were green," I said. "She twirled a key around her finger when I saw her for the first time in two years. She freed me from that piss hole of a dungeon in Edenvaile, and I paid back the favor at the slavers' camp."

"What the piss are you going on about?" Braddock asked.

I lifted my eyes from the floor. Apparently they did a proper job of reflecting the blend of rage, resentment and terror whirling inside me, because Braddock pulled his fat neck back inside his oversized shoulder guards like a turtle retracting inside its shell.

"Sybil Tath," I said. "That tree from the conjurers' world. It was tattooed on her back, branch for branch, color for color."

Attempting to make sense of this unfortunate revelation, Braddock did what most people do when confronted with an ugly truth: he tried to deny it. "Trees grow all over the world," he said, his words about as effective as the mad bark of a rabid dog is at making you pet it on the head.

"These trees," I said, holding my arms out wide as though the tent didn't hide the broad-leaved trees surrounding us, "are trees that grow all over the world. Tell me one time — just once — when you've seen a tree rise up from the ground, decide to fuck nature and slide sideways for a while, and then inexplicably jump one hundred feet straight into the air."

Good old silence.

"Go on," I said. "I'll wait. Actually, I can't wait, because apparently the daughter of Edmund Tath"— I smiled insanely while shaking my head—"is a *fucking conjurer!*"

Braddock emptied his gourdful of water. "Makes little sense for a conjurer to have been in a slavers' camp."

I shrugged. "Gaining my trust, I imagine. Knew I'd pursue Lysa in Vereumene, where her little birds would destroy my Rots and take me to her queen."

"Well," Braddock said, "our list of potential Vileoux Verdan's executioners has been narrowed down to one."

"About that. He's not dead."

Sheer and utter surprise doesn't appear as bulging eyes or a gaped mouth, but simply as what framed Braddock's doughy face: a firm, unwavering nondescript expression you would typically find when peering into the face of the recently deceased.

He swiped his gourd from the table and, despite it being empty, pressed it to his lips. He cleared his throat. "Not dead?"

"About as alive as you and me, save our minds not being possessed. I saw him, heard him speak. Looked just as decrepit and broken and sounded just as ancient and raw as he did when sitting on the throne of Edenvaile. So perhaps less lively than you and me."

"That's not good," Braddock said. The bluntness was nice to hear. "I can only imagine what they intend to do with him."

"I'd rather not imagine it," I said. "I need to find Sybil Tath. I can't let her corrupt Chachant more than she already has."

"Enlighten me as to your plan."

I clicked my tongue. "I told her to tell Dercy Daniser not to believe whatever whispers he hears from Chachant. She likely did not do that and instead embarked for Edenvaile from the slavers' camp. There are a host of messenger camps between here and there. Someone must have seen her."

"Your pockets look awfully empty," he noted. "Hard to buy off messengers without any coin."

"The Black Rot vault is not empty. You don't always need coin on hand to exchange payment for a favor, Braddock. Not when your word is as valuable as the currency you promise. By the way, keep this between you, Vayle and myself."

A smugness smeared itself across the king of Erior's face. "My, my. A secret the Shepherd wants to share with a pompous king but not with his own assassins? I feel so special."

"Do you feel special knowing our chance of surviving in this world has been cut off at the knees? No? I didn't think so. I don't want the others to hear about this. It'll breed in the back of their mind and weaken their resolve. Keep it between us."

"What about Patrick Verdan?" he asked.

"I'll get to Patrick, don't worry."

"What if you can't find Sybil?"

I took a step toward the entrance of the tent and looked back. "Then it's been not very nice knowing you."

CHAPTER SIXTEEN

My fondness for the horse I'd raised since she was a foal, Pormillia — who was still in bloody Erior — was never greater than when I was bouncing on the saddle of a steed named Kroon. Kroon seemed like a kind enough soul, what with his big brown eyes and affection for nestling up against you as you rubbed his snout. However, Kroon had a nasty addiction to chewing grass at inappropriate times, such as once every twenty steps.

It took six hours to cross the distance Pormillia could cover in two. Thankfully an inn sat along the way. I exchanged Kroon and one of my daggers — steel, not ebon, I'm not silly — for a horse named R. Or perhaps it was Are. Whatever the case, R had none of this grass-eating business that plagued Kroon, and we rode like the wind. And so too did Vayle, whose lively mare was raring to go after a short rest at the inn.

We spent most of our time cutting across the Haiden Grasslands, well-known for its sprawling meadows of golden grass whose stalks are thick and curly. Not brown-dead grass, mind you, but a healthy glow of gold, as if permanently burnished by a noonday sun. It's a place of serenity, but only for a few hours. After that, the calm goes right out of you like rotten meat. The mind can only take so much uninterrupted flatness and grassy pastures before boredom makes you wish you were in the mountains again.

On the fifth day of our journey, we came upon a small encampment with a towering beanstalk of a wooden post staked in the middle. It was nighttime, but still a flag could be seen soaring from the top, with the insignia of a golden galloping horse painted against a white sky. The walls surrounding the camp were made of short wooden posts, the tops gnawed down into spikes. The gaps between the posts were large enough for a person to fit between, but not a horse, which was exactly their intended purpose.

R trotted into the camp unimpeded, although he drew great interest from the vigilant eyes of a few messengers who watched with hands on their hilts. They relaxed once they saw the red hand of the Black Rot draped across the backsides of R and Vayle's mare. It may be an agreement among all civilized kingdoms and cities and villages and guilds never to harm a messenger, but agreements have funny ways of being forgotten.

A hunched man wobbled my way, holding a lantern. "How are you today, sirs and misses?" he said, taking R's reins as I dismounted.

"Just one sir, one miss," I said.

"Not so," he explained with a wagging finger. "Got yourself a sir horse and a miss horse too. Two sirs, two misses."

"Hopefully we won't be shacking up with the horses," I said.

An old guffaw exploded through the camp. "Not unless ya want to, no, sir. Our beds are taken tonight, but we have some straw laid out. Can put up a small tent for you, if you'd like. Standard gold piece for the straw, another for the tent."

The stable keeper secured R to a tie stall, then took Vayle's mare.

I walked over and patted the side of R, drawing attention to the red fist. "We've nothing in our pockets, but I believe you can trust that we will repay you."

The man tried to straighten his hunched back without success. "Of course, sir. The Black Rot is well-known among the messengers." He leaned in, lifted his hand beside his mouth and whispered, "Your payments are more generous than most, the riders say."

"Who is your commanding officer?" Vayle asked.

"Sir Daywrick is—"

"Sir Daywrick is right here," bellowed a man. He appeared beside the stable keeper. He was tall and athletically built, with a flowing red beard. A golden pin featuring a galloping horse was fastened to his cloak. "Black Rot, eh?" he said.

"Name's Astul," I said.

My commander nodded curtly. "Vayle."

Commander Daywrick beamed. "The Shepherd of the Black Rot." He turned to Vayle. "I'm, er, not as familiar with you."

She smiled. "I prefer it that way."

"Well, my men enjoy delivering messages to your, what do you call it — the Hole?"

"So I've heard," I said. "Do you have a moment to talk? Privately?"

He traded glances with the stable keeper. It was an unusual request. When you passed through a messenger camp, you did so to send a message or rest for the night, not talk to their commanders.

"Of course," the commander said at last, the courteous smile returning to his lips. "My quarters are right this way."

"Quarters" was certainly a hyperbolic term for the thing that housed Commander Daywrick. It was a shack of peeling wood with a flimsy door. It also reeked of must.

A candle limped to one side and the other, as if it was giving up on life. It provided for something better than total darkness, but not much. The commander sat at a table littered with stacks of parchments. Vayle and I stood, for that's what people do when there is only one chair in a room and it's taken.

"I'm hopeful you can provide me with information," I said, getting to my point quickly.

"About the messengers?" he inquired.

"About someone who may have passed through here recently."

An uneasiness stiffened the commander. "I'm afraid the messengers cannot divulge that information. Our code prohibits—"

"We know about your code," Vayle said.

"And we also know men are fickle creatures," I said. "They forget things occasionally, particularly when the flash of gold catches their eye."

The commander kicked his seat back angrily and stood up. "I cannot be bought."

"I'm not buying you. I'm buying your information. It's an age-old practice."

He slammed his finger meaningfully into the table. "I will not be influenced by—"

"Five thousand gold coins," I said, "delivered here within a month. My word, I'm sure you know, is as good as the gold that will soon be overflowing from your encampment."

The commander fell silent. Promising a man a mountain of wealth tends to make a mute out of him.

"Your horses look a fair bit ragged out there. Five thousand coins will buy a few strong, young ones. Or you could stuff your men's pockets, boost their morale. Or, hell, stuff your own pockets and enjoy the finer things in life. I won't tell, promise."

The commander looked around, as if tiny bee-sized messengers were flying about, ready to cast judgment upon him. "We talk within the order about messages that get sent," he said. "But it is known that these bits of information *never* leave the order."

"I understand. I've a made a life of burying secrets. All I want to know is if you've heard whispers of Sybil Tath, daughter of Edmund Tath, pass through recently."

The commander rubbed his knotted fingers together. "A messenger who rides a route from Rime to here and back came through about three weeks ago. Maybe a little more. He bore a verbal message sent from Lord Chachant Verdan to be delivered to Lord Dercy Daniser." He eyed the door to his shack. His voice trembled slightly. "There is to be an exchange of vows between Lady Sybil and Lord Chachant, held in the kingdom of Edenvaile. All of the major families were invited."

I shifted unconsciously on my feet. "When?"

"Ten days from now."

"Thank you," I said. "One month, five thousand coins. Count on it." I turned and walked out of the shack.

The night seemed much colder than it had just a few moments ago. Bad news has a way of altering your perceptions. Unexpected news has a way of crushing them.

"This is exciting," Vayle announced.

I lifted a brow and kicked a chunk of dirt. "You have an interesting interpretation of the exciting."

"I've always wanted to bear witness to a grand wedding," she said. "I assume we're going?"

"Oh, we're going." Whether we'd be wanted was another matter entirely. I did have to admit that seeing the confusion march across Sybil's face would be exciting. Discovering what she would do *after* the fact, however… well, that fell more on the spectrum of fear, loathing and general unhappiness.

I found the stable keeper spreading hay before a much-appreciative R.

"Sleep has been canceled," I informed him. "How many messenger camps are between here and Edenvaile, and where are they?"

The old man wiped a bead of sweat away from his wrinkled forehead. He counted silently on his fingers. "Hmm, roundabouts nine of them. Keep your steed's nose pointed straight here — well, as straight as you can, at any rate — and you'll run into all of 'em."

"Good man," I said, slapping his shoulder.

"Oh, and by the way. If you're wanting to shut your eyes for a wee bit on the way there, best camp is Hiven's Camp. Commander Hiven calls it Hiven's Fortress, which isn't far off. There's a great big inn with linens and all the fancy fixings. They even have daily hunts to invigorate morale, though I don't expect the Black Rot would be needing such things."

"Do they have wine?" Vayle asked.

His droopy eyes brightened. "Oh, yes. Lots of wine."

Vayle smiled. "Good."

He leaned in and offered a half-hearted whisper. "They even got a little special building there. The women inside don't wear clothes." He jabbed me playfully in the arm, and then turned serious as he glanced at Vayle. "Er, unfortunately nothing for the lady here... unless she enjoys the company of—"

"That's quite all right," Vayle said. "I enjoy the company of wine."

The stable keeper unbounded our horses from their stalls. I flipped him an imaginary coin and told him that although we did not sleep here, the debt would nevertheless be paid in his name, perhaps with a few extra coins thrown in. He thanked me profusely, and Vayle and set off for the wedding.

I hated weddings.

We crossed the Rime border on the fifth day of our journey. R's hooves thudded over a frozen tundra and beneath a slate sky whose clouds looked so thick and gray, one would be forgiven for believing the sun was eternally hidden.

Southern Rime was a blustery, pockmarked landscape with craggy hills and wisps of brown grass interspersed along the cracked ground of dirt and rock. It was a land of sheep and of buffalo and of people who apparently had no ambitions for finding happiness.

As Vayle and I pushed deeper into the misbegotten region, slushy flakes began pelting us in the face. Soon, as the air turned colder, the slush turned to snow that quickly reached depths of half a foot, with more on the way. Our progress slowed considerably. Thankfully, Edenvaile was a day's ride away. So too was the wedding.

Vayle and I rode abreast, occasionally exchanging looks to remind each other that we both we were tired, sore and bored. We traded off horses at each messenger camp we came to so that we'd have fresh beasts for the journey.

I was now fifteen thousand coins in debt.

On the morning of the tenth day, the curved walls of Edenvaile appeared through the haze of gentle snowfall and fog.

Vayle unbuckled her skin of wine from her satchel and she sipped.

"Give me that," I said, reaching over and taking a swig.

"Tangy," she said. "And a little sweet."

I inhaled the frosty air deep into my lungs. "I'm not drinking for taste."

"Neither am I," she said, licking the wine from her lips. She gave me a wink. "You haven't told me how we're getting in."

I sat back in my saddle and pulled the reins gently back, halting my steed. The looming castle of Edenvaile stared at me unrelentingly.

"Well," I said, uncertainty creeping into my voice, "we could wait for a market cart and steal it."

"That seems unlikely."

"True," I said. "We could scale the walls."

"That seems even more unlikely given we've no rope."

"Fair enough. We could…" I bounced my head back and forth, trying to jar loose a brilliant idea.

"Why not simply walk in?" Vayle said.

I considered this. "We're not what you would call welcome guests. Or rather, I'm not. Although Sybil did say Wilhelm helped her free me. But you can't really trust a conjurer, can you?"

"Chachant has employed you to find who killed his father. You're as welcome as any, I would imagine."

"The Chachant of old," I corrected her, "employed me to find his father's murderer. Since then he has slipped into an increasingly rapid state of insanity that seems to have been induced by his wife-to-be."

Vayle opened her mouth and caught a snowflake on her tongue. She swallowed it.

"Are you drunk?" I said.

"No. Why?" She looked offended at the suggestion.

"You're eating snow."

"I enjoy the coldness on my tongue. Walking into Edenvaile is our only option, Astul. Look around. There is no market cart. No secret passage into the sewers. There's only the gate."

I sighed. "If I find myself in that bloody fucking dungeon again…"

Our horses cantered up to the gate of Edenvaile and then slowed to a trot and then a walk. Atop the battlements were the city guard, dressed in silver steel breastplates and conical iron helmets with a thin nose piece running down the middle. They looked ridiculous. A black tabard wrapped around all of them, with the Verdan coat of arms featuring three golden swords pointing upward.

Those patrolling the parapet wielded bows, but those that greeted us below waved enormous swords and pikes in our faces. And greet, truly, is too kind of a word. They met us. With what seemed like unabashed resentment. There were ten of them, with more pouring through the streets.

They all had excitement in their eyes. This was probably their big day to shine, to put on a show for mommy Sybil and daddy Chachant. Poor bastards.

"We're here for the wedding," I said, smiling.

A guard with three golden swords fastened to his cloak straightened himself. "Black Rot was not invited," he said, taking note of the caparisons that covered our steeds.

"I assumed my invitation was lost."

An explosive argument boomed from inside the kingdom, near the frozen fountain in the large square courtyard.

"Fucking find someone!" a voice bellowed. A very familiar voice. "I don't give a fuck! Find someone with a hand."

"Wilhelm!" I shouted.

The commander of Edenvaile's city guard turned and, immediately upon seeing me, said something that looked quite foul under his breath.

The front of his balding head shined as the morning sun played a game of now-you-see-me-now-you-don't. The bags under his eyes were thick and dark, and he looked a good bit thinner than the last time I'd seen him.

He shoved his way between the city guards, coming to the forefront. "Go assist cock for brains over there," he told them, "and find me a goddamn butcher."

"Yes, sir," they said, all together. They shuffled their feet and went to assist cock for brains.

"I've got a fuckin' butcher who cuts his fuckin' hand off this morning," Wilhelm said, beside himself. "Can you believe it? A butcher cutting his hand off! What good is he then?"

"Why is the commander of the city guard concerned with that?" Vayle asked.

Wilhelm blew a puff of air between his cracked lips. "Because the commander of the city guard has become the commander of the kitchen, of the linens, of the drink, of the hunt, of the put-the-fucking-tables-over-here-you-fucking-vagrant-motherfucker." He sighed heavily. "This place isn't ready for a wedding."

"Did you try informing Chachant of this fact?" I asked.

Wilhelm burst into explosive laughter laced with sarcasm and irritation. "You have a better chance of stumbling upon a beach in this land than finding the king out of his bloody quarters. I haven't seen him in a week."

"Is he still alive?" I asked, partially joking.

"Servant says she saw him yesterday, so yes. We'll find out soon enough, won't we?"

I pointed at Vayle and myself. "Does that 'we' include us?"

"What are you here for?" Wilhelm asked.

"The wedding. It's such a magnificent—"

"Lies do you no favors. You're not well-liked here anymore, given a previous incident."

I rolled my eyes. "Is this about that stable boy? Gods, Wilhelm. Give it up. I didn't kill him."

"Gods? The Pantheon of Gods wouldn't help you here. They'd say your dagger—"

"I was set up," I said. "If I'm going to kill someone, it sure as shit won't be some little twerp tending horses. And I surer than shit wouldn't leave my weapon on the ground next to his corpse like some middling amateur."

Wilhelm wiped the falling snow off his steaming head. He clacked his teeth, deep in thought.

"If you believed I did it, you wouldn't have helped Sybil free me from your dungeon."

"Saying 'no' to a queen-to-be isn't something a commander of the city guard does," he retorted. "You were also present when a tanner here got his throat slashed, time before last. You slipped out the next morning, conveniently."

I guiltily unfolded my arms. "That *was* me. Had a bounty on his head. Borrowed some money from a certain lord. Never paid it back. Never had the intention of paying it back. So, he paid the debt with his blood. You know how it is."

"Is this your way of persuading me to let a known killer of the Edenvaile populace inside my walls?"

I side-eyed Vayle and chuckled. "Firstly, they're not *your* walls, so drop your balls down a few sizes, will you? Secondly, your king tasked me with finding the person who killed his father. Now, how do you think he would react if his commander of the city guard barred me from the city, cutting him off from potentially very valuable information?"

"You came here to talk to Chachant?"

I shrugged. "Sure."

The corner of his mouth curled into a seething frown. He shoved a finger in front of my face. "One misstep…"

"Right, right," I said, patting him on the shoulder. "And you'll have my head, or some such. Got it."

Vayle and I pushed past him on our horses, entering the city. Once we secured them to their stalls and kicked some roughage over for them, my commander and I took in the sights and sounds and smells of a kingdom on the cusp of a grand wedding.

It was rather mundane, actually. Wedding mornings apparently weren't something to behold. Sure, the smell of stews laden with rosemary and peppers and mutton and duck and all of the other deliciousness that goes into them wafted through the air on this cold winter morning. And servants bounded through the kingdom, mostly between different doors of the castle. And there was the clanging of steel as the city guard prepared for its big day, holding a rehearsal ceremony near their barracks.

But displays of grandiosity, of enormous bouquets, of chariots marching through the streets, of trumpets and drums — those were notably absent. There was something that greatly interested me, though.

I found Wilhelm prancing through the streets, steam sizzling from his bald head. "What is that?" I asked, pointing my chin at the immense balcony of cobblestone that curved from one end of the castle to the other, about midway up, level with numerous newly placed doors. Men with mallets and chisels were erecting a gold-adorned banister.

Wilhelm gave me a look that exhausted men give when they're about to quit on life. "That," he said, arms outstretched, "is the grandest of all grand balconies." He rolled his eyes and added, "It is where the wedding will take place."

He muttered something under his breath and jogged off again.

"Isn't that curious?" I said to Vayle, who poked her finger into the iced-over fountain in the market square.

"If I was going to have a wedding," she said, smirking at the mere idea, "I would have it in a place where I would not freeze my tits off."

"Unless… you wanted everyone to bear witness to your big day."

"I would not want that."

I made a seat out of the frozen fountain. "Let's think of people who would, shall we? I'll go first. Those who crave attention. Doesn't sound like Sybil or Chachant."

Vayle sat next to me and stretched her tired back. "How about an uncertain groom who may wish to plunge to his death after the exchange of vows?"

I laughed. "I think you're getting close. How about someone who wants to create a spectacle?"

"A spectacle would be wasted inside a candlelit castle," Vayle agreed.

"You would want it to be an unforgettable moment. One that would have people talking until they can talk no more." I slapped Vayle's knee and added, "By the Gods, Commander Vayle, I think we're on to something! Now let's see if we can't solve this riddle."

Vayle skated her nail across the ice. "Consider those involved."

"Chachant and Sybil."

"The marriage is happening unexpectedly."

"Quite unexpectedly," I agreed. "Why the rush? They can't possibly be prepared to host an ambitious event in such short time."

"Unless the marriage *must* happen," Vayle said.

I clicked my tongue. "Sybil gains nothing from this marriage, it would seem," I said, feigning ignorance. "Mydia is next in line if anything were to happen to my good friend Chachant."

"Unless something befalls Mydia."

"Ah," I said, lifting a finger into the air insightfully. "And if something were to happen to them both at the same time, why... Sybil Tath would become the Queen of Edenvaile and Lady of the Verdan Family."

"Unforgettable indeed," Vayle said.

CHAPTER SEVENTEEN

There were plenty of misfortunes that could have befallen Vayle and me as we sat at the fountain, pondering our revelation concerning Sybil Tath's wedding. For instance, the ice beneath us could have cracked, soaking our asses in water so cold we wouldn't have been able to feel our cheeks for weeks. Unlikely, yes, but possible and perhaps preferable to what actually happened.

What actually happened was that the doors of the Edenvaile keep opened, and a woman dressed in heavy wools from her neck to her toes stepped out.

Sybil Tath.

She looked as if she'd just woken up, her black hair askew and wavy. It was too bad she hadn't fallen into a permanent sleep.

She gripped the iron baluster that edged along the stone steps leading up to the castle front. She slowly descended into the market district courtyard, careful of her every step on the snow and ice that blanketed this city.

It was strange seeing her like this. The last time I'd laid eyes on her, dried mud had streaked her cheeks and days-old blood had dotted her chapped lips. I'd felt sorry for her. I'd felt... well, it didn't matter now. In the end, it was all a ruse. All a trick to gain my trust, and I had fallen for it.

Sybil picked her eyes up and a cast a narrow gaze into the courtyard. Her head cocked and her mouth fell agape.

"Astul? Astul!"

With a smile so fake not even the drunkest merchant would buy it, she shuffled her feet along the strips of ice hurriedly. It almost looked like she was skating. When she reached the fountain, she leaned down and embraced me in what was possibly the most uncomfortable hug I'd ever experienced.

Still, I had a job to do, and that job didn't consist of revealing my overwhelming need to stick a knife in her throat... yet.

"I'm so happy to see you," she said, holding my shoulders as she pushed away. She nodded at Vayle. "Commander Vayle. How are you?"

"Cold," Vayle said.

"I imagine you are. Would you like some more wools? We have plenty in the keep."

Vayle lifted the skin of wine she'd been nursing. "I'll be warm soon enough, Lady Sybil. My thanks."

Sybil shied away at the mention of her title. "Please don't call me that. You've more than earned the right to address me simply as Sybil. If not for you, I wouldn't be alive, much less marrying the man I love."

"This," I said, "is all a little surprising. After all, it was just a few weeks ago I questioned whether you two would ever marry. I believe that question came while you were freeing me from the dungeon. Thanks again for that, by the way."

Sybil inhaled the bitter air around her. "Chachant had intended on giving me the wedding of my dreams soon as he became king. But... his father's death delayed that. He spilled his heart to me, and I saw tears well in his eyes. Vileoux's death had consumed him. He apologized and made immediate plans for the wedding."

"What of his intent to go to war with Braddock?"

Sybil laughed. "Oh, my. That's all in the past now. It was an unfortunate mistake on Chachant's part, but one I think many of us would have made in his position. Would you like to walk with me? Standing here is quite cold."

Vayle and I traded glances.

258

"Go on," she said. "I'll stay behind and…" A raven cawed from atop a slanted roof. "Try to understand the language of birds," she said with a smile.

Smart woman, I thought. Sybil likely had no nefarious intentions behind her request to stroll through Edenvaile — at least nefarious physical intentions — but by staying behind, Vayle ensured one of us would remain alive and free in the event my assumption was wrong.

Sybil and I walked abreast toward the stables. The stable boy shoveled roughage from a wheelbarrow into each stall.

"Chachant is still deeply troubled by his father's… disappearance," Sybil said, keeping her voice hushed and her lips close to my ear. "As am I. Have you discovered anything more about the conjurers?"

Yes, disappearance was a good word. Because the bastard certainly wasn't dead. "Forget about the conjurers for a moment," I said. "How'd you convince him to stay his assault on Braddock's walls?"

"I didn't… not entirely."

My brows raised involuntarily. "You just said…"

"I know." She subtly scanned her surroundings. "There are lots of people here. I didn't want to alert anyone. He's still convinced Braddock is behind the assassination."

"He's managed to make a damned fool of himself over all of this," I said. "What of the mustachioed king of the sea, Dercy Daniser? Did your lover at least have the presence of mind not to beg him for his bannermen in a bid against Braddock?"

Sybil's lips tightened. "He's not marching to war, if that's what you mean."

"You met with him?"

"Of course," Sybil said. "I told you I would."

We strode past the stables and into the outer ward, where the curtain of stone walls besieged us. "You must have had one hell of a wind at your back to make the ride from the slavers' camp to Dercy's kingdom and then all the way back here in time to plan a wedding."

I watched Sybil's temple pulse as she subtly shifted her jaw. I was walking a very fine line. I needed her trust so that I could stay for the wedding, but I didn't want her to feel too cozy and comfy in my shadow. She needed to feel on edge. She needed to feel the terror that possibly someone knew her secrets — a possibility she couldn't confirm. That's where the terror breeds, in the uncertainty that the deep, dark secrets you've kept hidden for so long have escaped their prison and are out there for prying eyes to see.

"The weather was friendly," Sybil said, "and the steed the Rots kindly provided was strong and tireless.

Tell me about the conjurers. Have you learned any more?"

"I learned about them up close and personal," I told her, watching her face vigilantly for the subtlest reaction to what I was about to reveal. "Birds bathed in flames soared high above Vereumene."

Sybil stopped in front of a large forge. Her nostrils flared. "That sounds…"

"Similar to the description of the thing you saw flying high over Edenvaile the night Vileoux died? They're called phoenixes. Fierce as hell." I patted the scabbard at my side, smiled smugly and added, "As it turns out, however, they don't fare well against ebon and barbed arrows. I've yet to find anything living that does."

Sybil's face was unreadable. She'd perfected the art of masking her emotions. "You fought them off?"

"Killed them," I corrected her. Lying was so much more fun than telling the truth, particularly when the truth sees me in a bad light, or absolutely no light at all and locked in a rank dungeon with iron clasps binding me to a pillar. There is, I theorize, a indirect correlation between the number of times an assassin finds himself locked in a dungeon and his credibility.

Sybil sidled up to the forge and took a pair of iron forceps. She closed and opened them mindlessly before hanging them back on a rack. "I guess I shouldn't be surprised, given what the Black Rot showed me they're capable of." She turned. Sincerity tightened her face. "I never had the opportunity to thank you — the Black Rot, that is — for freeing me from that awful camp."

"Consider your debt paid so long as you keep your boy king in check."

"He wants to know who killed his father, but I'll do my best to blunt his raging emotions. I'm more concerned about the conjurers. Do you think they'll attack?"

One more lie. One more tale to spin, and it would be the grandest of them all.

"No," I said. "I think we scared the balls off their men and the tits off their women and the courage from both of their hearts. The phoenixes were a test. One they were not prepared for us to pass."

Sybil's shoulders fell and she sighed. "I hope you're right."

And I hope you believe me, I thought. When your enemy believes you're not prepared, they underestimate you. And belittlement is a tool that has delivered so many victories for those who should have never had a chance.

"I should go back to my quarters," she said, pulling the wools tightly around her as the wind picked up. "My... er... workers are probably getting nervous about the time. I need to bathe, dress up, and practice for the wedding."

"Just call them servants," I said. "We both know what they are. You're a queen now, or you will be very soon. You'll be sipping wine from golden chalices and flinging your hand at the nearest slave — sorry, servant — to fetch you some berries."

She let out a strained laugh. "That's not who I am."

"No? Then who are you?"

She shrugged. "I'm Sybil Tath. Luckiest woman in Mizridahl."

With a smirk, she ambled away, around the forge and back toward the keep.

"Pardon me," said a man with a thick drawl. He ducked inside the forge.

"Is this yours?" I said.

He rummaged through his tools that clattered together. "Ah, I wish. Property of Lord Chachant. But I run the thing. King requested a new helmet, fit with a black diamond in the center."

"Vanity shit," I said. "It's not good for a damn thing."

"King has to look good," the blacksmith said, placing his tools of choice on a table. He tied an apron around himself.

"What's your name?"

"Borgart," he said. "Master blacksmith, been shoving steel in fire and whackin' it with hammers for near thirty years now."

Borgart? Now that's a name I hadn't heard in a while, but one I was familiar with. I withdrew my sword from its hilt. "Does this look familiar?"

Borgart dusted the soot from his hands with his apron and laid the flat underside of the glistening black blade on his outstretched palms.

"An ebon blade," he enthused. He traced the mystical blue swirls down the fuller. The design naturally occurred when the ebon cooled. His thumb came to the crossguard, where a letter resembled an abstract *B*, its curves jagged, symbolizing the Black Rot.

His eyes flashed with excitement as he looked up at me. "Astul," he said confidently. "Yeah?"

"You got me," I said. "How'd you know?"

"The experience of making an ebon blade does not leave you," he said, paying it affectionate attention with his fingers. "I crafted these when I was the blacksmith for a little village."

"You had a reputation," I told him, "as one of the only blacksmiths who could reliably craft an ebon blade. I see your reputation has served you well."

Borgart handed me back my sword with great reluctance. "One of Lord Vileoux's commanders saw my work. He told the king, and here I am."

"How quickly can you forge an ebon blade?"

He snapped his fingers. "About that fast. Ebon is a straightforward process, unlike iron. There's no making steel out of it. No folding it. No hammering the damn thing for three weeks. You melt the ebon, you mold it, craft your edge, and you got yourself the best sword this world will ever see. See, problem is, it's extremely soft fresh out of the forge. Whack the thing a smidgen harder than you intended and it's ruined. Once it cools, it can never be reheated. It'll shatter. Not many blacksmiths have the subtle touch for it."

An erratic crow darted through the forge, cawed at Borgart and shot through to the other side.

"Damn birds," he said, waving it at five seconds too late.

"Can you make a few hundred — or more — in, let's say, fifteen days? You probably have more time than that, but let's play it safe."

Borgart crossed his fibrous arms over his stomach. "Oh, sure. Soon as you let me in on this little secret of yours."

"I am a man of secrets," I said. "Which one would you like to know?"

"The one where you're gettin' these bucketfuls of ebon from. I've made about ninety of the immaculate things in my entire life, and most of 'em were for your mercenaries."

"Assassins," I corrected him.

"Yes, well, point still stands. Where are you gettin' the ebon from?"

I'd figured that question would arise. Some historians claim ebon existed as plentiful as the trees when this world was first created, or mistakenly born, whichever the case. The evidence, they claim, is the unusual hollowed gaps in the nooks and crannies of mountains and the emptiness of old mines. They believe our ancestors took it from the earth to make their armor and weapons for war. Ancient poems refer to a blade that could sing sharper than a morning bird with an edge so black it could blot out the sun.

Thanks to our gluttonous ancestors, the mineral exists in tiny and increasingly rare quantities today. Funny thing, though. When I was young and angry, still running from the murder of my father and battling a demented mind that begged me to end it all, I came upon a square, stout hill that rose high above the ground below. And as proof that nature dabbles in art from time to time, the only way up was a flawlessly sculpted path that wound tightly around the hill. It had the sort of steepness and perilously sheer edges that goats enjoy bouncing around.

When I made it to the top, I decided that was where I would make my home. Soon, I decided to shovel out a trench so I could sleep in something resembling a bed, rather than on a flat chunk of land. As I pierced the dirt with the rusted shovel, something chimed, like a note struck from a finely crafted instrument. It gleamed a menacing black under the assault of a noonday sun. With a procuring of a pickax, I tunneled down a foot or so, scooping up all of the ebon that I could.

Vayle joined my side soon after. Fifteen years later, the Black Rot was a hundred men and women strong, and our little shit village was known as the Hole. The wooden boards that make our walls in that deep tunnel conceal a secret few will ever know.

Thanks to my happenchance discovery and the fortune of very wealthy merchants whose eyes bulged upon seeing the black gold, the Rots became richer than most kingdoms and better outfitted than every army in existence.

"Go south into Nane," I told Borgart. "Do you know where the Voll Inn is?" The infamous Voll Inn was where the son of Enton Daniser was poisoned seventy years ago.

"Roundabouts," he said.

"Continue due south from there, you'll come to a hill that looks like a demon had punched up from beneath the earth. It's in the middle of flat land, you can't mistake it. At the top, there is a hole. Go inside. If you value your life, you'll slide along the right wall. There are traps that have a tendency to puncture your lungs with darts if you straddle the middle or enjoy a nice walk on the left. Inside the last room at the end of the tunnel, there is enough ebon to make a blacksmith like you cry like a boy upon seeing his father return from the war. There is also plenty of food to be had."

Borgart was listening earnestly, his long fingers entangled in his muddy beard. "What kind of magic have you got yourself into, Astul?"

"No magic," I said. "There is a forge above ground. A few amateur blacksmiths in our ranks tell me it's quite nice."

He stuck a thumb between his eyes and shook his head in disappointment. "I can't just abandon my duties here, Astul. I live nicely here. I eat what I want, drink what I want, my wife isn't bound to servitude like so many wives."

I wanted to tell him none of that would matter when the conjurers soon swept across his comfy little world. But he would never believe that, so I had to borrow a remedy old as time itself.

"There is a vault in my hole," I told him. "In the room before the ebon. A key sits under a helmet in that room. Take what you feel is necessary, but do not rob me. I am not a man you want to steal from."

In truth, I had two vaults. The one with so much glittering gold you could submerge a catapult in it was tucked away safely in a corridor on the left side of the Hole. The one on the right held payments for various… debts.

Borgart stuffed his hands in his pockets and slowly turned, inspecting the forge wistfully. Indecision marked his face.

The air suddenly ruptured into a short but intense gust of bitterly cold wind. I hid my face in my shoulder of soft wool as a foot-high snowdrift fusilladed across Edenvaile. It stopped as abruptly as it began.

"You love your wife, no?" I asked him when the storm abated.

"Married twenty-five years now. She's my…" He searched for the words.

"Everything," I said helpfully. "Any children?"

"Two boys and a girl. My daughter beats the snot out of her brothers when it comes to blacksmithing. She's got the magical touch of her father."

I sidestepped onto the raised steel platform on which the forge sat and put myself as close to Borgart as possible. Personal space did not exist at this moment. He needed to feel nervous. Uncomfortable. Unhinged.

"If you truly love your children and your wife, you'll take them all to Nane. You'll make my ebon blades. You'll take your gold and you'll get the fuck out of here. There's a cloud approaching this world, Borgart. And it's going to pause right over this kingdom. You don't want to be here for it. Trust me."

"War?" he asked. "I haven't heard of a war."

"Do you have ears that hear whispers from the coast of Erior to the coast of Eaglesclaw? I don't request a few hundred ebon blades because I want to parade them around the kingdoms of this world. There is a war coming, Borgart. Your boys will be made to wield a sword and shuffle around with leather scraps dangling off of them for armor. And your girl and wife... well, who knows."

He lowered his head and pushed past me. "I'll leave as soon as I gather them. Where will I deliver the weapons?"

"Stow them away in the Hole. Then find yourself a little village far away from Vereumene, far away from Watchmen's Bay. Don't even think of coming North again. If we lose this war, little villages will be the last place they come."

He stopped. "Who?"

"You wouldn't believe me if I told you."

"I would."

"Conjurers," I said.

I could tell he was riffling through his mind, trying to reconcile the near-extinction of conjurers in Mizridahl with this new uprising.

Surprisingly, he asked nothing more. He simply nodded and ambled along, toward the gate. He must have lived in one of the villages on the outskirts of the walls.

I grabbed a straight-peen hammer lying on his workbench, looked it over and then slammed the heavy bastard as hard I could into the side of the forge. The resulting clink deafened my ears. My wrist recoiled behind my head, drawing the hammer inches past my temple.

All I could hear was a loud uninterrupted ringing. I dropped the hammer and threw my elbows on the tool table, burying my face in my nearly numb hands. Ever since I'd met Tylik and witnessed the atrocities done to that man, and the injustice... I... it changed me. I didn't like it. Didn't like feeling. I never used to feel. Just did what I had to do. And now, I displaced a man and his family so I could get a few hundred fancy swords to help for a war, and I felt like I'd committed an atrocity.

I needed to blunt my emotions. But how? How do you undo the changes that have altered your shape, that have reached in and obliterated the soul that made you who you were and molded it anew, for better or for worse? How do you return to the person that the world remembers you as and not the caricature you've become?

I had to remember who Astul was. He was a thief, a liar and a grand manipulator. He was an assassin, a man of gluttony and purveyor of sin. He was indifferent to injustice, inhospitable to the needy and insincere to every lover he'd ever fucked.

I considered this for some time, and then it dawned on me. A man like that wasn't the type of person to help save the world. Of course, I wasn't trying to save the world. I was simply trying to save myself and my Rots. That's what I told myself, anyhow. I had to retain *some* pride.

Time to fetch Vayle and prepare for the grand wedding. We had a conjurer to outsmart.

CHAPTER EIGHTEEN

Vayle was still sitting on the frozen fountain, but only after close inspection could I tell. The snowdrift that blew through had dumped a heaping of snow over her, and she didn't so much as shake one flake of the white stuff off. Hopefully the cold hadn't frozen the blood in her veins.

"Is my commander dead?" I asked.

A skin of wine rose from beneath the outcropping of snow like a paw of an animal trapped under an avalanche. That was a good sign.

"I will be soon," she said, "if we stay in this kingdom much longer. It's cold. Very cold. One of the many reasons I do not miss the North."

I clapped my hands and rubbed them together diabolically. "I've got some news that'll be sure to warm your bones. We get to hunt for an assassin."

Vayle looked at me, and the snow perched upon her shoulder collapsed, cascading onto her thigh.

"You look ridiculous," I told her. "You do realize that moving softens the cold, yes?"

"A paradox," she remarked. "The cold makes it so that moving is a painful thought, but moving is the only way to stay warm."

I blinked. "Right. About the hunt for the assassin…"

"Let's get on with it," she said, rising from her crudely made snow shelter.

"We're assuming Mydia and possibly Chachant are going to keel over during or after the ceremony. Death requires an assassin. Unless he's arriving on the wings of a phoenix, he's already here. I say we start our hunt for him in the kitchen."

She stared at me expectedly. "Explain."

"The easiest way to make someone keel over is by adding a dash of poison to their drink or dinner. If we keep our eyes on the preparations of food and drink, particularly Chachant and Mydia's plates, we can identify the assassin."

"And what if the assassin is someone who wields a knife and isn't afraid to plunge it into the belly of a king?"

"I've got that covered too," I said, smiling as widely and annoyingly as I could. I pointed to the recently erected balcony curving across the center of the castle. "We'll be up there with Sybil and Chachant."

"I envision two problems. Wilhelm is bouncing around here like a demented bunny. He *will* pass us while we're in the kitchen. I doubt he wants us there. Secondly, they will not let us on the balcony. Ceremonies are for the lords and ladies and those kind of people, not assassins."

"Just wait," I said.

"Wait? Wait for what?"

"Preferably a meteor to scorch the sky and suddenly plunge into the land of the conjurers. Failing that, we're waiting for Wilhelm to come back around."

Vayle pulled her undershirt up above her lips, protecting them from the cold. "Will you beg him to allow us entry to the wedding ceremony?"

I reeled back, quite offended at the suggestion that *I* would beg *anyone* for *anything*. She knew me better than that. "No begging necessary. He'll find our presence up there quite comforting after I reveal some information to him. Oh, and look there, the man of the hour is passing through now."

On second look, Wilhelm did resemble a demented rabbit looking for his next carrot fix. His head swiveled around as if the scent of orange, fibrous goodness surrounded him. He licked his lips in great anticipation and his eyes were narrow and focused. And he had quite the hop in his step.

"Commander Wilhelm," I called out. He stopped before me. "I wasn't entirely honest about the reason for our arrival. I've heard little chirps." I put my arm around his armored shoulders. "Little warbles and a few trills. Some whispers, if you will, that an assassin lurks about in Edenvaile."

Wilhelm's shoulders rose with tension. "And where have you heard these whispers?" he asked, his voice muted.

"If I revealed my sources, then I wouldn't have sources."

He shrugged my arm off and faced me, with a scowl cutting down his chapped lips. "Twice now you have lied to me about your reason for being here. Why should I believe this?"

"My need to talk to Chachant wasn't a lie, and we both knew I didn't want to be here for a bloody wedding. That was hardly a lie, more a jest."

Vayle stepped forward and rubbed her gloved hands together. "Hasn't one assassination of a king already occurred on your watch?"

Wilhelm regarded her coolly. He said nothing.

"It would seem," she suggested, "that it would reflect poorly on you if another assassin managed to fell another member of the court under your guard."

"Remember the assassination of Enton Daniser's son?" I asked. "I'd heard that the commander of the Watchmen's Bay city guard was in turn brutally reprimanded. Eyes plucked out and fed to him, and then his tongue was riven from his mouth and he was thrown out to the sandy coast, left to dry by the sun like a fish."

Wilhelm unfolded his arms and rested his palm on the balled hilt of his sword. "Is someone paying you to find this assassin, or has the Black Rot suddenly found the notion to play protectors of the world?"

"I want stability," I said. "Not a world that's plunged into chaos. What do you think the outcome of an assassination here tonight would be? Imagine if Mydia or Sybil get struck down. Chachant will lose his mind. He'll march straight to the gates of Braddock Glannondil or Edmund Tath or wherever his crazed mind tells him to march. Do you want that?"

Wilhelm rubbed his mouth in contemplating fashion.

"I want access to this wedding," I said. "Allow us to monitor the kitchen for any attempts at poisoning. Allow us access to the balcony where the wedding takes place. Notify your guards and tell them to keep watch."

Wilhelm looked past me. He forced a heavy sigh through the corner of his creased mouth. "Fine. But understand me, Shepherd. If you fuck me over, I will do to you what Enton Daniser did to his city guard and worse. I don't care what repercussions I face from the Black Rot. I'll face them at the gate. I will make you suffer for making me a fool."

I contained a smile that tried to consume my entire face. Wilhelm and his city guard wouldn't face my Rots at the gate. No, my men would destroy them from the inside. But I had no intention of dishonor, so I simply shook the man's hand and gave my thanks.

Vayle and I made way for the kitchen.

"If I may be entirely honest," I told her, "I'm not sure where it is."

"You've never been to the kitchen?"

"I've never set foot into any kitchen except the tiny hearths inside tiny homes in tiny villages."

"I imagine this one is large."

Once we finally discovered the location of the Edenvaile castle kitchen, I learned that large was not an apt description. The place was huge, massive, outright enormous. It featured several rooms, all of which specialized in a different mastery of cooking. They each had dirty stone walls and dusty stone floors, but that was where their similarities ended.

The front-facing wall of the first room had been converted into an immense hearth with iron hooks dangling from inside and menacing flames that licked at the iron bottom of one tremendously broad and deep-seated cauldron chained securely to two pairs of hooks.

There was a table upon which two cauldrons sat, servants pouring muddy broth inside both. It took two servants to heft each cauldron over to the hearth and chain it to the hooks. Once in place, they would add onions and celery and potatoes and various other vegetables, along with chunks of sliced beef, a large heaping of peppercorns, some spice that smelled similar to cinnamon, a dash of thyme and a host of other spices. There seemed to be one woman in particular who headed this fiasco of stew preparation.

She was angry. She stormed from the table, serrated knife in hand, and elbowed a young man out of the way. "Nononono," she said, speaking so quickly each word came out joined to the other like twins that hadn't separated from the womb. "Cinnamongoesinlater. Later!" she smacked him upside the head. "Dumb! Stupid! Howmanytimeshaveyoudonethis? Howmanytimesanswermenow!"

Visibly shaken, the boy, who couldn't have been a day over thirteen, stumbled back and spat out, "So—sorry, Miss Loeora."

"Ah!" the woman hissed. She spun around and her thin slits for eyes narrowed at Vayle and me.

"Whoareyou? Whyareyouinmykitchen?"

"Hmm," I said. "And what language are we speaking here?"

"Excuseme?"

Vayle stepped forward. "Commander Wilhelm sent us to oversee the feast preparations for today's sumptuous exchange of vowels between Lord Chachant and Lady Sybil."

I wished I had an inkwell and parchment so I could take notes on how I was supposed to behave around these people. Vayle had it easy; she grew up around nobles with sticks up their asses. Granted, she was their slave thing, so maybe easy isn't the most accurate description.

"Oversee what?" the woman asked, her speech slowing down considerably.

"We won't interfere with your duties," Vayle said, smiling graciously. "I assure you."

"Mm," the woman said, dropping her head and slicing a carrot like she was attempting to grind it into the chop board.

I began walking toward the open doorway of a second room connecting the first. "We'll have to watch all four pots," I told Vayle.

"Astul…"

"What have we here?" I said, smacking my lips together. In the second room, the front-facing wall featured three separate unlit hearths. On several long wooden tables were chunks and joints of bloody meat, bones jutting out. There were boar haunches being basted with butter and stuck onto imposing iron spits. There was a whole pig being rolled over, its belly sliced open and stuffed with seasoned apples and spices such as sage and basil and garlic. A couple of servants stuck a hefty spit through its mouth, rammed it through the other side and left it on the table for now.

I mentioned to Vayle about ensuring both Chachant and Sybil received the same meat.

Her reply was, "Astul…" but I ignored her and continued onto the third room, which was the spicery. A man expertly wielded a mortar and pestle, grinding herbs into fine dust.

The fourth room consisted of a servant preparing sauces, and the fifth a scullery where servants washed tongs and basters and chopping boards.

"Astul," Vayle said again, after I suggested the scullery could probably survive on its own without our intrusion.

"What?" I finally asked.

"We can't keep watch over four rooms simultaneou—"

She paused. The stew lady unleashed a flurry of words from a few rooms over.

"Nonono! Impossible! Impossible! Itisallimpossible!"

There was a jangle of armor and then the walls trembled as something stiff collided into them.

"Make it possible," a low-growling voice told her.

A few moments went by. The saucierer went to check on the hateur and returned with a wry smirk on his face. He shook his head and began slicing the crusts from a loaf of rye bread.

"Is there a problem?" I asked.

"Oh, nothing," he remarked scornfully. "The Lady Sybil has simply moved the wedding from this evening to noon today."

"That's only a few hours away," I said.

"Indeed," the saucierer said, pouring a small spoonful of vinegar into a bowl. "Indeed."

I tugged Vayle's hand and hurried out of the kitchen and through a door that led to the edge of the castle courtyard, where a thin strip of grass would typically lie in the summer months, along with bedazzling flowers and bulbous shrubs. Now, there were bunches of dead wood and snow. Not a desirable place to congregate, which meant it served well as a venue to exchange words you wanted no one else to hear.

"She moved the time because we're here," I told Vayle. "She doesn't want us to find whatever it is she's hiding."

"An assassin, you mean?"

"Or worse. You're right. Monitoring the kitchen for poison is a fruitless endeavor. It's much too large."

"Tasters," Vayle said. "They could help."

"Tasters aren't good for shit unless they're tasting wine. A good assassin buries the poison deep within the meal, where only his victim would eat from."

The heavy sound of crashing steel resonated through my bones. I turned to see the double-leaf keep doors open and a very familiar man step out.

"My Lord," Wilhelm said from a concealed position.

"Commander," Chachant said. "How are the wedding preparations coming?"

"Behind schedule, sir. We didn't anticipate Lady Sybil moving the time."

"I understand she's a handful sometimes," Chachant said. "But try to accommodate her, will you?"

"Of course, my Lord. Will that be all?"

Chachant bowed his head. "Yes."

There was a scurrying of feet from where Wilhelm stood. Chachant had a relaxing look around his kingdom, drawing the glacial air deep into his lungs. He sat on the icy steps leading up to the keep, his arms woven around his knees. An old heavy wool coat consumed him, and a pelt tinged with orange fox fur sat upon his shoulders.

He had the face of a stable boy. Cheeks full of freckles, wispy pale hairs curling out from his chin and neck. His hair was matted around his ears and his bangs glistened with grease.

"I'm told you don't make many appearances to the common folk anymore," I bellowed, slugging through the thick, lumpy snow over to the boy king.

Chachant flashed me a lopsided smile. "There's a voice and a face that I very much have wanted to hear and see."

"Consider yourself one of the few," Vayle said dryly.

"Commander Vayle," Chachant said with a nod of his terrifyingly perfect spherical head, "how are you?"

Vayle traded glances with me. It was a glance of steadfast aggravation, one that said, "Why do these buffoons continue to ask me how I am when it's quite clear how I am?"

"Cold," Vayle answered.

"Better than being ill and cold," Chachant said. "Malaise has kept me under the covers and inside my room for the better part of the last week. It is fortunate the fever broke yesterday."

I patted down the snow next to Chachant into a stiff seat of sparkling white crystals and sat my tired ass on it.

"From the stories I was told," I said, "I thought perhaps you fell victim to the avaricious nature of the crown and were locking yourself away, convinced there were thieves afoot who wanted to steal it all away from you."

Chachant rubbed a small pill of snow between his thumb and forefinger and cast it into the market square. It disintegrated in midair. "Have I ever been one to succumb to greed?"

"Greed takes many forms. It's not all about gold, you know? The annals of time are rich with those whose greed for knowledge undid them in the end. And greed for power. And respect. And *pride*."

There's a trick about broaching a dicey subject with someone who holds the power to have you dismembered at the time of their choosing, even if they used to be your friend and they still consider you theirs. You do not present the issue to them by taking it as if it were a wooden board and smacking it upside their head. You dilute it and serve it to them as if it were an abstract piece of art from which they can see the bends and turns you're attempting to take them on. If they decide to join you on the path, fantastic. If not, you drop the subject altogether, or you don't live long in this world.

Fortunately for me, Chachant wanted to tag along.

"It was strange, Astul," he told me. "I'd never felt the kind of hatred I did when my father was assassinated. It — or *something* — drove me to declare Braddock Glannondil responsible. Something drove me to damn near beg for Dercy Daniser's hand in the fight. I look back on it now, and—" His eyes cooled. They looked like dead steel that had been lying on the battlefield for centuries. "It was madness. I would never repeat my actions. The hatred then… it stole something from me. As a consequence, the North has become a laughingstock. All the respect my father garnered? I obliterated it."

I never imagined I'd have something in common with a king. But I knew the thief he spoke of. The one whose nails dig deep into the soft tissues beneath your skull. The one who picks apart your thoughts and infiltrates your mind. Sybil still had him in her grasp. She'd allowed him to think he had control again, but soon she'd reel him right back in.

"Hell," he said, "I expected this wedding to be ignored. Dercy's here, asleep. So is Edmund Tath.

Nearly every lord of the North is here too. I hope to mend my careless gaffes of the past over spiced mulled wine."

"And Braddock Glannondil?" I asked, wondering how much Chachant knew of his whereabouts.

He smiled. "Not here. Neither is my brother, but that..."

"Is hardly a surprise," I said.

"Hardly a surprise," he agreed. "But enough about me. What brought the Shepherd and his lovely commander here? Perhaps news of my father's assassin?"

Vayle forced out an uneasy smile in response to Chachant's compliment.

"Little progress on that front," I said.

"I see." Chachant's demeanor shifted from warm and congenial to icy and inauspicious. He shoved his pale fingers into his knees and heaved himself off the steps. "The wedding comes soon. There is much to do. Forgive me."

"Or perhaps even the king of the North isn't so fond of his weather?" I put in.

"The cold does make leaving my bundles of linens and thick blankets difficult. But I ventured out here to see my father for the first time since his death. Sybil thought it better that I view him after the wedding, in case it would stoke the hatred in my heart once again." He considered this proposition for a long while as the temperamental wind once again spewed forth a cheek-numbing blast of air. "I think she's right."

The boy king of Edenvaile tugged his yearning eyes away from the small mausoleum indicated by the statue of a sword-bearing king. It lay tucked away beyond the outcropping of rock and dirt the keep was built upon, far from the stable and market square. From our viewpoint, you could see only the tip of a masonic sword rising into the air.

Vayle watched Chachant drag himself back into the throne room like a lynx watches its prey meander away into the tall grass. Suspicion weighed down her thin brows.

"Sybil didn't move the wedding up because she was concerned we'd find an assassin," she said. "She was concerned about Chachant discovering his dead father isn't dead. Or discovering that he's here."

I buried my face in my hands. "Let's pray to every god that he *isn't* here."

CHAPTER NINETEEN

The last wedding I had attended was one that involved one hundred skins of wine, a barrel of ale, a rooster and a hen. Rivon had decided Griffon the rooster and Lory the hen had engaged in plenty enough promiscuous acts that it was high time the two exchanged vowels and begin a proper life together. Between the drinking, the duels, and a competition to see who could run the farthest balancing Griffon on their head, it was great fun.

As it turns out, matrimony between a king and his lady is taken a bit more seriously.

Firstly, there's the matter of clothes. While I was quite comfortable and considered myself sufficiently formal with layers of wool concealing my leather armor, Wilhelm informed me that was not appropriate attire for a wedding. I would instead wear, with great reluctance, mind you, a brocade cotehardie with rich mauve and tinges of gold woven throughout.

The servant girl, whose name I learned was Vivie, took me to a room within the keep. She sat me on a chair and meticulously combed the clomps of knots from my hair and then helped me out of my leather armor and into a white silk kirtle. She laid the cotehardie on a table and flattened out the wrinkles before dressing me with the lavish clothing. I felt distinctly uncomfortable during all of this. It seemed unnatural for anyone except the broken and the old to need assistance in clothing themselves.

Decorative golden buttons the size of cherries adorned the front of the cotehardie and the sleeves that stretched slightly beyond my wrists. Vivie pinned the excess fabric back.

To put on the final touches of this outrageous outfit, I stepped into cerulean-blue hose made of fine silk and a pair of burgundy leather boots that rose up to my knees.

When I finally emerged from the keep, carrying my old outfit in my arms, I found Vayle stroking the snout of a blond mare in the stables.

She looked at me and her nostrils flared. She desperately fought back a smile that carried on with unrelenting momentum, plastering a grin on her lips that I thought would eat her entire face. She cupped her stomach, hunched over and laughed hysterically, tears flowing freely from her eyes.

I blinked and waited for her to finish.

"You," she said, bursting into laughter again. She wiped her arm across her snot-covered nose. "You look a jester did you from one end and a rainbow drilled you from the other!"

Again she doubled over with giggles. Even the horse she was petting thought she'd seen the funniest goddamn thing a horse could see, tossing her head up and blowing air through her jowls.

I fingered the flamboyant buttons, moving them in circles as Vayle held her hands out as if she was pleading for the gods to not let her die of laughter.

"Do you need to me to find the chap who did this to you?" she asked. "The jester? I'll tell him to go easier on you next time so you don't have colors bursting from your arsehole."

I yanked my ebon blade from its scabbard. It hissed as it seared up the leather casing. "I may look the part of nobility, but I still am quite proficient at putting pointy things into fleshy stomachs."

Vayle wiped her nose again. "Are you threatening your commander?"

"Making myself feel better," I said, placing the blade back in its sheath. "Maybe you should be the one standing on the balcony and talking to these fucks instead of me."

We'd decided — or Vayle had decided — it would be best for only one of us to be present for the wedding. The other would play the part of a watchman. Or, in my commander's case, watchwoman. Vayle would stage herself between the crenellations of the wall and provide vigilance in case something unexpected were to befall the ceremony. And with Vileoux Verdan alive and well, my expectations hinged on the unexpected.

I hid my leather armor in the excess roughage of the stables. I didn't trust anyone here enough to keep it secure.

A short time before noon, Wilhelm led me to the keep. I'd faintly recognized most of the passages within the keep from my previous visits to Edenvaile. But there was one that looked new. The stone was freshly polished, the banners freshly ironed and stitched.

It was a dimly lit hallway that led to a door. Standing in front of this door were at least thirty colorful bastards just like me. Interestingly enough, none of them, except the guards interspersed throughout, bore swords.

We remained in the hallway for a very long time, which probably wasn't actually a very long time, but spend more than a few seconds with these jolly noble bastards and you feel your life slipping away five years at a time.

The brother of Edmund Tath was there, and he explained in excruciating detail about how his son — you know his son, of course, Quinn the Third — had begun archery late last fall. He could already hit the center of a target from fifteen feet out.

How utterly amazing! He obviously had a precocious boy on his hands. How many other princes trained by a lord's master-at-arms in archery could possibly hit the center of a target from fifteen feet out when the weather is calm and there are no bowmen pointing back at you and no predators chasing you to grind you up as their third meal for the day?

And then I was privy to some lord of the North's proclamation that his hunt for this weekend had been cut short because of this wedding and that if the wine wasn't to his liking, he would hunt outside the Edenvaile walls because Chachant wouldn't do a damn thing about it.

Nice to see Chachant have his bannermen so solidly behind him. That could bode well for me, though, if I could still go through with the plan to supplant the northern king with someone who could rally the men to my cause in exchange for his ass on the throne. Someone like… Patrick Verdan, who I very much hoped to see after this wedding.

I wondered how the Rots were doing on that front in the Golden Coast and Hoarvous.

Finally, the door opened and we filed out onto the balcony.

The veranda seemed considerably larger in person than it did from the ground, and far more regal. The floor was made of polished marble set with precious gems: rubies, emeralds, sapphires, topazes, amethysts and opals that harmonized with the marble in an admittedly alluring glint.

Having a look around, I began wondering how much the bank of Edenvaile had spent on this wedding. The banisters were indeed made from fine gold as I'd suspected from below. The silver balusters were intricately cut into varying shapes and sizes of swords and shields; every third sword was interrupted by a shield, to signify that you were indeed in the presence of the Verdans, in case the biting cold failed to remind you.

There were an array of tables covered with rich black cloths trimmed with gold, the center of each affixed with the Verdan trio of swords.

We were not permitted to sit, however. Not yet. Commander Wilhelm — or Wedding Planner Wilhelm — explained we would stand until the ceremony was complete.

I was positioned by the door, presumably to stick any assassin who wanted to try his hand at putting his name at the forefront of history. Next to me was an acquaintance who had apparently seen the monstrosity that was my attire and decided to outdo me.

He was a tiny man, with short stubby legs and even stubbier arms. The color of rich Tyrian purple dominated most of his regalia, including his cotehardie and a silk-trimmed hat. His tights were dyed indigo and his boots woad, two dyes which were acceptable. Purple, though? Ah, I suppose he could be forgiven. The mollusks which produce the dyes are plentiful where he is from, and his coat of arms is, after all, a purple shark thrashing about in an angry sea.

He was Dercy Daniser, Lord of the Daniser family, King of Watchmen's Bay, and Admiral of the Ships. Their family used to have a saying that went something like this: "He who controls the oceans commands the world."

They later discovered it is the man who is smart enough to discern an ambush from your closest ally who commands the world — something Enton Daniser failed to do. It's quite difficult for your ships to assist when the enemy is marching across your lands, unless your ships develop feet.

Dercy had a grizzled gray beard that looked like twigs and leaves had often nestled inside. His hat covered up the worst kept secret in Mizridahl. Some say he's been bald since his mother pushed him out.

He spoke deliberately and slowly, a master of stories and a commander of everyone's attention. "Shepherd," he said, his thick accent bellowing out the *p*. "Of all the men I thought I would find myself standing before at this matrimony, you were not among them."

"I am like mold," I said. "I appear in places you least expect, and desire." I smiled. The cold sunk into my teeth.

Dercy silenced his grin with a thoughtful forefinger across his lips. "Have you managed to take care of the savant who I requested eviscerated?"

"As I previously informed you, I do not eviscerate bodies. I simply ensure they can no longer breathe. And yes, he has been dealt with. He was not cooperative with my poison, I'll have you know. He almost got me caught."

"If you are pushing for a greater payment—"

"No, no," I said, quelling his worries. "Not this time." It was useless to negotiate payments when you've already been paid. That's the downside of demanding money upfront as an assassin. The upside is if the person who made the request kicks the bucket before you get around to putting their target down, you made off like a bandit. Admittedly, that happened about once every hundred times. But it happened.

"I'd heard a whisper," I said, keeping my voice low, "involving Chachant, your bannermen and a war. Although from what I've been told, you were not eager to march."

"Only a whisper?" he asked, side-eyeing me with suspicion. "Chachant made no effort to keep it secret when he visited me weeks ago. He marched with full bravado through my gates and loudly proclaimed Braddock Glannondil had killed his father and that the North would like my hand in capturing a king slayer."

What an idiot the boy king had made himself out to be. Inexperience at its finest. Only the youth think you can string together alliances by dropping your worries off at a friend's doorstep. Empathy only goes so far.

Chachant failed to understand that the way in which you forge alliances is by giving and taking, offering and receiving under the guise of friendliness.

Dercy, however, understood that quite well.

"I have little faith he can steer this kingdom well," Dercy confided. "But I am here today on account of tradition." He paused and smirked. "And to lend my wisdom to the boy."

I watched as someone important fidgeted in a hunter-green cotehardie. She did not tolerate the cold well.

"And what kind of wisdom might that be?" I asked.

"The finer points of the crown. Rallying your people, stamping out resistances... promising your firstborn son to Dercy's daughter."

I chuckled. "The finer points of helping the Daniser crown, I see. Tell me, since we're being so open with one another, would you have called your bannermen to war if Chachant had brought you irrevocable proof that Braddock was in the business of cutting down kings?"

"War can escalate," he said, massaging his dingy beard. "It can spiral out of control. I prefer to acquire my needs through a promise here and a debt there, not through force. But, if an ally needed help, things could be arranged. If, for instance, Braddock came knocking down his walls, then… perhaps."

Dercy had just proved to me why, despite his amicable disposition, I'd made the right decision for my Rots to usurp him. He had a massive army, on par with the Verdans' and dwarfed only by the Glannondils'. But the man would never participate in war until the threat was pounding on his gate, and that's simply too late to act when you're fighting conjurers. He would try to barter with them, which is all well and good, except when you're dealing with those who can claw their way into your mind.

The small villages surrounding Edenvaile had emptied out and poured into the belly of the kingdom. Thousands of peasants gathered, dressed in the finest clothes they could afford, which were usually nothing more than old cotton woven together and dyed haphazardly with colors they thought resembled those worn by the rich and powerful: deep reds and purples and blues and golds, utterly dull and sheenless. It looked like a sea of colored urchins had been whipped about in the market square and the stables and the forge and the inner ward and the outer ward.

After mostly everyone had settled into place, their bodies quivering as the cold ate through their thin fabrics, a symphony of trumpets and drums and stringed instruments erupted from… everywhere. I couldn't identify where the musicians were standing, but their melodies seemed to envelop the kingdom of Edenvaile like the gray snow clouds hovering low above the walls.

The ostentatious showing from every face in the crowd, from every note of the instruments and from the pitch of every voice of nobility on the balcony was enough to make me vomit in my mouth. And even if the vomit would have surged into my nose and out of my nostrils and dripped down my chin, that, I thought, would have been preferable to spending one more minute at this bombastic ceremony.

Fortunately, just as I'd had enough, progress was being made. The door I stood beside swung open. All instruments except the trumpets were silenced.

Dressed in a cotehardie black as onyx with gold trim and golden buttons and a matching cloak pinned to his ironed collar, Chachant strode out. He walked evenly and with purpose to the dais at the end of the balcony, where two pronged candleholders stood at either end. He stepped onto the dais, turned around and drew in a deep breath, expanding his already-broad shoulders and barrel chest.

His sleeves were rolled up slightly above his wrists, the underside of the brocade fabric dyed gold.

The boy thought he was hot shit, the biggest and most important bastard in Mizridahl at that very moment. Little did he know that most of his "important" guests were only here either to laugh at him silently or to secure favors his naivety would be all too eager to dole out.

A nagging stillness thickened the air as Chachant put his hands in front of his waist and clasped his wrist.

The door beside me opened again.

The trumpets blared.

The sea of people below churned with either real or faux excitement. Their chattering voices rose in pitch. The trumpeters, not to be outdone by a bunch of squealing peasants, bellowed loudly into their instruments as a pointed-toed boot appeared at the edge of the doorway.

The trumpets opened up into a warm, rapid melody, joined by the heavy percussions of drums.

Edmund Tath and his daughter, Sybil Tath, strode onto the balcony, her right arm joined to his left. Their strides were slow and stiff, a pace that was intended to draw as much attention to the bride as possible.

As much hatred as I had for the soon-to-be queen of Edenvaile, it would remiss of me to pretend she didn't deserve every eye that was affixed to her like clouds to the sky. Her beauty was unparalleled.

A cerulean-blue dress made of fine silk clung immaculately to every curve of her body, the hem flowing behind her like a gentle cresting wave.

Forest-green lace dotted her shoulders, with sharp gold woven beneath. An identically colored sash coiled around her waist. Diamond-colored threads were embroidered lightly beneath the surface of the dress, glittering like crushed ice in the sun. A flowered crown of cream and olive petals rested lightly upon her wavy black hair.

I'd always wondered where Sybil had gotten her beauty, a question that was at the forefront of my mind as Edmund Tath walked her across the balcony. The king of Eaglesclaw was about as pleasant to look at as my late Uncle Fredrick, a man who'd attempted to head-butt a fire on a drunken dare — much of my family was largely thought to be the product of inbreeding.

He had thin strands of salty hair that lay greasily upon his round, shiny head. His nose was much too small for his puffy face, and his cheeks were perpetually flushed. If the man had had the dignity to once in a while take in a hunt, or at least haul his ass off his throne, he likely wouldn't have had a body that resembled something between dough and chunky milk.

Thankfully, Edmund trailed off among the lords and ladies of the balcony, taking a seat next to Mydia as Sybil stepped onto the dais beside Chachant.

Savant Lucas stood before them in a loose-fitting white robe. His ancient hands trembled.

"Citizens of Edenvaile," the savant boomed in a craggy voice, "lords and ladies of the court, beloved guests from the illustrious kingdoms of Eaglesclaw and Watchmen's Bay, and loyal servants of the North, we are here today to celebrate a bond forged in love

and sealed in the unbreakable shackles of the
Pantheon of Gods."

The savant cleared his throat in attempt to quell
the climbing raspiness in his voice.

He unfolded his hand toward Chachant. "This
man, Chachant Verdan, son of Vileoux Verdan, Lord
of the Verdan Family, King of Edenvaile and
Immovable Mountain of the North, means to join
with this woman, Lady Sybil Tath, daughter of Lord
Edmund Tath of Eaglesclaw, in marriage. If any
present here today see foulness in either of their
hearts or betrayal in their eyes, speak now or face the
wrath of the Pantheon when you die."

There was enough foulness in Sybil's heart and
betrayal in her eyes that I was fairly certain it leaked
from her pores when she sweated. There was just one
tiny problem with standing up and shouting, "She's a
foul beast who needs to be struck down!" If you
didn't provide a small thing called evidence to support
your claim, you would suddenly find yourself without
a head. And that's not good if you intend to continue
on with living.

Apparently, likeminded nonsuicidal people
surrounded me, because no one said a word.

The savant continued with his scripted speech.
"Sir Wilhelm, please bring me the Sword of
Righteousness."

Wilhelm emerged from the line of lords and
ladies, his fingers wrapped around a leather-bound

hilt from which a lengthy broad steel blade arose, pointing toward the silt sky.

Savant Lucas took the sword in his wrinkly hands and held it high above his head.

"Lord Chachant Verdan, kneel and bow your head."

Chachant did as he was asked.

The sword in the savant's hands swayed like a thin tree that had grown tall but hadn't yet discovered how to branch out.

Savant Lucas spoke. "If you, Chachant Verdan, intend to take your betrothed as your companion for life, as a lover and a friend, as a partner to whom you are bound monogamously, and as a wife whom you will not taint with sin or wickedness, then you will stand tall before the Sword of Righteousness and you will grace it with the same dignity and respect as you would the Pantheon who demanded it be forged in their name, and you will uphold your promises. If you cannot uphold this matrimonial pledge, then remain kneeling and allow the Sword of Righteousness to grant you one last act of mercy, for the Pantheon will surely not."

While these empty words were booming in my ears — in all my years, I'd heard of no one stupid enough to admit doubt crept into their heart as they knelt before a sword intended to lop off their head if they did so — I made faces at Vayle, parroting what I assumed the savant looked like in his righteous glory.

Chachant predictably rose to his feet, and the formality continued in painful fashion. He straightened his shoulders, looked the sword hard in its figurative eyes and announced, "I will uphold my matrimonial promises."

The savant turned to Sybil and repeated the formalities with her. She stood at the end, looked the sword hard in its figurative eyes and announced, "I will uphold my matrimonial promises."

I half expected an angry fist from some god to pierce the sky and crack her right across the jaw for such a brazen lie. But only snow drifted down from the thick clouds, reaffirming my belief that if the Pantheon of northern gods did exist, they didn't give two shits for what happened below them. They were probably drinking barrels of cider and commenting happily on the swarm of diseases and rashes and infections each had thought up. Seemed like something a bunch of gods responsible for this reprehensible weather would do.

The savant instructed Chachant and Sybil to stand tightly against one another, shoulder to shoulder.

He carefully lowered the Sword of Righteousness and placed the flat side of the blade equally on their shoulders. "The Pantheon has declared these two as one. I present to you Chachant Verdan, Lord of the Verdan Family, King of Edenvaile and the Immovable Mountain of the North, and Sybil Verdan, Lady of the Verdan Family and Queen of Edenvaile. I now command the two of you to commence this celebration with a kiss."

Chachant and Sybil turned, joyous smiles picking at the corners of their mouths. He picked Sybil up in his arms, cupped his hands beneath her butt and kissed her for all of Edenvaile to see. Then he sat her down and winked at her, his mouth agape with a wry grin.

Edmund quickly handed her a bouquet of colorful wildflowers likely picked from the lavish fields of the West. She held the bouquet over the balcony and tossed it to the people below, who would fight over its petals for good luck and good health.

Sybil smoothed the wrinkles of her dress from where Chachant's hands had soiled it. She grabbed her newly wedded husband's hand as he attempted to leave the dais. She whispered in his ear and then waited for the cheers and clapping from the farmers and peasants below to quiet.

I looked for Vayle, who was crouched behind a crenellation. She'd seen the same thing I had and gave me a nod.

"Women, men and children of Edenvaile," Sybil announced. She turned to the nobles. "And the lords and ladies who were so kind as to travel from, in some cases, great distances to be here today. I have an announcement to make."

I hoped the announcement would be something along the lines of her finally realizing her dream to become queen and now that she'd accomplished what she wanted to in life, she would be pursuing other ventures, such as possibly discovering what it felt like to stab herself in the throat with a sword.

I had a feeling my hopes would be crushed.

And they were.

"It has been little more than two months since my husband, since the people of Edenvaile, since the world over has grieved the loss of a man whose greatness was so tremendous, Mizridahl has felt heavier and darker in his absence. I speak, of course, of Vileoux Verdan, the king of the North who was assassinated on a cold winter night."

She paused and expertly allowed the emotions to swell over the crowd like a thick fog. Half the art of speech is not stumbling over your words like a tongue-tied buffoon. The other half is presenting your palm to the audience and persuading them to eat from your hand. And there is no greater persuasion than the power of raw emotion.

"Or so we were led to believe," Sybil continued. She squeezed Chachant's hand and allayed the growing concern on his face with a warm smile. "But I had heard whispers a foul trick was in play. I had heard whispers that the poison that seeped into Vileoux's veins could only render him unconscious." She paused again, leaned her bosom over the banister and, with a heaping dose of exaggerated effect, said, "I had heard he was still *alive*."

Speaking of whispers... they rippled across the crowd now.

"Is he?" someone dared ask from below.

Sybil raked her teeth across her bottom lip. She stood aside and opened her hand toward the doorway. "See for yourself."

The door opened and a chill unlike any I'd ever experienced burrowed into my flesh and seemed to gnaw at my bones. My teeth chattered.

I saw the shadow before I saw the man. My teeth stopped chattering and my body stopped feeling. No cold, no fear. Just the unrelenting rush of excitement — the twisted kind — that you can feel surge into your throat and pound into your chest.

My hand instinctively went to the hilt of my ebon blade as Vileoux Verdan walked onto the balcony.

His acorn face was a tinge darker than I remembered it in Lith, like a man who had been forced to stay awake for centuries. But his white beard was as flawless as ever, his blue eyes as cold as the kingdom he had ruled for fifty years, and the crown upon his head as gold as a noonday sun.

The whispers rippling across the crowd were no longer whispers, and they no longer rippled. There were shouts and shrieks and cries of disbelief, and they rumbled and thundered and boomed.

"Gods below and above," Dercy said to me as Vileoux made his way onto the dais.

"Mind calling up some of your gods from the sea as well?" I asked.

With his quaking hand covering his mouth, Chachant gingerly touched his father's arms, inspecting them for perhaps worms, maggots and festered flesh — things a dead man would typically be slugging around.

"Father?" he said, bewildered.

Vileoux gripped his shoulder. "My son. You've become a man in my stead." He swiveled around youthfully and stepped up to the ornate banister. "Your king has returned," he shouted.

The people wept and cheered with affection. They should have run far, far away and prayed heavily to the Pantheon.

Sybil addressed the assembly, dividing her attention between the nobility behind her and the vast numbers of peasants below who ate up her words like seagulls suck down garbage.

"The whispers came from none other than an assassin present here today."

Oh. *Shit.*

She pointed to me with her sharp chin. "Astul, Shepherd of the Black Rot, informed me that your great king may have been held in a dungeon." She paused. "A dungeon operated by Dercy Daniser. And that is where I found him." She turned to Chachant. "*That* is why I stayed behind in Watchmen's Bay."

Chachant's face resembled the asperity of a chiseled rock as he looked at me. Fury reddened his cheeks. "You told me you knew *nothing* about my father's death!" His anger flung spittle across the balcony.

"I think it was a trap," Sybil said. "He hoped I would fall prey to whatever foul plan he and Dercy concocted."

Chachant shoved his finger angrily toward me. "Seize them both!"

"I don't think your daughter will be wedding their son," I told Dercy. I backed away and withdrew my sword. "Good luck."

The balcony shuddered as plated armor rose from the ranks of the nobles and stampeded toward me and Dercy.

Desperate for an exit, I opened the door only to see the pronged candles set upon the wall dragging unfriendly shadows, pursued by the sound of clanking armor, ever closer. I slammed the door, yanked a chair sitting next to Dercy and propped it up against the bronze handle.

It wouldn't hold long, but hopefully long enough for me to figure a way out with my guts still inside my belly.

Three city guardsmen slammed into Dercy. The Lord of Watchmen's Bay tumbled to the floor, his face thudding off the snowy marble. His eyes were open, but they looked like they were staring into oblivion.

There were three more guards on the balcony. They approached me with care, each of them advancing under the protection of a gleaming steel shield. Unlike Dercy, I had something in my hand that could inflict grievous harm.

And I knew how to use it.

I could probably take all three of the guards. The small quarters gave me the advantage; they'd have to file in like a cone rather than surround me. Plus, ebon has been known to cut through steel given enough whacks. But the door beside me that trembled under the pounding fists of more city guardsmen presented another problem. Famed as I was for putting sharp tips into spongy skin, I was no conqueror of an entire city guard.

But I really didn't want to pay a visit to the Edenvaile dungeon again.

What to do, what to do. I could jump off the balcony, but that would hurt. I could take Chachant or Sybil or Vileoux by the neck and escort them out of the keep under the pretense I would slice their jugular should their guardsmen attempt anything funny. But I probably couldn't reach them.

"Get down!" someone shouted, interrupting my devious planning.

An arrow tipped with fire whizzed through the air and struck the Verdan banner hanging upon the wall of the balcony. The flames raced down the banner, engulfing the fabric in a hungry inferno that contrasted quite nicely with the black background. Had my life not been threatened at that very moment, it would have been a nice time to pour a skin of wine and scrutinize the artwork flames can bring about.

Instead, I looked to Vayle, who dipped another arrow into what I presumed was oil. She then touched the tip to a torch between a crenellation, pulled the fletching back and let it fly. It crashed into the food and booze. Wine spilled onto the marble floor and quickly turned into a tiny lake of seething flames.

Wilhelm and his city guardsmen peeled back and shielded Chachant, Sybil, Vileoux and Mydia with their bodies. They hurried them along, keeping their heads below the banister.

The lords and ladies of various courts flocked to the door in panic. One of them in an olive cotehardie heaved the chair over the balcony and pushed his way inside the hallway just as a herd of guards pushed out.

"Seize him!" Chachant cried. "Seize him!"

A barbed arrow screamed past my face. It tinked off the mail chest of a guardsman. He grunted like a bear who'd just been poked with a hot iron. In a moment of foolish rashness, he reached for my arm. I pulled away, making him overextend. The plate bracer that protected his forearm and wrist slid up to his elbow, revealing a gap of flesh between his chain glove and his wrist bone.

My ebon blade sung as it slashed downward, between the fat flakes of snow. It flashed a midnight-blue wink at the guardsman just as the edge sunk into the first layer of skin and chewed through the remaining ones with precision and ease. It gnawed into his bone, stopping partway through. I knelt and ripped it like a saw across the remaining portion, and the guardsman stumbled backward with blood fountaining out of his arm.

A gloved hand clangored onto the marble floor.

Apparently a guardsman's curdling scream is like a battle cry for his fellow soldiers. They all wanted a piece of me, but I much needed my pieces if I wanted to continue living. So I sheathed my sword, jumped over the banister and lowered myself down so that I was hanging from a sword-sculpted baluster.

Below me lay a thick blanket of snow.

Sharpened steel glimmered at me from between the balusters. The hands that wielded the swords pushed closer.

Time to go.

I withdrew my ebon blade and let it fall to the ground. Then I released my hands from the baluster, spread my legs and tucked my hands behind my head for protection.

And I flew, in much the same manner as a goose in the throes of a heart attack.

Hopefully the snow was as forgiving as it looked.

CHAPTER TWENTY

There exists a type of snow so fluffy you could stuff it in a pillow and mistake it for the feathers of a duck.

This was not that kind of snow. This was the kind of snow that's compact and stiff. This was the kind of snow that splinters into icy fragments when a two-hundred-pound man falls on it from twenty feet up. This was the kind of snow that cracks like a sheet of frozen water. This was the kind of snow that hurt like hell.

The fall had punched the breath from my lungs, numbed half my arm and reopened the gashes Tylik had carved into my back. Much as I wanted to lie there and groan in self-pity, time was not a commodity I had.

I shook the pins and needles from my arm and got to my knees, coughing as the bitter air inflated my chest.

Pandemonium held Edenvaile in its clutches. Men and women and children scurried like a school of minnows in the shadow of a whale. Parents lifted their small children into their arms and yanked along the older ones, fleeing for the gates. Panic marked their faces, and dread scarred their shrill cries.

I crawled on my knees and swung my hands in front of me until the familiar soft leather of my sword was once again in my grasp. I picked it and myself up, stuffed it in my scabbard and tore off through the market district. There were guards down here, but none of them likely knew of the precise events that had happened on the balcony. They were hopelessly trying to organize the mass hysteria that unfolded before them. But it wouldn't be long before the soldiers who witnessed my dismembering of one of their brethren would make their way out of the keep and begin what I imagined would be a very thorough search and rescue. Or perhaps more accurately, a search and beat-the-shit-out-of-Astul.

I reached the stables and spun around, alert. No one had trailed me. One of the benefits of wedding days is that, so long as you are neither the bride nor the groom, you can typically blend in, which is a fantastic advantage if you intend to commit atrocities on that day. Or if you're unfairly blamed for committing atrocities.

Still, tight pants, an undersized kirtle and an oversized cotehardie are not beneficial for battle. My movement was too restricted. On my knees, I combed through the stockpiles of roughage for where I'd left my leather armor. A horse with a pink nose sniffed my arse while I did so.

"Would you mind?" I asked.

She blew air out her nose and continued sniffing.

"Yes, as you can see, I'm not one of yours. Apologies. Here. Eat some of this." I offered her a handful of roughage, which she investigated with her big brown eyes. She took it gingerly and left me alone to locate my armor.

I plucked my jerkin from deep within the roughage, along with an undershirt, breeches, socks and finally my boots and gloves.

"This is going to be brutal, old girl," I told the horse. She snorted angrily, and I gave a quick look at her anatomy. "Oh, sorry. Old boy. Well, here we go."

I held my breath, and I stripped stark naked, save my skivvies. Cold does not begin to describe what I felt. My nipples were hard enough to stab through flesh, my toes painful enough that a passerby could have cut them off and I'd probably thank him, and quite frankly, what that bitter air did to certain tools of masculinity, I may as well have not been wearing underpants at all.

Just as I was pulling up my breeches past my knees, a smooth, warm voice thawed my mind.

"Nice ass," Vayle said.

"Thanks for saving it," I replied. I jumped in an attempt to get a better pull on the breeches so they'd fit past my hips.

"This kingdom is crawling with city guardsmen," she said. "We need to leave."

"Can't leave just yet." I tied my breeches securely around my waist, then grabbed my undershirt and put it on. The stinging burns of gelid air were finally beginning to relent.

"Oh, I understand," Vayle said. "You want to experience life in the Edenvaile dungeon again, don't you? I very much do not, so if you don't mind, you can do so yourself."

"They have Dercy," I told her.

She raked her chocolate hair mottled with snowflakes out of her eyes. "That's Dercy's problem."

"It's going to quickly become our problem when Sybil takes his mind and uses it to call upon his bannermen for her war effort. That's my best guess as to why she wants Dercy."

"Let her have him. We don't need him. The Rots are going to usurp him anyway."

My commander had a special quality about her. She was the most optimistic person I'd ever met. Victory was always a possibility in her mind. Her pessimism when dissecting my strategies might have been unmatched, but her optimism for carrying them out was equally unsurpassed.

But sometimes optimism blinds you. It didn't often blind Vayle, but clearly it had cleverly stretched itself over her eyes this time.

"Vayle... that plan... it's spitting on a fire to put out the flames. It's digging a hole in the desert in hopes you'll find a pristine pool of water underneath. You have to understand...it's a strategy that has very little hope of succeeding. Our hope now rests with freeing Dercy Daniser. There are not many things that would bring the man to war... but I think this is one of them."

Vayle stared at me like a woman whose vision had retreated away from reality and was stuck in an endless loop inside her mind.

Finally, in a tattered voice, she said, "We should hide here." She cleared her wet throat and added, "In the roughage. There's enough to cover us. They won't look here, I don't think. Stay for a few hours, yes? Wait until the guards scatter a bit?"

Her breath rasped from her gaped mouth, and she sniffled. Was it something I said? She'd seemed fine moments ago. Hmm. I wondered. Her sudden change in temperament reminded me of a pane of glass I had once touched. It appeared pristine, structurally perfect. But the subtle graze of my finger shattered it into thousands of minuscule fragments. I learned that happens when a tiny, seemingly insignificant crack lurks beneath the surface. It only takes one meager prod to fracture the whole pane.

I'd seen Vayle like this only once before, after she revealed why she joined my side, those fifteen years ago. But I had no time to console her this time. Not now. There were angry men shouting and swords clanking together.

We were being hunted.

Vayle and I shuffled into an empty stall where all the excess roughage was stored. I covered her first and then myself. Her knee trembled against mine. Slowly at first, but as time wore on, it battered against my leg like shutters against a window.

A dank and musty air entrapped us within the roughage. It was wet to breathe in and lay thick in your lungs. Neither of us dared cough — there were too many steel boots stamping across the stables and patrolling the parapet behind us. After a while, the guardsmen complained we were likely out of the kingdom by now, halfway to the Hole.

The cavalcade of soldiers passing through grew more distant and predictable. I felt at ease enough to talk for the first time in several hours.

"Are you awake?" I asked Vayle.

She sniffled. "Of course I am."

"Not many things worry me on a personal level," I said. "But seeing my commander lose her composure will do it."

"You don't need to worry about me." She sounded like she was smiling out of embarrassment as she spoke.

"I've heard you're an excellent liar when it benefits your cause."

"Aren't all the Rots?"

I grinned. "It's one of the qualities I look for. But no one lies to me, least of all the greatest friend I have. So tell me what happened. What unhinged you?"

A long stillness was interrupted by a rustling in the roughage next to me. "I don't like to think," Vayle said. "My thoughts unravel and lead to places that are not kind. Places that make me feel things I do not want to feel. Fear and loathing. Restlessness. Panic. All of these emotions… I feel them in my chest. I feel them crushing my ribs, squashing my heart into my throat. I can't escape them — I could never escape them — unless I have a skin of wine in my hand. The sips, they chase away those dreadful monsters. They tidy up my thoughts, make the feelings go away. Far, far away, where they don't bother me anymore."

She paused for a while, and then added, "I'm all out of wine."

"I can find you wine," I said. "This kingdom overflows with barrels of the stuff. I imagine it's the only way they can keep their people from fleeing to warmer pastures."

"The conjurers," Vayle said, ignoring my offer, "I hate them. My very purpose for not killing myself after escaping slavery and servitude was to dole out justice. I wanted to bring an end to as many of those who deserved it as possible. The conjurers are the epitome of injustice. They come to a land that doesn't belong to them and attempt to reap its riches while exterminating its people. If they win this war, Astul…"

"They won't win," I said. "Now let's go find some wine and force Dercy Daniser into our debt."

The law of stealth says that your chance of succeeding is inversely proportional to the number of steps you take and to the number of eyes you must slip past. Only the Black Rot knew of the law's existence, mostly because I was the one who penned it.

If the law was true, the chances of Vayle and me succeeding in busting Dercy free were approximately — not quite, mind you — somewhere around… zero percent.

First was the not-so-small matter of getting into the keep. Vayle and I had crept out of the roughage at nightfall and discovered Edenvaile had more guardsmen than either of us remembered.

They posted up in pairs along the cobblestone streets of the market square, with no more than twenty feet separating each group. From what we could see of the keep — which was very little — it was much the same. More torches than usual illuminated the walkways, so drifting into the darkness as two shadows wasn't in the plans.

The only refuge from the armored presence was where Vayle and I were currently trapped: the stables. It made sense. The only way out of the stables was toward the gate or the market square, both heavily guarded and patrolled.

"This is problematic," I said.

Vayle's teeth chattered in sync with her shivering hands. Withdrawal was taking its toll.

"We need a distraction," she said.

"Shall I strip and streak through the market square while singing love poems? That would serve well as a distraction."

Vayle sported a grin that quickly disappeared. "Fire would be a more promising one." She licked her lips: a tic of hers when she was deep in thought. She shuffled through the snow, toward a horse. "Help me untie them."

I lifted my chin slowly as her plan became clear. Smart woman, that one.

I slid into a tie stall, where the horse who sniffed my arse was stationed. After undoing a rope with three knots in it that secured him to the feeder, I patted his long face. "No hard feelings on the mix-up earlier, yeah? You know how it is."

The steed blinked.

Vayle and I worked with haste to free the remaining horses from their rope. Thankfully, all of them remained in the stalls, none the wiser. One even lay down.

I met Vayle in an empty square stall piled high with excess roughage. She was kneeling, two daggers in hand. Affixed to the foundation of their leather grips was a charcoal-gray distention. This distention was present on the daggers of every Black Rot. It was a tool of survival: flint.

She held one dagger firmly on the roughage and struck the flint with the other. Flecked sparks licked the air and fizzled out. She struck the flint again and again, faster and faster. Sparks spat from the blade and settled onto the roughage, smothered into nothingness by the cold and snow. But it only takes that one special spark to conflagrate that one special piece of tinder, and then… well, you've got yourself a pretty little campfire.

With a few more strikes of the flint, a long stem of roughage sizzled and smoked. Vayle carefully cleared away the damp coating of snow that lay near it and protected it with her hands as the insignificant flame burbled in the wind. It slowly engorged the entire stem and began trailing along the top layer of the roughage.

Vayle backed away and proudly watched her creation grow into a hot fire that sent white smoke billowing into the black sky.

One of the horses picked her head up. Her ears were high and forward, but all the weight was on her back legs. She snorted a deep vibrating pitch and waddled backward unevenly, her haunches crashing against the stall. She pinned her ears back now. She snorted again and spun around, knocking against the stall. And then she galloped away furiously, tail tucked behind her butt.

The other horses took note of this and the growing fire and thought they too would bail out while they had the chance. There were suddenly fifteen horses galloping freely and wildly inside the Edenvaile walls. There would have been more — potentially a good hundred more, on account of the wedding visitors — but they were likely stowed away in the stables of nearby villages. Can't have the kingdom smelling like horseshit on the cusp of a wedding.

A guardsman hollered from across the market square. "What in the bloody hell are these horses doing?"

"There's another!"

"Three more," a third guardsman put in.

"I'm gonna slice the fuckin' skin off that stable boy's ass. Get these damn beasts wrangled up."

"Sir, there's smoke! By the stables."

"Fuck's sake."

Vayle and I slipped into a narrow alleyway that cut between a curtain of small stone buildings, the front of which faced the market square. It smelled like rotten fruit had been shat upon by bats with rotting guts. I gagged a few times before pulling my undershirt up above my nose and breathing in the sweet smell of sweat. You have to take what you can get in these situations.

There was a heavy clank of steel near the stables.

"Fuck me," the guardsman muttered. Or perhaps he was a captain. Seemed like it, with the way he issued commands.

"I need buckets!" he yelled. "Whole damn thing is going up in flames. Haul your asses!"

The hooves of a frightened horse pounded through the market square.

"Look out!" a guardsman said.

"I think he was aiming for me," another suggested.

They hurried past the alleyway.

We moved deeper into the alley and emerged into the market square. Merchant carts had been turned over, some of them splintered and beyond repair. A tavern door had been caved in and the wooden sign mangled. Probably from the resulting riot of frightened peasants, although the horses madly galloping around likely didn't help matters.

A guardswoman turned the corner near the fountain, where the square intersected with paths that led to the stables on one side and the barracks on the other. A grating voice stopped her.

"What's going on here?" That voice… straight from the mouth of the commander of the city guard, Wilhelm Arch. He probably wasn't a very happy man.

"Sir, the stables are on fire and the horses are running freely. Captain Quill has requested buckets."

"Get out of my way," he snarled.

The commander stormed past his soldier. Vayle and I crouched behind a broken merchant cart, although his tired eyes probably wouldn't have seen so much as a tail of our shadows.

"Quill," Wilhelm barked. "Get your men to the keep."

"This thing will burn to the ground!"

"Then let it burn. Get your men to the keep now and form ranks. Let the servants put the fire out. The Shepherd is still here."

Wilhelm marched back across the front of the square. He stopped a guardsman who bounded through with a bucket in hand. He snatched the bucket from the guard's grasp and sat it on the frozen fountain. "Go find some servants and tell them to put this fire out."

"Which servants, sir?"

"All of them! I don't give a damn if they're sleeping, washing, cooking or serving the fucking king. Get them down here now."

"Yes, sir, of course." The guard obediently loped up the steps toward the keep.

Wilhelm moved swiftly past the fountain. "Gods help you, Shepherd," he muttered lowly, "I *will* hunt you down."

"You know," I whispered to Vayle, "I much prefer when people hide from us. It's not as much fun the other way around."

"Damn," Vayle said, her face scrunched up in frustration. "Guess my plan didn't work."

Like ants coming to the aid of their queen, the city guard of Edenvaile formed ranks along the front of the keep and then around it.

"It got us out of the stables," I said, "and into the square. Which is where *my* plan now comes into effect."

"You have a plan?"

I smiled. "I do now."

I crept deeper into the square, treading carefully along the outcrop of shadows dangling outward from the buildings. Most of the city guard had positioned themselves by the keep, but there were still guardsmen and guardswomen who maintained their roving posts atop the parapet, and an eye in the sky is the most difficult of all to avoid.

Vayle and I made it to the outer ward, not far from the gate. From there we followed the snow-dusted cobblestones toward the forge and onward to the barracks that stood near the northeast part of the kingdom. Someone had apparently woken the stable boy, because he had one horse wrangled and tied to a post by the forge. He was in hot pursuit of the other, which made my foray into the barracks clean and quick.

I might have told Vayle I had a plan, but that wasn't entirely true. I had the fragments of a plan, the bits and pieces that make up the foundation of a plan. I just hadn't quite filled in the details yet. Which was a problem, because as we stepped inside the barracks, the conclusion to my plan was rapidly drawing near.

The building was made mostly of ancient timber dull as dirt, patched up over the years with fresher pine that looked out of place. Several rooms split off from the main hallway, most of which, from a cursory glance, stored armor, cloth, weapons and stale wheat rations.

The floor of wooden planks and the braced walls twisted and turned beneath ceiling joists appearing in dire need of repair. Eventually, the hallway spat us out into an enormous square room where the luminous glow of torches reflected off a marble floor. The walls were covered in stone, and on the back wall hung a large banner with two swords crossing a shield: the coat of arms of the Edenvaile city guard.

A man stood with his back to us, behind a desk littered with papers, candles and an inkwell. He was admiring a knight's helmet hanging upon the wall. It looked like it had come hot off the polishing stone, never having seen battle a day in its life.

"Nice helmet," I said.

He sucked in a silent breath, noticeable only because his shoulders damn near rose up over his ears for a moment. He turned slowly, a solid steel breastplate fastened to his chest. Plate bracers covered his wrists and matching gloves protected his hands. Half of him shined with the luster of gems, the other half dull with the muddiness of leather and old mail.

"Did I catch you while you were changing?" I asked.

"You did," he said, taking a meaningful step toward the table. "I was preparing for a hunt." His lips glowered from behind the denseness of his beard. He reached down and took a long, heavy-looking great sword from the table.

"Seems a weapon you'd want if you were hunting pigs."

He heaved the greatsword into his clutches, holding tight to the cracked leather hilt with both hands. "It is a weapon intended to be used while mounted. A weapon you need swing only once." He dropped it onto the table, where it crashed with a deafening thud. "I suppose it's not needed anymore. My prey has come to me."

He sounded mad. Looked mad, too. Had that empty, voided look about him that a person gets when their mind has fled, leaving behind a cold, dark husk.

"Listen to me, Wilhelm," I said, hoping that my plea with insanity would for once work. "What you heard on that balcony... none of it was true. Why would the Black Rot ally with the Danisers? Since when have you known us to be players in the game? We're hired swords, that's all."

"You've played me for the third time now," Wilhelm said. He took a pair of plate greaves from the table and fastened them around his legs.

"Vileoux is dead, Wilhelm. For all intents, he's dead. His mind is being controlled by the conjurers. He's a puppet. It's all a show. It's a front."

Wilhelm secured pauldrons around his shoulders. "Conjurers? That's your best lie?"

"Think about it," I said. "Truly think about what Sybil accused me and Dercy of. Forget for a moment the passion in your heart, the perceived deception you accuse me of, and instead question the logic of your queen's accusations."

Wilhelm turned and removed the knight's helmet pinned to the wall. "Vileoux will have me put to death for this. I failed him. Twice. My only hope for survival is delivering your head to his bedchambers."

"How long have we known each other?" I asked. "A good thirteen, fourteen years? Almost as long as the Rots have been around."

He put the helmet on. It fit loosely around his thin neck. When he spoke, his words reverberated off the brushed steel. "Fourteen long years of deceit."

Vayle stepped forward. "Commander Wilhelm, I know of a young man who had been part of your city guard many years ago, a young man whose name you will undoubtedly recall better than I. A night in a tavern that had run too long and seen far too much ale drain from the kegs ended with this soldier bedding a barmaid. His wife caught wind, and left for deeper into the North with their two children, back to her family. It drove the man mad, and in this madness, with passion disfiguring his thoughts, he murdered fifteen people and then himself."

"Eulys Torr was a coward," Wilhelm said.

"Only after passion had made him one," Vayle said. "Don't let the madness of passion turn you into something you may greatly regret, Commander. Something you may not return from. Astul tells the truth. The conjurers are coming, and they have Sybil Tath orchestrating their arrival."

"I saw the end of the conjurers," Wilhelm said, taking a large triangular shield made of hardened iron and covered with embossed designs. He produced a sharp short sword, marred with scratches and dents. "They don't exist anymore."

He moved slowly around the table. "This ends now, Shepherd."

Damn. This wasn't how my plan was supposed to conclude, with the death of a, for the most part, good man who I'd known for many years. I was supposed to convince him, to lure him in with the power of persuasion. People think an assassin's greatest strength is his blade, but it's not. Sharpened steel — or ebon — is only fitting for the throat you intend to slice. Often, lots of good men, proud women and innocent children stand between you and that throat. You can't just go along and kill everything in your way. You'll soon find yourself dangling from a rope, and if you evade capture long enough, all the death, the murder, the blood… it'll mess with you. It'll change you.

There was another reason I didn't want to duel Wilhelm. Iron clanking against plate is loud enough, but ebon smacking against the heavy shit sounds like the god of thunder erupting in orgasmic glory. It's a great way to give everyone in a half-mile radius the precise point of your location, which I suppose is wonderful if you're a merchant looking to hawk your wares or a whore eager to make your day's fill. It's less enticing for an assassin attempting to sneak into a heavily guarded keep.

"Give me a fair duel, at the very least," I said. "An honorable one."

Wilhelm laughed. "I know of the sword you swing. Don't take for me an imbecile."

I tossed my blade on the ground. It skittered along the wooden planks and banked off the wall. "Then give me a steel edge that your blacksmith has crafted, and remove all that silly armor and the shield."

Wilhelm lowered his guard suspiciously. "You don't care about honor."

"People always say that. But I do have standards, you know? See, I don't care about the manner in which I kill the arrogant son of some rapacious lord. But a man who I've known for fourteen years — or thirteen, however the hell long — that deserves a modicum of honor if a duel must decide who will continue to piss around on this world."

Wilhelm nodded his iron head at Vayle. "And her?"

"Oh, my!" I said sardonically. "The vicious Commander Vayle, renowned for the countless corpses her blade has strewn across the lands without mercy and certainly without honor." I rolled my eyes. "Do you think you can possibly help yourself, Commander? Or do you think your hunger for blood will overwhelm you and cause you to charge into this duel with your teeth gnashing and tongue hanging out?"

"I will sit here idly," Vayle said. "Nary a clap nor a jeer."

"And if I kill him?" Wilhelm said.

Vayle smirked. "Then you face me."

That didn't seem to worry Wilhelm as much as it should have. My commander was nearly as adept at plunging steel into soft flesh as I was. Some would even say more so, but those people are known for exaggerating things.

Wilhelm went about systematically removing his oversized and overpolished plate armor, stopping after unstringing or unclasping each piece to take a long, hard look at me, as if I might have the audacity to renege on our battle of honor. Smart man.

After dressing himself down to mail and leather, he retreated back to the wall that held various armaments and laid his shield on the table. He picked up a silver greatsword, the hilt shaped in ninety-degree downward curves that thinned to fangs.

He grabbed a matching blade and flung it at me. It fell at my feet, and I picked it up.

The shaft was weighty and much too long. Greatswords are nice when you want reach and impact behind your blows, but I preferred the blinding speed of shorter blades, the swords you can work with in close quarters. Still, I couldn't complain too much. After all, I wouldn't be swinging it.

Er, hopefully.

Wilhelm descended from the raised platform that supported his decorated table. He held his sword out like a chalice at an important dinner with the lords and ladies of the court.

"Think of it as a toast," Wilhelm said.

"Ah, a toast before death? I like it."

I tapped his blade with mine, and we pulled our weapons back. I heaved the sword into a guard position with both hands and shuffled toward the far wall to my left. Wilhelm matched my pace and my strides, a ceaseless focus bending his brows.

It sounded like we were dancing in there, our feet tip-tapping the marble floor as I retreated and he pursued — the eternal dance of predator and prey. The space between us was of cyclical light and darkness. The blackness trounced the flickers of torches, only to be burned into oblivion moments later.

When Wilhelm closed that space — when his mesh coat jangled a bit louder and his sword glimmered a touch sharper — I lunged and feigned an attack, pushing him back. And then I retreated farther along the wall, scraping the rough stone with my backside.

I leaped onto the platform and hunkered down into a defensive position near Wilhelm's table.

"An assassin with strategy," he remarked coolly as I had taken the high ground.

Of course I was an assassin with strategy. You don't live long as a reaper of life unless you have some wit floating about inside your fucked-up head. But the taking of the high ground in this duel was merely coincidence and not part of my strategy.

As Wilhelm contemplated his next move, I allowed myself a cursory glance at his table, and I inched closer to two objects that would seize me victory. One swayed in all directions, lurching and lunging. The other sat lazily inside the rim of what used to be living bone.

I lowered my sword, offering Wilhelm the opening he'd been looking for.

He took it.

His greatsword dipped to the floor as he lunged, back leg fully extended, front foot rising up onto the platform. The blade rose in an arc, sweeping furiously through the air. A burst of air climbed up my leg and broke against my knee.

The serrated steel continued onward. Had I been a fool, I would have put the tip of my blade at my shoulder and the hilt at my hip, guarding the soft flesh I left unprotected.

But upward strikes are so often feints, and so it was with Wilhelm's. His wrists rotated over one another as he moved the sword past my thigh. It was now charging ahead, straight as an arrow toward my gut.

I caught the underside of his blade with the top side of mine, lifting it away from the precious cargo inside my belly. With a powerful thrust, I pushed him back.

He stumbled unevenly as he awkwardly fell from the platform.

Now it was time to bring color to this room.

I dropped the greatsword. Before it hit the floor, I already had the hot wax candle from Wilhelm's desk in one hand. And then, as the sound of steel crashing against marble echoed throughout the room, I had the sheep's horn in my other. Cool wine sloshed against the rim, spilling out between my fingers.

Wilhelm saw what would unfold. Terror stampeded across his face. He charged onto the platform wildly.

I stepped back. Just far enough to avoid his reaching arm, the rushing summit of his silver blade.

It all seemed to happen so slowly, like a ballad of human frailties that erupts from the hauntingly laggard beat of snapping fingers and knuckles tapping against wood.

Imagine:

Snap. Tap. And the candle's raised.

Snap. Tap. And the flames burble.

Snap. Tap. And the fire draws jaggedly around Wilhelm's rugged face.

Snap. Tap. And the horn is hoisted back. *Drip. Drip. Drip.*

Snap. Tap. And my hand flings forward.

Snap. Tap. The melody ends. *Silence.*

Unavoidable, all-consuming silence as the fire intersected the wine and spewed forth a stream of flames into Wilhelm's beard. The orange warmth ate the thick hair like acid eats flesh. The flames spilled onto his neck, dripping off of his chin and nose like droplets of stagnant river water permanently infused by the color of the sun.

A shrill shriek brought me out of whatever stasis I'd been trapped in. Time moved normally. Maybe even too fast.

I grabbed a cloth sitting at Wilhelm's desk, jumped off the platform and tackled the burning man. Wrapping the cloth around his face and his hair, punching it into his throat and cheeks, I suffocated the flames. More importantly, I stuffed the cloth into his mouth, silencing his cries. The vibration of his wails trembled up my arms.

"Accepting an honorable duel with a dishonorable man doesn't make you honorable," I said. "It makes you stupid. Now, then, if you will stop crying, I'll let you up."

Wilhelm continued to moan.

I motioned Vayle over with my head.

335

"Sit on his legs when I flip him," I told her.

I turned Wilhelm over. Vayle sat on his legs, and I pinned his arms to the ground with my feet, keeping my hands free to ensure the homemade gag of burnt cloth didn't slip out of his mouth.

I flicked his singed beard and the hairs scattered like the petals of a dandelion in the wind. "Could have been worse. Your flesh could be melting off. As it is, it's just red. Turning white, maybe — blisters, you think? Probably."

Wilhelm grimaced. He tried hollering at me, but I stabbed the cloth deeper into his mouth.

"Let's set some rules, shall we? No yelling. No kicking. No punching. Be a good boy and it'll get you far, yes?"

Beneath the pain — beneath the hot, grotty blisters that were beginning to bubble on his cheeks and chin and neck and forehead and nose — Wilhelm regarded me with revulsion. Scowling, frowning and all other expressions of hatred were impossible for his disfigured face to form, but I could nevertheless sense it.

"I'm going to remove this cloth from your mouth. If you scream, I will rake my fingers across your face until your burnt skin piles high beneath the beds of my nails. Do you understand?"

Wilhelm said nothing. He expressed nothing, except perpetual pain and imperceptible hatred.

I plucked the cloth from his mouth and laid it on his chest. He was breathing heavily, lightly groaning with each rasp.

"Do you have rope in these barracks?" I asked.

No answer.

I splayed my fingers and lightly touched my nails to his cheeks.

"In the armory," he said hastily.

"Commander Vayle," I said. "Would you mind?"

Vayle got up and hurried out of Wilhelm's quarters and into the hallway, toward the armory we'd passed on the way here.

"Torture?" Wilhelm said, his teeth clenched. His lips were raw and crimson. "Is that when you intend to do to me?"

I chuckled. "Torture you? What would that gain me?"

"Enjoyment," he said.

"I take no enjoyment in this."

Vayle returned with a bundle of rope. We got Wilhelm to his feet and escorted him over to his table, sitting him in his chair. I stripped him of his golden cloak, then looped rope around his chest, his arms and his legs, binding him to the chair. I balled up the blackened cloth, stuffed it in his mouth, and secured about two feet of rope around it, tying it in an unbreakable knot around his head.

"This'll work well," I said, holding up his golden cloak. I looked at Vayle. "Go find yourself a fancy suit of armor from the armory. It's time to play dress up and free Dercy Daniser."

CHAPTER TWENTY-ONE

Deception. Deception. Deception. What a lovely lady she is. An easy one too, if you're using your tongue. I, however, was using my entire body. Or to be more accurate, passing the living sculpture that was Astul off as the old, weathered man the good folks of Edenvaile knew as Commander Wilhelm Arch.

This sort of deception isn't for the goat-brained and the scrambled-eyed. It would take ice in my veins and a steely resolve to even attempt. It also required a knife, a full suit of plate armor, a steel helmet with a straight nose piece and the ability to contort my voice into something more grizzled and raw, all of which — save the voice — were easily procurable within the barracks.

The knife chopped off half my beard that'd run rampant the past few weeks. Vayle helped me trim it down so the peppery spokes matched the length of Wilhelm's prior to his fiery accident.

Then it was on to the suit of armor, which was heavy and cold. The helmet squeezed my ears and amplified all sounds.

Vayle was dressed in a coat of mail and steel greaves she had obtained from the armory, along with a square shield streaked with oil and grease. A skullcap rested atop her head, her chocolate hair flowing out the back and down her shoulders. Looked like the quintessential guardswoman.

I approached Wilhelm, who was tied mercilessly to his chair and table. "Do I walk like a commander?" I asked, standing tall and absolutely straight as I paced. "Do I look like a commander? Do I talk like a commander?"

His eyes fell away, to the floor. Small blisters were stitched across his puffy, rosy face. His cheeks had a sort of shine to them, the kind your finger gets after a close encounter with fire.

"Where's Dercy being held?" I asked. He swallowed. "I know he's not in your lovely dungeon. Didn't see him being escorted into it, and if he was there, your entire city guard wouldn't be posted up by the keep. So where in the keep is he being held?"

He swallowed again, then clenched his jaw.

I shrugged. "All right. Have it your way, Wilhelm."

I stepped onto the raised platform, grabbed his skin of wine and poured a small amount into the sheep's horn. I lifted it indolently over Wilhelm's head and tilted it with a lethargic roll of my wrist. It spilled over the rim, a small stream of liquefied grapes, red as blood. Wilhelm gasped as the wine trickled onto his head, wetting his hair and drenching his face.

"Always a shame," I remarked, setting the horn on the table and reaching for a candle. "Seeing friends take this kind of path, I mean."

I crouched in front of the commander, held the candle up to his eyes and swept my finger leisurely through the flame. He twitched.

"I am a purveyor of information, Wilhelm. I will never rest until I get the information I desire. I will hurt for that information. I will kill for that information." I pushed the flicking flame closer to his face. "I will *burn* for that information."

Sweat dribbled into his eyes. Or was it the wine?

Vayle joined me on the platform. She put a hand on Wilhelm's damp shoulder. "Tell us where is. Pride isn't worth the pain."

Wilhelm's chest swelled. His arms trembled against the rope binding them.

"Fine," I said, sighing. "Trial by fire it is." I shoved the candle to where his face should have been. But he threw himself back against the chair, scooting inches away from a very painful ending.

"Wait," he pleaded. "Please. I don't want to burn." He licked his lips. Heaving, he whispered in a voice drenched in desperation, "I don't want to burn. He's upstairs. In the royal quarters."

I placed the candle back on the table and patted his knee. "Good. I'm going to stuff a rag in your mouth, keep you quiet. If you try to bite me…"

"No… no," he rasped. "Have the decency, Shepherd… have the kindness, I beg you. Cut me. Make me bleed out. If I'm found like this, I… I don't want to be tortured for my failures."

I stepped back and crossed my arms in quiet contemplation. Vayle nudged my elbow and gave me an affirming nod.

Seconds lapsed. But time regrettably did not pass silently. No matter your blade, it's never sharp enough to cut without making a sound.

We walked out of the commander's room without a word spoken between us. Vayle gulped down the skin of wine she'd snatched from Wilhelm's table and tossed it in one of the supply rooms. She seemed better. Good for her.

She stopped me before we reached the door that led back into the city. She grabbed my hand and wiped off dollops of Wilhelm's blood from my fingers.

"You missed a few spots," she said.

"Thanks," I muttered, pulling away to leave. She yanked my arm, rooting me in place.

"You were going to burn him. Why are you upset at giving him a proper ending?"

"You've known me for fifteen years. You really think I was going to burn him? I knew he'd turn away. I could've punched the candle farther if I wanted."

Her eyes narrowed. "I have known you for fifteen years, and I know that this isn't like you."

I put on a fake smile and said, "It's this fuckin' North. No sleep, always cold. Does things to you. I'll be all right."

Vayle remained unconvinced, but said nothing more. She'd prod me later, and maybe I'd tell her the truth then, but not now. No need to alarm her. Plus, I didn't know how to articulate it. All I knew was that seeing my brother die in my arms was not good. Watching my Rots butchered in an arena was worse.

Things were being taken from me. I knew what happened to people when everything they knew, everything they had, slipped from their grasp, leaving them alone and cold. That's how monsters form, how the dead look behind the eyes comes about, how madness takes over. It's how an assassin can go from killing for business to killing for pleasure. That terrified me.

I touched the hilt of my ebon blade as we paraded into the openness of Edenvaile. I sucked in a breath of frozen black air, held it deep in my lungs and let it slowly escape through drawn lips. There's something about the suddenness of the cold slamming into you like an unrelenting tidal wave as you exit the warmth of a building. It gets everything going. Sharpens your senses. Makes your heart thump a tad faster, beat a little harder. Makes you forget things, or at least allows you to stow them away in a deep, secluded compartment for a while. A compartment with a good lock that takes a while for demons to break.

Vayle and I climbed the steps to the keep, my golden commander's cloak — Wilhelm's golden commander's cloak — blowing in the wind. Every soldier straightened himself and herself as I walked past the ranks.

Don't make eye contact, I reminded myself. *Don't look at them. Don't give them the opportunity to question you.*

Of course, nothing I would do, save removing my helmet and showing them my true face, would make them question me. They were taught from a very young age to never question authority. The instructions were clear: tap your foot to the beat, nod your head and follow along. It makes for a mighty army and an enviable society that is highly organized. Question not, learn not, worry not. But there's one great susceptibility, and that's when the authority fails. Sometimes it's corruption that makes it fail, and sometimes, as in this case, it's deception.

Vayle and I moved effortlessly past the guardsmen and guardswomen, beyond the keep doors and to the kitchen attached to the side of the keep. Four guards moved aside, each saluting me with a nod. I returned the gesture as I stepped out of the naked cold and into a kind of cold that was mysteriously deeper and broader than that of the outside.

The stone walls of the kitchen seemed to snag the iciness throughout the day and suffuse it like pollen from blooming amaranths at the end of a southern summer. The door shut behind Vayle and I, and we drifted through the dark kitchen, avoiding the blunt silhouettes of cutting tables and mantels. Some of the embers in the hearths still smoldered, but most were blackened ash.

We moved through familiar rooms. The smell of bloody meat met onions and cinnamon and pepper. My stomach pitched and yawed like wine in a barrel, telling me in no uncertain terms it wanted food. Now. I'd gone without eating for longer than this, but I hated it every time.

A trio of voices whispered softly through the stone walls.

"Dangerous man like that ought to be chained and smoked," a woman said.

"Smoked? You don't know what you're talking about," a man said.

"Oh? And I'm sure you do?"

"My granddad worked in the prison fields of Ollaroy, way up North. Says they'd never smoke any prisoners they got till they beat all the information out of 'em. All that smoke kills you. Most of the time."

The voices grew more distant. "That's what he needs, to be killed. Kidnapping kings and starting wars." Gray stone separated us, but I envisioned the woman shaking her head unabashedly. "If that don't get you death, then nothing will."

"No wars yet," the man said.

"Won't be long," another voice said. "I pray to the Pantheon it will be short."

"Her boy's of age," one of the women said.

"Ah," the man huffed. "They won't need him. North is plenty powerful enough as is. Danisers won't stand a chance, if you ask me."

"I'm sure Lord Vileoux will ask his washer of linens for an opinion!"

The women giggled.

"Only here till the summer, thank you very much," the man said. "Ran out of coin passing through, that's all. When my father gets enough — and that'll be this summer, like I said — we're riding for the beaches. Gonna fish our lives away. I'm not like you. I know things. Got lots of experience."

The voices trailed off, and I continued on through the kitchen.

"What if Sybil is there with him?" Vayle asked.

Hm. I hadn't considered that angle.

"Would you kill her?"

Now, the death of Sybil Tath I had considered. It was a muddy mess, though. If I slid my sword across her throat, would that prompt the conjurers to attack immediately? We weren't ready for such an attack… but neither were they.

Perhaps more importantly: *could* I slide my sword across her throat? This wasn't an existential question set in a moor of morals and values, as the contemplation of ending Wilhelm's life had been. It was quite literal. If Amielle could rive the sky, buckle the earth and command the wind, could Sybil do the same?

"I'd prefer to wait until she left," I said.

Vayle couldn't possibly understand the unnatural and the macabre world that I'd seen conjured by the hand of Amielle, but she nevertheless nodded knowingly, as if she had some faint notion.

We exited the kitchen into a great hall with wide walls and vaulted ceilings. The castle of Edenvaile was mostly a square monstrosity with five paths to every destination. The royal quarters could be reached from a winding staircase that sat just outside of the throne room, and also by way of a less appealing set of stairs that tunneled deep through narrow halls and low-rising ceilings. There were more paths to be sure, but those were the two I knew.

We would be taking the path less traveled, because I had a premonition of my head falling off my shoulders if we tried cutting through the throne room. The fewer guards we encountered, the better, particularly if those guards were officers. Regular guards may not have the balls or tits to question authority, but officers do… because they are authority.

We walked along the great hallway that led into a smaller snaking corridor with forked paths every twenty feet or so. We passed several roving patrols along the way, all of whom tipped their brimmed skullcaps in recognition and continued on.

The flames from wall-mounted candles whished and whooshed as we walked by, their faint golden glow splashing the silk banners draping the hallway.

One of the forked corridors we walked was suddenly pinched off at the tip. At the end lay a doorway wrapped in a still sheet of blackness. I ducked inside, the soles of my plated greaves touching down on uneven steps of rotting wood. A creak here and a dreadful moan there, the ancient risers crying out under our pressure. If you'd put your hand above your head, you'd feel the cold wetness of rough stone beneath spongy mold.

The candles had all dried out since my last visit through this pathway many years ago, when the grand spiral staircase was still under construction. It wouldn't be long before the mold would eat this rising tunnel into rubble.

If you were lucky enough — or put your nose far enough up the king's ass — you got pampered up here in the royal quarters. Got yourself a nice room with windows overlooking… well, snow most of the time. A nice bed with feathers from geese or ducks and enough pillows that your poor nose would never feel stuffy when it was time to lay your head down to sleep. Got unlimited wine and a handmaid at your service who would bathe you, feed you and maybe even fuck you. What was she going to do? Say no to a powerful lord? But the Verdans did not discriminate.

It was all the same with ladies of the court, just put a pair of balls on the handmaid and there you go.

Bunch of worthless fucks. But I wasn't here to cull them, so I walked right on by their rooms and ignored the orgasmic moaning from within.

All of the ladies and lords of the court resided on the right side of the hallway. Or left, depending on which way you approach. Point is, the Verdan family resided on the opposite side. Yes, there was a sort of invisible line that silently proclaimed, *We are better than you.*

Which room would Sybil place Dercy in? Probably not Mydia's. The chambers of the king and queen were a possibility, but one that I didn't want to investigate quite yet. Chachant would likely be brooding in there, or sleeping, possibly along with Sybil. I hoped to find Dercy alone.

She very well could have stowed him away in her old room. Or Chachant's, but that was less likely given Vileoux probably took up residence in his son's quarters for now. Or she could have put him in one of the various rooms that had been empty for seventy years, since back when a litter of Verdans ran amok. That was unlikely as well, though, given none of the royal guard stood watch over the empty rooms.

It all came down to logical deduction. And so I stopped in front of the archway of rock that hugged an imposing door made of cedar. It was Sybil Tath's room. Two guardsmen, as always, were posted there. Their faces where sheathed in brushed steel that wrapped around their necks and sat upon a suit of silver plate. A protective slit grate covered their eyes, which stared ahead without yielding.

"Commander Wilhelm," one of them said, with a slight nod.

Not too raw, not too ragged, I thought. "Step aside, men," I said, thrusting each word out from deep within my chest, parroting Wilhelm's voice the best I could. "I have an audience with the queen."

I saw the whites of both men's eyes as their pupils slanted toward Vayle.

"She may be joining you as the newest royal guard," I said. "If Lord Chachant and Lady Sybil permit."

Even if my voice may have lacked the visceral edge of Wilhelm's, my manners were spot-on.

The guard to the left spoke. "The queen has forbidden entry until the morning."

And in predictable fashion, I thought. The royal guard was part of Wilhelm's city guard, but he held little sway in their lives. Directives issued by the Verdan family trumped Wilhelm's orders.

"How long have you men been here?" I asked.

"Since the morning, sir."

"Impressive."

I turned to Vayle and asked if she thought she had the endurance to stand on her feet for a day straight. While she answered, I took a gander. The remaining rooms were far down the hallway, beyond large swooping walls that interrupted your vision.

Poor planning there by the architects of this city. Of course, they probably didn't envision anyone assassinating a couple royal guards and freeing a king inside their illustrious keep.

I slapped a gloved hand on the steel breast of each guardsman. "Good men. You do your commander proud. Remove your helmets. I wish to see your faces. The Pantheon knows I could use a good reminder of what some of my men have gone on to accomplish."

Without hesitation, without questioning authority, the guardsmen took their helmets off and curled them in their arms.

I shook the hand of the young man in front of me and said, "Good man, indeed." Then I pulled him close, his steel frame crashing against my chestplate, the pimples on his chin bopping up against the softness of my beard.

His nostrils flared at the sound of ebon singing its lovely song as it scraped against the leather innards of its scabbard.

He yanked himself back, but my fingers were coiled around his wrist. I was latched onto him like an iron clasp. The panic of finding himself seized, unable to wrestle his own blade from its sheath — it paled his face to the color of cold milk.

This was all part of the job, the very thing he signed up for: giving his life to the kingdom he loved in a bid to protect her. But when the end comes — and it often comes so early for men like him — the courage, the bravado, every brash emotion shrinks in the shadow of death and the embrace of fear.

His warmth coated my fingers and my wrist and my arm. It sputtered, spat and splashed into my face, dotted my hair in red paint. The taste of burning iron leaked into my mouth as his eyes rolled and his mouth filled with blood.

I eased him to his knees and then to his stomach. Vayle had done the same with her guardsman.

Unwanted thoughts about this young man, his blond hair soaking in a deepening red pool, infiltrated my mind. Was he forced into the city guard as a slave? Were his parents still alive? Did he have a sister or a brother? I quickly pushed those thoughts aside as the two bodies bled out into a river that slowly snaked its way down the marble hallway.

The door to Sybil's room opened without resistance, and a small, squat man jumped off the bed in surprise. I removed my helmet, revealing my face.

Dercy Daniser put a finger to his lips and waved us in.

"Help me pull them in," I whispered to Vayle.

We lugged the dead-weighted bodies inside and shut the door.

Dercy stood near a tiny opened window, no larger than a slit for a squirrel to fit in and out.

It overlooked the snowy courtyard that lay behind the keep. Dressed in thick wools and Verdan regalia, Chachant and Sybil were sitting under a tree whose vast arms of needles and pinecones kept its trunk mostly free of snow.

They talked. I listened.

"It's not right," Chachant said. "Magic is uncontrolled. It's unpredictable."

"It's not magic," Sybil said. "It's a state of mind. It's something you already have inside you! You haven't learned how to use it, that's all. Do you want me to prove it to you?"

Shadows hid the features of Chachant's face, but I watched him pick his head up slowly from the ground, a mix of curiosity and concern.

"Come on," Sybil said, jumping to her feet. She grabbed his hand and helped him up. "Come out here, in the open."

I leaned in to Dercy and whispered, "I think you're meant to hear this. She wants to break you. She's going to show you what the conjurers are capable of. She wants to strip the spirit from your fight. I'm told they go down easier like that."

"They?"

"Those whose minds the conjurers want for their own. Look, if you feel yourself slipping into a void or falling or not at all present in this world anymore, bloody do something, will you? Flail your arms, shake your head, whatever, and I'll shut the window. When it happened to me, this realm slowly slipped from my grasp… you won't mistake it for anything else."

Dercy's eyebrow inclined. "You were taken by a conjurer? You seem fine now."

"I am fine. Now. I think. Long fucking story. I'll keep talking to you, prevent her from reaching inside your mind farther than she already has."

"Does that work?"

I shrugged. "I've no bloody idea. Can't hurt."

Sybil and Chachant stood in the middle of the courtyard.

"Hold me," she said.

Chachant stood behind her and wrapped his arms around her belly. She leaned back onto his shoulder.

"Do you see that raven there, in the tree?"

"Yes."

"Close your eyes," she said. "Are they closed?"

"Yes."

"I want you to imagine something." She rolled her head from side to side on his shoulder, looking into the sky. Finally, she stopped. "I want you to imagine the raven just as you saw it," she said. "Imagine it perched upon a snowy branch. Suddenly, it's flying. It soars against the midnight sky, your eyes barely able to trace its blurry black outline. Imagine it slowing, as if the wind is pushing it back."

In the midnight sky of Edenvaile, a raven drifted across the sky like a barrel across the sea, slowly rolling along the black waves.

"Now," Sybil said, "it's resting before the moon. Imagine, Chachant: this insignificant speck suspended in the sky, this marring of the moon. But you have its mind, my dear. And you can turn its insignificance into brilliance. It seems to be growing larger now, engorging itself on the brightness of the moon that's suddenly shrinking under the raven's massive wings and its elongated talons that are ripping at the curtain of the night, pulling it closed, shuttering the moon into oblivion."

The moon was no longer visible. A single entity of wings blotted it out.

"It moves as you will it," Sybil said. "It pitches down, screaming toward the ground. As it plunges, the moon becomes visible again, but it looks so small, so… insignificant compared to this creature. This creature that now powerfully lifts itself back into the air. Its yellow eyes spark like a freshly struck fire. Its wings of ink are burning now, melting off as the yellow flames chase away the night. It combusts! An enormous bird of fire, blue flames rippling across the surface of the yellow ones. It gently eases itself to the ground, the fire drinking up the snow and ice as it lands softly in a frozen courtyard."

Sybil's head rolled lifelessly back onto Chachant's shoulder. She gasped.

"Now, my love… open your eyes."

Chachant jumped back, but curiosity pulled him in again. "That can't be real. It's just like I imagined."

Sybil sidled out of Chachant's embrace on wobbly legs, toward the phoenix whose fiery tail swooshed about.

"It is real," she said. "I know you felt it."

"I felt it in you," Chachant said, trailing through the snow after her.

"It was in you too," Sybil said. "You helped shape it. You helped fly it. You helped create it."

"It's magnificent," Chachant said, childlike excitement drowning out the fear that had thickened his voice.

"Touch her. She won't hurt you. Your mind influences her."

The phoenix's fiery body illuminated Chachant's face. He sported the stupid grin of a man who had no idea the evil he was touching. The flames receded as Chachant's hand passed over the bird's body.

Sybil curled her arm around his shoulder and kissed his cheek. "The conjurers *chose* us. They *trust* us, the Verdans and the Taths — the families of divinity! That's why we must do this. I'm sorry I hadn't told you the truth before, but… I was scared. Scared of the gifts they'd given me, scared of what you would think. Scared of war."

"There's still a war to be had. You said so yourself."

"Yes, but it will all be over soon. Conjurer spies have eliminated the Rabthorns; the South is in disarray. My father is confident his bannermen will join him, and with your father returning, much of the North will fall in line. The only fight lies with Braddock."

"Not all of the North will fall in line," Chachant said. "My father will pull in a few, but my brother's abdication fractured the North. He has the allegiances of several families... powerful ones. And the North is always fickle. If they see power sway his direction, all of the families may join him."

Sybil traced her nail down along Chachant's jaw. "The needle of power will never point toward your brother. Not when the conjurers show their hand. But it will be a lot less bloody if you could maybe... mm, convince your brother to see our point of view."

A wind caught hold of the phoenix's flames, ruffling its spine of blue flame. Chachant smiled at it maniacally. "I could fly there tonight."

Sybil laughed. "Dercy and I are going to enjoy this girl tonight. He needs to see the power of the conjurers with his own eyes. But ride for your brother in the morning. I will meet you there."

Chachant pulled her in and kissed her lips, his fingers burrowing into her back.

Not one to play voyeur, I closed the window and looked at Dercy. "Feel all right?"

"Slightly ill," he admitted. "Never mind the fact I was under the assumption conjurers were almost extinct, I did not know they had the power to do... this."

"There's plenty more you don't know," I said. "Commander Vayle can inform you of everything while the two of you fly to Watchmen's Bay."

"Er, fly?" Vayle said.

I smiled. "We're going to steal a bird."

CHAPTER TWENTY-TWO

People generally do not go around stealing birds. Even in the remote villages where relationships with wildlife are questionable at best and promiscuous at worst, and where fowl are valuable commodities, thievery of the feathery things is not something that often occurs. The reason for this is simple: birds are bloody hard to steal. Try to steal something that can fly, squawk, tear into your skin with talons, peck your eyes out with terribly sharp beaks and shit all over you *and* themselves without second thought. Sounds like a sort of insanity most would much rather stay away from.

Thankfully, phoenixes were not like most birds. They seemed highly intelligent, affectionate, lively. Perhaps they could be reasoned with. I didn't have much of a choice but to risk it. This bird was a weapon, one that could not fall into the hands of Sybil or Chachant.

I crouched down inside the decrepit tunnel. Stale air whirled around me. "To the kitchen," I told Dercy. "When we exit the kitchen, we'll come to a courtyard. Lots of guards around. Stay sandwiched between Vayle and me when we come out. With any luck, we won't pass an officer."

"I can do you one better," Vayle said.

I looked in her general direction but saw only shadows. "Then lay it on me."

"Take Dercy yourself. I'll bring you a horse."

"A horse?"

"I'm sorry," Vayle said. "Did you intend to fly as well?"

"I've had my fill, thank you. There's not enough room anyway."

"Right. So you need an escape."

"Well… I was, er — you see, my plan—" I cleared my throat. "Fuck it. I can't think of a good excuse. I was too focused on ensuring freedom for both of you."

A small hand patted my shoulders. "Isn't he growing up so fast, Dercy, putting others before himself?"

"Shut it. If you find yourself in trouble—"

"You'll know it," Vayle said.

My hand swam in the darkness, till my fingers curled around the collar of a mesh shirt. Vayle clung to my plate, and we whispered the Rots hymn to one another.

"Strong sword," I said.

"Strong sword."

"Sharp eyes."

"Sharp eyes."

"Cold blood."

"Cold blood."

"Healthy fear."

"Healthy fear."

I shook her gently. "See you on the other side."

"I'll be there first," she said, and I imagined she was grinning, like always.

She shuffled past me, and she was gone.

I unhooked a dagger from my leg. "How long's it been since you held a blade?" I asked Dercy.

"A few nights ago," he said nonchalantly.

"Ceremonial blades don't count. I'm talking true steel, something you wield with the intention of cutting deeply into flesh."

"As am I. A vagrant stumbled onto our caravan camp on the way here. He was caught stealing salted boar flanks. I took off both his hands so he could never steal again. Beyond that, I practice my swordsmanship for one hour every day in Watchmen's Bay; a king cannot afford to lose the wit of his blade, just as he cannot afford to lose the wit of his mind.

"I know you regard my crown as weak and pacifying, Shepherd. But my reluctance for skirmishes and distaste for war does not speak of my weaknesses. I am seated on a coast where bandit ships prowl, where ancient tribesmen hold a special hatred for people like me, where vassals and lords of ancient strongholds and villages grow in power every day and so often wish to take the crown the Daniser name has clutched for two hundred years.

"I am seated in a kingdom where our stone walls are fortified with a mixture of steel because they were under siege eternally during my grandfather's reign and during my father's reign. I am seated in a kingdom that for the first time in its history has seen peace soothe its plains and its mountains and its shores for the thirty-some-odd years I've sat in that seashell-constructed throne. *Peace.* Do you hear that word? It's a word my people did not know for more than a few weeks at a time. Anyone can swing a sword, Astul: a conjurer, a drunk vagrant, a hopeless wanderer. Anyone can stab, blunt, poke. Real strength comes in pacifying those whose existence is driven by bloodshed."

I never thought I'd be lectured in a crumbling castle keep passageway, but here I was, beaten down by the king of the sea.

"Truthfully, I was just curious to know if you could handle yourself in case we were attacked."

"I'm well aware," Dercy said. "But I am equally curious if you know the truth as to why the Danisers will be your saving grace in this... what apparently is the beginning of a great war. And that is why you freed me, is it not? You want my army."

I shrugged. "Better to have you on my side than on the conjurers'."

"Know that it won't be for the steel that I bring, the horses I march or the bodies of young men and women who will overwhelm whoever and whatever they face. It will be for the past thirty years of peace; the past thirty years of strengthened alliances; the past thirty years of growth my people have enjoyed. It's because of that peace that I will have all the steel, the horses and the bright-eyed men and women who thirst to become warriors like their mothers and fathers, aunts and uncles. You take care of the North, and I promise you victory."

A familiar feeling bubbled up inside my stomach. When I was sixteen and met Vayle for the first time, I thought I understood the world and what she offered. Sarcasm and biting wit were the preeminent qualities of my repertoire. It wasn't until speaking with Vayle that I learned I was very ignorant of the world. She taught me words I never knew, history I'd gotten terribly wrong, cultures I didn't know existed… things a young boy growing up in the wild cannot hope to know. It was a sobering experience, one that made me feel, at the time, that I was a stupid boy who only survived because of luck. But I taught her how to hold a sword, whet the blade, plunge it straight and true, and through this I learned no one knows precisely how this world operates: the bits and pieces of its inner workings are littered in the minds of all its inhabitants.

Maybe I'd forgotten that over the years, but the conjurers and now Dercy had reminded me of it, and I once again felt like a very stupid boy.

"Let's work on getting out of here alive first, shall we?" I said.

Dercy smiled and took the dagger. He hid it inside his sleeve. "Lead the way, Shepherd. Or should I say, Commander Wilhelm."

I grinned, tightened my helmet and crawled out of that hideous tunnel for hopefully the last time.

We passed two roving patrols on the way to the kitchen. Each guard took great interest in Dercy, but they quickly dismissed their suspicious glances when I lashed out at them and told them to focus on finding the assassin. *I'm getting quite adept at this Wilhelm voice,* I thought.

We were halfway through the kitchen when the bells went off. One bell, then two, then four, then ten, all clashing like cymbals in a hollow chamber. It was the annoying, ear-ringing, headache-producing alarm of Edenvaile.

"Two of 'em up here, dead!" the voice screamed, and then trailed off.

It sounded like a stampede of animals with iron greaves on their hooves in the great hallway outside the kitchen.

A panicked voice broke in. "Lord Edmund's here! Lady Mydia too."

"The king?"

"Here!" a distant voice shouted.

"Get them into the cellar," a familiar voice barked. It was the officer in charge of dousing the fiery roughage and horseshit. "Where the bloody fuck is Wilhelm?"

"He passed us, sir, saw him with Dercy Daniser."

"Get off of me!" That voice belonged to none other than Sybil Tath. Her screech... oh, not pleasant.

"Let her go," Chachant hollered.

Voices bled in with one another, syllables drowning out vowels, hoarse cries erupting over calm and gentle orders.

"Take your men and find Dercy Daniser," the officer said. "I want Wilhelm Arch as well, alive or dead. Treasonous bastard."

"Lady Sybil!" a guard yipped. "Milady! We haven't cleared that... way... yet."

"Take *your* men to the royal quarters," the officer ordered. "Assist the royal guard."

"Sir! Lady Sybil ran off toward the courtyard."

"Fuck's sake. You and you, go chase her down. Now!"

"Let her go," Chachant roared.

I took off my helmet and sat it near a spice table. "Won't be needing this anymore. Can't see shit half the time anyway. Sybil's going for her bird. Let's play race the conjurer, what do you say?"

"Go," Dercy said.

I busted ass through the kitchen, hauling off toward the door and throwing it open, ebon blade in hand. I turned the corner, looked back to make sure Dercy was keeping up, and sprinted through the shin-high snow.

My calves burned. And my chest stung. Someone screeched, but from where? The ground glittered with flakes and ice, but the night seemed to hang extraordinarily low. It was black and cold, visibility blurred by falling snow.

Something crunched from behind. A pair of feet — no, two pairs.

Three pairs.

More than that now.

Their breaths rasped in my ears. Their shouts made my skull tremble. They called for archers. They called for everyone. They'd found us, they said.

"Stop!" they shouted.

We didn't stop. Dercy and I, side by side now, kicked over the mountains of snow and tripped over hills of ice. We picked ourselves up, and we ran. We ran hard enough to crack the frozen sheets beneath our boots, ran hard enough that we seemed to suck away the blackness of the night. The horizon beamed at us as we turned another corner, dimly lit but growing hotter, fiercer.

Oranger, bluer.

A tail flicked about anxiously, its flames cutting across patches of snow, melting them into puddles.

A shadow flung itself across the crystallized ground. It shed its skin, thinning its fat. It left heavy wool coats in its wake.

Sybil ran toward her bird, determination searing her face. Her arms were bare, her chest almost naked save a thin kirtle. She was faster than us. Closer to the phoenix. She was lightning zipping, shooting, dancing.

But just as thunder chases lightning, a shadow chased her. A much larger shadow with muscular legs that could stomp in a skull. A shadow that exploded through the snow like a rolling boulder.

Sybil spun around. She threw herself to the ground, somersaulting out of the way of a romping steed whose reins were held by my commander.

A platoon of guards banked around the far corner of the keep, closing us in on both sides.

I powered through the snow, urging Dercy on. Vayle and I held eyes for a moment. We both knew the plan had changed.

"Ride!" I told her.

She tugged on the reins. Her steed grunted and wheeled around. A pair of heels struck the horse hard in the ribs. Again and again. She charged toward the guards, skirting around their swords and vanishing beyond the keep.

Heaving and hacking, Dercy and I reached the phoenix. We climbed onto her back, her flames receding. I took the engulfed reins that cooled in my hands like hot steel plunging into ice.

There was a shriek that shivered across my shoulders. I turned to see Sybil on her feet, her face demented and swollen with anger. Had she the time and the energy, she would've grasped the phoenix's mind and likely turned Dercy and me into human pyres.

But finally, for the first time, I had the advantage. I took the reins and I pleaded with the bird to take us far away from here. The phoenix lurched forward, rising into the air. She ascended slowly toward the suffocating black sky.

"How do you control this thing?" Dercy asked.

The bird continued rising straight and slow, her wings flapping steadily. I stuffed my hands into her plumage and held tight.

"Excellent question," I said. "I'm not sure."

Suddenly, the bird that was once a raven tumbled toward the gate.

"How'd you do that?" Dercy asked.

I didn't want to tell him.

Spurts of orange flames lanced out from the phoenix's smoldering face. She tucked her wings into her body, gaining speed. A moment later she unfurled her wings and flapped them gently, carrying us like a lazy cloud across the sky.

"What?" Dercy said. "Fueled by magic?"

Again I said nothing. It wasn't that I couldn't articulate it, but rather that I didn't want to believe it. It felt very, very wrong.

"Look!" Dercy said, his stubby finger pointing toward the ground far below us.

At first glance, it looked like an agent of the night moved swiftly atop the snow. After a few blinks to clear out the blurriness and teariness that flying apparently inflicts, it became clear this was an agent not of the night, but of the Black Rot.

Vayle guided her galloping steed between the wall-to-wall buildings of the market square, dashing through the thin strip of snow covering the cobblestone streets. Taking advantage of the farce the city guard thought would foolishly lead us into their waiting hands, she bolted for the opened gate.

"She best weave," Dercy said. "Otherwise those archers on the wall will string her up."

"She's waiting," I said.

The archers thought they had her. I may not have seen their faces, but I was certain proud smirks pushed up the edges of their mouths, and their tongues probably slithered between their lips like snakes. She was heading right for them. Right for their barbed arrows that would sink into the chest of her steed and the flesh of her neck.

Each guard had nocked an arrow. They drew back just as the phoenix carried Dercy and me beyond the wall. I willed us back around, keeping close watch on my commander.

Their aim was on. Their hands steadfast. Their eyes pinned her down, waiting for her steed to take one more step.

Just as the archers of the Edenvaile city guard released a barrage of steel-fanged tips, fletchings and wooden shafts into the night, Vayle tugged on her steed's reins, vaulting out of the way. Another tug and the horse shifted its weight again, as agile as a cat. Vayle weaved like haphazard lightning through the snow, never allowing the archers more than a guess as to which way she would dance next.

She sped through the gate, continuing to weave as the hooves of her steed pounded the ground into a fine white dust. Once she was far enough away from the gate, she rode hard and straight into the freedom of Rime. Freedom, however, is a fickle lady. Or maybe it's a man? Or maybe a goat god, hmm? Whatever personification it prefers, it often vanishes just as quickly as it appears.

The Edenvaile city guard poured from the gates like pissed-off bees whose honey had just been snatched by a clever bear under the guise of their queen. About fifteen cavalry galloped after the woman who'd just made a fool of their archers. There would be more soon, but the remaining horses were held in the nearby villages, and it would take time for those on foot to reach them.

Vayle had a good start on the cavalry, but I needed the horse she was on, and she needed my bird. If we tried an exchange now, the city guard would be on us within minutes. And I was not eager to ride to Patrick Verdan with an army sniffing at my heels.

How do you rectify that little problem? Given my position, I had only one logical option, and it involved something people had been doing since they'd first come to this world, or were dropped from the sky, or were gifted by a god, or however the hell people got here in the first place. Something that brought smiles to the faces of the children and maniacs alike.

I would burn shit.

With nothing more than my thoughts, I made the phoenix turn in a wide, arcing fashion. Head down, wings tucked, she barreled downward, beyond the galloping cavalry, and then looped back around.

The poor bastards probably saw her coming, what with the white of the snow burning away and an apocalyptic sky steadfastly approaching them from behind, but what could they do?

With a flick of my mind, the phoenix spread her wings. She edged herself along the cavalry and showered every last one of them in sticky, broiling fire.

They flailed and they fell. Screamed and cried. They doused themselves in snow, but the elements betrayed them and turned to boiling water, scalding the skin from their faces and the brows from their eyes.

My thoughts raced the phoenix low over the snow like a mosquito over water. The bird caught up to Vayle with ease. My commander slowed her steed and eventually came to a stop.

The wind had wrangled her hair into a nest of tangles and knots. Her cheeks were red and her lips cracked.

"That will be one for the book," she said, patting her horse appreciatively.

"And which book is that?" I asked, stepping off the phoenix.

"The one I will write involving my near-death experiences," Vayle said. "They will all have a common theme: you."

I laughed. "More of me is a good thing, wouldn't you say?"

Vayle stepped down from her horse. She walked over to the phoenix but kept her distance.

"An alluring creature," she said, tiptoeing around its seething tail.

"You appear scared," Dercy said, as if he wasn't shitting himself when we first took to the air.

"I do not know if I am scared," Vayle said. "I have never flown before."

I put my hand on the bird's head. The flames peeled away from my palm. "Your thoughts control her actions."

Vayle's head cocked, almost imperceptibly. "That sounds very… conjurerish."

"Don't think about it too much. Get to Watchmen's Bay with the king here, and let him work his magic he claims he has vats of."

"There is an ongoing complication in Watchmen's Bay," Vayle said. "If you recall."

"What kind of complication?" Dercy asked, alarmed.

I rubbed my eyes. It didn't do much for the pain in my head. "This may sound…"

"Bad," Vayle put in.

"Treasonous, even, if you consider us loose friends."

"Horrific if close friends," Vayle said.

"Yes," I said, "thank you, Commander. I think he gets the point."

"Get on with it," Dercy said. "What happened to my kingdom?"

"Nothing," I said. "Well, perhaps something. It can't truly happen without you, let's put it that way. You're the big missing piece," I said, slapping Dercy on the shoulder, trying to loosen him up.

He looked at me in the way a father looks at his child while the boy is holding the shattered pieces of a family heirloom and attempting to explain that while this *is* as bad as it looks, consider the positives.

"The Black Rot proposed to assassinate you, along with your family, and lift one of your bannermen to the throne in exchange for a promise of supplies and men for the war effort. I was convinced you would not agree to war against the conjurers unless I had empirical proof. I believe my assumption was correct, until that nasty incident we've left in our wake."

"You are a bold man," Dercy said, as if paying me a compliment.

"Very bold," I agreed, chuckling uneasily. He was taking this well. "And you know what they say about boldness: it's the bold that… er, well. Lots of good sayings about boldness. I'm sure you've heard them all well enough."

He fingered his wiry beard. "And stupid."

"Occasionally stupid," I agreed.

"And an idiot who would have had twenty claims for the throne and no real support for a war few would believe in."

I shrugged. "It was a long shot to begin with."

After a long pause, Dercy cleared his throat. "Consider it forgiven."

What a fantastic conclusion. If this had been Braddock, I would have endured threats of my head being chopped off, my cock being clamped by a vise and injected with poison and so forth. Dercy Daniser — he was an understanding man. Calm, cool, collected.

"*If*," he said, "you inform me which of my bannermen agreed to your proposal so that I may hasten their meeting with their maker."

"Consider it done."

"Let us talk for a moment about logistics," Vayle said. "When should we march?"

"How long do you need to mobilize your bannermen?" I asked Dercy.

"Ten days," he answered. "I can make it to the walls of Edenvaile in thirty days, provided we don't get interrupted by a conjurer army."

"They're unlikely to attack you in the open," Vayle said. "Sitting inside a castle is the safest course."

I climbed off the phoenix and made my way to the horse. "You're sure your bannermen will march?"

"The North had kidnapped their king," he answered. "Pride, if nothing else, will move them. They don't need to know we're fighting conjurers, not until they see the bastards with their own eyes."

I patted the horse's long face. "This isn't part of the conjurers' plan, but as soon they see you march — and I'm assuming they have scouts posted everywhere — they'll come to the aid of Edenvaile. They have to. The North is their only hope."

"What of the South?" he asked.

"Braddock and Kane Calbid are taking care of that. Hopefully."

"Kane Calbid?"

"Long story," I said. "Rabthorns are out of the picture, that's all you need to know." I put a foot in the stirrup and slung myself up over the saddle. "I'm going to find Patrick Verdan. See if we can't steal the North right out from underneath Sybil."

Vayle stretched an experimental hand toward the phoenix. Her flames retreated, and she almost seemed to purr like a kitten as Vayle stroked her. "Where will you go from there?" my commander asked.

"Back to the Hole. I've other business to attend to before this war gets underway. Come look for me in about ten days, will you? I'd appreciate a flight back." I clicked my tongue and added, "Assuming I'm still alive."

CHAPTER TWENTY-THREE

The Black Mountains' mere name evokes a sense of dread, but they're like any other mountains: tall, looming, craggy and unforgiving. The Black Woods aren't any blacker than most, and the Deep Marshes aren't any deeper than those found in Writmire Fields. Names are mostly pretty things, that's all.

But the Widowed Path, now there's a pretty name with a rather haunting past. Like a river sucked dry by the sun, it winds its way through the western ridge, emptying out into Hoarvous, and throughout the way is the only path to many mountaintop villages and kingdoms, including Patrick Verdan's.

A long time ago, when the mountaintops weren't dotted with small villages, tribes of scantily clothed men wearing goat horns and drenched in goat blood — or elk horns and sheep blood, depending on which tales you believe — would pour from the deep crevices of the mountain and prey upon merchants and travelers who had heard of riches buried deep in the heart of the West.

Now, authors have been known to exaggerate, but most of them say there's never been a time in the great history of Mizridahl when so many wives were left behind as widows.

Fortunately for me, I wouldn't join the proud tradition of letting the Widowed Path live up to its name… if only because I didn't have a wife. There's always a morbidly positive way to look at things.

It took me about three days to reach the mouth of the path, sleeping for no more than two hours in messenger camps. I had traded off ten horses and now owed more than twenty thousand gold coins to the messengers. If I survived this mess with the conjurers, I'd have to go back to selling ebon to make my living.

An enormous curtain of wavy rock edged along both sides of the path, sometimes thinning the passage to allow no more than a single horse through at one time. At other points, it would open up like the sea, and you very well could have steered a ship between its bosom, provided you had enough water to fill the gully.

The sheer face of the mountain seemed to streak straight upward for miles, mottled with clomps of snow and ice that bespeckled the cracks and ridges. Spikes and pillars of rock were at the forefront, surging into the clouds until the thickness of the sky concealed them.

My horse, who was given the rather boring name of Chester, scooted along the lumpy roads of dirt, snow and stone, swaying as its hooves discovered just how deep the gashes ran along the passage.

Chester trotted slowly along for four days, covering about a hundred miles in total. The deeper the passage ran, the higher the peaks curved over top of us like a ceiling of bone. Scythes of ice would sometimes break off for a two-mile-long descent. The only warning you got was a slight whistling, which in the language of the mountain means "haul your ass."

I camped for a few hours a night. Longer than I would have liked, but an exhausted horse — or worse, a dead one — would serve me about as well as a cat in water.

We came to the gate of Icerun on the fourth day in the passage, or the seventh since I'd parted with Vayle and Dercy.

Gate in this case is a metaphor, because you can take a gander for as long as you please and you won't find any steel doors or wooden beams or levers or anything that resembles a gate. Not down here, at least. The gate to Patrick Verdan's kingdom was what looked like an unending slope apparently crafted by the hands of either a winter god who thought it would be hilarious to create the world's largest sledding ramp, or Mother Nature when she was on a bender.

At the top lay the kingdom of Icerun, hidden behind a veil of fog and snowdrifts.

I clambered down from Chester and took with me my hulking burlap sack with two trekking poles tied to the strings. I'd bought the supplies from a messenger camp near the mouth of the Widowed Path. I offered Chester a couple stale carrots, which he chomped down eagerly, and then patted him on the butt.

"Thank you, friend. Off you go, now." I slapped him on his haunches hard and shouted, "Go home! Go home! Go home!"

As he was trained by the messengers, the lemon-colored steed wheeled around and trotted back the way he had come. Hopefully the good man would reach the camp he came from without starvation setting in.

The morning sun poked its head out of the clouds, and slivers of golden light swam across the glacier shelf in front of me. Frozen crystals winked at me with prisms of blinding light, as if the mountain was taunting me.

"What are you?" I asked it. "A big pile of rock with decorative frosting, that's what. Not so scary now, are you? You're just an oversized wedding cake. How does that make you feel?"

It whistled back at me haughtily as a powerful wind swept over its peaks and broomed off a large drift of snow.

"We'll see about that," I said. I opened my burlap sack, dug through stale bread wrapped in sieve cloth, ointments that supposedly sealed cuts, oils to keep my blade singing a sharp tune, and other various purchases I'd made at messenger camps. At the bottom of the sack was a pair of snowshoes.

They were simple looking, but highly efficient for when the need to climb a mountain struck you. The soles were of expertly stitched leather lattice, ensuring your feet did not sink five feet beneath the snow, thus rendering you the next human statue upon the mountain.

I untied the trekking poles from the sack, put my feet in the shoes, threw the sack over my shoulders and drew in a deep, calming breath.

"Fuck!" I spat, coughing on the bitter air. "When am I going to learn not to take deep breaths in the North?"

The mountain whistled again, as if in laugher.

Silt crept across the sky from below the mountaintop. Hopefully a storm would not be in my future. There were few places I was less eager to camp than on the middle of a bloody mountain.

I shoved my trekking poles into the snow and propelled myself forward.

Ice crunched under the iron feet of my poles, and snow flattened under the lattice of my shoes. I was a conqueror of this mountain, beating it into submission with my primitive tools.

At least until nature decided to show me just how insignificant we two-footed, blabbering idiots truly are.

From barbed clefts came a wind so fierce, it howled like a symphony of female cats being mounted by their mates. Snow and ice convened into one, blasting into my cheeks, sanding the protective layer of skin from my face until what lay beneath was raw and burning. Snot leaked from my nose and froze almost instantly on the curl of my lip, and my eyes had been sucked dry.

My calves ached, my ass felt like I'd been a naughty boy and endured five hundred spankings, and my toes… what happened to my toes? Where did they go? I couldn't feel them any longer.

The ascent steepened with each step I took. I stumbled and fell and tripped, ate snow, chowed down on ice, and swallowed frozen crystals through my nose. I coughed up something thick and yellow and tasted iron swirling on my tongue. A tightness clamped my chest, numbness toyed with my fingers and sweat dripped from my balls. My breath climbed out of my lungs like a stricken animal desperately clawing itself out of the hole its predator had dragged it into.

Everything hurt. Everything burned. But some hours later — many hours later — I stood with a snowy beard, icy brows and a cold tongue hanging out of my mouth and looked at the grotesqueness that was Icerun.

Most kingdoms are constructed with aesthetics in mind just as much as they are with defensive advantages. After all, how would the people of Mizridahl know your kingdom is grand unless you have perfectly symmetrical walls, soaring towers and — *gasp* — a castle to die for?

Icerun was not like most other kingdoms. Personified, it would be considered a freak. A mangled mess that by chance alone was permitted to survive in this world.

Its malformed, uneven walls spread across the choppy mountain like lines drawn in the sand by a skittering crab. A gargantuan blockade of stone here, and then a stubby finger's worth here, joined together by cylindrical towers that sat precariously upon sloped hills. At least the keep was square and mostly normal.

It should have been comforting to find myself in a place where a king didn't give a shit about how his land looked to the rest of the world — you rarely find such a distant disposition in those with power — but something bothered me.

Something was wrong.

Something wasn't quite there. That is to say, *no one* was quite there.

Snow drifted along the battlements like wheels of sand and straw and sticks in an empty desert. There were no threatening displays of aggression by archers whose bows should've peered from the slits of the towers, no demand from guards to declare my name and my reason for visiting.

This kingdom felt empty. Abandoned.

The gate was open, so I went inside.

There were houses. Many, many houses, because this kingdom served not only as the castle, but as the refuge for all villages that would normally flock to fertile, nearby lands in most kingdoms.

The houses were empty. Doors were shut and there was no smoke billowing from the chimneys.

Snow thickened in the center of the city. The last time I made an appearance here some six years ago, the inhabitants of Icerun had kept not only their streets plowed but also their alleys. Huge fire pits had sprawled across the vastness of the city, and torches affixed to the keep had roared fiercely, always under assault from the wind but never bowing to its power.

Snow had covered the fire pits now, and the torches were barren.

The mountain whistled eerily, and then stopped.

Weariness churned my stomach and sent a shiver across my shoulders. Could the cold have taken them? Were there bones beneath this ocean of snow? Frozen flesh?

No, couldn't be. The houses would have been covered, and the unruly snowdrifts would have masked their doors. This looked like a city that had been bustling and teeming with life not long ago. The cold doesn't take a populace in a matter of days or weeks. It's a slow, torturous process.

And disease? That can be quick, but there always those few who are resilient to its effects. A handful would have survived. But a handful can't clear the streets. Can't keep the fires going, wouldn't have the mind to light the torches. They'd need to keep warm, huddle together, keep fed.

The keep, I thought. Maybe that was where they were. I trudged through the uneven terrain, up to the doors of the keep. They opened without resistance, creaking into the darkness of the castle.

"Hello?" I called out.

My echoing voice replied.

"Is anyone here?"

Again, the lonely echoes.

It was cold in there, certainly no sign that a fire had been struck recently.

I backed away, shut the doors and surveyed my surroundings.

That's when I noticed a peculiar sight.

The dungeon of Icerun lay beneath the ground, on an island of flat rock. A bridge had been constructed to connect the island to the city, spanning a gap where the mountain fell away a good hundred feet.

On this island, snow did not exist. In fact, a subtle wave of warm breath appeared to float low across the ground.

When you find yourself in a suddenly abandoned kingdom where shelves of ice surround you and white powder rises up like a swollen sea, it is not a comforting feeling to see a patch of dry, hot dirt. It's spooky as fuck.

Ebon blade in hand, I crossed the bridge at the pace of a snail, because I'd be damned if my death came from falling off a bloody bridge. Once I reached the island, I laughed.

Not a sincere laugh where you put your hand over your belly and you slap your thigh because the hilarity of the situation is just too much to handle. No, a laugh that slowly tumbles out of your mouth and falls lamely to your feet. A laugh that a man might cough up when he finds himself surrounded by three hundred foreign pikemen who do not understand what the word "surrender" means.

The ground was burning. I touched the dirt lightly with the back of my hand. It was a soothing kind of warmth, much like bathwater. Snow that fell upon it melted instantly.

Part of the island was still snow-covered; the burning patch seemed to be focused mostly in the middle, but it wasn't in the form of a circle. There was a broad vertical strip. Jutting out from the sides of that strip were much broader, much longer horizontal swaths.

If you looked at it long enough, it somewhat resembled a bird. A very large bird.

Something began rumbling beneath my feet. A voice.

I hurried over to a square cutout in an overhang of rock, the entrance to the dungeon, and listened. A boorish voice sang a song.

Piss on your bruises
Piss on your cuts
I've gotta fuckin' eat
So I'll eat your fuckin' guts

Piss on your mother
Piss on your father
I've gotta fuckin' drink
So I'll drink your fuckin' blood

And on and on it went.

"Think you'll eat my guts and drink my blood if I come down there?" I hollered.

The singing stopped abruptly. "Hey! Hey! Get me fuckin' outta here. They left us to rot. Get me outta here. I ain't even guilty of what they say."

That's a favorite saying among prisoners.

The steps spiraling into the dungeon were cut crudely from the frozen earth and the ribbonlike rock that colonized Icerun. Most proper dungeons are deep, hollow and dark. And you've really got to hit all three of those qualities. Otherwise, you have what is more a little hole in the ground than a dungeon. And no one's ever confessed to their crimes for fear of being stuck a few feet beneath the dirt, where the light still reaches them. It's deep down, where only the bats and sightless creatures venture, that'll shiver your teeth right from your gums.

But, as I quickly came to discover, the dungeon of Icerun was an exception. It was shallow, but no less dark than Edenvaile's and inexplicably more rancid than that of Lith.

The rotten stench of carcasses and old, festering blood hung in the air like the hot stickiness of a swamp. It clung to the hairs on my arms. It drizzled down my face. It percolated through my pores and seeped into my mouth, where the foulness of death and engorged maggots made me gag.

"You get used to it," the man said.

I waved my sword around, letting it be my guide in the all-encompassing blackness. I stepped on something slimy and wet. The sole of my boot squashed it, and a noxious gas sizzled and oozed from its wound. I gagged again.

"Yeah, that's foul," the man said, coughing. "That there is really fuckin' foul. Don't do that again, eh?"

His voice was very near, and so I stopped.

"What's your name?" I asked.

"Gorf. Goofy fuckin' name, yeah? Father thought it unique, thought I was going to grow up to be some warrior that'd topple kingdoms." He laughed a mucousy laugh and coughed. "Drank too much, got in too many fights, became a wanderer instead. Ended up here some years ago. The Lord Patrick Verdan took me in. And now he throws me in here for stealing. *Stealing!*"

"Consider yourself lucky you didn't have the mind to head south and steal something from Dercy Daniser. I hear he chops off the hands of thieves to solve their addiction."

"I didn't steal! Didn't take nothin' that wasn't rightfully mine. Now I'm sittin' here. I've been forced to kill to survive because those bastards up there left us here."

"Your song wasn't much of an exaggeration, was it?" I asked.

"What was I supposed to do? A man's gotta eat to survive. No difference in eating the leg of a goat or the leg of a man. Just… you know, you feel sick after eating a man's leg. It's cold, squishy, and chewy. Tough. Not good meat at all."

"How long have you been here?"

"Two weeks," he answered.

Well, well. That meant Patrick Verdan and his people had not vanished before then.

"Let's talk about Patrick Verdan," I said. "I assume that he didn't suddenly get a sensible notion to move to lower ground. He seemed to have liked having visitors hike up a bloody mountain to reach him."

I heard chains being thrown around, as if the man shrugged. "Let's talk about me gettin' outta here."

"Fine," I said, automatically and without thought. Anything he wanted, I'd give him… in the full confidence of my word. "I'll set you free after you divulge all information you have."

"You know where the key is?"

"No. But I have an ebon blade. Works all the same."

"Fancy man, are we? All right, all right. I'll sing you a song."

"No songs, please."

Gorf sighed. "It's a saying, a way of spillin' information. Where I come from, any sort of talking we do is singin' a song. It's kind of like — ah, you know what, forget it. A day or two after I got locked up here, there's this big noise up above. Sounds like an earthquake. Lots of vibrations. Rocks shaking, things like that. So I look at Erath and I say it sounds like feathers flapping. Big fuckin' feathers, yeah? And he says, hey, Gorf, I think you're right.

"Then all of a sudden, my wigglin' toes are getting warmed up, and my hands are thawing out. Hells, it feels warm down here, I tell Erath. Then we see this water dripping from above — lucky for me too, or I would have been dead way long ago. Snow's melting, I figure. Snow never melts around here, sticks around like a bad disease. Like a case of those fuckin' pimply scratchy things you get on your balls, yeah?"

"I wouldn't know," I said. "I choose my whores carefully."

"Well, anyway, that's it. All the story I got. Soon after, whole fucking kingdom just up and left, or so we figured. Couldn't hear no one anymore, and the guards went missing. Vanished, like…"

"Like you wish those pimply scratchy things would vanish?" I suggested.

Gorf snapped his fingers and laughed. "Like that, yeah!"

"Thanks, Gorf. It's appreciated." I turned and walked back up the steps.

"Hey! Where you goin'? What about setting me free here?"

I continued trekking up the crooked stairs. "We'll see about that when my commander comes and takes me off this abandoned mountain."

"Hey! You fuckin' lied to me. Don't leave me…"

His voice trailed off as I came out of the dungeon and walked across the crispy island, back toward the mainland of Icerun.

Gorf seemed like a nice enough lad, but I was alone and I had prized possessions, like food and an ebon blade. I couldn't trust him, not enough to shut my eyes and sleep, which was something I would do as much as I could until Vayle arrived.

I went into the keep and rummaged around for some timber, which I found stacked in a room, along with tinder. I made a small fire in one of the many sunken pits throughout the keep. I placed my burlap sack on the floor and unwrapped the sieve cloth from a loaf of honey bread. I sawed off a piece with my teeth. It was stale, tasteless and dry, but better than a human leg.

I washed the bread down with some cold wine, had a look around at my surroundings and laughed. What kind of insane idiot do you have to be to build a kingdom that requires the keep to be festooned with fire pits so your blood doesn't freeze and your bones don't shatter?

I laughed again, and I laughed some more, each subsequent chuckle quieter than the last, until the only sound in the keep was the burbling fire. I hoped to find more distractions, something else with which to occupy my mind, but my eyes insisted on returning to the flames.

Fire itself is supposed to be the epitome of distraction. It's a mystical thing, tails and sprites tinged orange and splashed with yellows and dashed with reds, flickering sideways, licking the air as if they're tasting its quality. You can find yourself lost in the flames as they rise and fall like tranquil ocean waves that soothe even the most battered minds.

Thing is, fire had scarred me. It drew me away from any and all distractions. Fire had become a harbinger of the conjurers, what with their flaming monstrosities that landed in Vereumene, that brought my twisted, subservient self back to Mizridahl, that altered a fleeing raven into an obedient tool.

And what of the bird that landed here? Had to be another phoenix, but whose? If the conjurers knew that Patrick Verdan was the missing piece to unite the North — something Vileoux very well could have told them during his stay in Lith — then sending one of their finest here to take Patrick's mind made sense. But surely Sybil would have heard. She wouldn't have wanted to send Chachant here otherwise, unless she wanted him out of the picture. Maybe she figured he'd die or suffer grievous injury on the mountain. But her little boy toy was more a blossoming flower to her than a pricking thorn.

Even if I went with the theory that the conjurers had clawed their way into Patrick's mind, it didn't explain why the whole kingdom was abandoned. The logistics of moving a thousand-plus women, children, the old and the sick, down its slopes... it was unthinkable.

It didn't add up. What was I missing? What piece eluded my grasp?

I gazed deep into the fire and rested my chin on steepled fingers. "Where did you go, Patrick?"

The fire spat and hissed, the only answers it ever gave.

Three days. Three very long days and longer nights in which I slept for an hour and woke for two, drenched in sweat. Then I'd shiver myself to sleep and inevitably wake again. It was a few hours past noon when ribbons of fire seared the cloudy sky,

rising over the Widowed Path and ascending to
Icerun.

The phoenix landed in the city center, and
Vayle climbed down into a puddle of slush.

"I wondered if I had come to the right place,"
she said, alluding to the emptiness around her.

I tossed my burlap sack around my shoulder
and approached her. "Back to the Hole. I'll tell you
about it on the way."

Vayle had no more theories than I about why
Icerun had been abandoned. But like an owl flying
back to its babies with a mouse in tow, she did bring
good news. Dercy had rounded up twenty thousand
soldiers between all his bannermen, including five
thousand cavalry. He would be ready to march in
three days, after receiving enough food and supplies
for the long road.

Vayle and I reached the Hole by late afternoon.
I jumped off the phoenix, knelt on the dirty ground
and kissed the mud.

"Thank fuck for dirt," I said. I spread my arms
out and spun around maddeningly. "It's wonderful,
isn't it? No snow. No cold... well, maybe a chill in the
air, but you can feel your toes and your fingers!"

Vayle remained seated on the bird, peering at
me queerly. I was surprised she wasn't shivering,
given she'd spent the past few days in the balmy
Watchmen's Bay, where they say the sun drowns out
all your worries, until a crab pinches your nipple or a
gale wind pushes the sea into your living room.

"Tell Dercy to march when he's ready," I said.

"How should I explain our fearless leader's disappearance?"

I chuckled. "Fearless leader? Right. Tell him I'm strengthening the war effort."

"Is this the day I see Astul beg a lord for help?"

"This is the day you see me buy a lord and everything he has to offer. Well, truthfully, less lords, more sellswords, but you get the point. I'll reconvene before you reach Edenvaile."

The phoenix cocked its head at a hundred-legged bug skittering across the ground.

"He's named you lord commander," Vayle said. "Don't get the wrong idea, though. He's the highlord commander, apparently. One step above you."

"I suppose you'll have to act in my stead, then. And even if I were there, we both know who the true commander is, Vayle. I get our Rots to do the shit I need them to do, but you're always the voice of reason. The true fearless leader. I know you've wanted this for a very long time."

Vayle lifted her brow. "I have never wanted a war."

"Deep down you have. You were born in this world for one reason, and that is to lead. You led your northern girls out of slavery. Led yourself down here and found me. Led us across Mizridahl to find new recruits. You led those recruits and taught them to become the most fearsome assassins this world knows. But you've always wanted something more. I could sense it smoldering inside you, a fire that only death could extinguish. You want to lead the world, to leave your mark on this pitted place.

"Here's your opportunity to march on and dismantle the conjurers, to sap them of morale, to still their wicked hearts, to end their hopes and crush their dreams. Here's your opportunity to play a very large role in saving the world, to show that a lanky slave girl from the North can conquer, to instill hope and courage in those who face a dreadful life like you faced. Here's your chance. Take it, Lord Commander. And run with it."

Her jaw shifted like tumultuous mountains. Then she smiled and said, "See you on the other side, Shepherd."

And she lifted the phoenix high into the air. It flapped its fiery wings and aimed its beak toward the sea.

I turned to the hole in the ground.

Time to empty out the old vault and see what the world had to offer.

CHAPTER TWENTY-FOUR

There were dusty inns, stuffy hovels and dimly lit taverns; there was the taste of sour beer, fruity wine and black smoke; the sounds of harsh voices like heels scraping against unpolished stone, drunken laughs and angry snarls; the feel of smooth gold slipping from my fingers; a weathered hand gripping my own, and depleted eyes flashing to life as the old soul awakens once more.

I bought a horse from a village elder near the Hole, and I rode that mare south to the edge of Nane, stopping in every dusty inn, stuffy hovel and dimly lit tavern I came across. We rode around the border, gold coins clanging in my pouch. I'd reach back and exchange a hundred or two hundred, sometimes even more, for good men, for bad men, for old men, but most importantly for men who had met Death before and knew how to satisfy the bastard Reaper by promising him northern corpses.

I eventually went back to the Hole, stuffed some more coins in my pouch and rode off again, to recruit the blades of more lads and lasses.

The sobering fact was, sellswords weren't going to position Mizridahl for victory. Victory was lost the moment I arrived at Icerun. Without Patrick Verdan at our side, the Verdans would have the might of the North at their disposal. At least forty thousand. Add in another fifteen thousand or so from Edmund's bannermen, and you've got a war in which one side outnumbers the other fifty-five thousand to twenty-some thousand, and that's without the involvement of the conjurers.

Maybe Braddock and Kane Calbid would obliterate the South, but then what? They would have to march on an army that had probably consumed tens of thousands more by that time.

Mizridahl was lost, unless one held on to the hope that Patrick Verdan would appear from the netherworld. I suppose it was that hope, however faint, and the pride of taking down as many of those bastard northernmen, as many as those bloody bannermen who swore allegiance to Edmund… as many as those fucking conjurers as I could that pushed me onward.

After ten days of traipsing around Nane and its nearby provinces, I'd gathered sixty-two mercenaries, fifty-five horses for the mercenaries without them, heaps of wool coats and pants, because apparently sellswords rarely venture North, and four wagons for carrying goods. In all, I had nearly emptied the Black Rot vault. Sellswords aren't exorbitant in Nane, but sixty-two of them will run you a pretty coin, and fifty horses will cost you a pretty chestful of coins. And paying off three messenger camps, now that's expensive.

That payment was not for my previous debt, but rather for yet another favor. Three messenger camps stretched between where Nane meets Rime. I offered fifteen thousand coins to be split between the camps in exchange for any information of caravans leaving Rime on a course for the North.

Vileoux Verdan had a history of silent alliances with minor families in the province. Several years ago, when the Ollesean family waged war against the quickly expanding Wendals, Vileoux supplied the Ollesean army with weapons, armor, food and horses. The Olleseans promptly crushed the Wendals, whose strongholds near Edenvaile gave Vileoux grief. He had a history of similar proxy wars in the past.

There are only two good reasons to dole out favors in this world: to protect your interests, and to stockpile yourself a handsome supply of debts you can call in just in case uncertainty arises in the future. And uncertainty had certainly arisen.

My sellswords and I were at the Hole, readying ourselves for our northern excursion, when under a blistering sun, a horse trotted carefully up the winding ridge of my plump little hill. The messenger's white coat hung over the saddle.

I met him at the jagged edge of the plateau, out of earshot of the mercenaries, who were mostly lying in the grass — who knew sellswords required sunbathing?

The messenger clambered down from his steed. I'd seen him before, at the border camp. He had a dimpled face, broad forehead and stringy hair. He relaxed his hand on the spherical hilt of his sheathed sword and leaned to one side. His name was Alear.

"Your discretion is appreciated," he said. "The messengers *are*, above all else, honorable and free of corruption. I would not want anyone to think otherwise."

I smiled. "Of course they are. And in my mind, they always will be."

"Your gold was not spent in vain," he said. "Two caravans have left the Ollesean stronghold of Ikkyl. They're aimed toward the North." He shifted uncomfortably on his greaves. "Messages have been infrequent lately. There's been talk of the five families using their own couriers for fear of being spotted in a messenger camp and having their messages intercepted. It might be heresy to come to blows with a messenger, but in war everything is heresy. I've heard rumors that war is coming."

"Don't believe everything you hear," I said, patting him appreciatively on the shoulder. "Thank you for the information."

Informing him that his world would end — or *could* end — in twenty days wouldn't be beneficial.

Better to let him live out his days in ignorance than consumed by fear.

He nodded, tapped his hilt and said, "Well, good day to you, Shepherd."

The messenger mounted up and guided his horse back toward the precarious slope, navigating the equally precarious descent with perfection.

I gathered the sellswords up. Sun-kissed faces stared at me, above crisply burnt arms and shoulders. Bastards probably hadn't seen the outside of an inn in over a year. Most sellswords took their gold, drank it away, and then went on off in search of another payment, another drink, till the day their bodies revolted and they dropped dead.

"I have it on good authority," I said, "that a couple Ollesean caravans have left Rime and are en route for Edenvaile. I want ownership of those caravans transferred over to my name. The transfer will be done in blood. You have one hour to collect yourselves. Then we ride."

I didn't care what kind of weapons and armor and supplies the caravans carried. Disrupting a few caravans wouldn't spoil the northern war effort, but their wagons could very well be used to gain entry into the frozen city of Edenvaile.

From within the city walls, Amielle and Sybil and countless others would probably rive the sky, churn the earth, rent the wind. The good soldiers of Watchmen's Bay would suffocate beneath the dirt or have their skulls caved in by falling volcanic rock.

And the battle would end, repeated again soon as Braddock lugged his fat ass up to our graves.

We needed to besiege them, to crumble their walls, to disrupt their peace and eradicate all sense of safety within the city. Send them scrambling... conjure up a little bit of chaos. And the best way in which to lay siege isn't with fancy ladders, thick ropes, sharp hooks, massive rams or powerful trebuchets.

No, it's to become a parasite: infiltrate the city's innards and then annihilate it from the inside out. Explode through its walls like worms through the belly of a pig. Anyone can see a fist coming for their face. But few ever expect to find themselves on their knees while their liver is being eaten alive and their kidneys are being torn asunder, and oh my — what is that wiggling out of my belly button and swelling my stomach?

The sellswords and I marched northeast, across miles of flat grassland with twisted green stalks visited frequently by bees and dragonflies. I'd taken two wagons with us, leaving the other behind at the Hole. They'd be used for greater purposes later.

As we passed into Rime, the sun winked a long goodbye as it rolled behind the Black Mountains. The air got colder and the ground firmer. Soon our horses were trampling on snow, and we dug out the heavy wools from the wagons.

It was day three — more importantly, day thirteen since Dercy's armies would have departed Watchmen's Bay — when we sniffed out a path the messengers cleared, one I assumed the caravan would be taking so as to avoid feet of snow slowing their trek. We followed it North until night fell. In the morning, we were tracking fresh indents of wheels, hooves and boots. Hours later, sometime after we crossed into Edenvaile under a blustery but thankfully dry sky, the stark outline of a gray horse was drawn tightly against a sea of powdery snow.

We clicked our heels, and our horses broke into a gallop.

Swords were drawn as the sight of two covered wagons lolled uneasily along the shoveled path.

There's nothing like hearing steel rasp against leather in an embittered wind — the cold seems to amplify its hauntingly beautiful threat.

A head swiveled in the distance, and then more. Probably thought they were under attack from bandits. As the ominous cloud of bearded mercenaries drew closer, I wondered what they thought. They didn't have much time to sort out their thoughts, in truth. We were on them, circling them like pack-hunting predators, the summits of our swords aimed at their throats.

"No guards?" I said, pulling up on the reins of my horse. She huffed at me and tossed her head back wildly, but obediently came to a stop. "Strange caravan, don't you agree?"

A woman and man sitting in one of the wagons stared ahead, their knuckles white and jaws clenched.

I climbed down from my saddle and approached them. Several horses trailing the caravan trotted my way, their riders brandishing weapons, but the sellswords intercepted them swiftly.

"Ah, there they are," I said. I hopped onto the small wheel of the wagon, gripped the wooden sideboards and peered beyond the frightened carriage drivers, into the bed. "Nice cache you have there." I poked my head in and put my face a few inches away from the woman. "Must be a handsome reward for delivering, oh… what do you think you have? A good three hundred swords, couple pieces of armor? Some other little steel knickknacks."

"Same in this one," said one of my mercenaries who had boarded the other wagon.

"We come from Ikkyl," the woman blurted out. The man next to her looked enraged. She passively held out her hands in attempt to placate him. "We were heading for the great kingdom of Edenvaile."

"I like you," I said. "You don't make me get my hands dirty for good information. But I'm afraid we have a small problem."

"Don't kill us!" she pleaded, her small round face sagging with fear. "I have a girl in Ikkyl, please, sir. *Please.*"

One of the mercenaries licked his lips. "Pretty girl, there. Wot do you think, Astul? Could share her fifteen times before sunset, eh?"

Terror poured into her chest and lungs. I could feel it on her heavy, warm breath. "If I release you," I said, "you will wander into a messenger camp or a nearby village. You'll send word to Ikkyl that your caravan was raided. Ikkyl will send word to Edenvaile, and then I find myself in a heap of trouble."

Her teeth shivered, and her eyes puddled with tears. "I won't. I promise you, swear upon the Pantheon, swear upon my daughter, I won't do that."

"If there is one thing men, women and children all share, it's that they lie."

The girl closed her eyes, hard, jettisoning a tear down her cheek.

The deeper I got in this game, the less I liked it. In my younger days, I'd raided plenty of caravans. Somewhat for the wealth aboard, but mostly for the thrill. My reputation as an assassin preceded me, but I never once put ebon to the throat of an innocent woman or man or child. Because what did it matter if I allowed them to live? I didn't care if they told their fearless vassal or their boastful lady with her furs and jewelry. No one would cross me, and if they did, my agents of death would quickly dispose of them.

But now? Now I had to worry about a fucking lord in some abhorrent stronghold informing a fucking king that the caravan which entered his kingdom carried with it assassins. Vileoux would sniff out my men — my parasites — and so would go my grand siege. I *depended* on people now. People who influenced my actions. People who stripped me of my freedom.

This war couldn't end soon enough, one way or the other.

"Step out," I ordered the drivers.

The woman's nostrils flared, and the dull skin stretching across her forehead tightened. The white of her knuckles glowed like a pale moon, and she snapped the reins. "Go, go!" she screamed.

The two steeds pulling the wagon stumbled forward exhaustedly. Just as the wooden wheels spun in the snow, I lacerated the thin vein that pulsed with excitement on the woman's throat. I pushed the ebon deeper into her soft tissues, crushing and severing muscles and tubes.

She glugged as blood gushed from the flap of flesh my sword had incised, the red warmth surfing down her chest like a ripple of water down a flooded stream.

The man beside her jumped from the wagon and made a run for it. He took about nine steps before a sellsword cut him down and fouled the immaculate snow with the color of strong wine.

A couple mercenaries boarded the second wagon and hurled its occupants, two mustachioed men, out into the snow. The sellswords circled them like vultures, managing a few swift kicks to the drivers' heads before I stopped them.

"End it," I said. "We have an appointment to keep."

Swords were raised, and swords were plunged. No cries, no desperate wails. Just some blood, a petering series of gasps and then a forceful wind blowing through, as if to collect the souls we'd just strewn.

"Look inside the beds," I said. "Take what you want, but make it quick. We're leaving in ten minutes."

Like a flock of birds clamoring for a few morsels of bread, the sellswords pushed and shoved one another at the front of each caravan. They pulled hair, shouted and threatened. They reminded me of my brother and me when we'd spotted what we thought was a gold coin tucked away in a thicket. I punched him in the jaw and leaped on top of it. He picked himself up, dropped an elbow on my head, called me some choice names and kneed me in the ribs until the pain rolled me onto my side. Anton thought he'd won when he had the glittering gold between his fingers, but I bit his knuckle until I tasted blood and heard him scream like a little girl. In the end, what we found for our efforts was not gold but rather a flattened piece of duck shit covered in pollen.

Thankfully, the mercenaries withheld physical violence, and they calmed down after getting their grimy hands on some new iron.

While they inspected their new weapons, I took stock of the goods inside the wagons that lagged behind. Food was still plentiful, if stale and cold, and we still had rows of wine skins, which meant morale would remain stable, unless we had a teetotaler sellsword amongst us, which is a rarity along the lines of seeing a eunuch bending over a whore. After all, if you live to kill, you better have some wine to chase away the nightmares.

But while our goods were well-stocked, the horses did not fare as well. Many were heaving at their sides, heads drooping, nostrils flaring. Their backs and bellies were frothing beneath the saddles, a milky glaze that leaked down their thick coats.

So much for leaving in ten minutes. Half my horses would probably keel over by the time we made it twenty miles farther.

"Stoke some fires," I hollered. "We rest here tonight and leave in the morning."

"Wot about guards?" a man asked. "In case some wanderers or barbarians come looking for a poach."

"Figure it out," I said. "I'm not your fucking father."

I missed my Rots during times like these. The Black Rot was the most organized and lethal fighting force this world had to offer, and I'd back that claim even in the face of the Glannondils' Red Sentinels, the Danisers' Blue Wave, the Verdans' Royal Guard and all the highly specialized killers across Mizridahl. The Rots would never ask silly questions like who was standing guard. It was figured out before the first fire was even lit.

Perhaps I was being too hard on the mercenaries. After all, it is their intrinsic nature to be disorganized buffoons. They're crude fighters, ones who can stab and poke, but asking them to make strategic decisions beyond that is useless. I didn't have time to babysit them, though. I had maps to look at, thoughts to think, a blade to sharpen, and most importantly, wine to drink.

And I drank my wine, and another. Two skins' worth coursing through my veins. I felt pretty fuckin' sloshed as I raked a whetstone up the edge of my dagger, laughing to myself as I dropped the blade for the sixth time in my lap. I picked it up again, held it steady and caught the reflection of a small band of equally drunk sellswords approaching me. They crouched before my fire.

"Thought I'd introduce myself if we're going to be killin' together," a man said. Scars zigzagged across his face, and a dense black beard hung to the middle of his chest. Caught within were flakes of snow and soot and splinters of twigs and crushed leaves.

"Story is Mama called me Art as I popped right out of her, but then she said I looked more like a Pog, so that's my name. Pog."

Two women and three other men huddled around Pog. They introduced themselves in order. There was a Crillean, a Svella, and the others I couldn't remember. Didn't care to remember, either. They weren't my Rots. They were only sellswords. Buy 'em up, put 'em to work, and if they die, then you have simply lost an investment.

I laughed to myself. I liked the way the wine made me feel. Took away all that sentimental shit that wrenched my gut and made me question who I was.

"I like this," Pog said. "It's different for me. For all of us. Assassins like you, they don't hire us. No, we get these pigheaded lords and ladies who haven't seen a real fight in their whole lives. They think they can hold a sword just because their master-at-arms taught them how to parry once or twice. They come to us, lay some gold in our hands, and we follow 'em west and east and south and north, wherever they're goin'. Make sure they get there safely."

"You should hear the stories they tell," Svella said. She rolled her eyes. "One time they drank wine that was sour, and it gave their tummy the cramps."

"A little lord from Sedan bitched about the quality of his boots," Pog bemoaned. "Said he hadn't gotten new ones made in over a year. I told him I'd been wearing the same ones for eight years now. Shut up him real quick. Wealthy fuck probably couldn't even patch a hole in the sole."

I took a swig of wine. "I'm sure they pay well nevertheless."

"Ah," Pog grumbled. "You pay better."

"As I should. Because this may cost you your life."

Pog shrugged. "Don't matter. Makes me feel alive again, camping in the wilds, hunting down caravans, storming walls. I got a savage's heart, Astul.

We all do, including you. We're nothin' but a bunch of ragged monsters loping around in search of blood."

I grinned and took another gulp of wine to the face.

"I've heard some tales about you," Pog said, "don't tell me they're not true."

"The better a tale sounds," I said, "the taller it likely is."

"Heard you were a murderer," Pog said.

"Assassin," I corrected. "Murderers are novices. You would never call a seasoned blacksmith an apprentice, would you?"

Pog flicked away debris from his beard. "That's all fine and good, but still stands that you're responsible for lots o' graves. Also heard you were a liar."

"Who hasn't spun a story once in a while?" I retorted.

"And a thief."

"Occasionally I have borrowed items and not returned them," I confessed.

"And a kidnapper."

"When the job calls for it, I suppose."

"A broken, disparaged monster just like us," Pog said. "But gods, it's not our fault. Some of us were born to the wrong name, destined to plow fields. Some were pulled aside as little boys and girls by their lords, forced to sing songs, serve the nobles and maybe even forced to suck a few cocks. Some of us were captured by slavers, run ragged till we escaped. Life has chewed us up, Astul. Chewed us up, ground us into real mushy morsels, and then spat us out into what we are now. All we got left is to take as much revenge as we can before we eat some dust and take the eternal nap. That's why we kill, pillage, rape — to take from others what was taken from us."

Svella had a smile on her face that spread to the other mercenaries. They all nodded their heads as Pog talked, as if he was reciting their motto.

"Had a little princess approach me a few weeks ago," Pog said. "Thirteen, maybe a few months older. She got separated from her lord father on a journey west. She had lots of gold on her, asked for my help in reuniting her." He grinned maniacally and swept his snakelike tongue across his teeth. "I put her up on my horse, and we rode about twenty miles into the deep woods. She was clutchin' my waist like she wanted it, pressing her little nubs against my back. So I stopped before a great big oak.

"Climbed down off my steed, and I reached up and put my fingers around her pretty little throat. Stripped her naked, threw her on the forest floor and I fucked her till she bled for the first time in her life. Took that princess's innocence and I wrapped it around my cock and slammed it into her. By the time the sun rose, she had crusted thighs, and she was damn near bloating with my seed. With teary eyes and a hoarse voice, she asked me why. And I looked at her, and I told her, 'Because you need to know what it

feels like to be me. To be empty, ravaged and lifeless.'
She called me a monster, and I thanked her, then I
took her gold and left her to wilt."

"Well," I said, "your reputation *is* everything."

"That it is."

I took a final swig of wine. "If you'll excuse me,
I need to rest. Long road tomorrow."

"I can't wait to kill me some Verdans," Pog
said, smiling. He picked himself up and walked away.
The remaining mercenaries followed him like cattle.

I looked beyond the spitting flames of my
campfire and followed the splash of blinking stars
that threaded themselves into the fabric of the night
like flashing buttons, all the way up, till I was lying on
my back.

I thought about the story Pog told. I'd heard a
lot worse over the years — spend a few nights among
drunks in a tavern and you'll get your fill of horror —
but it gave me pause, which was something the wine
was supposed to prevent. I wasn't like the sellswords.
I still had people to live for and a cause for which to
fight. But if those were stolen from me… what would
I be capable of?

The Astul I knew, the one I strived to become
again, was no monster. A bold man, yes. Cold and
cutthroat, yes. Merciless, often times. But murder,
lying, stealing, kidnapping — they were the tools of
my trade, not acts of impetuosity carried out under
the very dangerous and always-shifting guise of
revenge. But if I had nothing meaningful to fight for,

and everyone I cared about was gone tomorrow, would I become Pog? If I was emptied out, ravaged and lifeless, would I become a monster like him?

I'd seen enough good men succumb to insanity that I already knew the answer.

There was a chance I wouldn't die in this war. Maybe I'd take an arrow to the back or a club to the head. Dercy's army would retreat from the Edenvaile walls, desperate to live another day, and they'd take me with them. Or maybe the North and the conjurers would take me prisoner. One way or another, I'd live in a world that wasn't mine any longer. I'd look for revenge. I'd look for ways to strip those of the life that had been taken from me. I'd become a monster.

I reached deep into my pocket and eased a finger along a tiny bottle I'd brought from the Hole. It calmed my racing heart, and if I opened the cap and I tilted the oily liquid down my throat… it would still my racing heart. It would thicken my blood, idle my thoughts. It was the only certainty I had that I would never become a monster.

I slid my fingernail beneath the cap, popping it off.

I licked my lips and I laughed.

Then I replaced the cap and closed my eyes, for tomorrow would be a long, hard day, and it would be immeasurably longer and unfathomably harder if I had to go through it dead.

CHAPTER TWENTY-FIVE

A mercenary by the name of Logan stood back, hacksaw in hand, proudly admiring his work.

"Clean cut," he said.

There were a few sniggers amongst the sellswords, and after poking my head inside the wagon I saw why.

I blinked, hoping that with each shutter of my eyelashes, a new vision would appear before me. "Logan," I said, "we're going to play a game. Are you ready?"

"Er. Sure."

"It's called yes or no. You told me you were adept at woodworking. Yes or no?"

"Yes."

"You understand what the word adept means. Yes or no?"

"Of course."

"And you know what woodworking means. Yes or no?"

His eyes creased. "What're you tryin' to get at here?"

I peered inside the wagon again. Logan was supposed to cut the bed out of the wagon so we could place a false bed below for four or five sellswords to lie inside. A new plank of wood would be fitted on top, ideally in perfect alignment with the original, so that when the Edenvaile city guard glanced inside, they wouldn't suspect a thing. Logan, however, had decided to make this problematic.

"Well," Logan said, "you can't expect perfect precision."

"Some semblance of precision would be wonderful," I said. "You're about as precise at cutting a straight line as a virgin is at fucking. 'Am I hitting the right spot? No, how about now? Over here, maybe? What about this side?'"

The mercenaries slapped their thighs as they hurled out booming laughs.

"I'll fix 'er up," one of them said. "I used to build walls as a lad."

"Hopefully you didn't practice under the same master as Logan over here," I said.

The former carpenter went to work salvaging what he could of Logan's hack job. By the end of his sawing, hammering, whacking, clawing, swearing and knuckle-busting, he delivered a passable false bed, so long as the Edenvaile city guard didn't examine it too thoroughly.

He then repeated the process on the second wagon.

When he finished, the morning sun was a ripened melon gushing with flavor and spilling its orange juices across the crystallized landscape. A sun like that ought to put some warmth in your bones, but here in the grasp of winter — beginning of spring or not throughout the rest of Mizridahl, it was always winter here — it was just a pretty bulb in the sky that sometimes blinded you.

The groups were set. The eight sellswords who would hide inside the false beds — four in each — wiggled their way in. A flat sheet of wood covered them, on which the promised delivery of weapons and armor was piled. The drivers were chosen based on who best resembled the Ollesean people — at least that was the reason I gave to placate the unrest that broke out amongst those who deeply wanted to have the lead roles. In truth, I had about as much knowledge of the average Ollesean person as I did of naked mole rat hierarchy. Were they all pasty white like those we butchered? Were their women all so slender and shrill? And surely their men couldn't have been so old and frail. Who knows? Hopefully not the Edenvaile city guard.

I put Pog in charge of the mercenaries who would sneak inside the walls. The man was disgusting, vile and, yes, utter filth, but he seemed like a man who could lead. A man who could get things done, particularly when those things included chopping off heads.

We marched off toward the North, the lot of us, but only for another night. The morning after, the caravan with two wagons continued on, toward the gates of Edenvaile.

The fifty-some sellswords I retained devoured a stew of cabbage and boiled bread heated over a large campfire. After their bellies were full, I rounded them up.

"I paid for your swords," I said, "but now I need your eyes and ears."

I unfolded a large map I had taken from the Hole, and I flattened it over the frozen snow. I struck my fist at the eastern border of Rime.

"Edmund Tath's bannermen will be coming through the Widowed Path, here." I glanced up and scanned the mercenaries. I pointed at ten of them. "Let's call you boys and girls… spy group one."

"That's a shat name," one of them remarked. "What about the Eagles?"

"The Eagles?"

"Yeah, yeah. The Eagles. 'Cause eagles fly around all silently, you know? See things that no one else sees, like spies do."

Some heads turned, most of them cocked to the side.

"The eastern spies," a woman said.

I snapped my fingers. "There you go, the eastern spies." I looked at Mr. Bird Brains. "*Fucking eagles.*"

"Better than fucking spy group one," he shot back.

"All right," I said. "So you jolly lads and two ladies will position yourselves here." I trailed my fingernail just beneath the mouth of the Widowed Path. "Some hills, forests, places to hide about. This is day seventeen — remember that. I need you to return on day twenty-six. Go due west of here till you see an army that looks like a mobile city. You'll find me there."

One of the sellswords cleared his throat. "What're we supposed to do there in the, er, forests and hills and all that?"

A woman turned to him in disbelief. "Are you shtupid? We're the eastern spies. We're spying."

"I want to hear about every soul who passes through the Widowed Path," I said. "What they're wearing, carrying and how many of them there are. Watch yourselves for roving bands of soldiers who try to sniff out scouts."

I organized another ten and ordered them to scout near the Mount Kor, at the far southwest of Rime. Another ten would remain here in the hills on lookout for Ollesean forces and other families who were in debt to the Verdans. Finally, the remaining twenty-some mercenaries would come with me, simply because I had overcompensated and bought too damn many of the sellswords.

The scouting groups took what supplies they needed to survive. I grabbed what I could and abandoned the wagons because lugging them around would slow us down, and they weren't necessary any longer. And then I fled south. And then east. And then south. Back to the east. A little toward the west, and then south again. It's bloody annoying traveling across mountainous terrain.

On day nineteen, I made it to the Hole. There, I gathered up the ebon blades that Borgart had crafted, loaded them up into two wagons and left again.

On day twenty-three, I established contact with the armies of the gods. At least it looked that way. Felt it too.

The rolling hills of ugly gray bedrock wavered under the roiling blight that swept over them. Thunder rumbled the rocks and fractured the air, splitting the thick humidity like an ax splits wood, dousing your skin in a cold sweat. It wasn't the kind of thunder that strikes without warning, the kind that seemingly cleaves your ears in two and then retreats like a yapping dog. No, this thunder was constant. A low, relentless throaty roar that pimpled your skin. It wasn't a threat, but a promise.

It looked a mountain shifting across the landscape, leaving behind disrepair and toil. There were pikes aimed toward the heavens, spears glinting as the moon and sun played a game of hide-and-seek. Thousands of foot soldiers marched at the head, and behind them archers, and behind the archers trotted the cavalry, the proudest of them all.

My sellswords and I remained on the small hill overlooking the foreboding scene below. We waited for a good hour and finally the horizon of muscular horse flanks and sharp armor abated. Oxen came into view, hauling innumerable wagons of coveted supplies. The logistics of war can boggle the mind. Ensuring you have enough food for twenty thousand men and some five thousand horses is no small matter. Those who plan accordingly can win a war against a much larger force without so much as swinging a sword.

Well, perhaps not if you're laying siege to a castle which has enough supplies for a good six months. You certainly need to swing a sword in that case.

I waited for night to fall, and when it did, Dercy's army predictably settled down and set up camp. I led the mercenaries down steep earthen steppes and rode for the middle of the army, just behind the cavalry, where the officers would gather. Thin drops of water fell from the sky now, soaking my hair.

A handful of cavalry met me midway, dressed in royal blue tunics with a Tyrian purple crest of a shark. They demanded my name and intentions. Despite me giving them both, they eyed me suspiciously and informed me I would follow them to Commander Vayle and that if I or my men put a hand on our weapons, they wouldn't hesitate to strew our entrails across the dirt.

"Well," I said, "you bunch certainly have more gusto than Glannondil soldiers, don't you?"

They ignored that and led me through the suffocating walls of their army. One of fog or steam snaked lazily across the ground, rising up slowly around us like we were boiled fish in a covered pot. Judging from the sweat that dripped from my fingers, we may well have been.

Most of the cavalry were resting beside their horses, eating hardened crackers and washing it down with small sips of wine. I'd eaten those crackers before — you bite down too hard, and you'll be eating a tooth as well.

Slaves in rags had the joyful backbreaking duties of digging latrines and fetching supplies from the wagons far in the back. They weren't new to this kind of work; their spines were misaligned, their shoulders were permanently slouched, and their knuckles were swollen and busted. Most were likely prisoners serving their punishment.

Finally we came upon a mishmash of purple tents illuminated by hungry torches whose receding fires fought a losing battle against the rain.

The cavalry stopped in front of one of these tents.

"Lord Commander Vayle," a soldier announced, "there is someone who claims you will see him."

With her chocolate hair pinned up and a quill in her ear, Vayle emerged from the tent. She had a spry smile on her face, undoubtedly amused. If she really wanted to fuck with me, she'd say, 'Take him away!'

"That man," Vayle said, "was chosen as the true lord commander by your king."

Each of the cavalry straightened themselves.

"I'm sorry, sir," one of them said. "It was with no ill intention that—"

"Pipe down with that proper 'sir' shit," I said. "Listen, there'll be two wagons coming into the camp soon. They're bringing a special delivery for the war effort. Direct them here when they arrive."

"Yes, si— I mean, yes."

The cavalry scattered.

"Look at you," I said to Vayle. "Quill in your ear, hair tied up, bags under your eyes. Correct me if I'm wrong, but it looks to me like you just finished interrogating a map."

Vayle smiled a tired smile — the kind of smile you flash with your eyes closed, while you rock back on your feet, thinking how nice it would be to fall asleep right then and there.

"War planning," she said with a shake of her head. "I haven't worked my mind this hard in a long time." A faint smirk touched her lips, as if she had just dipped her toes into a hot bath.

"It's like planning an assassination," I said. "Just on a much larger scale."

"*Much* larger," she said. She pointed her chin at the sellswords. "Who are they?"

"Some of the mercenaries the vault of the Rot paid for."

"What do you do?" she asked them, immediately stepping back into her commander role.

"We kill!" Ivor said. Then quickly, "If you want us to. We also protect."

"Which usually involves killing," I reminded him.

"I understand what a mercenary is," Vayle said, "but *what* do you do? Are you cavalry? Foot soldiers? Archers?"

"Anything but archers," Ivor said.

Vayle wiped the dripping rain from her brows. "Join the men on foot up front. Leave your horses here."

After they were gone, Vayle invited me inside her personal tent. We walked to a table where a few candles flicked a mellow orange into the room. There was also a map on top of a map on top of about ten other maps.

"Does someone have a cartography fetish?" I asked.

Vayle leaned over the table. "I marked up the other ones too much."

She picked the quill from her ear and laid it in the inkwell, then she rubbed her face and stared at the map, clicking her tongue.

There were ink lines… everywhere. It looked like someone had stabbed the night sky and then squeezed out every ounce of black blood it had to offer.

"I'll be honest," I said. "I've no idea what I'm looking at."

Vayle sighed. She bent down, grabbed another map from beneath the table and unfurled it on top of the others.

"Dercy and I have been working on this since we landed in Watchmen's Bay. I think I've finally broken through with something."

"Er, where is Dercy?"

"Sleeping," Vayle answered. "He hasn't slept in three days. And I haven't slept in two." Her eyes slanted upwards toward mine. "It's my turn tomorrow." Revisiting the map, she drummed her nail on Edenvaile. "Northern castles are nightmares to lay siege to. All the mountains and hills act as walls. The reinforcements hide behind them. When the wounded and the dead pile up in the castle and in the field, the reinforcements pour out like ants, and they resupply. Anywhere else, where the terrain isn't as fierce, the entire army often gathers within the castle. If you can manage a good rush at the wall and send soldiers over, you create chaos. There's no time to issue orders or catch the attackers by surprise.

"But the North — they'll time it perfectly. They'll wait until your men are over, and then they'll send in an overwhelming force to flush you out. It's a battle of attrition, and that never favors the attacker."

Vayle looked at me with an inclining brow and crossed her arms.

I cleared my throat. "Ah, yes. The ever-clever resupply tactic of the North. One that you always have to prepare for, hmm?"

She chuckled. "Dercy admitted that he gave you — and then me — the title of lord commander as nothing more than a reward for our help in rescuing him. It would give us little influence over the war. It wasn't until I offered better strategies than all of his officers and held better sway with his men that the title gave me the power the name represented. And I think my newest scheme will justify that decision. Do you remember Grimm, a lord at the border of Nane and Rime?"

"Grimm… Grimm…" I searched my mind for the name. "Ah, the sheep fucker? No, no, that was someone else. Grimm…"

"You, me and Big Gruff assassinated his wife and her three secret lovers."

I snapped my fingers in recognition. "Oh, that was a good one. Funny bastard, that one. Had a good sense of humor to him. Well, after we brought him the head of his wife and the cocks of her lovers."

"I wrote him a letter recently, requesting any help he could spare. Unsurprisingly, he could promise no soldiers."

"He could if he really wanted to," I said. "But his liege — who is it, Lord... I can't remember his name — probably wouldn't appreciate it."

Vayle opened a fresh skin of wine and threw it back for a good three seconds. She smacked her lips and sighed refreshingly. "Probably not. But he *does* have something else waiting for us in his village. A battering ram."

"What the fuck is a little village vassal doing with a battering ram?"

Vayle laughed and drank more. "Claims he has had it for twenty years. During a weeklong bender, he drew up plans to invade his liege's stronghold. He bought the ram and ladders, then sobered up. It's been sitting in his armory ever since."

"Dercy didn't think to bring a battering ram or other siege equipment? Seems like a necessity when you're laying siege."

"Six hundred miles is a long way to carry siege equipment. It would not make it."

I snatched the skin of wine from her table and gulped some. "Before you inform me of your grand plan that involves this ram, allow me to divulge my plan. It's much simpler. There will be mercenaries inside Edenvaile. When I give the word, they will butcher as many archers as they can."

428

"Excellent," Vayle said. "That means I don't need to waste as many footmen as fodder." She removed the wet quill from its well and began drawing circles and lines and arrows.

"Every foot soldier will be here, all fifteen thousand of them. One-third of the cavalry will remain behind, here, and an equal amount of archers will idle on the sides, here. In the middle of the infantry is the ram." She drew three long lines toward Edenvaile. "The infantry will march toward the gate, shields over their heads, protecting themselves and the ram carriers, who will be marching with them. When the cavalry and footmen pour from Edenvaile, we deploy our cavalry to the wings, meeting them. The ram will hammer at the gate and—"

"Vayle," I said.

"And hopefully with your sellswords cutting down the archers from above and all the panic on the field—"

"Vayle…"

She frantically tapped her finger on the map. "The ram will level the gate. From there, we—"

"Vayle…"

Barely taking a breath, she continued. "We swarm the castle, flood it with everybody we have, push back, dismember and kill every northernman we come across, create chaos, force the reinforcements to retreat, and then we gather on the walls, fortify the rear gate and we hold the castle. We take it. We become the defenders. Maybe we can kill or capture

Vileoux, Sybil, Chachant, Mydia, someone. We can turn the tide. We can—"

I slammed my hands on the table. "Vayle! For fuck's sake, breathe."

My commander's uncharacteristic excitement abated as she regathered herself and took a drink. "I've been at this for three weeks now. It's testing my sanity."

"All I hear is the northernmen this, the northernmen that. What about the conjurers, Vayle? You can outwit and outsmart and outduel the northernmen, I trust that. I don't know if it will be enough to compensate for the two-to-one disadvantage we have in available men, but I'll share your positivity and say it can. But none of this accounts for the sway the conjurers will bring to this war. You haven't seen the will of a conjurer buckle the earth and make it quake, but I have. You haven't seen a conjurer compel the wind to come alive and thrash about like a wicked sea, but I have. You haven't heard their voice rape your mind, silence your thoughts and instill their desires inside your soul. But I have. How do you account for that? How do you defeat something like that?"

Vayle folded her hands on the table. "In the past, there were only a few who could control the elements."

"All it takes is a few."

She played a grating melody with her gnashing teeth, and then pushed herself away from the table. "I know that," she said, the optimism from her voice falling away like cheese from a grater.

"It's not as if we can't give courage and hope a try," I said, feeling somewhat shameful that I'd once again driven my commander into those awful pits of dismay. Not a good place to be in, and it feels even worse when someone leads you there. She was a very intelligent woman who undoubtedly knew her plan had no regard for the conjurers. She likely didn't need me to throw in that bit of information.

"It's a question I have no answers to," she said, her back still turned. "How *do* you account for an enemy you've seen in only small skirmishes, whose tactics are not written in books, whose weaknesses are as invisible to you as the land they hail from?" She hung her head.

"This isn't a war we can win. I understand. But it feels wasteful, Astul. It feels wasteful to ignore the good life I still have and not prepare for the battle ahead like I would if victory was kneeling inside those walls, waiting for me. It feels wasteful not to mount an assault that will eliminate as many of those who make us hurt as possible, if only in the name of justice.

"I know that justice means little to you. But it is the only pursuit that has fully governed my life, and if I must die pursuing it, then... it must be a good death, yes?"

Her words were faint and shallow, dripping out of her mouth like water from a thawing cube of ice. I sidestepped the table and snuck up behind her, taking her softly by the shoulders.

"Most agree that I'm not a good man much of the time. But you are a great woman, Vayle. The world will surely miss you more than it misses me. If we both must bid this place goodbye in the coming days, I could take no greater pleasure in death than standing beside you as the Reaper comes swinging his scythe. You are my friend, Vayle. My partner in this dark world. It's not love that binds us, and I'm glad. Because love is wild and unpredictable, here one moment and gone the next, so rarely sustained for eternity. No, it's respect that brought us together. Unbreakable respect, like rock forged in deep, abandoned caves where the pressure and heat of long-forgotten molten lava had molded mountains and walls, invulnerable and immortal."

Vayle turned in my arms, her head lolling to the side. She straightened herself and withdrew her ebon blade, just as I withdrew mine. We threw them on the table.

The blue of her eyes swirled around like turbulent winds. She tucked her fingers beneath my belt and wound me in.

"We have eight days on this world," she said, unclasping my buckle. "Let us extract what pleasure we can." She winked uncharacteristically and added, "Not for love nor for respect. Not for anything but the savage and the primal... the finer things in life.

Like we used to, before this world spun out of control."

Some call it making love, but I preferred the time-worn term of fucking. It sounds rawer, animalistic, the perfect word for the obscene manner in which we stripped each other of clothes, the filthy way we ran our hands up each other's body, mine over the humps of her pale breasts and hers down the length of my bulging cock, the unscrupulous sounds of kissing and sucking, of moaning and crying, of flesh slapping flesh, of gasps and thrusts.

Vayle and I did not make love. We fucked. And it was good, great, even, as it always was. While her loins ached after, my heart cried out in pain. I did not wish to leave this world quite yet. It was a good world, all things considered. Lots of wine still to taste, lots of assassinations to be carried out, lots of gold to stuff in my vault. Hells, maybe even another friend still to make — much like the friendship Tylik and I had struck.

Where was he now? If his gods existed and they were finally tired of playing cruel jokes, maybe they'd swept him far away from the conjurers. Far away to a sandy shore, where the sun always shined and the sea was always blue and the fish were plentiful. A shore where you didn't need feet to get around, only knees and hands. He could crawl about until old age finally took him, feasting on crabs and fish until his belly could fit no more.

I fell asleep on that note, my arm over Vayle's shoulder, cradling her breasts.

A heavy pulse of chaotic noise awakened me sometime later. I'd been asleep for precisely the amount of time it takes you to question whether you have slept for two hours or twenty-two.

Vayle sprung up like a suicidal woman upon a pyre who just ascertained the meaning to life, which was: your woes may never go away, and you may well slip farther into the void, but *fuck* fire burns.

"What's going on out there?" she asked, stabbing a pair of fingers into her sleepy eyes.

I yawned. "A party, perhaps?"

She spun around the room like a cyclone late for its appointment to level a small village, snatching up her clothes and attempting to put them all on at the same time. "I'm in charge here while Dercy's sleeping. If we're being attacked..."

Oh, right, I thought, *we're in the middle of a war camp*.

That sudden realization shook the swampy grogginess from my mind. I jumped up and got dressed alongside Vayle.

Two men burst through the tent, clad in full plate armor, immediately turning their attention elsewhere as Vayle was still naked from the waist up.

"Commander Vayle," one of them said. "A fiery bird swooped down from the mountains. It made landfall approximately half a mile outside of the infantry. There were two men on it. One of them claims he is here to see the Black Rot, and if luck would have it, its shepherd."

Vayle and I traded glances.

"What are their names?" Vayle asked.

"My Lord Commander, that information was not relayed to us. The patrols did, however, inform us that one of the men upon the bird is missing his toes."

CHAPTER TWENTY-SIX

The impact of disbelief can be felt in several places: in your racing heart that you may, depending on the improbability of what has just transpired, paradoxically feel in both your stomach and throat, but strangely not your chest. In your mouth, which will often delude you into believing your lips, tongue and the inside of your cheeks have turned into a sandy desert which no water will ever moisten again. You can feel disbelief in your eyes, which tend to bulge and stretch in ways eyes are advised not to bulge and stretch. You can feel it in muscles that seize and tremor and your shaky fingers that make it quite difficult to properly hold a sword.

But you feel it most prominently in your mind. Upon seeing or hearing or smelling or feeling or tasting something so utterly unlikely, the large spongy thing inside your skull has but two choices: end all of its processes, which I believe accounts for fifty

percent of all sudden deaths, or accept the fact that
life is a very funny bastard sometimes.

I coughed out a dry laugh so massive, it forced
one half of my heart back down my throat and
punched the other half back out of my stomach,
framing it as a whole piece in my chest once again.

"You're a fucking crippled magician!" I cried,
running forward and embracing Tylik. Mister No
Toes was riding like a child on his nephew's back. I
relieved Karem from his plight and carried Tylik over
to a chair, sitting him down.

He seemed so much more broken in the light.
One eye was nearly sealed shut, with bright pink
pustules clinging to the lid. Profound black ovals, like
severe bruises that could never quite heal, dotted his
forehead and cheeks and arms and legs. He was
balding in some areas, with stringy hair in others and
a misplaced lush mane zigzagging across his temple.
The rot of his missing toes looked much improved,
however. Gone was the wretched green slime and
inky leakage.

"I've heard some good fucking stories over the
past few weeks," I said, "but I think yours is going to
top all of them. How the piss did you get here,
Tylik?"

Tylik coughed up a wet ball of mucous, which
he quickly swallowed. "It's a story all right, and a
good one! Me and Karem here, we heard the horses
come tramplin' after us in the woods that night we

broke free. Took 'em a good long while, though, didn't it, Karem?"

Karem reclined as much as a stiff wooden chair allowed a man to recline and put a skin of wine to his lips. He sighed, tilted his head up and said, "Mm hmm."

"Luckily for us," Tylik said, "we weren't bouncin' up and down on some horses. Might be quick, y'know, riding on saddles, but anyone with half a brain in 'em can track those big paws in the mud. So anyways, we hide out behind some trees, inchin' our way through the forest when the sound of racing hooves quieted, and then darting behind more trees when they returned. My poor nephew damn near broke his back carrying me. Tryin' to shorten this story up now, but lots of things transpired. Biggest one of 'em all, I'd say, happened when we reached a little village tucked away inside a bosom of a mountain. How long it take us to reach, Karem?"

A soft snore burbled through the tent.

"Karem?"

No answer.

"Karem!" Tylik hollered.

Karem jerked sideways and spilled a pool of wine in his lap. "Bah!" he spat. "What? I'm tired, Uncle."

"How long did it take us to reach Dorral?"

"Four days."

"Four days!" Tylik said exuberantly, holding four of his skeletal fingers up. "And that was with the help of a friendly merchant who wagoned us on up there most of the way. So we get there and — now, this is the village my family ran away to, see? Don't want to confuse you. So we get there and I reunite with my little children, who are now big children, and I see my wife again, and it's the greatest moment of this broken man's life. But I can't rest. I know that. My wife says it was some god who gave me another chance, but... but I know it was you, Astul. You and Karem. I couldn't sit on my hands now. I was given the opportunity to do somethin', and I was gonna do it."

The massive, goofy smile on my face seemed stuck there perpetually as Tylik talked. It was a strange feeling, being happily sucked back into a past in which I should have held absolutely no nostalgia for — a past where I slept against a pillar, where iron clasps gnawed at the flesh of my ankles and wrists, where a friendly voice helped me through the dark days and the sightless nights. Of course, it was also a past that had hope, however minuscule and however fleeting.

"Allow me a guess," I said. "You made good on your promise to do something with that opportunity by procuring a phoenix?"

Tylik erupted into a coughing fit. The sickly pustules on his eyelids bobbed up and down like stitching needles as his body convulsed. He regathered himself and cleared his throat.

"If only it was that easy. See, word had gotten around that the conjurers had taken a wee little village a small ways up north. According to some good merchants, it was pretty bare, not a lot of protection. Still, put us in lots of danger. We could have been next. So I convinced all the strong men and women to put on their boots and grab hold of the sharpest things they could. We were goin' to war. Bless the hearts of the kids, they wanted to help too. Put some slingshots in their hands, wrapped 'em in good quilted armor, and we marched north."

"A farmers' march, hmm?" Vayle said.

"Oh, we were more than farmers," Tylik said, his nose scrunched up and his one good eye lowered. "Butchers, dyers, tanners, saddlers, blacksmiths, armorers, grandpas, grandmas, fathers, mothers, fierce protectors, angry freemen. We were much more than farmers."

The jovial tone always present in his words was strangled by an undercurrent of hatred and loathing.

"And we showed them conjurer bastards what good old-fashioned justice is all about. Not one of 'em was left standing." His eye began to twitch, and his lips tightened. "Not one 'em had a head left on their shoulders!"

"And the phoenix?" I asked.

"Two of 'em were there," Tylik said, the tenseness in his shoulders and face slipping away. "Used those big fiery birds to take everyone way, way far away, to the sand. See, we hadn't heard squat about conjurers bringin' villagers from the beaches around the East, so that's where we went. Then Karem and I, well, we knew we couldn't just well stay there. What if the conjurers won this war you were talkin' about? They'd be everywhere! Like the clouds in the sky! So we took a phoenix, hoped I remembered correctly that you said Mizridahl lay to the south, and we steered her that way."

Vayle stood. She had a curious look about her. "How did you defeat the conjurers?"

Tylik waited for her to continue on, but when it became apparent that was her only question, he said, "Well, we swung sharp things across their throats."

My commander contemplated this for a moment. "Did the ground not move under your feet? Did things not fall from the sky? I know for a fact some of them can bend the elements to their will."

"Oh, yes, yes," Tylik said. "A few of them can, seen it myself more than I'd care to admit. But most of those under the conjurer banner, they're just like your soldiers outside here. They swing swords and sing songs while they march. Now the actual conjurers themselves, they pick at your mind and do terrible things to it. Or great things, as they would have you believe. The ones who can move the earth and all that wickedness, no... there aren't many. Stuff like that can kill you, did you know that? Seen it once before. Young man tried to make the earth swallow a rabbit, and his head *exploded*! Swear it did!

"By the gods, I bet you even the queen Amielle would only be able to open up the sky once or twice — and only for a short while — before her mind would be so tired, she couldn't tell you the difference between a donkey and a cow. 'Course, with the sudden lack of donkeys and cows in the past thirty years, not a lot of people could. 'Least on my world."

"It won't take much to turn the war clearly in their favor," Vayle said. "We're already severely outnumbered."

Tylik appeared confused. "But I am not done sharing my story. I recalled Astul telling me while we both suffered in that awful dungeon that a man by the name of Patrick Verdan was the key to winning this war. He was somewhere in the North, but as Karem and I discovered, the North is a very big place. But people here are very accommodating and will answer most questions you have, as long as they don't see the fiery bird you arrived on. Stuffed to the brim with directions, we flew toward and eventually landed in a place so cold and snowy, I could not breathe. And I talked to this very elusive Patrick Verdan."

"When?" I asked.

"Oh, has to be about four weeks ago now, I'd say. 'Course, I talked to him just yesterday too."

"What's he doing away from his kingdom?" I asked.

Tylik cleared his throat. "He's preparing for a very large war."

Justin DePaoli

CHAPTER TWENTY-SEVEN

The architect of fear is hope. Without hope, without the possibility of a better tomorrow, what is there to fear? The best outcome and the worst are one and the same — either way, you've got no fucking chance. So you go out with one last spectacular showing, that one last prodigious burst of light that flares as bright as a meteor streaking across a dark sky before the night smothers it.

Six days ago, I had no fear. Regret for having to leave this world, sure. But not fear. And then Tylik comes, reveals a little secret and pumps me full of hope once again. A hope that intensified when the sellswords who served as spies informed me four days ago that no one had crossed the Widowed Path. That meant Edmund Tath's bannermen weren't arriving in Edenvaile, at least not on time.

Hope cut through me like an ebon blade on the thirtieth day of the march. It was probably a day fitting of the brumal North. In all likelihood, the clouds were low and thick and chunky with the color of sour milk and smoke. Probably wasn't any sun, because this place didn't fuckin' deserve it. Snow was probably falling — tears from the poor bastard gods who had to watch over this pathetic land.

Or maybe the sun did come out. Maybe it burned abnormally hot, melting the flakes as they fluttered down and stuck to the brims of helmets. Maybe you could smell the sweetness of grass thawing beneath the ice as the last days of winter retreated.

Maybe, possibly, probably — I couldn't tell you what the weather was like. Hope had cut me open, and just as decay settles inside a fresh wound, fear weaseled its way in. Couldn't tell you what the weather was like because I had the shakes. Had the grumbles in my stomach and the booming percussions of thumps and thuds in my heart. Had the crushing doubts, the what-ifs, the don't-you-dare-fuck-ups racing through my mind.

Couldn't tell you what the weather was like because who has the fucking time to look toward the sky when an enormous wall of stone and crenellations, of legs and arms, of bows and arrows, of thin eyes and tight lips, of people who just want you bloody fucking dead — who has the time to look toward the sky when you're staring at that?

I stood at the forefront with Vayle and Dercy and a few other officers, far out of range of the archers. I had nothing to say, no advice to give, no real reason to show my face up there. It was all about selfish curiosity, a twisted thirst for what war was all about.

See, assassinations are one-and-done. You kill a single man, maybe a couple more here and there, but it's small stuff. War, though? It's big. Massive. Incomprehensible and imperceptible. Fifteen thousand infantry stood behind me. Swords at their sides, pikes pointed toward the heavens. Their stoic faces looked chiseled from stone. The absence of terror in their eyes wouldn't last. In even the best scenario, half of them would be trying to stuff their guts back inside their bellies and choking on blood as arrows punctured their lungs. Over seven thousand men dead. More than likely it would be ten thousand, twelve thousand, possibly every last one of them.

The mind can't possibly reconcile the scale of obliteration that war delivers. At least mine couldn't.

A voice as chilling as the frost that thickened the air sailed across the field. It came from the balcony that had hosted Sybil and Chachant's grand wedding.

"Lay down your weapons," Vileoux Verdan said, "and I will allow these men to march peacefully back to their homes. My grievance is with you, Dercy, not the innocent souls you bring to my walls."

Dercy responded, but I didn't listen to his words. It was all a formality, and I was more interested in identifying those who joined Vileoux on the balcony. Unsurprisingly, Chachant and Sybil stood by his side. Farther on down the line were a few men and women I'd never seen before — conjurers, undoubtedly. But the tall, slender gal who centered this little gathering… oh, I'd seen her before.

Her voice had once echoed inside my skull. Her dungeon had nearly broken me. Her arena murdered my friends. They called her the queen of the conjurers. I'd never killed a queen before. It was time to change that.

I turned the reins of my horse over in my hands, guiding her back through the horde of shields and leather and mail and swords and pikes and axes that gathered in square clusters of forty deep and forty wide. The glint of silver stretching across the field probably looked like stalks of freshly planted white sage to a hawk.

Although the hawk would question what a couple of wooden beams mounted upon wheels were doing in a field of foliage. That, of course, was the weapon of the day — the big-ass battering ram Vayle had procured. The ram itself sat idle above the wheels, suspended by chains. A canvas canopy enclosed it, stitched with cold, wet hides that would have a good chuckle at any fire-laced arrows the North would hurl from their wall.

My mare trotted past it, past the remaining infantry and beyond the archers who stacked behind, arrows already nocked, fingers nervously prodding the twine.

A small distance behind the archers, Dercy's remaining officers gathered, along with Tylik and his nephew. It was also where my Rots made their stay. We'd sit tight until we were needed.

My mare reared around and faced the Rots, who were seated on their horses. There were twenty-one of us in all. Vayle had managed to round up the few who'd combed through the Golden Coast in search of a usurper, but there was no time to bring back the ones who had gone to Hoarvous. I wondered what they were doing there now. Perhaps they were responsible for the lack of Edmund Tath's bannermen, against all odds.

"Fuck me," Slick said. "Thought I'd gotten away from this shit years ago."

Slick wasn't a particularly stealthy assassin. He'd gotten captured more than eighteen times since joining the Black Rot, but that's precisely how he got his name. He managed to slip out of any confine, slick as oil and crafty as a fox.

"You never leave war," Rimeria said. "It follows you around like a hound fly."

"'Least you can kill a hound fly," Slick retorted.

I smacked him lightly on the cheek. "Cheer up, Slick. You're not a feeder for indispensable knights like you were for your uncle's militia. You're the indispensable one now."

"Yeah," Rimeria said, "who else could we bet on getting roped up and thrown into a stockade every time he has a job to do?"

The Rots chuckled and had some more fun at Slick's expense, but the jokes soon ended as Dercy returned.

Dercy's steed huffed a steamy wisp of rotten horse breath into the air and lowered its face of menacing plate. A warhorse in every sense of the word.

Its rider didn't look too bad himself. The short and squat King of Watchmen's Bay was dressed in a suit of plate that glistened from his boots to his gorget. No helmet, though — somehow that made him all the more intimidating. After all, it's not often you see a little man in plate armor with a balding head, sitting atop a horse fit for a mountain of a man. It's disconcerting sight.

Dercy side-eyed Tylik. "Let us hope you are not being misled, hmm?"

"Been around for a long time," Tylik said. "Got me a good eye for insincerity, promise you that."

"I would never question it," Dercy said. "I have a healthy distrust of all things northern, that's all. When you're raised in a place like this"—he looked around, judging the gray sky and the bitter air with contempt—"it does things to a man. Have to fight for your food when you're little, or you'll starve. Only the most cunning make it out alive."

The snow crackled under the heavy hooves of Vayle's horse, who appeared from the thicket of archers.

"Ram's ready," she said.

The steel plates protecting Dercy's fingers clinked as he fastened a tighter grip around his steed's reins. He drew in a deep breath, held it, and then let it pass slowly through his flared nostrils.

He regarded the officers and the Rots with a quick nod. "Men... women... today we bear a great responsibility. Take a look now at the vastness of life before you and behind you. There are twenty thousand beating hearts standing on this field today. There are soldiers, savants, tailors, tanners, blacksmiths, servants, prisoners, husbands, wives, fathers and mothers. Twenty thousand who have entrusted you with the safety and fortitude of their world. You cannot consider a single one of their lives, or indeed twenty thousand of them, more valuable than the survival of this good world we've come to know, but you will not dare let one of them go to waste. Today you lead so that tomorrow you can rebuild."

Dercy unsheathed an ebon blade — a gift from yours truly. He jerked the reins of his warhorse, and it trotted to the outer edge of the infantry. He held the silver eye of his blade high in the air, clicked his heels and galloped down the ranks.

"Go!" he screamed. "Now! Tear down their walls! Go!"

A chill skittered up my spine as the swarm pressed forward. The wind was drowned out by thousands of pieces of clanging armor, fifteen thousand boots rumbling through the ossified sea of snow and ice, crunching and splintering the frozen earth.

A carnal cry of bravery and honor billowed up like chimney smoke from the marching footmen.

I watched the Edenvaile parapet in equal parts anticipation and dread. "Come on, you bastards," I whispered to myself.

Vayle said something, but I ignored her. The wall was more important. The archers had their elbows cocked, ready to unleash pure hell on the unlucky soldiers at the very front.

A couple stray arrows whizzed down from the Edenvaile wall, the mark of nervous men — their intended targets were still too far away. Wouldn't be long, though. Wouldn't be long before the barbed tips would needle their way into flesh, or if our men were lucky, deflect harmlessly off their armor.

A bit of chaos would be good right about now. Some unexpected fun along the battlements, a few surprises gift-wrapped in steel. That was my contribution to the first part of the siege: to deliver agents of chaos.

But where were they? Where were my little agents?

Right *there*.

A speck trailed up to the parapet, and then another. And another, and another. It was a blur now, a pod of stars streaking across the sky, flashing pinpoints of black light as they raced onward.

Some of the archers turned alertly. Others toppled over the crenellations, somersaulting slowly with the wind beneath them, till their bodies fell below the horizon of soldiers that marched upon their walls. I knew when they struck the unforgiving sheets of ice because the taunts and cheers and hollers from the footmen flared up like a fire being fed fresh needles.

I smiled. Chaos had been born. My sellswords cut through the clumps of archers effortlessly. The bowmen may have had swords at their hips, but they were caught off guard and too closely packed together. By the time they realized the threat was on them, they were dropping over the wall like sick baby birds from a nest. And they couldn't well shoot at their attackers without sending iron tips through the backs and necks of their fellow archers.

But good things never last. Reinforcements were sent in, and the mercenaries were mercilessly beaten down. I'd told them our footmen would storm the wall with ladders they could use to slide down in case of danger, but that was a lie. A lie I knew would cost them their lives and one that I would tell again. This was war. There are no promises of safety in war.

There is no mercy in war. The footmen knew that well enough when they came upon the gate. They stepped over the corpses of their friends. They found the man they walked shoulder to shoulder with writhing in pain as an arrow gouged the gap between his shoulder and breastplate.

This was war. There is no humanity in war. If it existed, I wouldn't have heard the high-pitched wails of agony as cauldrons of boiling water poured over the wall, sizzling the cold air in a bath of steam and splashing on the men below.

Flesh was melted on this day. Scalps were scalded and skin fused together, topped with blisters like cherries on a pie.

This was war. There is no time to brood. You make decisions quickly and live with them. Vayle understood that. There was no hesitation in her voice when she called the cavalry to action.

They swooped in from behind us, the soles of my feet rattling as two thousand horses stampeded out in a U shape, quick to greet the mix of cavalry and infantry who bounded out from behind Edenvaile. They all wore the jagged *C* of the conjurers. Five hundred of ours wielded ebon blades, giving them the distinct advantage.

My mouth felt like cotton. Had it been open this entire time? Maybe. My eyes were dry too. Probably would have helped to blink. Didn't have time, though. A crack of thunder stole my attention.

The double-leaf gate of Edenvaile trembled.

Another bellow of thunder.

And the gate trembled once more. Amielle and the other conjurers on the balcony crossed their arms, as if they were waiting impatiently.

I took my horse closer to the action. The action was nothing but terror: clashing steel and spurts of blood. Screams that could curdle milk fresh from a cow's teat.

I imagined myself at the forefront, fighting off the cavalry and rushing guardsmen. What would I do? What they all did, probably: kill and move.

Swords clang, shields splinter, and you move.

Blood spatters your face, tinges your tongue with the taste of burning iron.

And you move.

You see the eyes of your friends roll back, the whites flash at you like a lake of pale milk under the moon. Sometimes you don't see eyes at all, only empty sockets with red spongy cords dangling, misplaced, strewn.

And you move.

You move because it's the only thing you can do. Till you come upon the enemy. Then you kill.

Man looks like you, walks like you, talks like you, probably has a family like you. Problem is, he's holding a pike and dressed in different clothes. You don't think about his wife, or his children. Or his problems or the fact he's out there to pocket a bit of gold to afford some salted fish for his next dinner. If you don't parry his blow, sidestep him and shove your blade deep into his belly, twisting the steel up around his ribs, ripping and tearing at his flesh… he'll do it to you.

And so you kill.

And you move.

If these men survived, most of them would slip away into madness. But for now? They needed to live, and living meant killing.

A loud cheer erupted from the front lines.

The gate was splintered. And like the rotting foundation of a house, it collapsed inward.

This was where the real war began. And if Tylik was right, where it would end.

A battery of conjurer and city guard cavalry stormed out of the gate, trampling over the footmen who stood in their way as fodder. That's all they were, a distraction for those behind them who hurried to the wall with wooden ladders to augment the men and women who rushed through the gate.

One of Dercy's officers shouted out orders to his archers, and Vayle barked at her cavalry, deploying the remaining three thousand on the wings.

Suddenly the mix of conjurer soldiers and city guardsmen reared around and fled deep within the castle walls, as if a horn bellowed a retreating boom.

I turned to the Rots. "Should I embark on a speech like Dercy? Or should we just go in there and kill the cunts?"

Expecting smiles, I was disappointed to see what could only be described as unadulterated horror on their faces.

Then I heard it. And I turned, and I saw it.

Half of the godforsaken wall uprooted itself and flung its tons of stone frame outward, crushing cavalry and footmen alike. A bloated geyser vomited dust and snow into the air, obscuring my vision.

Warhorses raced out of the fog, heads down, hooves exploding through the snow. Some were painted in splotches of bright pink from where their flesh had been sawed off. Others collapsed in a heap, as if the snow had wiry tendrils that coiled around their thick legs, yanking them down. Most either had no rider or were dragging the man who used to sit atop them.

Thousands of heartbeats gone, just like that. Thousands of voices chanting courage and bravery silenced. It felt like the world had idled, as if everything out there — the wind, the cold, the stars, the sun, the moon, the sky, the great unknown — had stopped to witness what we were capable of.

And then like cows in a field resuming their consumption of grass and roughage after deep reflection, they all went back to work. The wind whipped, the cold stung, and I was sure the stars glittered and the sun continued on its arc below the mountains.

The second portion of the front wall wrenched itself out of the iced-over dirt, spilling reverberations across the field that rippled through the white powder like the wake of a boat on the ocean.

And then… *boom*. It leaped outward, every square stone falling in perfect harmony with one another. More dust, more fog. More silence, more death.

My eyes swiveled back and forth across the field, mindlessly sweeping along the debris of collapsed stone. And then squinting at the effervescent white smoke concealing the horde of corpses. Thousands more remained alive — if you stretch the definition — frantically searching for some semblance of hope.

This was all part of the plan. We knew the freaks wearing the jagged *C* would use their demented minds to wreak havoc on the battlefield, although evulsing an entire wall and shattering it on the skulls of our men... well, that was a bit more than expected.

"Round up the cavalry!" Vayle shouted. With a quick pull of the reins, her steed pivoted and began galloping toward the right wing of the battlefield.

The officers behind me pulled off to the left. I could hear them shouting as they drove their horses hard through the snow. "Back, back, back, back! Back, back, back, back!"

"I feel as useless as a blind man's eyes," a Rot said.

"You won't for long," I told him.

A few battlements of our archers advanced ahead. I clicked my heels, spurring my horse onward after them. I circled around in front of them.

"Get your asses back there," I yelled.

One of the archers pointed ahead. Looked no older than a baby-faced eighteen-year-old. "If we got the cavalry and infantry comin' back toward us, northernmen'll be on 'em like hungry hounds. We're their only defense."

Pointing the tip toward the back line, I lowered my eyes into a glowing glare and said very slowly, "Get back, now."

He held my stare for a few seconds. Then, "You heard him. Pull back."

I met back up with the Rots, shaking my head. "Thought I was going to take an arrow to the throat there for a moment."

"We woulda fucked 'em up for ya," Klon said.

Vayle and the other officers soon returned, and behind them trudged a much smaller company of warhorses than were sent out to meet the conjurer and city guard cavalry. The footmen followed in short order. Many of them were dashed with specks of blood, and some of them were mortally wounded. Their helmets were askew, their faces streaked with sweat and powder from crushed stone.

From behind them, like a beam of moonlight thinning through a black forest, ambled Dercy on his mighty warhorse. When he got to us, his breathing was labored. He sat hunched over in the saddle.

"A wall, huh?" he coughed out. He wiped his arm across his mouth. "Never told me they were capable of doing that, Astul."

"To be fair," I said, "I did tell you Amielle crumbled a shelf of rock that I was standing on."

"Couldn't pick her out of the crowd up there," Dercy said, pointing his tiny dimpled chin toward the balcony, which was hazed over still with dust. "But I saw at least five hurling their guts over the banister after the first wall fell. One collapsed, and then the dust came up and I couldn't see a thing."

Interesting. It took five to uproot one wall, which meant it probably took ten in total. There weren't many more than ten conjurers on that balcony, so unless more were in reserve... they may well have blown their load. Although Amielle and Sybil surely had a few surprises remaining.

Everyone watched in silence as the sheet of white soot hanging over Edenvaile began to methodically settle back into the snow. Still couldn't see a thing.

Dercy sat back in his saddle. "Hear that?"

"Hooves," Vayle answered.

"I was going to suggest steel," I said.

"You're both right," Dercy said. He turned to Tylik. "Let's hope you are as well."

Like serrated daggers of lightning piercing a gray sky, pikes and swords charged through the obfuscating cloud. It was something out of an occult nightmare, the muscular frames of horses peeling back and climbing through the dust as a demon might propel himself from a portal of the underworld.

I felt the storm brew in my legs and then my thighs, swirling up my arms and echoing in my skull.

"Steady, now!" Dercy advised his men. Most of them probably couldn't hear over the steady growl of thunder.

There were enough horses coming through the fog to level every man in Dercy's army, continue on to splinter his wagons and stamp the slaves into the snow without ever circling back around. You'd be hard pressed to find one city guardsman within the group. The thousands of cavalry all wore the jagged *C* of the conjurers. It was as if Amielle and Sybil had forced Vileoux to hold his men back just to show us the full power of the conjurer army.

But first, they'd have to reach us. The uneven terrain that boots and warm blood had turned to slush wouldn't prevent that, and neither would a bunch of brave soldiers who wore faces flushed with anger. Nothing would prevent them from turning us into ink on the pages of history except Tylik's promise.

And what a promise it was.

The promise was a fleet of warhorses.

It was the charging banners of an ominous mountain upon which Icerun had been built.

It was a faction of disgruntled vassals who Vileoux Verdan had never sought to mollify.

It was a testament to just how easy the North is to fracture.

It was a blizzard winding through the snow, thrusting out from the rear of Edenvaile.

The armies of Patrick Verdan and all the northern bannermen he'd gathered galloped and ran and roared with a singular voice. They poured out around the walls. There were tens of thousands of them, a mix of cavalry and footmen. There were slingers, swordsmen and pikemen. Knights, lancers and some good old-fashioned grunts clad in quilted armor.

The brigade of conjurers charging us peered back. Their advance slowed, and then utterly stopped as they learned a rather well-known secret among the inhabitants of Mizridahl: trust does not exist, and the truth is as capricious as the wind.

The initial push of the northern armies drove into the middle of the conjurer cavalry, halving them and forcing the two sides to split off, where the remaining northernmen rounded them up and cut them down.

I glanced at the Rots. "Now we have some fun."

With a few kicks, my mare whinnied and plotted a course down the middle of the battlefield. She dashed through the snow, shoveling clumps of it behind her. Most of the fighting was a good two hundred feet away, to either side. There were some leftover conjurers wandering through the middle, but they paid a small band like us little attention. We had to be a bit wary of the northernmen who pursued them, though — in war, everything and everyone looks the same. You swing first, apologize later.

We arrived at the corner of the Edenvaile wall. Well, where the corner of the Edenvaile wall *used* to be. The Rots and I climbed down from our horses, smacked them on the butts and sent them off.

"It's a fuckin' graveyard," Kale said.

We stepped over mashed corpses and pulverized stone alike. Tops were detached from bottoms, legs from hips, heads from necks. Chalky bones jutted out of mangled flesh. Red syrup, like the filling of a sweet cake, had swallowed the white of the snow. It stuck to the soles of our boots and smelt heavily of copper.

"Go, go," I urged them on. Conjurer and city guard reinforcements were flowing from the center of the city into the field. Around the side walls still standing came a swarm of northerners who I had a feeling were not on our side.

"Kale," I said, "wait. Lend me a hand."

A wooden ladder lay in the snow, still intact. It was obnoxiously large but curiously light. Kale and I carried it to the other Rots, who stood by the forge.

"Seems quiet here," Rory said.

I craned my neck around the corner, to get a better look at the balcony. It was empty. "People don't tend to gather around forges. They're all probably holed up inside the keep, which we need to get to. Figure all the doors to be barricaded, and behind the barricades we're probably going to find more than our fair share of guards." I kicked the ladder gently. "Luckily for us, we've got this giant fucking thing. Balcony door probably won't be barricaded."

"Trick is getting there," one of the Rots said.

Light as ever on my feet, I inched toward one of the snow-cleared paths that eventually ran perpendicular with the keep and intersected the market square.

If I had some gold jingling in my pocket, I'd bet it all on coming upon a couple cavalry or a platoon of city guardsmen. But I reached the path without confrontation. They must've been gathered near the market square, ready to spill out in the form of more reinforcements if called upon.

I continued down the path, listening intently for the unmistakable sound of a snorting horse or crunching snow.

Nothing.

A few more steps. Still nothing. No voices, no shadows flicking across the ground.

A few more steps and I stood at the edge of the market square, directly in front of the fountain and the steps leading up to the double-leaf doors of the keep.

The belly of Edenvaile growled hungrily as a furious wind slapped my cheeks. I returned quickly to the forge.

"Well," I said, "everyone's gone."

Kale motioned toward the field. "I'd say everyone's fightin'."

With the mishmash of clashing swords and the blurs of horsehair blending together, you couldn't tell friend from foe, not from where we were. But if what we'd seen exit Edenvaile, both from inside the city and its rear, were all the reinforcements this kingdom had… they were outnumbered three to one by Dercy's remaining men and Patrick Verdan.

Even if Vileoux Verdan and Amielle and the others were very poor at math, they understood this would not bode well for them. That was why they'd retreated into the keep: one last stand. Or in the case of Amielle and Sybil, more time to craft a little surprise.

I snatched the ball-peen hammer from the forge and smacked it off the anvil. "Listen up. Your primary targets are Amielle and Sybil. Vileoux and Chachant are your secondary targets, Edmund Tath your third. Any conjurer you come across will have a jagged *C* painted on their chest. Kill them."

"Wots 'bouts thems lads and girls?" Iggy said.

I looked at his rotund face and repeated what he said, which was something I had to do every time he spoke. Not only did his accent add esses to nearly every word, but the bastard never made sense. Good with a sword, though.

"What?"

"Thems lads and girls that lives here. Young'uns."

"Doubt you'll encounter them near the royal quarters, which is where we're going. They're probably stuffed in a basement. If you do see them, leave them be."

A Rot named Slenna unsheathed a dagger and hugged the blade with her hand. Blood trickled down her wrist and sunk into the snow. She wiped the crimson liquid on her face like it was makeup.

"Makes me look fiercer," she said, winking.

"Let's move," I said, "before the rest of you get it in your mind to start dismembering yourselves."

Kale and I lugged the ladder along, him on one end and me forty feet away on the other. It was awkward to hold, awkward to carry and awkward to turn. We smacked the legs off a tavern roof at one point, which woke up an angry mound of snow sitting atop, causing it to fall on our heads and down our backs.

We danced the rest of the way to the keep, attempting to persuade the icy powder to evacuate. It instead fell in my pants. A whore whose kinks outnumbered the leaves on a tree once told me it felt good to put ice between your cheeks, right up against the opening there. I was drunk, so I let her do it to me. It didn't feel good then, and it certainly didn't feel good now.

Uncomfortable sensations aside, we made it the keep safely. I tilted the ladder up, resting it against the balcony, and punched the legs solidly into the snow.

"Don't worry if you fall," I said. "You won't die. Trust me, I know."

I climbed up first, and the Rots followed one by one. About half of us were on the balcony when the quietest assassin in the world, as I termed him, uncharacteristically stammered.

"What… the piss is that, Shepherd?"

I was looking down the ladder when he said my name, steadying it for Slenna. I glanced up. Then squinted. Then my jaw fall away from my mouth.

As in life, war is full of ebbs and flows. You only stay on top until the wave crests, and it always crests. Although we were winning this battle, I expected something to interrupt our momentum. It's just that I anticipated it coming from the minds of Amielle and Sybil, and not through the sky behind us.

A molten glow broiled the clouds, transforming the sky into a sullen furnace. If there was an end to the world, where brimstone would sail through the sky like migrating birds and everyone had approximately six seconds to live, this was what it would look like.

At the forefront of the cataclysm were, one could suggest, phoenixes. But these monstrosities were to phoenixes as a sapling is to the tallest pine in a forest. They were massive, hulking distortions of birds whose wings must have spanned a hundred feet. When they flapped, the air hissed away in fear.

Within their talons the size of a small man, they held swollen cocoons encased in flames.

They lumbered along, not at all like the agile phoenixes I'd known. They lethargically aimed their beaks toward the ground. Lower and lower they descended, before suddenly dropping their cocoons.

The sacks of fire splattered on the ground. Hundreds of conjurer soldiers burst out, wielding swords and mauls and maces. Soon there were more

— several magnitudes more — and the clumsy transports that delivered them bumbled away, high into the air.

The reinforcements took our new allied northerners by surprise. I couldn't wait around to see the aftermath, though. I had a job to do.

A rustling drew my attention back to the city of Edenvaile. Two mounted royal guardsmen, clad in plate, stormed toward my Rots on the ground.

"Iggy!" I hollered. "Cut 'em down!"

It was too late. Iggy took a blade edge across the back of his neck.

The quietest assassin in the world, Moor, tried jumping out of the way. But horses are quick, and the swords of royal guardsmen are quicker.

Two of my Rots were down, and four more were being chased. One of the guardsman circled back around and kicked over the ladder, trapping them down there.

Rimeria and a few of the others who were up top with me drew their bows. I lifted a pacifying hand to stop them. "Don't waste your arrows, you can't shoot through plate. Come on, we have a job to do."

I opened my mouth and filled my lungs with the vitriolic air of the North, holding the breath as I walked to the balcony door. Deep breath in, calm breath out. Deep, calm. Easy does it. You learn early on as an assassin that breathing is vital to your career. It steadies your hands, eases the nightmares that wake you, prepares you for another day of killing. Most of the time it works.

Sometimes it doesn't.

I wiggled the brass handle of the door. It didn't budge.

"If I want inside your keep," I said, licking my lips, drawing back and hauling off with a tremendous kick to the frame, "I'll get inside your bloody keep."

Another kick, more ferocious than the first. And another. The sudden jolt of my foot crashing against the wood pulsed up my entire leg, to my hip. Hurt like hell, and I didn't give a damn. I kicked again and again and again. Finally, the frame splintered, something cracked, and I shoved that fucking door right off its hinges. I punched through the twisted fragments of wood still in my way, withdrew my ebon blade and stepped into the hallway.

Fifteen of my Rots followed. Down six from when we started.

"Only one way to get to the royal quarters," I said. "Through this hallway, make a few right turns, and the stairs are right there. If we get separated, always stick together, in teams of two. Royal guards are tough bastards with their fancy plate, unless you're dressed as their commander."

I continued through the hallway for a few paces, then stopped. "If any of you find Chachant, Sybil, Vileoux or Amielle without me… I want you to kill them slowly. Make them suffer. Make them hurt. Understood?"

No one nodded, but they all understood. We weren't torturers; we were clean-cut assassins. You go in for the kill and leave just as quickly, no time to stick around and cut out tongues or eyeballs. No reason for it, usually. But when our brethren are cut down... well, we can make time for that sort of thing.

I sifted through the darkness of the hallway, hand along the cold stone wall. It became mustier and danker the deeper I tunneled, and it felt much colder than it had when I walked this hallway during the wedding. Emptier, too, and not so much in the absence of chatty voices and festive wedding colors, but a detached emptiness... something neither here nor there, not quite connected to the fabric of reality.

The hallway stretched on, seemingly forever. Had I missed a turn?

I stopped and listened intently. No sound of parading boots behind me. No noise at all, in fact, except the disturbing huff of my own breath.

My fingers unconsciously coiled tighter around the hilt of my sword as I shifted slowly around.

A black smog blinded me.

"Kale?" I called out. "Slenna?"

No answer.

"So this is your little trick?" I said aloud. "I can stay here all day, Amielle. All night, Sybil, whichever one of you is behind this. At some point, you'll tire. Or your keep will be stormed and your throat slashed."

A peculiar sound droned far away. *Tink-tank.* *Tink-tank.*

There are not a lot of things that tink-tank in this world. Tink? Sure. An arrow will tink off a breastplate. And a drop of water splashing into the bottom of a chalice may tink. But those are singular sounds. This was a melody. A predictable and consistent harmony.

Tink-tank. Tink-tank. It became louder.

Heavier.

It was crashing now, like cymbals at a climax. There was a theme as it drew closer. *Tink-scrape-tank.* *Tink-scrape-tank.*

I drew my finger across the wall. There was a small space of flat stone, then an indent of mortar. And again, a small space of flat stone, then an indent of mortar.

I pushed the tip of my sword against the wall and traced an identical line.

This was what I heard: *Tink-scrape-tank. Tink-scrape tank.*

CHAPTER TWENTY-EIGHT

A warm glow chasing away the void is supposed to be comforting, but the flecked orange tails that scoured hungrily down the walls did not comfort me. Maybe it was because of the sound that followed those feathered tails. Or maybe it was because I had the perspicacity to notice it wasn't so much that the darkness departed as that the light was unsheathed. The blackness, the night, whatever had surrounded me — it gave the impression that it had complete control and it would return whenever it wanted.

As it allowed the room to bask in the burnished embers of a sunset, a shadowy figure sauntered down the hallway, his sword tinking and scraping and tanking along the wall.

His shape reminded me of someone. He was tall and unwieldy, arms flinging uncontrollably as he

Justin DePaoli

walked, much like a foal who stumbled and bumbled around with the gracelessness of stilt legs.

"Led me to death," he said, "but not a grave."

"Rivon?"

He smiled, but it wasn't a smile that Rivon Eyrie would flash. It was a cadaverous smile — one unbound by the tightness of flesh and lips. Just a mouthful of teeth and a jaw of pale bone.

"Oh, fuck you," I spat. "You're not real."

He stopped and cocked his head. "Not real? What makes a man real?"

"A beating heart, for starters."

He put his hand to his chest. Skin unraveled from his fingers, drooping over his knuckles. "There's something in there." He pulled his hand away, and the flaps of skin flopped back over his skeletal appendages loosely and crookedly.

"All I wanted," he said, "was to take good care of my roosters, get good eggs from the hens, enjoy their morning calls. Get far away from the life the Rot gave me. The nightmares followed me, y'know? Never could outrun them. Woke up in a cold sweat every night, swore the eyes of my victims were peering at me through my door… voices were in my hut. I told you the life wasn't for me. I told you I was done killing. Then you show up and you take me away from the life I loved. You take me on your warpath, and then you don't even have the decency to let me die in peace."

473

He drummed his cadaverous knuckles on the flat side of his sword and approached me.

"That's not how it was," I said. "Believe whatever lies you want, Rivon, but you won't make me believe them. Saving my head in Erior was a choice, one I appreciate. Joining me was a choice, another that I appreciate. But I never made you do either."

He came to a stop a few feet in front of me. He raised his sword vertically, till it was flush with his fleshless face. "All I want is an eye for an eye. There are no more nightmares to worry about now, because sleep is not something that I know any longer."

"Ghosts cannot kill me," I said. In her bid to recreate my friend, Amielle — or Sybil — had stripped all humanity from Rivon. Even his festive style of tripping over his words had been sucked right from his voice.

He laughed sardonically. "A ghost? I wish that's what I was. No, I'm still chained by the physical realm. I wonder… will you die in peace, or will you suffer my fate?"

He lunged forward, cutting his sword horizontally across the air. I met it halfway, erupting a vicious clang down the inescapable hall. We held position for a moment, until I slipped a free hand away from the hilt and punched Rivon square in his nose.

We both reeled back, him clutching his face, me clutching my knuckles.

"Fuck!" I said.

"Fuck!" he said.

Who knew a dead man could feel pain? At least I had that on my side. I took grip of my sword again and waited for the fallen Rot to lash out. But he didn't. With the patience of someone who had an entire lifetime to wait, he tiptoed around the hall, sidestepping like a crab to one wall and the other. It was a good plan to keep the blood flowing. Mm. Poor choice of words there, perhaps.

"Suppose you're real," I said, matching his dancing feet. "Who brought you back from the dead?"

His tongue orbited the empty space where his lips should have been. "Who raises a carrot from a seedling to a fully grown vegetable?"

"Probably a farmer."

"Think the carrot knows that?"

He faux-charged me, grinned and then dashed with purpose. I side-stepped his blow, and we traded sides.

"Rivon Eyrie, ever the philosophical man," I mocked. "Come to the tavern at night to hear his deep thoughts, which include 'If a rooster can see you, can it look into your soul?' and the timeless comparison between growing food and rising from the dead."

"Whoever brought me back," Rivon said, "it's greater than anything either of us can comprehend."

I wagged my finger disapprovingly. "I don't think so, old pal. Amielle is the one who did this, and I still don't believe you're real. She has a knack for creating nightmares that trap you. You're just a vestage of my past. Good as dead in the real world."

The balls of his shoulders rolled back, and he sprinted forward again, this time carving a wicked pattern through the air. He brought his blade up, down, across, diagonally, jabbed it, faked it, swung it quick and swung it hard. I parried each blow and kicked him the gut, driving him back again.

"Funny thing is," I said, breathing laboriously now, "she recreated you damn near perfectly. The same flaws you had as a Rot have become even more obvious in your tenure as Braddock's rooster bitch. You telegraph every move a half second too early, and your feet couldn't outdance a clubfooted drunk. Tried teaching your old ass, but you never could learn."

Holding my blade at guard, I took a step, and then another, moving fluidly across the floor. Rivon backed away, his boot scraping and dragging. All you heard from mine was the gentle tap of the toe kissing the wooden planks, effortlessly carrying me across the way much like foam hitches a ride across a river.

"I've taken down giants," I said. "Cut off arms that were bigger than both of mine. Lopped off heads that weighed as much as a ripe pumpkin. Doesn't matter your strength or your speed or your shit-eating grin. Technique and fluidity, Rivon — that's all you need. And you've got neither. You were a good man. Funny, kept the Hole in order. We would've snipped you loose a long time ago if you weren't."

"I assassinated my fair share," he asserted.

"You botched your fair share too. Anytime you took a job on your own, you returned with excuses as to why the job didn't get done. Today, your excuses run out."

With the panache of a haughty sword master and the grace of a limber dancer, I sprung across the room. With spry steps and quick flicks of my wrist, my black blade sung a series of sharp notes as it eviscerated the air with its steely blue swirls. He parried one, two, three and a fourth and a fifth, but as I changed direction without warning, twisting around his shoulder, his ankles tangoed with one another.

He stumbled. He straightened his arm, a desperate attempt to brace himself against the wall as he was falling.

He never got the opportunity. A murderous cry, and then a black edge ripped apart the flesh of his chest and violently slammed him into the floor. He lay there, impaled on my sword, his bony face shivering.

"Don't worry, Rivon," I whispered, yanking my blade out, "I know you weren't truly alive. I refuse to believe."

A rotten crimson jelly mottled with streaks of jet black, like coagulated blood, painted the edge of my sword. It was as thick as honey, but smelled like meat that a bucketful of maggots had gotten to weeks ago.

I tried shaking it off, but it was inspissated across the ebon edge. Expecting — or perhaps, hoping — it would vanish with this abyss Amielle or Sybil had trapped me in, I tucked my sword back inside its sheath and continued walking.

The darkness pursued me, from either side. But just before it blotted out the last remnants of light Rivon brought in his wake, the illusion that entrapped me shattered.

Or more accurately, it tucked its tail between its legs and scurried off. There was no great explosion, no twisting and collapsing ether that made the air vibrate and the walls shift. Just a whimper.

Black carpet, trimmed with gold, lay beneath my feet. And an overpowering scent of pine that one only finds deep in the forest or within the keep of Edenvaile wafted through the air. It was a much more pleasant smell than the acrid jelly-blood-infested repulsiveness that fouled my blade. Speaking of which, I wondered if it had disappeared, or…

I'd have to check on that later, thanks to a little thumping that sounded quite similar to panicked feet hurrying down steps.

More noises: some voices echoing off the walls, shouting naughty words, and the clangor of angry steel.

"Fuck off!"

Something crashed above me, shaking the ceiling.

"He said fuck off!"

My Rots. I looked up and followed the muddled sounds of their racing footsteps with my eyes. They trailed off, toward a staircase that wound around and emptied out into the hallway I stood in. It was on those stairs where the urgent pattering of feet from moments ago had now blossomed into a slim figure who turned the corner and ran.

Someone chased her. No, someone followed her.

Faces flashed in my mind. There was my brother's face, flat and empty as I rent his throat with a rusted dagger. There was my father's face, mouth agape, eyes shinier than marbles as I cried and cried and stabbed and stabbed, sucking the blood from his rotten heart. There were the faces of my Rots, pale and still as the stench of death emanated from their spoiled organs.

A profound anger pulsed inside me. The tingles and shivers climbed across my shoulders and down my spine. My arms were pimpled and my teeth were clenched. I didn't go through all of the shit in my life to sit here and play the role of a dazzled spectator.

My predatory instincts — the kind of savageness that idealists and do-gooders like to think men have cast aside for intelligence and morality — propelled me forward. I was a wolf, and these gals were my prey.

Ebon blade in hand, I hunted them down, eyes fixed on the dragging hems of their white cloaks like a jackal pursuing the swaying tail of a fleeing fox through the dark of night.

Sybil Tath's mess of black hair flung to one side of her shoulder as her head swiveled around. The fear... oh, it percolated in her eyes like beads of sweat through pores. I was faster, stronger, hungrier. And she knew it. Magic wouldn't save her now.

She turned back around, shoulders bobbing, arms flinging.

I readied my blade, lowering it to my side.

The royal Verdan carpet beneath my feet became a blur. The torches affixed to the walls coalesced into a canvas of bleary sunsets. I wasn't running, I was soaring. Felt like I wasn't even touching the ground.

With another stride, I drew back my sword.

A second stride, and I held my breath.

With a third, I swung.

With a fourth, there was a yelp, and my arm shuddered. Serrated ebon sunk its teeth into the soft tissue of Sybil's calf. I leaned away and dragged the blade across the muscles and tendons, careful to avoid bone. I wanted her in disrepair, not to bleed out. Not yet.

Her ankle twisted, and her knee bent in disturbing fashion. She crumbled to the ground and rolled onto her back, clutching her leg, beating the air into submission with her squeals.

I went on, not missing a stride. Had to keep running, keep hunting, because the true prey was still trying to get away.

Amielle curled her fingers around the edge of a wall, and then she disappeared, down another flight of stairs.

Sybil's howling faded behind me as I turned the corner. I bounded down the steps, skipping every other three.

Amielle's auburn curls bounced springily on her shoulders as she raced away from a wicked grin. She was being chased by a cold-blooded killer, she thought, one who wouldn't hesitate to chop those pretty little lips right off her face. Let her think what she wanted. Better for fear to push her on.

She jumped from the fifth step and landed stiffly on the floor below. She said something, and then darted to the left. Had she made it all the way down that narrow hallway, she could have pushed open the doors and been greeted by the frosty air of the rear courtyard. Maybe she could have hidden, signaled a stray guard, something to bide her time while she searched for a pair of wings in the sky to pervert into a submissive beast of flame.

Could have — those are the two great words of finality.

I leaned my shoulder down and brutally drove Amielle into the wall, shielding her head so body parts of lesser importance would take the brunt of the force. The wall met us with the same kindness of a fifty-foot wave. We fell backward and rolled in each other's arms, till the thick carpet beneath slowed us.

My arm had caught a few rugged ridges of rock along the wall, splitting the skin. And my shoulder... boy, felt like a party of gremlins inside there, taking turns at gnawing on my tendons.

But no amount of pain could stop me now.

I fisted Amielle's hair and yanked the bitch to her feet. Her once-baleful eyes that had looked as frightening as the center of a maelstrom were now dull and marred with the fogginess of defeat. She shied away from me, until I pinched her thin chin and wrenched her sandy face toward mine.

"You know, I've never been big on words when someone's going to die. But you and I," I said, tapping the center of her head with my finger, "we need to talk."

"Shepherd," Kale called out from down the hallway. "Got her." He heaved a wounded Sybil Tath onto his shoulder.

"And him," said Slenna, who appeared from the stairs holding a dagger to the throat of one Chachant Verdan.

"This one too," said Ervin, pushing Vileoux Verdan along. He slapped the old man's face and said, "Come on now, look alive."

"Can I cut the tongue out of this one?" another Rot asked, tracing the tip of his dagger along the gaunt mouth of Edmund Tath. "He fuckin' spit on me."

A few more Rots followed down the stairs, dragging conjurers who appeared a few hours away from death, and some northern lords who apparently weren't eager to take to the battlefield.

"I told you to kill them," I said.

Kale shrugged. "Once you up and vanished, Slenna said you were talkin' out your ass, passion and all that."

I counted the number of Rots silently. And again. Two were missing. "Where's Flint and Treddle?"

Kale pointed his thumb toward the ceiling. "Bled out. Royal guards *are* tough bastards, you weren't lying. Got me on the shoulder and I think Ervin is missin' some skin from his back."

"Whoever's not holding a prisoner," I said, "go retrieve them. They may have died here, but they will not rest here."

I twisted Amielle's head around. "You on the other hand, dear…"

She shook her head, as if out of pity, and said, "You can kill me. But you cannot kill an idea."

We'd see about that.

CHAPTER TWENTY-NINE

We emerged onto the balcony under a sad sky, but the sight on the battlefield was one of joy and victory. Stray battlements of conjurer reinforcements were fleeing the field, and the small number of bannermen who had taken to Vileoux's side sat in a heap of snow as prisoners in the face of Patrick Verdan and his mighty army, which had a few curious colorings mingled within.

Pastel green colorings, those made famous by various shaman sects of Hoarvous. Interesting.

The plume of dust and snow had finally settled back into the earth. Swords from the field aimed toward me, and then a small contingent of horses trotted toward what used to be the gate of Edenvaile. Dercy Daniser, Patrick Verdan and my commander were among them.

I turned to the Rots. "Escort the captured downstairs, into the throne room. And open the doors for our friends. I'll be down there shortly — a former queen and I have a few things to discuss." Once the Rots departed, I inhaled nature's glacier breath deep into my nostrils. "Colder here than you imagined?"

Amielle watched the contingent trot inside the walls her conjurers had evulsed. Her shoulders slumped, and her head hung. She said nothing. Had her head not been a little bloody, and had the exhaustion of this battle not beaten her down, I might've been wary of a one-on-one confrontation, given our last meeting hadn't ended in my favor. But she was too weak now. Too feeble.

"You don't particularly seem dressed for the occasion," I said, noting the thin linens her cloak was pinned to. Her hands were clenched into fists inside the sleeves of her shirt.

"Are you attempting to woo me?" she asked. "If you are, I would suggest starting off with a bang, not mindless chatter."

"I'm afraid not. I've always been of the mind that you shouldn't romance a woman who won't be around to see the sun rise tomorrow." After some time, I added, "How's that for a bang?"

"Better," she said blankly, moving to the edge of the balcony. "Shall I lean my head over?" Catching the queer look on my face, she added, "For the clean cut, of course. Or do you intend to make a mess of me?"

I unsheathed my blade. "Eager to die, are we?"

She watched the contingent move closer. Or perhaps she was dredging the depths of her ruined dreams, as people who look mindlessly into the horizon are wont to do.

"This isn't about me, shepherd of assassins." She turned. "You're the one who's eager for death, always."

I chuckled.

"Did I miss a joke?" she asked.

"It's just that… look at us. You're dressed all prim and proper, and I'm a mangy mutt with a beard that needed trimming six months ago. You have your fancy spells, and I swing a sword like a dumb-fuck ogre. You're a bloody queen! And me? I shepherd a bunch of misfits and outcasts. Isn't it funny, then, that we're driven by an identical passion?"

"What drives me," she said, "is—"

"Absolute power," I said.

Her eyes narrowed. "My people—"

I interrupted her with a dismissive wave of my hand. "Oh, fuck off with all the savior shit. Maybe a little part of you wanted to save your people. Rescue them from the droughts and whatever else plagues your world. That's not what drove you to this, though. You got a whiff of power, and you loved it. You'd do anything to keep it, right?"

"I'd do anything to keep my people alive."

"Of course you would. Because if you didn't, you'd have a revolt on your hands."

Amielle shunned me, offering me the view of her cloak as she paced down the balcony.

"Look," I said empathetically, "I understand."

"I was eight when I learned the ways. By fifteen, I could conjure phoenixes. I snuck away from the domiciles at night to ride them and visit my friends hundreds of miles away." Her chin rolled across her shoulder as she peered back at me with a grim smile that faded like a good memory long lost. "By eighteen, most of my friends were dead. Famine and drought hit the northern provinces first. I decided then I would use everything power would grant me never to let another girl or boy go through the hardships I did."

Three horses walked abreast beneath the balcony. My commander glanced at me for a moment before proceeding into the keep with the others.

"You made some hard choices to get to where you are, didn't you?" I asked. "Did some things that maybe the ten-year-old you wouldn't be proud of?"

"I don't think you understand," she said.

I traced my nail up the snaking rivulets of steely blue that adorned my sword. The markings had been with me since the beginning, one of the few constant reminders of my past — a place where I do not like to go, but one where I often visit to remind myself.

"I have my own lust for power," I said. "It masquerades as a lust for freedom. I committed unspeakable acts of terror when I was a young man. Killed, maimed, tortured, kidnapped, brutalized, pillaged — all of my own accord, mind you. I set my own contracts in those days.

"I would tell anyone that I did it in the name of freedom, to create a reputation and a band of assassins no one would dare fuck with. Fat lords would swallow hard when we came by, and laws didn't much apply to us, because goddammit, we were fearsome! We could do anything we pleased! *That*, I would say, was freedom."

A ghastly wind blew through and strung wisps of auburn hair across Amielle's eyes. She brushed them out of the way and leaned on the banister, listening attentively.

"Of course, that's not freedom," I said. "Freedom's sleeping your nights far away from the confines of walls and uptight vassals. Freedom's a jingle in your pocket, a skin of wine whenever you want it. Freedom's spontaneity, a horse ride to the west and a stay on the beaches while you fish up some good food and tell some good tales."

Amielle crossed her legs and rested her chin on her palm. "From what my spies told me, you've enjoyed your fair share of freedom."

"Only recently," I said. "My crusade for power turned me into a very foul thing, and make no mistake, I was a thing — not a person. If I had continued, who knows? I might have assassinated a king just to show the world that I owned it. Would've started a great war, probably got all my Rots killed, and me? I'd be long gone, facedown in some ditch, fizzled out like a fast-burning flame."

Amielle straightened herself and crossed her arms. "And look at you now," she said impassively, clearly unimpressed.

I held my arms out and spun around, glimpsing into a panoramic world that I stood atop of. "Look at me now," I said, smiling. "I parlayed my reputation and my deeds into contracts. And here I am today, a man whose blade lords call upon so they can quietly ascend the ranks, who's hired to rectify miscarriages of justice, who families big and small alike need to stamp out competition and sniff out enemies. All for business, mind you, nothing personal. I have all the power I want and all the freedom I want, and I will do anything to preserve it."

"Including killing your own brother," Amielle said, drawing her lips tight in mock disapproval. "Murdering a king too, and butchering each and every one of his enlisted guardsmen. What was the final count, Astul? Two hundred?"

I strode over to her meaningfully. With an indolent brush of my hand, the edge of my ebon blade clacked up the buttons of her tunic and idled beneath her chin. With a subtle flick, the black tip lifted her head high into the air. She licked her lips and smiled wide.

"Sacrificed fifty of your dear Rots," she said. "Marched how many mercenaries to their death upon these walls? I'm sure you didn't inform them that their heroism would end with blood pouring from their necks, did you?"

I pressed the summit of the sword more firmly into her chin. Blood sprinkled out.

"My, my," she said, "it sounds like the lust of power has claimed you yet again."

The sword dug deeper into her flesh, lifting her onto the tips of her toes. She grinned like a skull.

"And that's precisely why I won't kill you," I said, lowering the sword and sliding it inside its leather-bound home. "You've taken a lot from me. You've made me feel the familiarity of losing myself again. It ends now. I've preserved what I wanted, and I'll take nothing more. Not your life, not Sybil's. I'm done. But I do have a lingering question. What did you think forcing me to kill the mirage of Rivon Eyrie would do to me?"

Her head cocked. "I've never heard that name. And I did not conjure a mirage."

I didn't know why I bothered asking. Of course she'd play dumb. What would the truth get her now?

I hooked my arm around Amielle's. "Let's go. I'm sure you have some eager visitors downstairs."

"You won't ever eliminate the conjurers," she said.

"I'm sure Dercy and Patrick and Braddock — wherever the hell he is — will draw up some plans and lay siege to whatever remnants you left behind in Lith."

I tugged her arm, and we walked.

"We're like ants," she said.

I stopped and attempted some mental acrobats so I could harmonize conjurers and ants, but the pieces weren't fitting. "Ants?"

"Ants," she reiterated. "Have you ever attempted to kill them? They keep coming back. Unless you snuff out and eradicate their colony, they march on endlessly, no matter how many you flick off your arm or stamp into the dirt."

"Colonies aren't difficult to locate. You just follow the trail."

A conceited smile touched her lips, and her brows flicked upward.

I chuckled to myself. One last charade to evoke a mind-breaking fear within me, that's all it was.

"Move," I barked. "I've still got one last bit of business with this frozen kingdom before I leave."

CHAPTER THIRTY

With the collapsed wall of Edenvaile a good mile behind me, I crossed my arms and watched as forty mules dragged twenty wagons full of glittering gold through the snow. They slogged their way toward the Hole. A handful of Rots accompanied them.

A pair of feet crunched through the ice behind me.

"Have you spoken to Braddock?" Vayle asked.

"Briefly."

Braddock, along with a small battery of Red Sentinels, had marched into Edenvaile a few nights ago, chasing those monstrosities of fire that burned the sky and dropped cocoons of conjurer reinforcements onto the battlefield. Apparently they were the remnants of an army that had fled his and Kane Calbid's forces.

"He went on about his proposition," Vayle said, "to unite the realm under one crown. I've heard Patrick is *very* interested."

I locked my fingers behind my head. "Mark of a good king there, make you feel he's interested in whatever you wish to talk about."

"Only the king of Icerun at this moment. But I don't imagine he won't make a claim for the throne of Edenvaile."

"Of course he will," I said. "He's got the support. And he doesn't want a fractured, war-mongering North made up of ten different claims. Kane Calbid will claim the South, no opposition there. Eaglesclaw will be unstable — especially since the Rots managed to spur a rebellion of Edmund's bannermen — but it's good to have some instability. It'll make the Rots a pretty coin."

Vayle pointed her chin at the lethargic caravan in the distance. "Speaking of coin, how much did you take from the Edenvaile vault?"

"Four times what I was promised," I said, grinning. "After all, we did a lot more than just discover who assassinated Vileoux Verdan."

"He's to die tomorrow," she said. "Along with the others, even Mydia, who seems to have had little part in this."

"Tomorrow," I said, rubbing some warmth back into my frozen hands, "I'll be fifty miles away from here. Will my commander be joining me?"

Vayle rubbed her tired eyes. "I do not mean to cause inconvenience, but I am in dire need of a month away from everything I've ever known." Her chapped lips remained parted slightly. She drummed her hand along the leather of her thigh, eliciting a consternating tune. "Ah," she said, pushing a deep breath out. She shook her head and flashed me a frustrated grin.

"It's fine. I don't need to know everything, Vayle."

"You deserve to," she said. "I, er—" Her hands revolved around one another, trying to churn the words out. "You know I've never accepted a job unless it resulted in justice. An assassination must be in good faith. I thought this war would end in the greatest capture of justice I'd ever experienced. And… it did, in a way. But, Astul, I…"

I reached out and held her hand. "It's all the dead, isn't it?"

Her eyes were closed. "The snow hasn't covered them yet. And the cold, it… I thought it would—"

"Cover the rot?" I suggested.

Her teeth sawed across her lip. "I can still smell them."

"I know," I said quietly, closing her fingers inside my palm.

"I just, well — I feel very strange."

"Am I going to lose you?" I asked.

She swallowed and looked up, eyes reddened and moist. "Let me go away for a while. I'll return. I promise."

After the lengthy silence, Vayle regathered herself. "And you? Where will you go?"

"I made a promise to Tylik that we'd rectify the small problem with the guard who burned his toes off."

"What problem is that?"

"That he still has his toes."

"You may want to get there quickly. Braddock, Dercy and Patrick are organizing a large force to sail for Lith soon. Well, in the general direction of where they believe Lith lies."

"First I'm paying a visit to my brother's grave."

"I didn't think you believed in talking to the dead."

"It's my brother, and on the off chance the dead have ears, I suppose a, er... well, a brief hello wouldn't be out of order."

Vayle embraced me tightly, patting my back. "Stay safe. I'll see you back at the Hole soon enough, I promise."

As my commander fled back toward Edenvaile, I felt cold and empty. Funny thing that, since I had enough gold to buy a kingdom, had earned myself a reputation as the death knell of the conjurers, and hell, I'd accomplished everything I set out to do: preserved my freedom and the Rots' way of life. Thing is, this grand chase had ended. Throughout it, my nearest companion was Death. And now? Now I was safe and secure. The adventure and the peril had fled from my life, and I... well, I missed them.

And that was why I made plans to go visit my brother. Not to say hello to the dead, as I'd told Vayle I would. No, morbid curiosity drove me. Or perhaps less curiosity and more hope. A hope that I could recapture the adventure and the peril. A hope that maybe there was something greater and more dangerous out there than the conjurers. A hope that whatever words I would say at my brother's grave wouldn't fall on the ears of the dead.

My eyes fell to the hilt of my sword, still smeared with a small chunk of gelatinous blood from Rivon's belly. I spat on my finger and wiped it off, till the blade ran clean with black ebon.

ABOUT THE AUTHOR

Justin DePaoli called Pittsburgh home for twenty-one years, but now lives in Kentucky with his fiancée, stilt-legged German shepherd, two cats, and a company of fish.

Beginning his career as a freelance writer, he now writes fiction full-time.

When he's not writing, he enjoys playing guitar (quite poorly), running, lifting, playing video games, and spending time with his fiancée and menagerie of pets.

Made in the USA
Middletown, DE
17 March 2018